Death Spirits

Allan McLeod

Lulu Books

Death Spirits

A Novel by WA McLeod

Dedicated to my readers for whom every word is written and to my darling wife for whom I exist.

I wish to acknowledge the efforts of many people who provided editorial input and encouragement, but specifically those of our friend, Barbara Kramer, for her tireless work and optimism. Remaining errors are mine, not hers.

I would be remiss if I didn't mention Paddy Hatt, a soul mate for over thirty years who always seems to know when to wedge in an encouraging word.

Northern Exposure
Empire Diner

Movie

To order a copy, visit http://books.lulu.com/browse/

For Wanda and Gabe and Diane and Gideon…and in
memory of Julie

Chapter 1

*M*y name is Zoë Brown. I was murdered on Saturday, May 14th at 4:33 a.m., exactly one month before my twenty-fifth birthday. That the same night I made a promise to Victoria Otto, a woman who had been murdered eleven years ago, a woman who, in the flesh, I had never met nor seen, but whose spirit had, for some inexplicable reason, attached itself to my soul.

Victoria Otto made herself known to me ten months ago, the Tuesday morning after Labor Day, the same morning I stood in front of my brand new grade twelve history class in Largeville, North Dakota, looking at twenty bright and shiny young faces peering at me expectantly; the same morning a voice whispered a name I didn't know, a name I'd never heard, a name that became seared into my brain as surely as though it had been etched there by a red-hot branding iron.

VICTORIA OTTO! The name ricocheted inside my skull. VICTORIA OTTO! I stood there transfixed, momentarily unaware of anything else—for that brief span of time, Victoria Otto occupied my total being, she was my total being.

"Miss Brown, are you OK?" The voice belonged to one of my new students, a busty blonde with the devil in her big brown eyes.

"Yes, yes, I'm fine," I replied, as though emerging from a trance and not sure at all that I was fine. I inhaled deeply several times until my breathing slowed. Then I approached the girl's desk in the first row and tried to focus on the cardboard name sign hanging from her neck. SARA PETERSON it said, and was adorned with hearts and pithy sayings, the more prominent being, 'School Sucks' under which a different hand, a boys I assumed, had written 'And so does Sara.' "Yes Sara,

I'm quite fine, and I think your sign has served its purpose."

Two boys seated behind Sara snickered. I pretended not to notice, certain Sara could devour them at will. I returned to the front of the classroom, struggling to gather my wits, wondering why I, a student of scientific logic, the only girl at summer camp who had thought Ouija silly, had experienced a powerful paranormal phenomenon, if indeed that is what it was.

Over the next several months Victoria Otto tried again and again to occupy my consciousness, but each time I successfully drove her away. In March she went quiet. April flew by and the next thing I knew we were half way through May. After awhile, I no longer dwelled on her silence—I had heard the last of Victoria Otto. And then last Thursday, I took my class on a field trip to Garrison Dam.

Since arriving in North Dakota the previous September, I'd wanted to see the Garrison, one of the largest earth filled dams in the world, but of greater importance was the lake it had formed, not for its 365,000-acre size and fifteen-hundred-mile shoreline, but for the woman who gave the lake its identity.

Sakakawea. I had my class practice saying her name. Sakakawea, Sakakawea. Even the boys, though grudgingly at first, became interested in this Shoshone woman who had played such a key role in the success of Lewis and Clark's expedition to the Pacific.

When we arrived at the dam and stood atop the two-hundred foot embankment looking out across the mirror-like surface of the lake that seemed endless, I asked my class to hold hands and close their eyes, to feel Sakakawea's spirit, to see her in their minds, to imagine what she looked like, to think about her not only as a woman and a mother, but an Indian woman who, two-hundred years previous, had worked alongside and advised an expedition of men, long before such things as equal rights and equal employment opportunities had become seeds in anyone's mind, a woman without whom Lewis and Clark may not have succeeded.

As I talked, a vision began forming in the mists of my mind, a vision of a young Indian woman so beautiful she took my breath away. She had blue-black hair that hung to her waist in double braids that ended in a feather-laced circle at the back of her head. Her piercing black eyes that seemed to be asking 'Why?' were recessed under peaked, prominent eyebrows. High, delicate cheekbones and a long, lower jaw gave her the look of a bronzed Cleopatra. Her white dress and moccasins were made of a fine animal skin imbedded with thousands of colorful beads in intricately woven patterns. She extended her hand.

"Sakakawea," I whispered, reaching out to touch her fingertips.

"No," she said, "my name is Victoria Otto."

I yanked my hand away as though I'd stuck it into an open flame and popped my eyes open. My students had gone. The power boats that dotted the lake grew silent and became canoes slicing noiselessly through a rushing current. The sun scooted behind a dark cloud. The air grew cold.

"Why are you doing this?" I shouted. "Why have you occupied my soul? How dare you use the power of Sakakawea's spirit to break down my walls of disbelief?"

I glanced around expecting to see Victoria Otto standing there, but there was no one. I ran to the water's edge and touched its coolness with my hand. I touched a rock. I ran back to the roadway and touched the dirt that became asphalt. A bird chirped. The trees turned from gray to green. I felt the warmth on my back as the clouds moved away from the sun. Blue sky, endless blue sky, and voices, wonderful human voices.

"Did you feel her?"

"Did you see her?"

My students were abuzz with wonderment. I gathered them around and we talked about what they'd seen, what they'd felt. They all described sensing Sakakawea in varying forms. Some saw her working alongside Lewis and Clark. Others saw her carrying her child strapped to her front, blazing trails through thick stands of forest. One saw her weeping, but didn't know why. When they'd talked themselves out, I asked if any of them had seen Victoria Otto or felt her presence.

"Who's Victoria Otto," they wanted to know.

That night, I went to the usual Friday dance, but my heart wasn't in it, so I left early, 12:30, and came home. I lay awake in my bed for the longest time, unable to find sleep, unable to quiet my mind. Every few minutes I'd look at the red numbers of the clock on my bedside table, hoping, praying I'd dozed off, wishing for morning. At 3:30 I got up and sat by my window, staring out into the night, watching the leaves of the large elm trees flickering in the yellow glow of the streetlights. The air smelled after-rain fresh, but it hadn't rained. A calf bawled in the distance. It seemed to be calling for its mother.

I thought of my own mother and father in Chicago and wondered if they would hear me if I called into the night. My mother would probably want to know why I hadn't called sooner.

A dog barked. Then another and another. One could always hear dogs in Largeville. Everyone owned a dog. They all barked at night. I thought of closing my window to shut out the noise when a set of headlights rounded the corner and went dark. The car slowed and then stopped. I couldn't see whose it was. Two car doors opened and closed. Two shadows moved across the road. I thought it must be the other two teachers living in the building, though I wondered why they were out so late and where they'd been.

I listened for their footsteps on the creaky stairs. A tingling sensation ran through my body. A face appeared at the window. I jumped back and screamed, though no noise came out of my mouth. My body began to shake. I stopped breathing, and then I heard a sob.

"Please," she cried. "Help me."

My cellphone rang. I answered, but no one was there. The face disappeared. I returned to my bed. As I lay staring up at the ceiling, wave after wave of goose bumps ran up and down my legs and arms and spine, Her whispery voice floated in the air. "Promise me, you've got to promise me."

"Promise what?" I asked, paralyzed.

"Find my killer. Release my soul to the spirits of my ancestors."

She took my hands and pulled me from the bed. I felt her sweet, hot breath on my face. "Promise me," she cried. "You're the only one..."

I shivered. She wrapped a throw around my shoulders.

"Please...please..."

"I promise," I whispered back. "I promise I will find your killer."

My cellphone rang again.

"Yes, who is it?" I peered into the dark corners of my room hoping to see her. I wanted to make sure she'd heard my promise.

"I know it's late, but I need to see you."

"Pardon, no, it's OK. I mean I don't mind that's its late. Are you in trouble? You sound like you're in trouble."

"No...yes...I don't know."

"Where are you?"

"Out front. Please hurry."

Chapter 2

Kate Flanagan answered the intercom without looking up from the paperwork scattered across the top of her desk.

"We got a call from up in Largeville," her boss, Deputy Police Chief Harry Carson, said. "Some kid's found a body."

"You say Largeville like I'm supposed to know where it is."

"Straight north, spitting distance from the Canadian border. You can't miss it. Well, actually you can, but don't."

"I'll tell Bob. He'll be overjoyed." Bob Hutton was her partner. Harry Carson and Bob Hutton liked to pretend they didn't like each other. Maybe they didn't.

"Where is he?" Carson sounded dour.

"He's picking up the SUV." The SUV, one of four that belonged to the Police Department, had been in the body shop, its third trip in six months. A week ago, Hutton had smashed the right hand side into a speeding car. Five weeks ago, a drunken hunter shot out the windshield and half the hood with his high-powered rifle. Six months ago, a week after the SUV's had been purchased, Hutton had been broadsided at a roadblock. None of the other three had so much as a scratch.

"Tell him from now on you'll do the driving."

"You tell him."

Kate Flanagan was a junior detective with the Investigations Division of the Minot, North Dakota, Police Department. She'd been on the force for six years and had been Bob Hutton's partner for a year. Hutton was a ten year veteran and considered the top detective on the force, even grudgingly by his long-time nemesis, Harry Carson. Except for not yet giving her the chance to lead an investigation, she felt lucky to be working alongside the great one, as she secretly called him. He willingly shared his knowledge and was quick to jump to her defense if questioned by Caron or the chief.

"I'd like to see the look on his face if he got his driving privileges yanked," Carson said.

"Well I wouldn't."

Carson ended the call. "Shit!" She'd planned on spending part of the day buying paint for her living room now that she'd finally decided on Peach Cooler, an agonizing process of paint chip elimination that had taken six months. Well, so much for Peach Cooler. She called Hutton to give him the good news.

"I'll pick you up in five minutes," Hutton said.

By the time she got outside, Hutton was sitting at the curb in the shiny, black SUV.

"Looks new," she said, climbing in.

"Rattles and pulls to the right."

"You want me to drive?"

Hutton tossed her a 'you kidding' look. "You call the ME's office?" he asked.

"Isn't that your job?"

He tossed her another 'you kidding' look.

"What, you can't call?" she asked.

"Hey, no need to be testy."

"I like being testy, and you didn't answer my question?"

"I can call. I just thought since you had all that time waiting for me to arrive that you might have made the call."

"Relax, I made the call. He should be here in a minute."

A dark green Buick pulled in behind the SUV. Flanagan recognized Stan Jackson. He didn't seem pleased to be out at 6:30 a.m. on a Saturday morning. Flanagan nodded. He didn't nod back.

"Looks like he's nursing a hangover," Hutton said.

"He's just pissed because I called."

"I suppose he thinks we like this shit?"

"Speaking of testy, you got something you want to get off your chest?"

"Nah, just being bitchy like everyone else."

Flanagan wanted to fire back, but something in the way he replied made her keep her mouth shut.

They headed north on Route 83 with Jackson glued to their back bumper. Hutton periodically touched the brake pedal and laughed when the Buick bucked as Jackson slammed on the brakes.

"You'd better hope he never does your autopsy, or pray for a closed coffin."

Hutton laughed again.

They rode silently for a few miles. She tried to amuse her mind by counting cars, and then telephone poles, and then white cows. And then she wondered if Hutton and his wife, Dorie, had patched up their differences. She wanted to ask, but wasn't sure how he'd take to her poking in his personal affairs. Probably about like you'd take to him poking in your personal affairs, she told herself, as if you had any personal affairs to poke into. She glanced at the side of his face, fixing on the scar on his cheek where he'd been shot.

"You ever been to Largeville?" he asked, as if sensing her probing eyes and wanting her to stop.

"No, you?"

"A few times, hunting pheasants and Canada Geese. You'll like it."

Five long minutes later they pulled onto a gravel road that led into Largeville.

"Dear sweet Jesus," Flanagan said, as they drove down the town's main street past a collection of small stores and shops that needed painting and cleaning.

"I told you you'd be thrilled. Hey, there's Pete's Café. Why don't you run in and get us a couple of coffees and some donuts?"

"I'll tell you what: Why don't you run in and get us a couple of coffees and some donuts?"

Hutton grinned and flipped his notebook open. "According to the caller, someone named Joe Peterson, the two guys who found the body are waiting on the road just north of town in a green 1991 Ford Taurus with a red right front fender."

"Gee, do you think that could be them?" Flanagan asked, pointing to a solitary green car sitting on the side of the road a hundred yards ahead with an older man and a younger man leaning against the right front fender that just happened to be red.

"No one likes a smart ass."

"That would account for your total lack of friends."

They pulled up behind the green Taurus and got out.

"You Joe Peterson," Hutton asked the man with the deeply lined face that hadn't seen a razor for a day or two. Flanagan guessed him to be fifty, about five-foot seven or eight, and judging from his pot belly, either a heavy beer drinker or a baking wife. He wore a spotless white apron and white flat top hat that Flanagan figured had to be the whitest garments in Largeville. With him was a younger man, not yet twenty Flanagan figured, in white sneakers that looked new, blue jeans that look like they'd been ironed, and a red checkered shirt that had definitely been starched and ironed. His brown hair had blonde high-lights, his eyes were too blue and darted around too much, and he was too good-looking and knew it.

The older man pushed away from the car and nodded, eyeing Hutton and then Flanagan.

"What's your name," Hutton asked the younger man.

"Tommy," the young man said, his lip curling into a snarl.

"Tommy what?"

"Tommy Striker."

Tommy continued leaning against the car, a sprig of ryegrass hanging from the side of his mouth.

"He's the one who found her," Joe Peterson said, nodding at Tommy. "Down there in the drainage ditch." He motioned over his shoulder with his thumb. Thick, waist-high rye grass lined both sides of the narrow road.

A black SUV, the same as Hutton and Flanagan's except covered with several layers of mud, roared up and skidded to a stop, churning up a cloud of dust and bits of gravel that momentarily caused them to shut their eyes and cover their noses and mouths. The driver's door flew open and a bantam rooster of a man dressed in khaki shirt and slacks jumped to the ground. He shoved his brown Stetson back on his head, pushed his aviator sunglasses up the bridge of his nose a notch, and stepped forward in his fancy cowboy boots. "Just what in the Sam Hill is going on here?"

"Sir, please stand back," Hutton said.

"Now you all listen here, besides being mayor of this fair town, this here's my boy and I want to know what 'n tarnation is going on?"

Flanagan stepped forward before Hutton and the man in the Stetson decided to get into a serious pissing contest. "Sir, are you Mr. Striker?"

"Yes I am. Now—"

"Sir, your son reported finding a body. We're here to investigate. Perhaps you'd care to help."

Others from town must have gotten wind that something was going down because a scattering of men and women had arrived, and more were coming up the main street on foot, by bicycle, and in cars. Flanagan figured the senior Striker could play road cop.

Striker puffed out his chest. "Yes ma'am, of course. I'll do what I can."

"It will help if you can keep the others back," Hutton said.

Striker glared at Hutton, and then looked back at Flanagan. "That what you want, ma'am?"

Flanagan nodded. Behind her, she could feel Hutton beginning to steam.

Striker said to Tommy, "You OK boy?"

"Yeah." Tommy looked down and kicked the toe of his sneaker at the road, his earlier cockiness gone.

"You look at me when I'm talking to you boy, you hear?"

"Yeah," Tommy said, raising his head slightly.

"Mr. Striker," Flanagan said, nodding toward the townspeople getting closer.

"Oh, yes ma'am," he said, and started off.

Flanagan glanced in Tommy's direction. No love lost there, she thought, and took a step toward the edge of the road. As she did so, her body began to quiver and then shook violently. She managed to take two steps back and get her hand against the front fender of the SUV. The shaking stopped. She shook her head to clear her mind, glancing across at Hutton hoping he hadn't noticed.

He had. "Nice going Flanagan. You going to be all right?"

"Yeah, sorry.

He started to walk away.

Her hand shot out, grabbed his arm, and spun him around.

"What the hell—"

A fire burned in her brain. She heard herself say, "I want you to listen to me."

He tried to pull away. She tried to let go, but couldn't. Something had taken control of her motor functions. She tried to speak, to say she didn't know what was happening. Instead she said, "I want this case."

Hutton studied her for a moment. "I don't think so. It's not time."

Her hand tightened until her arm started to tremble. She was afraid, but she knew her eyes were boring into him and her voice was deep and confident. "I…WANT…THIS…CASE."

"I said it's not time, and this isn't the place to have this discussion."

She felt her hand squeezing tighter. He winced.

"I'm past ready," she hissed. "You know it and I know it and the only way we're not going to have this discussion right here right now is for you to give me this case."

Hutton glanced at Joe Peterson and the kid and then at Striker. Flanagan followed his eyes. Peterson and the kid seemed to be looking everywhere but in the ditch. Striker was charging off up the dusty street as fast as his bow legs would carry his round body, waving his arms at the approaching townspeople.

"All right," Hutton said, turning back to face her, "you want it, it's yours."

Her fingers opened. He rubbed his arm and looked at her in a way she hadn't seen before.

"Thank you."

"Hold your applause—you might curse me later."

Her stomach told her he might be right.

"If you two are through," Stan Jackson said, "I'd like to get started."

"Normal ritual," Flanagan said.

"Yeah," Hutton muttered, and walked over to Joe and Tommy.

Flanagan walked to the side of the road. A breeze came up and rustled the tall grass. It seemed to be trying to tell her to stay back. She took a step forward. If there is anyone down there, she thought, I'll be on top of them before I see a thing.

"Is this the right place, Tommy?"

"Yes ma'am. Right down there."

She took another step and stopped. She sniffed the air. Hutton came up behind.

"Do you smell that?"

"What, the pig shit?"

"Orchids?"

"I smell wet green grass and stagnant water and dirt and pig shit, but there ain't no orchids growing anywhere in North Dakota."

A voice whispered in her ear and worked its way inside her head, at first cool and gentle like a breath of air, and then a sirocco, searing hot, etching a name in her mind: Zoë Brown, ZOË BROWN, ZOË BROWN!!

"Shit!" she cried. The embankment gave way and she fell backward. Hutton tried to grab her but missed. Her head bashed onto the road's gravel-strewn shoulder.

"Jesus Flanagan, sorry. Are you OK?"

"Nice catch," she said. "Pull me up."

He grabbed her outstretched hand.

"Stay here," she said to Hutton, and waded back into the tall grass, now accompanied by a splitting headache and a voice that continued whispering: Zoë Brown, Zoë Brown, and then a picture of a young woman began to take shape in her mind. She tried to push it away, but it wouldn't be deterred.

"Careful," Hutton shouted.

She stopped and looked back. Hutton's eyes followed every move. She looked past him at Stan Jackson. "Down here," she said to Jackson, whose mood hadn't improved. "The bank is tricky. Take Hutton's hand."

"I'd sooner fall in," Jackson snorted.

"Suit yourself," Flanagan said.

Using her arms, she parted the grass and inched forward. "Walk in my footprints," she said to Jackson, who was sidestepping his way in. She tried to take another step but something, a hand, pressed against her chest and held her back.

"What is it?" Jackson asked.

She looked down. One more step and she'd have fallen into the water-filled ditch.

"The ditch is right here."

He peered around her. "I don't know how you saw it, Flanagan, but goldang lucky for us you did or we'd be up to our butts in slime."

She dropped to her haunches and shoved the grass back from the swampy smelling brackish water. And then she smelled orchids again. She nudged another clump of grass.

"There," she said, almost to herself. Two bare white legs with red high heels stuck out through the blanket of green seed pellets that covered the water's surface.

Jackson snapped several pictures and bent down, placing his thumb and finger on either side of the victim's Achilles tendon. A handful of water striders scooted away; one of the victim's legs moved. Jackson seemed not to notice. He stepped back and took more pictures.

The aroma of orchids continued to fill Flanagan's nose, so much so she could almost taste them. She looked at Jackson. He only smelled death.

The ambulance arrived and Jackson motioned the attendants down the embankment, warning them to step carefully. They soon had the body out of the water.

Flanagan gasped when she saw the young woman's face, the same face she'd seen in her mind a moment earlier. She gripped Jackson's arm to steady herself.

"Goldang it," Jackson said. "Flanagan, I thought you'd be past that by now."

"No, it's not that; I thought I recognized her."

Jackson threw her a questioning look, but said nothing other than, "She's had a nasty smack on the side of the head."

Flanagan looked where Jackson pointed. The whole side of the victim's head had been caved in. And other than the red high-heels, she was nude. Jackson took more pictures, pinched the victim's skin in several places, took her rectal temperature, checked her vagina and breasts, and instructed his aides to bag her.

"How long she been in there, Doc?"

"Four hours max, judging from her feet. Harder to tell from the underwater parts. Temperature says less, but the water affects that."

"Anything else?"

"No signs of violent sex. We won't know the rest until we cut her open, though I suspect she was dead from the head wound before going in the water. She doesn't look full of water."

Flanagan accompanied the attendants to the ambulance. When they had the body inside, she asked Joe to volunteer a look. He didn't want to, but said he would. She looked at Tommy. He shook his head. Striker swaggered up, having deputized several townspeople to keep their friends and neighbors at bay. She asked him. He didn't hesitate. That gave Joe extra courage. She escorted both to the back of the ambulance and asked the attendant to show the victim's face.

"Jesus Christ," Striker said. "It's Zoë Brown."

Joe groaned something that sounded like, "Oh my god."

Flanagan's knees gave way. Joe Peterson caught her under the arms and held her steady until Striker and Jackson each managed to grab an arm. Between the three of them they got her upright.

"Maybe we should take you in too," Jackson said.

"I'll be all right. There's just a little too much of last night in my system."

Jackson frowned.

Flanagan took a moment and then asked Striker and Joe if the victim had lived in town.

"Up at Howard and Hilda Vole's place," Joe said.

"Yeah," Striker said. "In the teacherage up behind the Baptist Church."

"Teacherage?" Flanagan raised an eyebrow.

"She taught at the school there," Striker said, and pointed to the school-like two-story brown brick building that sat back from the town's main road two hundred yards off to their right.

"We'll want to see the school and where she lived."

"I can take you to Howard and Hilda's place any time you want," Striker said. "But we'll have to contact Ed Gregory—he's the principal—before we can get into the school. I mean I can get us in, but to be politically correct, as they say, Ed should be there." He forced his face to grin.

Flanagan nodded, and asked Hutton if he wanted to come to Howard and Hilda's place, knowing he had nowhere else to go.

"You want to ride with me," Striker said to Tommy.

"Nah, I'm going to the café."

"Don't go running off. I'll need help later."

"Yeah." Tommy pulled a pack of cigarettes from his shirt pocket and shoved one into his mouth.

Striker seemed about to say something else, and then climbed up into his SUV and flew off up the street in the same cloud of dust and flying bits of rock that he'd rode in on.

"Is he always in that big a hurry?" Flanagan asked Tommy.

Tommy struck a match and lit his cigarette. "Mostly," he said through a cloud of exhaled smoke.

Jackson pulled up and rolled down his window. Flanagan asked him to call as soon as he had the autopsy results.

Hutton and Flanagan followed Striker's trail of dust up Main Street, heading back the way they'd come in. In the side mirror, Flanagan saw Joe Peterson park his car in the center of the street facing Pete's Café and watched as Joe and Tommy got out and went inside.

* * *

She smelled orchids. She closed her eyes and rubbed the tips of her fingers into her temples. She saw Zoë's face, not her cold dead face, but her alive and vibrant face, a face she wanted to reach out and touch, a face that brought tears to her eyes.

You are troubled.

Who did this to you?

I don't know.

Chapter 3

Striker stood on the road adjusting his cowboy hat and sunglasses and hitching up his pants when Flanagan and Hutton pulled up.

"That guy's got more moves than a batter in a slump," Hutton said.

"He doesn't strike me as a baseball player," Flanagan said. She got out of the SUV and looked up at the large, two story white frame house with black roof, trim, and shutters. "Big enough for a hotel," she said. She made a mental note of the three cars and a pick-up parked in the graveled area in front of the two-car garage.

"That's Zoë's car," said Striker, pointing at the gray BMW.

"Nice wheels for a young teacher," Hutton said.

"You mean a young female teacher," Flanagan shot back.

"Hey, it'd be nice wheels for me, OK?"

"Nice try."

One of the garage doors was open. Besides hoses and tools and bicycles and a riding lawnmower and several garage sales worth of other junk, Flanagan noticed a snowmobile and a new-looking Kawasaki motorcycle. A large boat with an outboard motor sat on a trailer along one side of the garage; a camping trailer that looked new sat on the other side.

"A lot of equipment," she said to Striker.

He shrugged. "Some of it belongs to their kids, four girls and four boys, all married, they hardly visit any-more." He shook his head.

"That bothers you."

"They could visit more, if you know what I mean."

Flanagan felt like saying, 'No, what do you mean?'

"You want me to come in? I know Howard and Hilda real well. I won't tell them what's going on, but I can make introductions and then get out of your way faster than you can say 'Jack Robinson.'"

She wondered who Jack Robinson was.

"Did you say other teachers live here?" Hutton asked.

"I don't think I said that, but yes, Joan Foster and Betty Hale live here. I'm not sure what grades they teach. They're in the elementary school. They're going to take it real bad. So are Howard and Hilda."

Flanagan saw a white lace curtain on the front window move aside. An older woman with a round face peeked out. "They know we're here."

Striker and Hutton turned to look. The face disappeared.

"That's Hilda," Striker said. "Salt of the earth; so is Howard."

Striker led them up the sidewalk to the front porch that was partially hidden behind a growth of creepers. The porch was filled with large earthen pots stuffed with robust geraniums and miniature petunias that seemed to have a million flowers. A double swing at one end creaked in the swirling wind.

Striker pushed the doorbell and cupped his hand to the window. Door chimes sounded. Striker pushed the button again.

"Yeah, yeah, hold your horses," a woman's voice said. Someone coughed. The curtain moved aside and Hilda's round face peered out. She flashed a row of yellow teeth, tugged the curtain back into place, and opened the door.

"Strike," she said, covering her mouth as she wheezed out another cough and then wiped her mouth with the hem of her apron. "This damn asthma's going to be the death of me." She eyed Flanagan and Hutton for a moment and then turned her attention back to Striker. "What the hell brings you out ringing and ringing my bell so early on a Saturday morning—you running for reelection already?" Her inky black hair, the kind that only comes from a bottle, was stacked in big rollers, and her green print dress and apron hung from her shoulders like a big tent.

"Morning Hilda," Striker said, touching a finger to the brim of his hat. "Howard up?"

"Oh merciful heavens yes, you know him—he gets up with the sun. Come on inside. He's out on the deck having his third or fourth cup of coffee and trying to decide what to do with the rest of his day."

They stepped into a spacious foyer that had three French doors. Hilda opened the one straight ahead that led into a long hallway with glistening hardwood floors.

"After you ma'am," Striker said, motioning Flanagan to follow Hilda.

Flanagan's feet stuck to the floor and a tingling began to run through her body. "What's through there?" she asked, pointing at the door on the left.

Hilda turned. "Oh, that one leads to the second floor where our girls live. On the weekends, Howard and I try to be quiet though I sometimes think they could sleep through an earthquake."

Flanagan saw a shadow move behind the curtain. She sniffed at the air. Orchids! Like it was an entity separate from her body, her hand moved to the door and twisted the knob. The door swung open. She went up the two stairs that led to a landing where sweaters and jackets hung from wooden pegs. She pulled the sleeve of a yellow sweater to her nose.

"I don't think she should be going up there," Hilda said to Striker.

"They're the police."

"Oh my."

Flanagan sniffed the other sweaters and jackets and then the yellow sweater again. It clung to her face. She brushed it away and started up the stairs. At the top, the hallway led to four closed doors. She walked to the one farthest down on the right and stood for a moment, her heart pounding in her ears. The door opened. She pulled on a pair of latex gloves and stepped inside.

She moved to the center of the large room. Framed posters of gallery showings, Broadway musicals, and ballet performances lined the walls. The bookcase was stuffed with hardcover and paperback books, magazines, and papers. She glanced at the large-screen television set that wasn't on and the Bose radio that sat silent; she touched the body-sized indent on the puffy comforter that lay across the made up bed.

She walked across to the front windows where a computer sat on a small desk. As though in a state of weightlessness, a space-themed screen saver caromed within the confines of the flat-screen monitor. She nudged the mouse. A web page came into view. She leaned closer. It was an article about an Indian woman by the name of Sakakawea, something about the Lewis and Clark expedition.

From Zoë's dresser, she picked up a gold-framed picture of a man and woman who looked to be in their fifties. 'Love, Ma and Dad' it said. A set of delicate glass figurines occupied every available surface. She glanced around the room one more time. Where were the clothes that should have been strewn across the chairs and bed? Where were the shoes that should have been lying here and there? She ran her finger along the top of the headboard. Where was the dust?

The floor creaked. She whipped around. No one was there. She went back to the door and looked down the hallway. Downstairs she heard Hutton talking to Hilda and Striker. She listened for another moment and returned to Zoë's room.

* * *

It was I.

"I gathered as much. Maybe it's time you told me what is going down here."

I'm not sure I know.
"Give it a shot."
You have to believe I exist. You can't push me away.
"I don't know what to believe."

*   *   *

Flanagan crossed to the bathroom and switched the light on. The floor and walls were white tiles, four white bath towels with an embroidered pink Z hung next to the old-fashioned tub with big claw feet, and two matching hand towels and face cloths hung from brass rings next to the pedestal sink.

A large, mirrored medicine cabinet with six globe lights across the top was mounted above the sink. Colorful bottles of bath oils and shampoos were perched on a ledge next to the tub and more sat on a shelf below the small window. She pushed the curtain aside and peered out. Below were the two SUV's, theirs and Striker's, and the cars in the driveway. A dog sounded a throaty howl as if following a scent.

A healthy-looking fern hung from the ceiling on a gold-colored chain. She removed her glove and pinched the dirt, not surprised to feel the moistness. To get rid of adhering particles, she brushed the tips of her thumb and fingers together. She touched the towels. They were dry.

The medicine cabinet was stuffed with toiletries, and the like. She picked up a pack of birth control pills and examined the dispenser. It hadn't been used. She closed the door, turned out the lights, and returned to the bedroom.

"May I help you?" A pretty young woman, five-foot ten and thin as a rail, stood in the doorway, arms folded defiantly.

Flanagan pulled her badge from her waist clip. "Detective Flanagan...what's your name?"

The young woman cocked her head as if wondering whether or not to reply. "Joan Foster," she finally said, and stepped toward Flanagan, her narrow hips thrust forward and her toes pointed out like a ballerina's.

Flanagan snapped off her rubber glove and shook Foster's hand. Foster's spindly legs jutted from red short-shorts and a white blouse tied at the waist exposed a wafer-thin midriff. Flanagan figured her borderline anorexic, but her husky voice was warm and her smile, though cautious, appeared to be sincere. Her dark auburn hair was cut short, like a man's, and parted on the side, and her dark eyebrows were plucked to pencil thin lines that arched high on each end like question marks.

"What are you doing here?" Foster asked, as if not wanting to know the answer.

"Are you the only one here?" Flanagan asked.

Foster nodded her head toward the open door. "Betty Hale is in her room."

"Would you mind getting her? I need to talk to the two of you."

Foster didn't move. "Has something happened to Zoë?" Her eyes grew big and round.

"I need to talk to the two of you, downstairs, with Mr. and Mrs. Vole."

Foster backed away two steps, then turned and glided from the room, though not before tossing a concerned look over her shoulder.

A bit of red caught the corner of Flanagan's eye. She pushed the bed skirt aside and retrieved a sequined handbag. Inside, she found Zoë's wallet containing two-hundred and thirty-six dollars, a collection of make-up accessories, and the array of items normal for a woman's purse, including a birth control pack with a pill taken yesterday.

Flanagan closed the handbag and stood as Foster returned followed by a sleepy-looking young woman.

"This is Betty Hale," Foster said, stepping aside.

Hale, a chubby, five-foot five, wore a short purple housecoat that wasn't long enough to hide her brown leather sandals that did nothing attractive for her flabby feet. Her middle finger constantly poked at her glasses that kept sliding down her pug nose. Her hair looked like a stack of wind-blown straw, her skin was too pink, and her smile more of a self-conscious snort.

"I'm Detective Flanagan."

"Hi," Hale said with the voice of a young girl.

Flanagan ushered them into the hallway and closed Zoë's door. "Who has the keys?"

"Zoë probably had one," Foster said, "but they're never locked. Howard...Mr. Vole...has extras."

Flanagan led them to the foyer where Hutton, Striker, and Hilda waited.

"I didn't know you were going to get the girls," Hilda said to Flanagan.

"We need to talk to all of you," Flanagan said.

"Where's Zoë? Don't you need Zoë?"

"Not for the moment," Flanagan said. "Why don't you take us to see Mr. Vole?"

"Yes of course dear, if he's still there. I didn't know you were going to get the girls," she said again.

"I'm sorry, but they need to hear what Detective Hutton and I have to say."

"Well what about Zoë?" Alarm began to register in Hilda's eyes.

"We'll get to her later."

Hilda mumbled, and proceeded down the hallway.

Flanagan whispered to Hutton, "We need to lock and tape Zoë's door. Mr. Vole probably has keys."

Hutton nodded.

Hilda led them through a closed-in back porch and out onto a raised deck covered with Astroturf. A man with gray spiky hair reclined on a lounge chair, his back to them.

"Howard," Hilda said. "The police need to talk to us."

Howard jumped up and slopped his coffee down the leg of his khaki slacks. "Damn it woman, how many times have I told you not to sneak up on me like that—you trying to give me a heart attack?" He brushed at his wet slacks. Hilda grabbed a roll of paper towels from the deck table, tore off a few sheets, and dropped to her knees, daubing at his pant leg and the Astroturf carpet.

"Not now woman," Howard hissed, waving his arm in dismissal and spilling more coffee in the process.

"If you don't put that cup down you'll soon have us all splattered," Hilda said, still daubing. "Now stand still while I finish up."

Foster snatched the cup from Howard's hand. Hale bent to assist Hilda. Howard continued to fume.

"Howard, sorry to sneak up on you like that," Strike said, "but I'm afraid Detectives Flanagan and Hutton here have some bad news."

Howard stared hard at Flanagan and Hutton. Hilda and Betty Hale stopped their daubing and stood next to Foster.

"I'm very sorry," Flanagan said, "but Zoë has been murdered."

Howard collapsed into his chair. Hale started to sob, her body shaking mightily and big tears tumbled everywhere. Foster pressed her lips together. Her eyes were damp. She put her arm around Hilda's sagging shoulders and led her to the chair next to Howard's. Hilda clutched Howard's quivering hand and tears dribbled from his eyes. Hilda bit at her lip. Strike looked down and kicked at the Astroturf with the toe of his boot.

"We know this is a bad time," Flanagan continued, "but we need to ask a few questions."

They stared statue-like, except for Hale who couldn't stop sobbing.

Striker walked down off the deck. At the bottom of the steps he turned and said, "Folks, I'm awfully sorry about this. Howard, I'll call you later."

Howard didn't respond.

"Thanks for your help," Flanagan said. "We'd like to talk to you when we've finished here."

Striker said he'd be at the town hall at the end of the Main Street.

Flanagan turned her attention to Howard. She guessed he, like Hilda, was in his late sixties. His huge ears sprouted shrub-like tufts of gray. Sitting slumped back in his chair, his feet barely touched the deck.

"Were you home last night?" she asked.

Hilda said, "Howard and I watched TV, the baseball game, The Seattle Mariners were playing, that's our favorite team."

Flanagan nodded, and made a note in her book.

"After the game ended we went to bed."

"What time was that?" Hutton asked.

"Howard, she wants to know what time."

"Eleven-thirty," he said. "They played an extra inning."

"Seattle won," Hilda said.

"They're not interested in the goddamn baseball game," Howard said.

"Oh now don't be so grumpy. We're all sad you know, not just you." Hilda had another wheezing fit and Foster patted her on the back.

"Was anyone with you?" Hutton asked.

"We don't have an alibi if that's what you're asking," Howard said.

"What about the two of you?" Flanagan asked Hale and Foster.

"I was in my room all night," Hale said, looking so guilty she couldn't possibly be.

"Alone," Flanagan asked, knowing the answer.

Hale's face turned bright pink. "Yes, of course. We're not allowed to have men...yes, alone."

Foster said, "Betty and I had dinner with Zoë at Pete's Café here in town, as we did every Friday night, and then the three of us walked home together."

"What time was that?"

"We got to Joe's around seven and got home just before nine. We all went to our rooms."

"Did you go out after that?" Hutton asked.

"No, first I bathed and then watched TV."

"And like Miss Hale, were you also alone?"

Foster eyed him coolly.

"They know the rules," Hilda said, "and they're all real good girls."

Hutton kept on with Foster. "Did you know Miss Brown intended to go to the dance?"

"She went every Friday."

"Did you see her leave?"

She shook her head.

"About what time do you think she might have left?"

Howard said, "10:30—she always left exactly at 10:30." Foster and Hale nodded. Hutton and Flanagan took notes.

"Well not exactly 10:30," Hilda said, "but it's always around that time."

"I tell you it's always exactly 10:30," Howard said. "You can set your clock by it."

"What time did she come home?" Flanagan asked.

Hilda pointed at Howard with her head. "He told me he heard a car at one o'clock."

"What I heard at one, woman, was Zoë coming home. The car was later."

"What time did you hear a car?"

"Closer to four."

"Did you see Miss Brown when she came home?"

"Didn't have to—I heard her going up the stairs."

"Maybe it was Miss Foster or Miss Hale."

"He knows their steps," Hilda said. "If he says it was Zoë, it was Zoë."

"At four, did you see the car?" Flanagan asked Howard.

Howard nodded.

"He got out of bed and went to the window," Hilda said. "I told him to stop snooping before the neighbors saw him, but he wouldn't listen. He never does."

"It wasn't the neighbors," Howard said.

"He said he didn't recognize the car, of course he wasn't wearing his glasses."

"Didn't need my glasses to know it was a car."

"What kind of car?"

"By the time I got my glasses it had gone, but it was red."

"He told me it looked like a sports car," Hilda said. "And he heard a car door slam."

"When was that?" Hutton asked.

"When he went for his glasses—when he got back he asked me if I'd heard it, but I hadn't. He took another look and told me the car had gone. I didn't hear it leave. He called it a ghost car. I told him if it came back, we shouldn't be watching."

"How about either of you," Flanagan said to Foster and Hale. "Did you see or hear anything?"

"No." Foster said. "Our rooms face the back. We rarely hear any street noise."

"I didn't hear a thing," Hale said.

"I can't believe Zoë's dead," Howard said. Hilda began to rub his arm.

"You're certain you didn't hear her leave after she got back from the dance?"

They both shook their head. Hilda said, "She might have gone out without our knowing."

"I would have heard," Howard said.

"He always hears the girls," Hilda said.

"Do any of you know who might have done this?" Hutton asked.

"Oh my goodness no," Hilda said. "Everyone liked Zoë; she was everyone's favorite. Not to say anything against Joan and Betty, mind you, because they are lovely girls too, but even they will tell you that Zoë was special."

"They want to know who killed Zoë," Howard said, "not what you think of everyone."

"Don't mind him…he's upset," Hilda said. "We're all upset. This is such terrible news."

"Miss Hale, what about you?"

"It's like Hilda said. Zoë was everyone's favorite. Everyone loved her."

"Miss Foster?"

"I can't imagine anyone doing this," she said, putting a hand on Howard's shoulder. "Not to Zoë, not to anyone. It's all so horrible." Her thin body shivered. Howard reached up and patted her hand.

"Striker said the BMW belongs to Zoë. Do you know where she keeps the keys?"

"If they aren't in her purse," Foster said, "they'll be in the car. She usually didn't bother removing them."

"And a key to her room—I want it locked."

Howard pushed up from his chair and took a couple of stiff-legged steps. "I can get you a key to her room."

Flanagan followed him inside the back porch. He fished a key from a row of hooks hidden behind the deep freeze. "This is Zoë's," he said. "The rest are for the other doors, the garage, and the vehicles, in case the originals get lost or someone gets locked out—seems someone is always losing a key."

"Are there others besides these?"

"The girls each have a key for their rooms, and Zoë must have had one somewhere, but they never lock their doors. No one, not even the missus or me, ever goes in uninvited."

Flanagan ran up the stairs and locked Zoë's room. Hutton could tape it before they left. Back downstairs, she went out to Zoë's car. The keys were in the ignition. She pulled on a pair of gloves, checked the inside of the car and the trunk and then locked all the doors.

"Make sure no one tries to get into her room or her car," she said to Howard, who stood on the front porch watching. "One of our lab people will be out later today to do a detailed inspection."

Howard nodded.

She rejoined him on the porch. They walked back to the deck where Foster and Hale were kneeling in front of Hilda, their faces buried in her lap. She stroked at their hair and told them everything was going to be OK. Hutton was busy checking his handheld for messages.

"Anything?" Flanagan asked.

"Not much. Doc's still in the basement." That meant he was still busy with the autopsy.

* * *

My parents need to be told. I need to be with them. You must take me.

How do you propose I do that?

Please...you must promise.

In her mind she saw the two people from the photograph in Zoë's room. They began to cry. I'll do what I can.

* * *

"You OK?" Hutton asked.

"Yeah, I'll be fine. Would you mind taping the door to Zoë's room and her car? I need to make a call."

Hutton left to get the tape from the SUV. Flanagan flipped her phone open and hit a number. When Jackson answered she said, "Yeah Doc, it's me. Have the victim's parents been notified?"

"Not by me. What's up?"

She wasn't about to tell the chief medical examiner for the State of North Dakota that the victim's ghost wanted her to personally deliver the body. "Can you let me know as soon as they've been notified?"

He mumbled something that she took as yes.

"Also, can you send McManus out this morning? I want her to go over the room and car."

He mumbled another something that she took as yes.

"I gather you're in the middle of the autopsy."

"Started. The blow to the head killed her. No signs of recent sexual activity, consensual or otherwise."

"She took birth control pills."

"I didn't say she was a virgin, she just hasn't had sex recently, at least not within the last forty-eight hours."

Join the club, thought Flanagan. "Listen Doc, tell McManus to check in when she arrives. We'll be at the Town Hall at the end of the Main Street—we haven't been there yet, but it can't be hard to find."

She ended the call and walked over to where Howard and Hilda remained huddled with Foster and Hale. "We're leaving now," she said, and gave each of them one of her cards. "Thank you for your time, and again, we're sorry about Zoë. If you remember anything at all that you feel might be useful, no matter how incidental you might think it is, please contact Detective Hutton or me. Often, it's the tiniest clues that tell us what we need to know."

*   *   *

It wasn't any of them.
How can you be sure?
I know their smells.
What does that mean?

*   *   *

When she got to the SUV Hutton had finished taping Zoë's car.

"Where to?" he asked.

"Main Street, Town Hall—let's hear what Striker has to say."

Chapter 4

The freshly painted black and white sign hanging above the door of the graying clapboard building said 'Largeville Town Hall.' New window boxes with blue and pink and white petunias were mounted under each of the two large front windows. Flanagan studied the other buildings. None had visible recent additions or refurbishments except possibly the storybook-looking red brick bank that sat on one corner of the town's main intersection.

Striker stood on the sidewalk, thumbs hooked into his belt, talking to a large man in overalls and a John Deere cap so sweat stained dirty that it no longer had much of its original green color left. Unhooking one of his thumbs like he might be drawing a pistol for a shootout, Striker poked a finger in the big man's chest.

"That's an aggressive discussion," Flanagan said.

"Do you think he stands out there all day?" Hutton asked.

"Well he did tell us he's the mayor."

Hutton pulled in and stopped next to Striker's SUV.

Striker waved. Hutton flashed the police lights.

"That'll make his day," Flanagan said.

"Who, besides Striker, do you think we should see?"

"Actually, I'd like to start with the kid, then Striker, and then Joe. They'll point us to others."

"We'll have lots of time. Nothing much else happening here for the next few decades, except church tomorrow being as how I saw a Baptist Church and Baptists don't miss church on Sunday."

"Voice of experience?"

"Dorie's family is all Baptist."

Flanagan was about to say, "You've got to be kidding!" but noticed his mood had turned pensive. Instead she said, "So we don't interfere with church. Besides, I think I'll to go to Chicago tomorrow."

"Other than the Cubs, who's in Chicago?"

"Low blow."

"Better bet than the Mets."

She didn't know why she was a Met's fan. She'd never seen them play other than on TV. Always the underdog to the damn Yankees, she guessed. "Casey says the victim's parents live in Chicago."

Hutton turned to look at her.

"Please don't question my approach."

"What did I say?"

"I know what you're thinking."

"What I'm thinking is that you're more dedicated than most cops I know, including me."

Flanagan's face grew hot.

"Apology accepted," Hutton said.

"I didn't apologize."

"Your face flashed red."

She brushed at her cheeks and reached for the door handle.

"Know what I'm doing tomorrow?"

She looked back.

"I'll be sitting with my feet up drinking beer and watching at least six baseball games on my 36-inch HDTV."

"I didn't say I planned on going alone."

"You wouldn't?"

"I would."

They got out and joined Striker. The big man in the overalls and the dirty John Deere cap had already started off up the sidewalk toward the center of town. Flanagan watched as he crossed Main Street. He looked back once and hesitated, but then kept on going.

"Your friend isn't happy," Flanagan said.

"Oh, that's big Johnny Burke—he's always that way. C'mon, let me show you around." Striker ushered them inside. The small building had two rooms separated by a hallway. "This here's my office," he said as they entered the room to their left. "Over on that side"—he jerked a thumb—"is a conference room that you might want to use, assuming you'll want a place to talk to some of the folks here in town."

He made a big production of sitting in the big, expensive looking leather chair that sat behind the battered wooden desk.

"The mayor has a nice throne," Flanagan said. The four wooden chairs, side table, and desk were old and rickety.

"In case anyone asks, I bought and paid for it with my own money."

"How long have you been mayor?" Hutton asked.

"Got elected twelve years ago, and I'll probably be mayor until I die or move…no one else in town wants the job, that's for sure."

"Why is that?" Flanagan asked.

"Too much bitchin'—excuse me ma'am—and moanin'. Everyone's got a complaint about this or that or the other."

"And you don't mind?"

"Hey, I like this town. I like the people. I like hearing about everything that goes wrong."

"You're the problem solver," Hutton said.

"Don't solve many problems, but I'm a good listener and they think I do." He laughed, too loudly Flanagan thought, and when he'd recovered from his fit of mirth, he said, "I had those babies done for our Centennial." He pointed at three large photographs in depressingly dark wooden frames. The brass plates tacked on the bottom identified them as aerial views of Largeville taken in 1993 for the state's centennial.

"A little late, aren't they? I thought the centennial was in 1989."

"Better late than never I always say. And this here's my rogues' gallery." He got up and walked to a clutter of pictures on the side table.

Flanagan took a closer look. The common thread was Striker's face and pushed back cowboy hat and lots of red and white and blue balloons.

"These are some of the people you might want to be talking to." He pointed to the larger picture in the center. "But not him, he's the governor, and that's the governor's wife, and that's my missus, except you can't see her face because of the balloons. She always hides behind the balloons."

"Why is that?" Flanagan asked.

Striker looked at her as though he'd never thought about it before, and then shrugged it off. "And that's big Johnny Burke—he's the one I was talking to when you drove up—and that's his missus." Striker's finger whipped back and forth as he continued naming various people. Flanagan paid more attention to his finger that looked as though it had been broken several times. Maybe he'd poked it in Big Johnny's chest once or twice too often.

"Let's take a look at the conference room," Flanagan said.

Striker led them across the hallway. Four captain's chairs with foam pads sat around an old rectangular table. She gave the table a shove with her hip fearful it might fall over, but it seemed sturdy enough. Hutton clicked the wall switch and the two overhead neon lights buzzed and zapped to life.

A dozen gray metal chairs sat stacked against the back wall. Duplicates of the aerial photographs that hung in Striker's office hung in the conference room.

"That blind work?" Flanagan asked, looking at the Venetian blind hanging in the front window.

Striker went to the window, raised and lowered the blind and closed and opened the slats. "Seems OK," he said.

"This will do just fine," Flanagan said. "I assume there's a washroom?"

"Yeah, in the back. It's unixex, but it's clean and everything works."

Flanagan and Hutton put their cases on the table and removed their laptops.

"I was wondering what you had in there," Striker said. "Thought maybe it was extra guns." He grinned.

"Just tear gas and hand grenades," Hutton said.

Striker stopped grinning.

Flanagan chuckled to herself.

"Well, I guess you'll be wantin' to start with me," Striker said, and gripped a chair, swung it around, and raised a leg as though he were mounting a horse.

"Actually, since Tommy was the one who found the body, I'd like to talk to him first, provided it's all right with you of course."

Striker's leg stopped in mid-air. "Well, yes, of course, I just thought…he's with Joe. I'll call the café and have him report straightaway."

"Thanks. I promise we'll get to you as soon as we've talked to Tommy."

"Yes, of course." He retreated to his office.

"I think you broke his heart," Hutton said. "Not nice to fool with the mayor."

"Look who's talking—grenades and tear gas? Give me a break."

"It'll give him something to tell his loyal subjects."

They turned the computers on and checked the recorders to make sure they were working. Hutton tossed his notebook on the table. Flanagan flipped hers open, but left it in her case.

"You want them facing in?"

She nodded. Hutton placed his case on the chair facing the window. Then they removed their hats and placed them on the case so that anyone could plainly see that the only empty chair faced away from the window.

Striker stuck his head in. "I have to run this up the pole." He had an American flag folded under his arm. "Tommy will be here in a minute."

Flanagan went to the window. Tommy ambled up the sidewalk puffing on a cigarette. Through the open door she heard Striker say, "Give me a hand with this flag, boy."

Tommy flicked his cigarette into the street.

"Come on boy, I haven't got all day."

Tommy didn't increase his pace. Striker reached back and closed the door. Flanagan could no longer hear what they were saying, but could still see them. Her stomach churned when Striker gripped Tommy by the back of the neck and gave him a shove along the sidewalk. It was as if she were back on her father's farm, as if it were her father's hand slapping her across the face and knocking her into the horse stall, ripping off her jeans while he took off his belt and smashed its buckle across her buttocks and thighs until she bled. She made up stories about having trouble with her period so she didn't have to take phys-ed until the welts and black and blue marks healed.

"Bastard," she said.

"What?"

"Striker grabbed the kid by the back of the neck and gave him a shove."

Hutton came to the window.

"I'd like to go out and kick the old man's ass," Flanagan said.

"Hey, the kid probably deserved it. My old man was always shoving me and my brothers around, cursing at us, kicking our ass, whatever, mostly because we deserved it."

"No kid deserves to be shoved around."

"Hey, take it easy, it's no big deal."

"It is to me."

Hutton stared at her for a moment and then said, "You want me to bring him in?"

Flanagan nodded.

Chapter 5

The voices inside his head started and he was nervous, but he wouldn't let them notice.

Listen to me Tommy, this slut's no different than the others, her eyes all over you like that. Curl your lip the way that you do, let her know you're in charge.

What am I supposed to do?

Don't do as they say; do the opposite.

"Please sit there," Flanagan said, pointing to the chair facing away from the windows.

She won't let me pass.

Show them you're the boss. Refuse. Sit where you want, not where they want.

"I'd like to sit at that end," Tommy said.

Now the guy is pissed. So's the broad.

Sit there," Flanagan said. "Please."

Tommy shrugged. "Whatever." Slut.

That's not how to show them you're in charge . I'm extremely disappointed in you.

Shut up. I know what I'm doing. I'm in control.

Flanagan stepped around Tommy, closed the Venetian blind, and returned to her chair. She and Hutton turned on their recorders.

"These are recorders, Tommy. We record all of our interviews."

No shit.

Flanagan opened her laptop and typed the date and time into a blank interview page.

"For the record, please state your full name."

"Uh, Thomas George Striker." God, I love your smell.

"Everyone calls you Tommy?"

He nodded. I love your nice round ass.

"How old are you Tommy?"

"I'm eighteen." I love your gorgeous tits.

She folded her arms across her chest and stared hard.

You know I'm checking your tits. Please don't hide them. Did you know your blouse is open? I can see your bra? It isn't fancy. Maybe it's police issue, maybe you have a knife tucked inside like that black bitch detective on TV, the one with the giant tits that fall out of her blouse.

"Mr. Striker...do you mind if I call you Tommy?" Hutton's deep voice resonated like that of a local TV newscaster.

Tommy faced Hutton.

Yes dork, I do mind, but like I have a say in the matter. "No, that's OK."

"Thank you for agreeing to talk to us." Hutton clasped his hands behind his head and stared at the ceiling. "We're going to break the back of this case. The person or persons who did this will be brought to justice, they will not escape the long arm of the law, and we're counting on you to help us."

Jesus, what's your name, Detective Cliché?

"And another thing, everything within these walls is confidential so feel free to tell us everything you know."

"Yes sir." You think because I live in this shit hole town that I have shit for brains. Here's a newsflash, Dickhead: anything I tell you will be written down, either by you or the slut lady, entered into your shitty police-issue laptops, and transferred to a mainframe where it will be available for any amateur hacker to see.

Flanagan pushed at the mop of reddish-blonde hair pinned on top of her head.

You're not a great beauty, not like Miss Brown—you're too pale and your nose is pointy and spattered with too many freckles, maybe you have freckles on your tits, maybe I'll lick them off. Miss Brown had been around...she'd been with a lot of men, not like the girls in this dump who don't know how to please a man. How about you Detective, have you been around? Do you know how to please a man?

Flanagan shifted in her chair and crossed her legs. Her foot protruded past the end of the table.

Nice boots. Miss Brown didn't wear boots, always sexy high heels that made me want to lick her feet. Tommy stared at the curve of Flanagan's thigh. Jesus, I'm getting such a boner. He patted his shirt pocket. God I need a cigarette. He looked around. Not one fucking ashtray. Thank my old man for that. He looked back at Flanagan.

What are you—twenty-five, thirty? You're not sexy. Miss Brown was sexy, especially when she put on her tight shorts with no panties and t-shirt with no bra and paraded around town advertising her juicy wares, just waiting for some guy to jump her bones. You ever go braless, slut lady? I'll bet you always wear panties. Maybe you're still a virgin. Maybe you need the big cherry ride.

Flanagan glanced at Hutton.

What, you think he's some kind of god? You two got something going? Riding around in that big SUV every day, stake-outs—lots of time to fuck your brains out.

Flanagan glanced back at Tommy.

Yeah, I feel the electricity. I know you want me bad. He smiled. OK, don't respond.

"Tommy, how long have you lived in Largeville?" Hutton asked.

"Since I was five or six."

"That would make it twelve or thirteen years."

No shit Einstein. "Yeah."

"Are you still in school?"

"Yeah."

"You know, Tommy, if you volunteered a little information, I wouldn't have to ask so many questions."

"OK." Asshole!

"What grade?"

"Twelve."

Hutton shook his head.

Tommy returned his attention to Flanagan.

Your fingers are delicate though, like Miss Brown's.

Her finger twitched.

I'll bet that's your trigger finger, the one that you use to kill. Have you killed anyone? Now that's a turn-on, knowing the woman you're fucking is a killer. Your nail polish looks like dried blood and my boner's coming back big time. Please tell me you've killed someone.

"Tommy," Hutton said, "I realize this is probably making you nervous, but why don't you start by telling us how and when you found Miss Brown?"

Yeah, I'm scared out of my frigging mind. Tommy leaned back in his chair, put his hands behind his head, and stared at the ceiling. How do you like it Prick Tracy, me acting like I'm you?

"Don't hold back, Tommy. Tell us whatever you want and let us worry about what's important."

OK dumb ass. "Well, let me see. I found her early this morning, around six."

Flanagan asked, "Why were you out that early?"

Hey slut bitch, how am I supposed to tell my story if you keep interrupting me? "I went to meet my friend, Dale. He wanted to look for bottles and cans. Every Friday night there's a big dance…next day there's always lots of bottles and cans."

"Why does he look for bottles and cans?" Hutton asked.

"His old man won't give me money for cigarettes."

"Does your father give you money for cigarettes?"

Tommy smirked. "He gives me money. He doesn't know what I spend it on."

"And that's why you were out on the road?"

Tommy nodded. "Yeah, me and my dog, Zinc."

"When we arrived your friend wasn't there," Flanagan said.

What can I tell you? He's an asshole. "I guess he slept in."

"Have you spoken to him?"

"I got his voice mail."

Flanagan recorded some notes into her laptop.

"The grass is pretty thick along there," Hutton said.

"Yeah, I guess."

"You couldn't see from the road."

"I stayed on the road because the grass was still wet, but Zinc doesn't care about wet grass. He heard mice or something scurrying around and raced in. Then he reached the edge of the ditch and stopped cold. From his stance, I knew he'd found something. I told him to come, but he wouldn't budge so I went after him, trying to follow one of his trails so I didn't get soaked. I felt him quivering when I grabbed his collar. That's when I saw…well, you know, that's when I saw her feet sticking out."

"What did you do then?" Flanagan asked.

"I got the hell out of there—I yanked Zinc's collar hard and ran to the café."

"Why there?"

"Joe was there. I saw him open up."

"And then?"

"After Joe called 911, we went back to where I'd seen Miss Brown."

"Did he see Miss Brown?"

"Joe said he didn't want to go anywhere near the ditch."

"So you just stood there and waited?" Hutton asked.

Tommy nodded. What the fuck else were we supposed to do? Tommy took a cigarette from his shirt pocket. "Do you mind?" he asked Flanagan.

"We'll soon be finished," Hutton said. "Then you can smoke outside."

I wasn't asking you, asshole. He tucked the cigarette behind his ear and shoved the pack back into his shirt pocket. He flicked his lighter a few times.

"What made you think the person you saw was Miss Brown?"

"Her red shoes."

"There are lots of red shoes."

"They were the same ones she wore to the dance. I knew they were hers."

"So you saw Miss Brown at the dance," Flanagan said, flipping through her notes.

"Yeah, she was there."

Go ahead, tell them how that little whore wore red high heels with the sexy straps around the ankles; tell them how she wore that low-cut dress the same color as the shoes; tell them how flaunted her long, slender legs so luscious and white; tell them how she showed off the tops of her milky breasts that bounced up and down when she walked. Tell them how she let her dress fly up when she twirled so everyone could see her thong, black it was so everyone would think they'd caught a glimpse of her succulent pubic hair. Go ahead big man, tell them how she kept coming on to you, how she wouldn't leave you alone. You thought you were in control...what a laugh.

Shut up, just shut the fuck up. I was in control. You don't know what you're talking about.

"Was she with anyone?" Hutton asked.

"She always came alone, but there were always a bunch of guys who wanted to dance with her."

"Did you dance with her?"

"No."

Because the little boy was afraid to ask—he was too much in control.

I wasn't afraid. I could have rubbed against her. I could have felt her breasts pressing to my chest. I could have felt her pressing into my crotch. I could have felt her throbbing pussy brushing up and down on my legs.

That's another laugh. You make me sick.

"Were you there alone?"

"I went with my friend, Dale."

"The same one supposed to meet you on Saturday morning?"

Tommy nodded.

Tell them about his girlfriend, Karen, the one you'd like to fuck if you had the nerve to ask.

I've got the nerve.

Yeah big boy, in you dreams, just like all the others?

"Did you and Dale leave together?"

He nodded.

"What time does the dance usually end?" Flanagan asked.

"Usually three or four. The band is supposed to stop playing at two, but someone always gives them fifty bucks to play longer."

"Is that why your friend didn't meet you, because you stayed until the end of the dance?"

"Nah, we left around midnight."

Hutton chuckled.

Hey asshole, I don't always go home early if that's what you're thinking. Sometimes I hide in the ball diamond across the road behind the fence and watch the leading citizens of Largeville switch partners and screw each other's wives in some car or right out there on the ground. Sometimes they come over to the ball diamond, and I get a close up look. One couple did it in the visitor's dugout while I hid under the bench. They did it on the bench, right in front of my face, and while they were doing it, I was whacking off.

That's about as close as you're going to get.

Shut up! SHUT UP! SHUT UP!

"Was Miss Brown still there when you left?" Hutton asked.

"Yeah. She's always there."

Because you haven't got the nerve to ask if you can walk her home; you're afraid she'll laugh and tell you to come back in a few years, after you're a real man.

She would've come with me. I didn't ask.

"Tommy, is something wrong?" Flanagan asked. "You seem distracted."

"Uh, no, I'm OK."

Flanagan made a few notes, studied the computer screen for a moment, and then asked, "Tommy, do you get along with your father?"

Tommy glanced at the closed door.

Here's your chance: tell them how he's always embarrassing you in front of your friends by grabbing your neck and marching you down the street and by telling everyone you wet the bed until you were fourteen. Tell them how he punched your buttocks until they were black and blue. Tell them how you cried from the pain when you sat at your desk. Tell them how he punched your mother until she couldn't take any more; tell them how he punches the squaw between her legs and on her arms because she won't have sex.

"He's OK, I guess."

You're a coward.

"Like all fathers?"

"Yeah, I guess."

"Does he hit you?"

Tommy looked away.

"I saw him push you on the sidewalk."

"He told me not to say anything."

"Does he hit your mother?"

"My mother's dead!"

That's the way. Give her the blast.

"I'm sorry, Tommy, I didn't mean to upset you."

"I'm not upset."

"So there's just you and your father?"

Tell the nosy slut it's none of her goddamn business.

"Lottie lives with us."

"Is she your father's new wife?"

"I guess."

"You don't sound too happy."

How would you feel if your father married a twenty-year old squaw? "No, it's OK."

It's not OK. She's a fucking Indian, a smelly, greasy Indian. You know what they call you: little chief Tommy? They call your father a squaw fucker.

Tommy studied Flanagan as she wrote in her notebook.

Flanagan looked up. "We'd like to talk to your friend. Have him stop by later this afternoon."

Tommy nodded. "Is that all?"

Hutton said, "That's all for now. We may need to talk to you again in a day or two, after we've talked to some of the others."

Tommy got up, put his cigarette in his mouth, and started for the door.

"Don't tell your friend what we talked about," Flanagan said, joining Tommy at the door.

Tommy turned, brushing hard against her breasts. Thank you Jesus.

"Uh sorry," he said. "No ma'am, I won't."

Chapter 6

Hutton said, "The kid's a pervert. He sat there the whole time wondering how you'd be in the sack."

Flanagan's face grew warm. She knew Tommy had been staring at her breasts and suspected his brushing against them hadn't been accidental, but still, that didn't give Striker license to use him as his personal punching bag.

"He's an eighteen-year-old boy whose father smacks him around—cut him a little slack."

"Let's not forget what our job is here."

"And what would that be?"

"You should know by now."

"Oh I know, but you seem to think I don't so please elucidate oh wise one, please tell me what our job is."

"You're being a smart ass, Flanagan, but don't lose sight of the fact that we're here to find the victim's killer, not play nursemaid to some kid with hormones for brains."

"I'm not playing nursemaid. There's nothing in the manual that says we can't empathize with our suspects."

"You want to empathize, empathize with the victim."

If you only knew, Flanagan thought. "Listen, I feel sorry for the kid. My old man kicked me around. I know what it's like."

Hutton seemed about to say something more, but instead decided to stare at his computer screen. Figuring silence the best route for her also, before she said something she knew she would regret later, she turned and stared out the window. After a moment, she turned back to Hutton and said, "Let me ask you a question."

"I'm not sure I want to hear this."

"It's not what you think, or at least it's not what I think you think."

"You're getting way too complex for me, Flanagan. I'm just a simple cop."

"Yeah, and I'm Elliott Ness. Do you think Tommy told us the truth...about how he knew it was Miss Brown?"

"You have doubts about the all American boy?"

"Sometimes you really piss me off."

Hutton made a little grin.

"So do you?" she asked.

"Yeah, I think he told us the truth."

"You don't sound like you'd stake your life on it."

"Don't get me wrong, I think the little dirt bag would lie to his parish priest, but I also think, despite the curled lip and tough-guy front, that he's scared shitless."

Flanagan stared at him for a moment wondering when he'd reached that conclusion, wondering if she felt the same way or was she using his years of experience as a crutch to help her feel something more than she did.

"I don't like you doing that," he said.

"Doing what?"

"Staring. Tell me what's running through your mind."

"I'm not sure if I feel the same as you or if I think he's been clobbered so many times by his old man that he's become a pathological liar—saying what he thinks will keep him safe, keep him from pain.. I think he told us exactly what he thought we wanted to hear, true or not."

"That's deep Flanagan."

"I should've known you wouldn't get it."

He chuckled. "Here's what I noticed: he kept digging at his nails, and other than tossing around an odd glare as part of his tough-guy persona, he wouldn't look directly at either of us."

"And that tells you..."

"That shows me fear."

"Maybe he wouldn't look directly at us because he chose to stare at my breasts."

"Well, and please don't take this as sexist, but we can't accuse him of bad taste."

Flanagan threw her pencil. Hutton ducked. The pencil sailed past his ear and hit the wall. "Good shot," he said. He plucked it from the floor and handed it back. "You think the kid's best friend...what's his name"—he flipped through his notes—"Dale Kiley will provide any answers?"

"I think he'll help us decode Tommy Striker."

"You really think he's that complicated?"

"I think there's a lot going on in his brain, things that Tommy will never tell, at least not truthfully."

"I wonder if he and the victim had a little something going."

"Who's reaching now?" Flanagan asked.

"You saw how he reacted when you asked about the men in her life."

"That doesn't mean they were lovers."

"Oh come one—the kid was flipped."

"That doesn't make it reciprocal."

"Think about the red shoes," Hutton said. "Tommy seemed too certain. My bet: he's seen her in them more than at the dance."

"Your mind is as sexually fanciful as his."

"Hey listen, I toss it on the table for what it's worth."

"Consider it tossed."

"I'll remember this when we learn otherwise."

"Make sure it gets into your report."

"Page one, Flanagan. You know me."

"Tell you what: If I begin to think otherwise, about Tommy and the victim I mean, you'll be the first to know." She walked to the door.

"Don't leave on my account."

"I hate to deflate your ego, but McManus has arrived."

Hutton got up from the table and joined Flanagan as she walked out to McManus's blue Chevrolet with a large State Medical Examiner's sticker on both front doors. McManus rolled down the window. Flanagan welcomed the rush of cool air and leaned forward, resting her arms on the door.

"You know Detective Hutton?" Flanagan asked McManus by way of introduction.

"We've met," McManus said. "How are you, Bob?"

"Fred," Hutton nodded. McManus's name was Fredericka; most everyone called her Fred. Even in her severe blue ME uniform, Fredericka, with her high cheekbones, thin face, and tall, shapely body, definitely wasn't a Fred.

Flanagan told her how to get to Hilda and Howard's place.

Hutton said. "I sealed her room and car."

"How decent of you." The look on McManus's face asked why Hutton and not Flanagan had performed that menial task, akin to vacuuming and dusting.

"It's her case," Hutton said.

"About time," McManus said to Hutton. "Congratulations," she said to Flanagan.

"When you've finished there," Hutton said. "Come back and we'll take you to the school."

McManus drove off with a flip of her hand. Flanagan and Hutton walked back to the town hall.

"We should have sealed the classroom," Flanagan said.

"You mean I should have done that."

"I should have made sure."

"You mean I should've done it without being reminded."

"You want me to agree?"

Hutton took out a coin. "Heads or tails?"

"Heads or tails what?"

"You call it, I'm wrong. You don't, you're wrong."

Hutton flipped the coin.

"Is this why your record is so inconsistent?"

"Call it." He grabbed the coin and slapped it on the back of his hand.

"Heads."

He removed his hand. "You win," he said.

"I feel so much better now."

Hutton stopped and poked his head in Striker's office.

Striker looked up from his phone and waved them in. After a few seconds, he ended the call and hurried from behind the desk. "You ready for me?"

"We are, but first we'd like you to take us to the school."

"Oh." Striker seemed disappointed that it wasn't his turn to be front and center. "Well we'll need to get Ed Gregory. He's the principal. I can't just go barging in without him. I mean I can, being mayor and all and this being kind of an emergency, but to be politically correct, he should be there, if you know what I mean."

"Fine, call him. He needs to be told anyway."

Striker punched a button on his speed dial, talked for a moment, and grabbed his hat. "He'll meet us there," he said, and headed for the door. "We can walk if you want, or you can ride with me."

"We need to keep our vehicle close by," Hutton said. "We'll meet you there."

"Whatever you say." Striker swung up inside his SUV and tore off up the road the two blocks to the school.

Flanagan chuckled. "We need to keep our vehicle close by? I'll be sure to remember that one."

"Watch and learn, grasshopper," Hutton said.

Ed Gregory met them ten minutes later. He was short and bald and wore thick, rimless glasses. His stylish blue jacket and grey slacks seemed out of place in Largeville, particularly on a Saturday morning. He

explained he'd only just returned from a State principal's convention in Minot and hadn't had a chance to
change.

Striker introduced Flanagan and Hutton. It was obvious from the big question mark that took up residence
on Gregory's face that he hadn't heard about Miss.
Brown.

"Mr. Gregory," Flanagan said. "I'm sorry to have to
tell you this, but one of your teachers, Miss Zoë Brown,
was murdered this morning."

"Oh my goodness," Gregory said, clutching at his
chest. He reached for the edge of his desk. Hutton
grabbed Gregory's free arm and helped him into his
chair.

Flanagan gripped Gregory's shoulder. "Mr. Gregory,
are you going to be OK?"

"Such an upsetting thing," Gregory said, his eyes
staring blankly.

"Mr. Gregory, look at me," Flanagan shouted. "Are
you going to be OK?"

Gregory raised his head and stared at Flanagan as if
wondering what she was doing in his office. "Such an
upsetting thing," he muttered.

"Ed," Striker said. "You want a drink of water?"

Gregory nodded. Striker came around behind the
desk and poured a paper cup full of water from the silver
thermos sitting on the credenza. He gave the cup to
Flanagan who held it out for Gregory to take. After a
few moments, Gregory seemed to recover and asked
what he could do to help.

Flanagan told him they needed to see Miss Brown's
classroom. Gregory led them down a pale green hallway
that needed repainting, past rows of lockers that looked
new, to a closed door that had 12C painted in black letters on the opaque window. Gregory stood aside as if
afraid to open the door.

"Is it locked?" Hutton asked.

Gregory seemed unable to take his eyes off the latex gloves that Hutton pulled on.

"Mr. Gregory," Flanagan said sharply. "Do you have the key?"

He blinked several times. "It's not locked."

Hutton opened the door and he and Flanagan gave the room a quick inspection. "Can this door be locked?" Flanagan asked, returning to the hallway where Mr. Gregory and Striker stood talking in low voices. "Our investigator will want to give everything a thorough going over."

Gregory went to his office to get the keys. By the time he'd returned, Hutton had sealed the door with yellow 'crime scene' tape.

"Our investigator's in Largeville now," Flanagan said, seeing the frown on Gregory's face. "She'll examine Miss Brown's classroom this afternoon. After that, it can be released so none of the students need see the tape."

"Such an upsetting thing," Gregory said for about the tenth time. "I don't know how I'm going to tell the others."

"Miss Foster and Miss Hale already know. We had to check Zoë's bedroom earlier this morning."

"Yes, of course, but the others, I don't know how I'm going to tell them."

"I don't know either, but if you don't figure it out soon, they'll find out on their own. Is that what you want?"

"No, of course not, but—"

"Mr. Gregory, I'd recommend you get on the phone right now and tell them. Call Miss Foster if you need help. She impressed me as a strong person."

He gave Flanagan a look that said, 'I hate you for making me do this.'

Flanagan and Hutton left Gregory to make his calls and returned to the town hall. Striker followed along behind and pulled in beside them. She asked Hutton if he wanted to interview Striker.

"You're giving me a promotion?"

"I want to watch his reactions."

"What if I miss something?"

"I'll jump in if I think you're not doing a good job, or you can always flip another coin."

Chapter 7

"You sure shook up old Ed," Striker said.

"Murder does that," Hutton said.

"Yeah, I guess it for sure does that," Striker said, shoving his hat back and scratching the furrows in his forehead. He looked over his shoulder toward the interview room. "Well, I guess you're ready for me now."

Hutton nodded and motioned him inside. He swaggered in, eyes darting between the two of them. Hutton pointed him to the chair Tommy had occupied.

Hutton and Flanagan turned on their recorders. Striker shifted uneasily.

"Standard procedure," Hutton said. "Unless you object."

"No no, that's fine. I just thought it'd be a little more informal like. This is a small town. Everything we do here is informal."

"Mr. Striker, before we start, we want you to know that everything you say within these four walls is confidential. That means we want you to feel free to tell us everything you can that may help us find the killer, to not be concerned that someone will find out what you told us. In other words, they won't find out unless you tell them, and we don't want you to tell them because we want everyone we question to tell us what they remember, not what they may have heard from you. Is that clear?"

Striker paled a shade and nodded.

"For the record, please state your full name."

"Yes sir. My name is Strike, uh Newton Striker, Newton Thomas Striker." He chuckled. "Sorry if I seem nervous. I'm not used to dealing with the police all formal like this." He glanced at the recorders.

"Yes," Hutton said. "Just pretend the recorders don't exist."

Striker nodded.

Hutton forced a smile that disappeared as quickly as it had appeared. "Mr. Striker, what is your age and how long have you lived in Largeville?"

"What? Oh, I'm forty-seven. I've lived here in Largeville for the past thirteen, no, let me think, it's twelve years now. There's just my missus, Lottie, Loretta actually, and the boy, Thomas George, Tommy everyone calls him. He's going to college in the city in September. Hard to believe, they grow up so fast. His mother and I never went to college. Not many did back in those days, at least not where we're from."

"Where is that?" Hutton asked in a way that said to Flanagan that he didn't care.

"Huh? Where are we from? West Texas originally, just outside Odessa. Yeah, Bush country, that's for sure, but I never met any of them. I'm a card-carryin' Republican though. Maybe that's what got me elected mayor. Most everyone in Largeville is Republican. We don't believe much in spending hard-earned money on a bunch of illegals. I say if they need help, send 'em back to Mexico. Same as all the others that have no business being here, like them Muslins over there in the Middle East, killing Americans and stealing our oil, and what do we do? Well I'll tell you what we do: we let them come here, invite them with open arms, look after them if they get sick. They live in tents all their lives, walk around half-starving, ride around on camels, then come over here, and we give 'em houses to live in and money to buy food and cars. Something's screwed up, that's for sure, and we have the Democrats to thank for that, but don't get me started."

"No we wouldn't want to do that," Hutton said.

"I'm not complaining, mind you. I'm happy to have a real job that pays real money."

"What is your real job, Mr. Striker?"

"I've been in the oil patch all my life. Right now, I work for Tex-Cal, an oil company out of Houston, checking properties, making sure production levels are maintained, figuring out how to squeeze more oil from the ground on these old wells, shutting down wells that can't get up to minimum requirements, that sort of thing. I keep log books. It's like meter reading only weekly instead of monthly."

"Not much oil in North Dakota," Hutton said.

"More than people think. Not like Texas or Louisiana, not by a long shot, but enough to keep me busy. Some of the leases here are on Indian lands where I've had experience, so I guess that's why Tex-Cal asked me to come."

"Hmmm," Hutton said, and scribbled in his note pad. Flanagan knew it was just for show.

"For the record, Mr. Striker, please confirm that it was you who identified the victim."

"Uh, yes sir. Joe and me. Joe Peterson, he owns the café."

"And it was your son who found the victim's body?"

"Yes sir."

"Did you know who the victim was before you made your identification?"

Striker worked his forehead with his fingers, his eyes glazing over.

Flanagan asked, "Did Tommy tell you he'd found Zoë Brown's body?"

"Huh? Oh, no ma'am, no he didn't. Fact is I didn't see him 'til I came up the road there. I didn't know what in tarnation was going on."

"What did you think was going on?" Hutton asked.

"What did I think was going on? I thought Joe and Tommy might be in some kind of trouble, that's what. I saw when you drove past my house on your way into town and said to my missus, 'What're the cops doing in town' but she didn't know, so I jumped into my SUV and headed off up the road to see where you went. We don't get many cops in Largeville."

"Why did you think Joe and Tommy might be in trouble? Has Tommy been in trouble before?"

"Huh? Trouble? Him? Might be good if he did, always sitting around doing nothing. No sir, no trouble for Tommy, but a parent is always the last to know, they say."

"Yeah, that's what they say. How about Joe Peterson? Has he ever been in trouble with the police?"

"Not since I've known him. Joe's a pretty straight-laced guy, working day and night at the café."

"Mr. Striker," Flanagan said. "Do you think Tommy knew who was in the ditch?"

"Huh? No ma'am. As I say, he didn't tell me. Maybe he told Joe. Did you ask Joe? What did Tommy say? Did he say he knew? I hope he didn't say he told me. If he did, he must have been confused."

"When you saw the victim, were you absolutely certain it was Miss Brown?"

"What? Yes sir. No mistaken her, poor thing. Such a pretty girl too. Most of the teachers kept to themselves, cliquey like, so no one really got to know them all that well, but Miss Brown was different, more outgoing. Whenever I'd see her on the street or in the store, she'd always come over to say hello, ask how I was doing, ask after the missus and the boy, said she hoped all was well. It seemed like she meant it, not just making conversation if you know what I mean?"

"No I don't know what you mean," Hutton said.

Flanagan shot Hutton a look. He was looking for ways to get under Striker's skin.

"It's just that some people ask but don't care. They look right past you when they talk, as though you aren't there."

"Mr. Striker, please tell us more about Miss Brown," Hutton said.

Striker's eyes went blank again and he rubbed at his forehead, traits that Flanagan already knew meant he'd missed the point of Hutton's question. She kicked Hutton's foot under the table.

"Like when she came here, what her interests were, how she spent her free time, if she had a regular boy friend, that sort of thing."

"Oh yeah, well sure, whatever I can, but you got to understand we weren't close or anything like that."

Hutton nodded. Flanagan made a few notes in her pad.

"Well, Miss Brown came to Largeville last year—September I think—at least she started teaching in September, but maybe she came in August to get settled and all that kind of thing, you know, before she started her new job."

"I thought she'd been here longer."

"No sir, this was her first year. Ed Gregory can tell you about that a whole lot better than I can. I'm sure you'll be wanting to talk to him some more, him being Zoë's, er, Miss Brown's boss and all."

"Did you say Ed Gregory?" Hutton asked.

"Yes sir. Ed Gregory, the one who met us at the school."

Hutton scribbled a note. "Please go on," he said.

Striker scratched his head. He was lost again.

"Where was she before she came here?"

"Sir?"

"Where did Miss Brown teach before?" Flanagan asked.

"As I said, Ed Gregory—"

"Yes, I know." Hutton said. "Ed Gregory can tell us, and we will talk to him, but what do you know, what do the people of Largeville talk about when they talk about Miss Brown, what do you hear? You're the man in charge; I'll bet they tell you everything."

"Yeah well I have to admit they do tell me things."

"I'll bet you know more than anyone."

"Well you got that right. Listen, this is hearsay so I don't know it for a fact, but the story I heard was that she graduated from one of them big teaching colleges back east, Illinois, I believe, and then taught for a year in New York City. One thing I do know for a fact: the kids here loved her—she was like a breath of fresh air over at that school."

"Was she Tommy's teacher?"

"Tommy's teacher? No ma'am. I believe she taught grade seven. Tommy's in grade twelve."

"You said you knew the kids loved her," Flanagan said. "We thought maybe you'd heard that from Tommy."

"Well, no ma'am, as far as I recall he didn't ever come out and say anything direct like that. It was just something that I heard over and over from the parents and after awhile, you begin to know it's true. Well, what I mean is that you don't really know it's true, but you think you know it's true—if you know what I mean?"

Hutton grimaced. Flanagan nodded.

"So I guess the only time you saw her was outside the school," Hutton said.

"She taught one grade twelve subject, English I believe, so we saw her for the parent/teacher meetings, three or four of them, the last one was about a month ago."

"So she was Tommy's teacher."

"No sir. That would be Mr. Gregory and Mr. Perini, the vice principal. Tommy took most of his classes from them though I'm not sure who teaches what subjects, except for the one he took from Miss Brown."

"I'm confused. If Miss Brown taught him one subject, doesn't that make her one of Tommy's teachers?"

Striker scratched his head. "Well, technically yes, but when we think of teachers, we think of the main teacher, not the ones who might teach a subject. Last year

Tommy took shop, yet we never thought of his shop teacher as his teacher, if you know what I mean."

Flanagan wondered if Striker had ever considered a run for higher government office.

"And other than that, all your contact with her took place outside the school?"

"It wasn't really formal contact or anything like that. In a town this size, you walk down that street out there"—he nodded over his shoulder—"and you're bound to bump into a few people coming and going, buying groceries and the like. Most days, Miss Brown walked to school so I'd see her on the sidewalk over there twice a day. When she saw me she always waved. She had a great wave, lots of energy, just like her: lots of energy. Of course I wasn't spying or anything like that—it's just that with these big windows looking out, it's hard not to notice people going by, even across the street. Hell, I can tell you the names of most everybody that walks or drives past here on any given day."

"Yeah, I'll bet you can," Hutton said, and inhaled deeply.

Flanagan wondered what he was up to.

"I hope you don't take this the wrong way, Mr. Striker, but did you see Miss Brown socially?"

Striker's face flashed red. "Well now sir, I resent that. Miss Brown was a fine lady and I'm not one to be fooling around on the missus. I've gone through a lot of shit—excuse me ma'am—but I never socialized with another lady. That's one thing I can say for sure. Came close a couple of times, long months away on some job up there in the Artic or out in some goddamn ocean; always lots of hookers around, but I didn't want to take a chance on bringing a pecker rash or worse home to the missus. I've seen a lot of marriages end because some guy couldn't keep his pecker in his pants. That's not for me."

"What I meant—"

"Oh, I know what you meant all right. Let me just tell you about one of my wife's best friends, Tutti Nixon, who got VD from her no-good husband. Bob's his name. He and I weren't ever friends, not close like our wives, but we worked the same jobs so I knew what he was doing. I told him a couple of times to be careful. He drank a lot, shit we all drank a lot, and one night he laid a black eye on me for not mindin' my own business, so I never warned him again. A couple of months later my old lady phones me out in the North Sea—she never phones me at work, not even in the same town and here she is calling me in the middle of the friggin' North Sea—I thought someone had died, bawling her eyes out she was, saying that Tutti was getting a divorce, that Bob had given Tutti some disease."

"And your missus, as you call her, thought you were doing the same?"

"Worse than that, that prick Bob told Tutti that it was no big deal, that we all did it, that it was either screw each other or screw the hookers so Tutti tells the missus to be careful because I'd been screwing around also. Good thing I never saw him again or I'd have killed him, the dirty, lying bastard. When I got home I had to go to marriage counselors and spend time with the pastor at our church just to convince the missus that I'd been behaving. And I don't even go to church regular like. I felt a complete fool telling this young preacher about my love life. What the hell does he know? The missus was into it though. Shit, she told him everything. Embarrassed the hell out of me."

"Well, it must have worked." Flanagan said.

"Ma'am?"

"The marriage counseling must have worked. I mean, you're still married."

"Well it did and it didn't. It's a long story."

"Why don't you tell us about it?"

"It's just that my first wife, the one I went to counseling for, ended up getting sick shortly after, and I had to put her in a hospital."

"Oh, I'm sorry."

"Yeah, well that's what happens sometimes. She isn't dead or anything, but isn't ever going to get better. A couple of years after I put her away I met a new lady that I wanted to marry so I got a divorce."

"Have you ever killed anyone, Mr. Striker?" Hutton asked.

"Huh? Oh, you mean what I said about killing Bob? Nah, that's just an expression. I'm sure you've heard it before. Even in the army I was a mechanic so I never killed anyone, but Bob's the closest I ever came. Maybe if he'd shown up about the time my old lady called, I'd a killed him for sure, then we wouldn't be having this conversation because I'd be in jail somewhere, maybe on death row down in Texas. We don't put up with any killing of our people down there. No sireee, kill someone in Texas you get the needle, not like other places."

"You mean like North Dakota," Flanagan said.

Striker snorted. "Nobody gets nothing here, not with all those anti-death penalty activists making noise. There's over five hundred on death row in Texas and just as many that's been executed."

"That's the best way," Hutton said. Flanagan glowered.

"Boy, you got that right."

"I guess with all those executions, there soon won't be any murders in Texas."

"It's the Mexicans and them other immigrants. Killing's a way of life for them. Nothing changes."

Striker folded his hands on top of the table and twiddled his thumbs for a moment, an activity that seemed to demand his full attention. Then he stopped and looked at Hutton. "Say, detective, I was just thinking how I need a coffee. What do you say I give Joe a call? What about you, miss?"

"I don't mind."

"No, I meant 'Can I get you something?'"

"I'll take a black coffee."

"Double that," Hutton said.

Striker called Joe. "Yeah," he said when Joe answered, "We need three black coffees up her pronto. Send the boy."

Joe showed up a few minutes later carrying three mugs of coffee on a round tray.

"Where's the boy?" Striker asked.

"It isn't busy right now and I needed air."

"How much for the coffee?" Flanagan asked, taking two dollars from her pocket.

"Put your money away," Striker said. "We never charge our guests."

Joe grimaced. Flanagan wondered how often Striker hadn't paid.

"Mr. Peterson, we want to talk to you next, say in about a half-hour?"

Joe looked at his watch and then at Striker.

"Give her a call," Striker said. "She's not doing anything."

After Joe had left, Striker said, "It's hard for him to be away near lunch time so usually my missus helps out."

"We can talk to him another time."

"He's open from six to midnight every day so he doesn't have what you'd call a mess of available time."

Hutton flipped through his notes. "Is Joe married?"

"Yeah, but his wife never lifts a finger to help at the café—too busy partying with the boys at the beer parlor."

"And Joe doesn't mind?"

"He used to, not for not helping, but for not looking after their daughter."

"Used to?"

"Sara—that's their daughter, a real looker like her mama, or at least like her mama used to look before the booze turned her old—anyway, Sara ran away to the big city a couple of months back, Minneapolis I think, taking up with every man she finds, so I hear."

"How old is Sara?"

"Oh, she's legal, if that's what you're asking, but just—she celebrated her eighteenth birthday on the way out of town."

"What is Joe's wife's name?"

"Won't do much good to talk to her; she drinks away half the day and night. Can't miss her if you go a looking though, with all that orange hair stacked on her head."

Flanagan looked back through her notes and added a few comments.

"Her name?" Hutton asked.

"Huh? Her name? Well, most folks that have known her for a long while call her Claudy, but her real name is Claudine. These days you hear about half of each, but back before she started drinking you never heard anything but Claudy. Pert thing she was too. Such a shame." Striker looked down as if in prayer and slowly shook his head.

"Since Joe's wife keeps company outside the marriage, how about Joe? Does he fool around with other women?"

"Who Joe? No sir, I'm pretty sure Joe's never fooled around. He ain't got the time for one thing. Always at the café, except for his doctor visits, something to do with his legs. They must be getting worse because my missus has been there a lot more than she used to. He goes to some sawbones over in Williston. I don't know the doc's name, but Joe'll tell you. Don't say I said anything, though. He doesn't like to talk about it much."

"As Detective Hutton told you at the start of the interview, Mr. Striker, everything you tell us is confidential."

"Yes ma'am, it's just that this is a small town and you don't want to be talking about your neighbors, if you know what I mean."

"We can imagine," Hutton said.

"Joe's a good one to talk to though. He's lived here for twenty years and hears everything that's going on, being in the restaurant every day like he is—probably more than he wants, the way that wife of his flits around."

"I guess your wife must hear a lot as well."

"My missus? You wouldn't want to talk to her. Of all the people in Largeville, she knows the least. Mostly she sits at home watching television—soap operas and games shows and Oprah. I got her one of them giant screen Sony's last Christmas. Course its good for sports too, so I let her have it during the day and I get it at night and on weekends. We stuck the little one in the bedroom in case one of us needs to watch something when it's not our turn with the big one. Usually that's her because I'm never home during the day unless I'm on my death bed."

"You don't strike me as the type that gets sick all that often." Flanagan said.

"Haven't missed a day of work in twenty years, and when I'm not working at my real job, I'm here running the business of the town. It's not much, but bills have to be paid and decisions have to be made."

"Always something," Hutton said.

"One person I do think you'd want to talk to though is Tony Perini, vice principal of the school. I used to see him and Miss Brown together all the time, but I think he's a faggot so I can't imagine there was anything going on between them, if you know what I mean."

"I'm not sure I do know what you mean, Mr. Striker." Flanagan said.

"I don't mean to upset you none ma'am and maybe I'm wrong, but it's getting so you just can't tell these days."

"You can't tell what?" Flanagan asked.

"Well, I mean they're everywhere: football, baseball, government's full of them. Most of them look like ordinary people. What I mean is they don't wear them bright clothes and talk funny and flip their hands around."

"There are homosexual policemen, Mr. Striker."

"Yes ma'am. I see that on TV. Gay and lesbian cops. Those lesbian cops are tough looking broads. I mean no offence or anything."

"Mr. Striker," Hutton said, "before, when I asked about you seeing Miss Brown socially, I meant at church or other social events in the town."

"Oh well now, that's a different story. Sure, Miss Brown, she was active in all sorts of things. Not church though, people always said they never saw her in church, but school projects like fund raisers and parties for the kids, and town events like the big Christmas show we put on and the Easter egg hunt for the kids. At Christmas, she helped wrap presents—every kid in town under age six gets a present—she even rode in the sleigh with Santa Claus. Some of her students were dressed as elves in green and red costumes. My missus helped make the costumes. For two weeks, we had nothing but red and green cloth all over the house and then the kids came for fittings. Pain in the ass, but the missus seemed to have a good time. Same with the Easter egg hunt. The kitchen was nothing but eggs boiling and cups of dye sitting all over the place and the stink of vinegar. Every year, big Johnny Burke—you might be wanting to talk to him—dresses up as the Easter bunny and hands out baskets of candy eggs."

Flanagan noted Burke's name.

"So she didn't go to church?"

"No sir, leastways that's what everyone said. Not that anyone cared; it is just one of those things that people in small towns notice and talk about. Most said she usually went to Minot or Williston on Sundays so maybe she went to church there, though I don't know why she'd go all that way when we got three perfectly good churches here in Largeville."

"Three?"

"Yes sir. There's the Baptists up at the other end of Main Street, near Howard and Hilda's place; then there's Central over here across from the curling and skating rink—that's where me and the missus go when we go, but we don't go often so maybe they talk about us too—and the Lutherans on the east side. The Lutherans and Baptists are a lot stricter than Central. They all go two or three times a week. Maybe they need more saving than the rest of us." Striker chuckled. When Flanagan and Hutton didn't respond, his chuckle evaporated.

"Did you ever see Miss Brown with a man?"

"Oh yes sir, she had lots of men friends. I mean not that she was a loose woman or anything like that."

"Did she see anyone on a regular basis?"

"Well now, come to think of it, no. The only time I ever saw her with a man was at the Friday night dances. I can't recall seeing her with a man other than that. Everything she did in town, she was always alone, you know like eating at Joe's or at town picnics, stuff like that."

"Other than Mr. Perini, what about the other male teachers—did she socialize with them?"

"I don't recall ever seeing her with anyone other than Perini."

"Is there a teacherage for the men?"

"Perini rents a small apartment across from John and Lizzie Burke's place up by the curling rink. Ed Gregory rents a house. Someone said he likes to garden in his spare time. To each his own, I say."

"Does he live alone?"

"Yes ma'am. As far as I know. The town wouldn't look favorable upon him living with a woman, him being a teacher and all. Send a bad message, if you know what I mean."

"What about living with a man?"

"Huh? No ma'am. That'd for sure be worse. We're trying to teach our kids to be normal here—none of them weird homosexual relationships."

"Do you think Miss Brown was a lesbian? You never saw her with a man and she lived with two other women."

"Well now ma'am, one can draw their own conclusions about anything, but there's no way in hell that Miss Brown was a lesbian. From what I hear, every young single man in the county used to show up at the Friday night dances just to see her—she just hadn't found the right one, that's all. I'm told a couple of our local boys, one's a farmer and one lad lives here in town, were probably as much in the running as any of the rest of them, including those big city boys. Yes ma'am, our boys are quality young men, through and through."

"What are their names?"

"Well sir, I can give you their names, but if you're thinking they had anything to do with Miss Brown's murder, I can tell you right here and now they didn't. No sir, not those two."

"Still, we'd like their names."

"The farm boy is Greg Adams. Farms his daddy's place; big spread, ten miles north of town. Greg's the only son, so he'll get it all one day. The young lad here in town is Dawson Richards. Smart as a whip, that one. He's off to graduate school in the east."

"But you never saw Miss Brown with a man."

"I think the main reason was that Miss Brown respected what people thought, what her students thought, so she wasn't about to be running all over the country with any old Tom, Dick, or Harry."

"But Greg Adams and Dawson Richards were OK."

"Yes sir, because everyone in town knows and likes them. If Miss Brown chose to go with anyone, we all hoped it would be Greg or Dawson."

"What about others in Largeville. Did anyone have any reason to want Miss Brown dead?"

"Maybe some of the women." Striker forced a chuckle.

Flanagan asked, "Some of the women?"

"Well, I didn't mean that seriously, of course, but Miss Brown was a mighty pretty young lady. Not many men in town that didn't have fantasies about her."

"Did you?" Hutton asked.

"No sir. I mean she was a beautiful lady and all that, don't get me wrong, but I'm a strictly one woman man. Lottie catch me foolin' with another woman, she'd just as soon kill me as cook me another meal."

"Did the women ever say anything?"

"When I said some of the women, I was just joking...I didn't mean anyone in particular—well, there was one, but she hasn't been around for few months."

"Tell us about her," Hutton said.

"Edie Coombs, a hot tempered vixen. She and her husband, Rick, came from Montana, Havre or one of them big cities, and lived in a shiny new trailer, one of those expensive Airstreams, up behind up behind Central Church. Some said his daddy bought it for them as a wedding present, hoping they'd move out of Montana. Anyway, that's beside the point. They hadn't been married all that long when they got here. No kids. A couple of them little fancy dogs, white poodles or something like that. I guess they took the place of kids, the way she fussed with them. She even bought them little fur coats for winter. That for sure had the people talking."

"Why do you think she had it in for Miss Brown?"

"Edie was a good looking girl, always dressed like one of them big city gals with fancy slacks and jackets, not in jeans like the womenfolk from around here. She was a big woman, not petite like Miss Brown, more like one of them big Italian women, either that or one of them other Latino types. I guess that's where she got her temper. Least that's what some of the womenfolk figured. I don't know how it got started, the problem with her and Rick I mean. No one ever does, do they? You think you got it all figured out and then BANG, something happens and you realize you don't know shit from shinola."

"Did Edie Coombs think Miss Brown had something to do with their marital problems?"

"I hear it started at a Friday dance. More shit gets started at those dances than anywhere else. Too much drinking. Even the women who aren't hot tempered like Edie sometimes beat the crap out of their husbands for foolin' around. Yeah, and the husbands beat the crap out of their wives. I never cottoned to the husbands beating the wives, though. A guy gets kicked in the balls for rummaging where he ain't supposed to, that's one thing, but beating on the ladies—give them a good talking to, that's what I say. It don't mean anything anyway, it's just the booze and everyone having fun."

"Your missus ever kick you in the balls for having fun?" Hutton asked.

"Huh? No sir, not me. As I explained before, I don't fool around. You meet the missus and you'll know why. Anyway, Rick Coombs, he's a good looking sucker, black curly hair, big brown eyes, like a Mexican except he's American through and through, not lazy, a damn hard worker, and smart. Anyway, the way I heard it, he goes and gets all liquored up at the dance back in January or February—I can't remember for sure except it was colder than a dead whore's heart, excuse me ma'am—and then disappears during a band break. When Edie discovers him missing, she starts roaring around like a crazy woman, cursing up a storm and screaming in some foreign language, Italian I suppose, but since no one in town speaks Italian they couldn't say for sure. Then about the time they thought they were going to have to tie her down to make sure she didn't hurt someone, Rick staggers in the side door, shirttail out, Miss Brown right behind, her dress and hair mussed up like she'd been in a wrestling contest."

"And Edie Coombs saw them."

"Yeah, she saw them all right because she screamed like a banshee in heat, charging at the two of them, fists flying like a windmill. Well, instinctively, old Rick steps in front of Miss Brown and Edie lands a boatload of haymakers on his chest and face, and before anyone can grab her, Rick goes down. Then she starts kicking him with her pointed boots and blood spurts from everywhere. Finally, big John Burke tackles her to the floor. John must weigh in about two-fifty at least, and even he has trouble keeping her down, so a couple of others grab her arms before she tears his hair and eyes out."

"And they got her under control?"

"They might have, but Burke's wife, Lizzie, joins the fray. She kicks the bejesus out of big John every chance she gets, but no one else better try so she grabs a handful of Edie's hair and tells her in no uncertain terms that she'd better keep her fucking mitts—sorry ma'am, just repeating what Lizzie said—off her Johnny or she'd not see the light of morning. Then she decks her out cold. That pretty much ended it, except for old Rick, who had to be rushed to the hospital. He got something like seventy-five stitches and a broken nose and a couple of missing teeth out of the deal."

"You seem pleased."

"No ma'am, I didn't mean to seem pleased, but it was a damn good fight."

"You mean except for Rick."

"Yeah, well as I said, Rick ended up in the hospital. On Sunday, when a few of us visited Rick, Edie still hadn't shown her face, and no one knew where she'd gone. Rick wasn't looking forward to ever seeing her again—he'd hired body guards to protect his room around the clock."

Striker grabbed his phone from his belt and peered at the number. "Excuse me for a moment. I got to take this call." He stepped across the hall to his office.

Flanagan reviewed her notes. Hutton went to the bathroom. By the time he got back, Striker had returned.

"Anyway," Striker continued, "Monday morning arrives. 9:01 a.m. Miss Brown is in her classroom facing her students for their morning drill or Pledge of Allegiance or whatever it is they're allowed to do these days, when the door bursts open and in barges Edie. To hear her students tell it, they could see fire shooting from Edie's nostrils and with a murderous look in her eye, she headed straight for Miss Brown screaming that she was going to kill her. Some of the students panicked and ran to the back of the room, but I'm told that Miss Brown played it totally cool. She kept herself in shape and was good at most sports so she managed to keep the desk between her and Edie, trying to calm her down, and then Ed Gregory and Tony Perini—they'd seen Edie tear up to the front of the school in her big SUV practically bouncing the steps—charged in and tackled Edie from behind. Lucky for them, Edie bashed her head against Miss Brown's desk on the way down and got knocked colder 'n a cucumber, otherwise she'd have likely beaten their cans off."

"That's quite a story," Flanagan said.

"Yeah, well Ed Gregory got all panicky thinking Edie might be dead and phoned for an ambulance, but by the time it arrived, Edie had come to. The fight had gone out of her, but that didn't stop her from taking off in a spray of gravel that broke a couple of windows in the school."

"What about the police?" Hutton asked.

"One of your fellows came looking for Edie, but Miss Brown wouldn't press charges and the school figured two broken windows weren't worth the trouble."

"And that's the last anyone saw Edie?"

"Last I heard, Edie was over in Vegas working some casino. Still had her fancy dogs. Rick never came back. His brother and father showed up about a month later and hauled the trailer away. I talked to them some. Decent people. They have a ranch in Montana. Said they didn't know where Rick had ended up, though I suspect he's on the ranch—he just didn't cotton to facing Edie. Not a very common name, Coombs, you could probably find them."

Striker glanced at his watch.

"I hope we're not keeping you?"

"No sir, it's just that it's almost noon. I have to get down to Minot by 1:00, and then out to check on some of my wells. I'll be back later this afternoon. Can we finish then, or tomorrow?"

*   *   *

Ask him if he knows Victoria Otto.

Who is Victoria Otto?

Her spirit resides in mine. I promised to find her killer, to free her spirit to journey to its final resting place.

Good of you to let me know. How many others are there, or do you plan on springing them one at a time?

No more.

You don't know who she is?

I never found out. I spent too much time trying to pretend she didn't exist.

*   *   *

Flanagan felt Hutton's kick. "Um, sure," she said to Striker, "but before you go, have you ever heard of Victoria Otto?"

"Can't say I have—she from around here?"

Hutton stared. He'd never heard the name either. "It's someone with whom Miss Brown may have been in contact."

Striker shook his head. "No, it's not a name I know."

Chapter 8

The instant the door closed behind the departing Striker, Hutton asked, "OK Flanagan, who is Victoria Otto?"

"First, I want to call Joe Peterson and tell him we'll see him at one instead of now. That'll give him a chance to handle his lunch crowd and give us a chance to grab a bite."

"Good plan," Hutton said, "so long as you tell me about Victoria Otto."

Flanagan nodded and called Joe Peterson. They agreed to meet at two. Flanagan made a reservation for three for lunch and tossed her phone into her bag.

"Do you think he lied about knowing Victoria Otto?"

"Don't try to change the subject."

"I'm not. Did he lie?"

"Yeah Flanagan, I got the feeling he did."

"I saw Victoria Otto's name in the victim's file."

"That's strange since we don't have a victim's file."

"While you were taping the room and car, I called Stan. He's started pulling information together." Her face felt warm. She'd never mastered the art of telling a convincing lie.

"I think you're making this stuff up as we go along. Not that I mind, just let me in on the play before you call it so I don't fumble the ball."

"It's there. Trust me."

"Flanagan, I never trust anyone carrying a gun."

"How about a bet then, a coin toss? That's more your style."

"What's the bet?"

"You're the master."

"Dinner. If Victoria Otto's name isn't in the file you owe me dinner—and an explanation." He started writing in his notepad.

"You're writing this down?"

He grinned and kept writing. "Oh," he said, looking up momentarily. "Dinner is to be this week."

She felt her heart beat faster. Since she'd started working with Hutton, she'd often fantasized about a romantic dinner, the two of them in some distant place where no one would know who they were, where his wife wouldn't show up and make a horrible scene...

She got up and went to the window, trying her best to inhale a few deep breaths without him noticing. A green half-ton stacked so high with hay bales that it looked like it might tip maneuvered around the larger potholes on the wide, dusty street. The driver was leaning forward, his arms wrapped around the steering wheel as if trying to make himself higher. He wore a battered brown hat that covered the back of his head and neck. The truck turned at the intersection and disappeared.

On the sidewalk across the street, an elderly lady in a green print dress limped along tapping her cane with each unsteady step of her march toward a building with yellow wood siding and a large red and white sign that said Cobb's Grocery.

She finally trusted her voice. "You'll have to think of something other than dinner. I make a practice of not socializing with co-workers."

"So I am right. You're admitting defeat."

"I'm doing no such thing."

"Why are you worried about dinner with a co-worker then?"

"A hypothetical, that's all."

"Don't give me that BS Flanagan. A nice juicy steak will do just fine and I know the perfect place."

She twirled the blind cord between her fingers, wondering what his idea of a perfect place would be. Her body began to feel warm. She started inhaling again.

"Hey, don't beat up on yourself, Flanagan. Everyone loses to me sooner or later. In your case, it just happens to be sooner." He laughed.

She remained silent, staring out, seeing nothing. After a moment she said, "OK, you win, there's nothing in the file so I'd like you to see what you can dig up. If there's nothing local, check with NCIC."

"National Crime Information Center? Not a chance, not until you tell me exactly who or what I'm looking for. I don't care if the State guys think I've lost it, but I'm not about to have the Feds, who by the way don't think anyone outside the FBI can tie their shoes and don't like me to start with, cart me off in a body hugger."

"Yeah, I've heard they have one or two in your size, custom made according to Carson." She turned to face him. "Seriously, I need your help on this. You know the State and NCIC better than anyone. If Victoria Otto exists, you're the one who can find her."

"Hey, I didn't say I wouldn't, I just don't want to look like an asshole."

She about said, 'Too late for that,' but bit her tongue.

"I know what you were about to say."

"You don't miss a trick." She couldn't help but laugh. He responded with a crooked grin.

"You got anything more than a name?" he asked.

"We're not looking for Jane Doe—how many Victoria Otto's do you think there are in the world?"

"We're not talking the Minot white pages here, we're talking a hundred million names, maybe more. How about an approximate date—this year, this century, sometime in the last thousand years, before Christ, when?"

"I'm not…"

* * *

She felt a tingling in her neck. She smelled orchids.
Saturday, May 14th, 1994.

* * *

"What's the date?" Flanagan asked.

"What's wrong with your nose?"

"Nothing, what's the date?"

"That's what I want to know, the date. What is this: 'Who's on first?'"

"No, I mean what's the date today?"

Hutton looked at his watch. "The 14th. You want month and year too?"

"When's the last year before this that we had a Saturday, May 14th?"

"If I could get on line—"

"Harry can check."

"You'd better call him. He doesn't like me much."

She got her phone from her briefcase and punched Carson's number on the speed dial. "You give yourself too much credit."

"It was a small dent."

"Yeah, a small dent in his new Jaguar, the car of his dreams, the car he'd been saving for all his life."

"Carson."

"Harry, when's the last time we had a Saturday, May 14th?"

"What?"

"The last Saturday, May 14th."

"You got something to tell me?"

"A hunch. Maybe not even."

"Hang on."

Hutton started his calendar program. Flanagan covered the mouthpiece. "Check 1994." Hutton looked at her curiously and punched a few additional keys.

Carson came back on the line. "We last had a Saturday, May 14th in 1994. Now tell me your hunch?"

"Our Largeville victim may be a connected to a young woman who was last seen on May 13th, 1994."

"You got a name?"

"Victoria Otto."

"I'll take a look. By the way, tell your friend Hutton he owes me a new Jaguar."

"He says you owe him a new Jaguar," she said to Hutton.

"Give him this." Hutton stuck his middle finger in the air.

"I saw that." Carson said.

"He says he saw that," she said to Hutton, "and I'm hanging up now. You guys can continue this on your own time." She ended the call.

"How did you know it was going to be 1994?" Hutton asked. "And while you're at it, I still want to know where you came up with Victoria Otto's name."

"That wasn't the bet."

He flipped back to his notes. "...isn't in the file and an explanation. It's right here, in black and white, 'an explanation.'"

She waited for the telltale tingle in her neck. She waited for the smell of the orchids. Nothing.

"Anytime you're ready."

"You wouldn't believe me if I told you. I'm not sure I believe it myself."

"Try me."

"Give me a couple of days."

Hutton gave her a sidelong glance.

"Two days," she said, not knowing what difference two days would make. She walked back to the window. "Well well, guess who's sitting across the street keeping an eye on us?"

Hutton joined her. They watched as Tommy got up and opened the grocery store door for the old lady in the green print dress.

"Say what you like, he's been taught some manners."

"I still say he's a pervert." Hutton said.

She smelled Hutton's cologne. A pleasant ache spread through her groin. "He likes you," she said, edging away, making sure no part of her throbbing body brushed up against him.

Tommy took out a cigarette, lit it, and blew a cloud of smoke as though blowing it in their faces.

"Pervert," Hutton said.

Chapter 9

Flanagan went out to the sidewalk. "Hey Tommy," she said.

"Hey," he said. He stood up and brushed the seat of his jeans, flipped his cigarette onto the road, and disappeared inside the store.

"You scared him off," Hutton said, joining her on the sidewalk.

"He's shy."

"He's probably watching as we speak."

She glanced across at the store windows. The idea of Tommy spying on them made her uneasy. Hutton and his pervert talk had started to get to her.

"It's closing in on twelve," Hutton said, glancing at his watch.

They started up the sidewalk toward the café. Flanagan called McManus and asked her to join them for lunch.

"She coming?" Hutton asked as Flanagan put her phone back in her bag.

"She isn't sure."

They crossed the street between the parked cars. "Looks like they don't lock their cars," Flanagan said, glancing at the keys dangling from the ignitions.

"They sure as hell don't wash them."

"Another day and ours will look the same."

They glanced back at the shiny black SUV that marked them as outsiders as surely as the bank of red and blue lights across the top.

"And so will we," Flanagan said, waving her hand in front of her face in a futile attempt to keep the grit from her nostrils and mouth as a car tore past and kicked up a cloud of dust.

"Someone needs to talk to that young lady about speed limits," Hutton said.

"You sure it was a young lady?" Flanagan asked.

"Long hair that looked washed. Guys with long hair let it get stringy."

"I didn't know you were a hair expert."

Hutton grinned. "Yeah, that's me, the hair expert."

"I'm glad we're within commuting distance," Flanagan said, nodding at the two-story wood-frame hotel that had a slight lean to the south. Along the side, a neon sign flashed "BEER PARLOR" in red letters. She thought of what Striker had said about Claudine Peterson. Four half-tons and three cars were already parked at the curb.

"Why did Miss Brown come to Largeville?" Hutton asked.

"Why did anyone come to Largeville?"

"Maybe that's a question we should add to our list."

"At least the bank looks solid," Flanagan said, glancing at the neat looking red brick building with green shutters. The large sign across the front said: The First National Bank, Est. 1942. Gold leaf lettering on the glass part of the front door said: FDIC Insured; Open Mon-Fri, 9:30 a.m. to 3:30 p.m.

"Must be farm money. The town doesn't look rich enough for a bank."

They arrived at Pete's Café with its two large front windows with blue gingham curtains.

"Joe's wife might not be helping out," Hutton said, "but some woman is, unless Joe's heavy into washing and ironing."

A sign on the door said they were about to enter Pete's Café. The aromas escaping into the street told them it might be worthwhile. Hutton shoved the door open and motioned Flanagan inside.

Six stools and a dark wood counter sat along the right, five booths lined the left, and three tables, each with four chairs, filled the center. Tiffany-like lamps hung over each booth, above the counter, and from the middle of the ceiling. Bright fluorescent glowed from the kitchen at the back.

More noticeable was the silence. Everyone had stopped talking and turned to gawk. They were all big men who wore either greasy looking baseball caps that said things like John Deere or Fram or STP, or battered and dirty cowboy hats that looked like they'd been in one rodeo too many. Flanagan got a creepy feeling like she'd stepped into a late night bar wearing an 'available' sign on her forehead. She was grateful when Joe rushed from the back and ushered them to the front booth.

"I saved this one for you," he said.

"I hope we're not taking anyone's place," Flanagan said. The other booths and tables were full.

"No ma'am, this here is Strike's booth. He's gone out of town. He told me to save it for the two of you."

"We'll need one more place setting," Flanagan said.

"Your investigator joining you?"

"Possibly," Flanagan said, surprised that he knew about McManus. The din of conversation resumed. "The privacy of small towns," Flanagan said to Hutton. "I wonder if they know everything we've talked about?"

"Probably," Hutton said.

The five foot, ninety pound McManus arrived a few minutes later and slid in beside Hutton.

"More room on that side, "Hutton said.

"She's in charge," McManus said. "Move your big ass."

Joe came back to their booth with a stack of warm raisin bread and butter and told them he had roast beef or pork chops. Both came with mashed potatoes, gravy, and corn, peas, and carrots. Dessert was apple pie, with or without ice cream. They gave him their order and he promptly disappeared.

"Anything interesting turn up?" Flanagan asked McManus.

"Nothing that rings bells. There were copies of her bank and credit card statements and phone bills neatly tucked away in a file in her closet. We'll need to examine the entries more closely but at first glance they appear ordinary."

"What about her phone records? Who does she call?"

"One Chicago number; numerous times, and several New York numbers, mostly random, but one pops up five times." McManus handed Flanagan a list.

She studied the details. "All dialed direct, all at night. Chicago must be her parents."

"I suspect you'll call the numbers," McManus said. "But I'll also run a check with our friends at ND Tel when I get back to the lab."

"Send me an e-mail one way or the other."

McManus made a note in her Blackberry.

"What about her car?" Flanagan asked.

"She gets it serviced at the BMW dealer in Minot. Since coming to Largeville, she's driven all of four thousand miles."

"I drive that in a month," Hutton said.

"Both Miss Foster and Mr. Vole said Miss Brown hardly ever went anywhere, mostly to Minot on Sundays, so I guess it's accurate."

"Did they say why she went to Minot?"

"They didn't know for sure. Miss Foster thought she visited a cousin in a nursing home."

Flanagan made a mental note.

The biggest of the big men sitting at the counter got up from his stool and lumbered to their booth. Flanagan recognized him as Johnny Burke, the man Striker had poked in the chest.

"Johnny Burke." He put out a big paw.

"Detective Flanagan," she said, feeling the sandpaper-like roughness envelop her hand. This is Doctor McManus from our lab and this is my partner, Detective

Hutton." Burke turned toward McManus and Hutton and nodded.

"Well, I won't keep you. Just wanted to say hello and hope you enjoy your stay with us. Going to be in town long?"

"Three or four days, off and on," Flanagan said.

"Bad business, this. Well, be sure to let me know if I can help." With that, Burke returned to his stool.

Flanagan watched as he talked to the men on either side who in turn talked to the ones beside them. Soon, two left their stools and walked to the tables and then to the other booths. Occasionally, a head turned with eyes cast in their direction. Flanagan couldn't hear what was being said, but suspected everyone would soon know that she and Hutton were going to be in town for three or four days, off and on.

She looked back at the kitchen and saw a trim woman in a hairnet and blue dress buzzing around. "That must be Striker's missus," she said to Hutton and McManus.

They craned around. "I'll bet she's a winner," Hutton said. "She's thinner than I expected."

"Not all Indian women are fat."

"How old did Tommy say she was?"

"Twenty-five?"

"I think he said twenty."

"Who are we talking about?" McManus asked.

They filled her in. She took another look. "I'd say twenty. Maybe she'll get fatter when she gets older. All the fat ones are older."

Hutton said, "I don't know—I've seen some young ones cast big shadows."

"You're both prejudiced," Flanagan said, just as the woman spun around and started out of the kitchen.

McManus said, "I'll bet ten bucks you weren't expecting that."

"Jesus," Hutton said.

A young Indian woman came to their booth, her arms loaded with platter-sized plates piled high with steaming food. "Sorry it took so long," she said, her husky voice warm and with no hint of an accent. "Pork chops for you sir and please be careful, the plate is hot, and for you too ma'am," she said to McManus, "And..." She swung toward Flanagan. "...that means the roast beef is for you." Her eyes locked on Flanagan's.

Flanagan tried to look away but sat frozen. She felt as though the breath were being sucked from her lungs. She tried to inhale and clawed at the table.

"Kate, what's wrong?" McManus started to get up.

Hutton grabbed Flanagan's hand.

The young Indian woman lunged forward and bashed the palms of her hands into Flanagan's chest. A gush of air rushed from Flanagan's mouth. She inhaled with a loud 'whoop'.

"She'll be fine now," the young woman said.

"My God," Hutton said.

Flanagan put her hand up to ward off further attention and patted the other against her chest. "Yes, I'm fine," she said, taking in several gulps of air, her eyes still fixed on the young woman, at her black intense eyes and sculpted cheeks and nose, at her black shiny hair that looked like polished ebony. "Thank you," she said.

The young woman nodded, a smile hinting at the corners of her eyes.

Flanagan tingled all over and felt a warm calm. She smelled the orchids and waited, but Zoë Brown didn't communicate. What's going on? What's happening to me? Is this part of what I'm going to experience? Unexplained black outs? Unable to breathe? You've got to give me some answers. You're the only one I can talk to. Am I going crazy? You've got to help me with this.

Hutton and McManus stared, mouths agape. The young woman turned and with the grace of a ballerina, floated toward the kitchen.

"Flanagan," Hutton said. "You're starting to spook me out."

"Ditto that," McManus said and gripped Flanagan's arm.

"Really, I'm fine. It was nothing."

"Well it didn't look like nothing from where I sit. This morning and now this. You get checked when we get back, or I tell Harry."

"Traitor."

"What happened this morning?" McManus asked.

"She fainted."

"I did not faint. I told you: too much beer last night."

McManus frowned. "Do as he says, Kate, or I'll tell Harry."

"Traitor."

"I'm serious, Flanagan," Hutton said.

"So am I," McManus added.

"All right, all right, I'll get checked. You happy? Now eat."

Flanagan was glad to see them dig in, to get their attention elsewhere for a few moments. Besides, she felt fully recovered, at least physically.

Hutton broke the silence. "That can't be Striker's old lady," he whispered.

"She's Indian," Flanagan said, "and she's young."

"Lottie, more coffee when you get a chance," Johnny Burke said from his counter seat.

"Seems as though it is," Flanagan said. "Striker said his wife's name is Lottie."

"I've never seen a more beautiful woman," McManus whispered.

Flanagan watched Lottie Striker pour Johnny Burke's coffee. Something didn't fit. How did she get stuck with a redneck like Newton Striker?

"It seems that Largeville is raising more questions than it wants to answer," she said to Hutton and McManus.

Chapter 10

After lunch, Flanagan and Hutton returned to the town hall. McManus went to the school to check Zoë's classroom. Flanagan contacted Doc Jackson in Minot to get an update on Zoë's autopsy.

"I may have told you some of this before," he said. "The blow to the side of the head killed her. There was no water in her lungs which means she was dead when they put her in the ditch."

"I wonder why she wasn't wearing clothes."

"She wasn't raped. No signs of struggle: no bruising, no broken fingernails, no cuts."

"From what we've learned so far, she doesn't seem the type that would voluntarily take her clothes off."

"Then they must have undressed her after they killed her," he said. "If she put up a fight, there should have been things like skin under her nails or bruising or even someone else's hair."

"What hit her?"

"Something metal, pipe, baseball bat—couldn't find wood slivers."

Flanagan ended the call and said to Hutton. "Did Tommy mention seeing signs of Miss Brown being rolled or dragged down the embankment?"

They checked their notes.

"He told us," Hutton said, "that he didn't want to go into the wet grass, and when he did go in, it was because the dog had knocked it down chasing mice."

"Her body had to be dragged or rolled or carried to the ditch. Why wasn't the grass already knocked down?"

"Two hours had passed; maybe it sprang back."

"I need to take a look. Besides, after that lunch, the walk will do us good."

"You walk; I'll meet you there."

The afternoon wind had come up and dust devils zigzagged up and down Main Street. Flanagan decided to ride. They stopped along the edge of the road where yellow 'crime scene tape' loosely encircled the area where Zoë's body had been found. She checked her watch. It had been six hours since they'd removed Zoë's body from the water. Flanagan got out and checked the grass. Six hours of hot sun had evaporated the morning dew, and while the grass had started to spring back from the trampling they'd given it, their activity remained clearly evident.

"If Miss Brown's time of death was 4:30 and Tommy found her at 6:30, he should have noticed the trampled grass."

"Maybe there were two of them and they stood at the side of the road and gave her the heave-ho."

"That's a long heave-ho."

Hutton peered down at the ditch. "I don't like giving the little perv the benefit of the doubt, but it's not an impossible toss. Didn't you say her legs were sticking out of the water?"

"They were."

"Well, if they went to the trouble of taking her down to the ditch they would have made sure she was totally submerged."

"Whose side are you on?"

"I said I hated giving him the benefit of the doubt."

"I think you're right. He might have some problems, but murder isn't one of them."

They got back into the SUV just as Joe Peterson came out of the café and headed toward his car. "There's our next appointment," she said. "Good timing."

Chapter 11

Without his apron and cap, it was a different Joe Peterson who entered the interviewing room. He wasn't tall, five-foot six, Flanagan guessed. His hair, though still black, had receded and thinned; the few remaining wisps on top brushed straight back. The V-shaped wrinkles on his forehead were constant, deepening to crevices when he raised his brushy eyebrows. His eyes were brown and intense. His prominent nose ended in a bulb that had copious vein lines beginning to show. Her mother used to say that heavy drinkers had one line for each year of alcohol abuse, something like being able to tell the age of a tree from its rings. Based on that analogy, Joe had been abusing for a lot of years.

A mat of hair from his chest popped up through the open collar of his checkered shirt, which, like the gingham curtains in his café, was starched and pressed. His faded blue jeans were clean and also look ironed. No one irons blue jeans. She glanced at his feet. He wore white socks and black loafers with crepe soles.

"Mr. Peterson, that was a great lunch," Hutton said.

"You didn't have to pay."

"It's against the law for us not to," Flanagan said.

"Oh, well I didn't know that. I didn't mean to suggest anything illegal."

"That's OK," Hutton said. "It was worth every dime."

The sides of Joe's face wrinkled into rows and a light flickered in his eyes.

"Thanks for agreeing to meet with us."

"That's OK, but I don't know why you'd want to talk to me. I guess maybe Strike told you to talk to me, though I don't know why. He knows I never have much to say."

"No one told us to talk to you, Joe. We're talking to several people in town who we think might help us figure out who murdered Miss Brown."

Joe nodded, and seemed to ponder what Hutton had said.

"For the record, please state your full name."

"Yes sir, let me see, well my name is Pete Peterson, Peter Peterson actually—it's Norwegian—though everyone calls me Joe. When we moved here, there was another fellow named Pete—he was always into trouble with the police, nothing big or anything, drinking and driving mostly…dead now. Anyway, a couple of the old-timers decided to call me Joe. I guess they thought one Pete was enough." Joe's eyes glazed over as though his mind had momentarily gone to another place.

"Joe, how long has it been since you moved to Largeville?"

"Oh yeah, well my wife, her name's Claudine, and I moved here from Minot right after we got married, eighteen, no, nineteen years ago. Our daughter, Sara, she was born in Trinity Hospital down there in Minot."

He folded his hands on the table. They twitched. His face flushed. "You'll probably find out anyway so I may as well tell you: Claudine was pregnant when we got married. We had planned on getting married anyway so it just moved the date up by a year or two."

"It happens," Flanagan said. "A lot don't even bother getting married these days."

"Yeah, I guess so. I couldn't do that though. Anyway, I loved Claudine and we sure did love that little baby girl."

"You could have moved here after she was born."

"Yeah, I guess so, but we're from another little place up near the Canadian border—that's where our families live—so we had to get out of there, you know, so we wouldn't have to look at their righteous faces seven days a week. They're all Pentecostals up there, figuring what we did was a big sin, the biggest, though it isn't one of the Ten Commandments. I wanted to tell them that, but Claudine, she said I couldn't."

"We didn't plan on staying here either; it was just a stopping off point, but Claudine's uncle, not one of the Pentecostals, took pity on us. He owns a small house up past the ball diamond and told us to use it for as long as we wanted. Well, we're still using it."

He looked at Flanagan. His face clouded over and the light that had danced in his eyes went dead. What caused his pain?

"You said your wife's name is Claudine?"

He nodded. "But she doesn't know Miss Brown."

"Your wife doesn't work with you at the café?"

"No ma'am. We don't see too much of each other any more. As I said, we still live in her uncle's house, but I keep the restaurant open eighteen hours a day, so she's usually sleeping when I leave and sleeping when I get home. That lady you saw today is Strike's wife, Loretta, Lottie—everyone calls her Lottie. She helps me out on most days. Strike's away a lot so it gives her something to do. Everyone likes her, and they never say anything about her being an Indian."

"Why would that be a problem?"

"Huh?"

"Her being an Indian."

"Oh well, you know, small town people and their prejudices."

"Is she the one who keeps your curtains washed and ironed?"

"Yeah, everything in the café that looks good, Lottie does, including the food." He chuckled. "You come there on a day when she isn't doing the cooking, and you won't have any trouble getting a seat."

"Looks like you sneak a shirt or two into the wash."

His face reddened and he changed the subject. "Of course I can't stop you from talking to Claudine, though it's best to catch her around ten in the morning. I may as well tell you this, because you're going to find out anyway: she drinks a lot and isn't coherent later in the day."

"I'm sorry," Flanagan said, thinking of her own mother who drank herself to an early grave.

"No ma'am, don't be sorry. That's just the way it is. We've been kind of drifting apart for a few years. It's gotten worse since Sara—she's our daughter—left. Claudine thinks the world of Sara. So do I, but they were real close, like sisters. They dressed the same, wore the same perfume, the same color nails, lipstick, some real wild stuff, but when Sara turned eighteen, she up and left in the middle of the night. She broke Claudine's heart when she did that. That's when Claudine started drinking more; now she's hardly ever sober."

A pang of guilt gripped Flanagan. After she left home, her own mother had started drinking heavily, but they'd never been close. "How long has it been since Sara left?"

"Three...no, maybe four months now. I wanted her to finish out the year at school, to at least get her diploma, but she said she wasn't going to pass any of her courses anyway, so there wasn't any point in hanging around. Miss Brown tried to talk her into staying."

"Did you know Miss Brown well?"

"Yes ma'am. Everyone in town knew Miss Brown."

"Except your wife."

"Well yeah, except her. Maybe one or two others."

"Have you heard from Sara?"

His eyes brightened. "She phoned me at the café last week. Needed a hundred bucks real bad. Isn't that just like a kid, always phoning the old man for money? She's in Chicago, working in a seafood restaurant just until she gets into modeling or acting. Then maybe she'll move on to New York or Los Angeles, she isn't sure, but her tips have been real lousy so I wired her the money. I don't know why she works in a seafood restaurant—the only seafood she ever saw out here was canned tuna. I told her she should find a good steak place. That girl sure knows her beef."

"Have you seen her since she left?"

"No, we just talk on the phone. I try to get her to call Claudine, but she won't. She sure sounds different now that she's all grown up. I can't wait to see her. I wanted to go to Chicago, but she told me she's real busy."

"Modeling and acting are tough. I hope she makes it."

"I think her chances are fairly good." He chuckled. "Fathers always think that. Anyway, she's met this guy who's a director or producer or something like that. He's promised to get her some appointments—auditions I think she calls them. She told me she might need a thousand bucks for pictures—head shots she calls them. They send out these head shots to everyone hiring models and actresses, kind of like a business card, hoping someone likes what they see. In Sara's case, that won't be a problem. She's a real looker, just like her momma used to look before...well, you know." He frowned and rubbed his hand through his almost non-existent hair.

Flanagan made a note to check on Sara Peterson, promising actress and model, Chicago, Illinois.

"Tell us about Loretta Striker."

"Well I'd rather you asked Strike. He doesn't..."

"I'm sorry, he doesn't what?"

"I shouldn't say."

"Joe," Flanagan said, "anything you tell us will be held in strict confidence."

Joe seemed unconvinced.

"Did Striker tell you not to talk to us?" Flanagan asked.

"Well he said I shouldn't talk about other people."

"No one will know one word of anything you say," Hutton said.

"Well, Lottie helps out at the café. She and Miss Brown were good friends. I know Lottie had Miss Brown up to their house for dinner once or twice, maybe more often, and Miss Brown always tried to come into the café on the days when Lottie worked—not when she was working though, Miss Brown wouldn't ever bother anyone when they were working—so they could talk and laugh, you know, like women do." He pressed the tips of his fingers together and studied his fingernails for a moment.

I hang around with the wrong type of women, Flanagan thought. My friends mostly curse and drink and look for guys to screw. "She's very beautiful."

"Her Indian name is Shower Cloud. It suits her better than Lottie." His wrinkly smile reappeared. Flanagan liked it when he smiled.

"Do you know where she's from?"

"I think she told me once that she's from the Athabaskan or Apache tribe over in West Texas. She used to teach on the reservation so I figured that's why she and Miss Brown always had a lot to talk about, you know, the teaching thing and all. Sometimes when I wasn't busy they'd invite me to join in, but then they talked about the restaurant, something I knew, I guess so I wouldn't be embarrassed by not knowing…well, you know, with me not having much formal learning."

"You probably know a lot more than you think," Flanagan said.

Joe grinned.

"What about Mr. Striker? He doesn't seem like the kind of man who'd like his wife to be working all the time."

"He didn't used to until he bought my building, not my business, just the building. I figured Sara might need the thousand dollars real quick if she gets into modeling, so I wanted to be ready. Anyway, I guess Striker figured

Lottie being there is good for business, that I'll be able to make the payments."

He rubbed at the furrows in his forehead. "This here's Strike's building too. When he got elected mayor, he bought this old place, used to be a little card shop that Mr. and Mrs. Stokowski ran. They retired from the farm and wanted something to do. Never made any money, but they loved having people come in and poke around and stay for coffee. Then Mrs. Stokowski, Nellie, passed on, about ten years ago now, and Mr. Stokowski went into that big nursing home down in Minot. Never did adjust—missed Nellie I guess, he passed on not long after."

Joe shook his head and looked sad. "They were good people—sorry to see them go. They're buried up in the cemetery north of town." He motioned with his thumb.

"Anyway, the building sat empty until Strike bought it and turned it into a town hall." Joe laughed. "That was after he got elected mayor. Strike being Strike, he had to have a decent office for the mayor. The most expensive thing is that big chair that he bought over the Internet. Everyone remembers the day it arrived—bigger event than the fourth of July."

He pointed at the aerial photos. "Strike paid some guy to take all these pictures, and his office is full of photos of dignitaries who've been in Largeville. Strike invited them all, in his capacity as mayor, them and maybe a hundred others. Most never came, but he keeps on trying. He even invited the president."

Joe laughed again. "To us, all these people are big shots, but to Strike, they're just people. Maybe it's because he travels around a lot and makes more money than anyone in town. He gets that big SUV from his employer, some oil company, Darko, or something like that, out of Houston."

"He told us he worked for Tex-Cal."

"Oh well yeah, if he told you that, that's what it is. His old truck, before he got the new SUV, had the company's name painted on the driver's door. I think it said Darko, but with so many of them companies getting bought and sold these days, it's hard to know who anyone works for. Most people don't even get paychecks anymore—the money goes right into their bank accounts. I don't think I'd like that. Not good for company loyalty if you ask me. Back in the days when I used to get a pay check, before Claudine and I got married, I always said a silent thank you prayer to my employer. It was like they'd granted me another two weeks to live. Now it seems there'd be nobody to thank."

"How did Miss Brown and Mr. Striker get along?"

Joe studied Hutton for a moment as if trying to decide what kind of answer to give. He seemed afraid of saying anything untoward about Striker.

"Well sir, I've never seen him talk to Miss Brown, and as far as I know, Miss Brown never came here to his office. Strike doesn't spend much time loafing around. He's always got something on the go, checking his wells or heading off out of town. He's gone a lot."

"What's a lot—one, two days a week?" Flanagan tried to imagine why someone whose job it was to monitor producing wells in an area not known for its oil production needed to spend so much time out of town.

"Always more than two days. Sometimes he's gone for the whole week. I don't know where he goes, Houston maybe. Everyone kids him about having a mistress. He always laughs so I don't think he has a mistress. You know, if he got mad, then everyone would be suspicious. Besides, Lottie's is a beautiful woman, well you saw her so I don't need to tell you that. She's keeps herself looking good, not like a lot of them who let themselves go." Joe looked off to his far away place.

Flanagan wondered if he was thinking about the old Claudine. "Have you ever seen Mr. Striker get angry?"

"Oh well, he's got a temper, that's for sure, anyone'll tell you that, but I never seen him angry at Lottie or the boy. Well, maybe the boy once in a while, but nothing unusual. Strike's been in a few fights, mostly at the Friday night dances, when a few of the boys got out of line and start cussing and misbehaving. Old Strike doesn't go for any of that, so he puts them in their place, sometimes with his fists. He seems to know what he's doing because he never loses."

"Did he ever use anything besides his fists?"

"No sir, never any weapon like a knife or gun, if that's what you mean—once in a while someone might use a whiskey bottle as a weapon, but that didn't scare Strike. He'd dance around and the next thing you knew, the guy would be out cold and Strike would strut around like he'd won a ten-rounder."

"Joe, tell us more about Miss Brown. Did people like her? Did she like it here? Did her students like her...that type of thing?"

"Well ma'am, the high school boys all had a huge crush on her." He chuckled. "Of course, she wasn't the first teacher that had that problem. I suppose it was because she didn't seem much older, and when you saw her wearing those skin-tight t-shirts and shorts, you'd think she was one of them. Until she talked, that is. Then you knew she was more mature; you got the feeling that this was a lady to be reckoned with."

"Was there ever any talk about the way she dressed, that maybe she was trying to make herself attractive to get attention?"

"Oh no ma'am, I never heard or saw anything like that. Miss Brown was too careful to have an affair with anyone in town, leastways one of the students, not after that woman teacher on the West Coast, what's her name, went to jail after one of her students got her pregnant." Joe's eyebrows shot up creasing his forehead with deep ruts. "Not that that influenced Miss Brown any, because she wasn't like that at all, but I'm saying it has to make one think."

"But she was friendly?"

Joe's eyes twinkled. "Some might say she flirted, though I'm not saying that in a bad way—in a friendly way—making a guy feel like he was special."

"Did she flirt with the high school boys?"

"I don't know that I'd call it flirting—once or twice a week when they'd be having a soda after school, mostly Strike's boy, Tommy, and Dale Kiley—he's Dan and Maude's boy. Anyway, the two of them'd light up like a Christmas tree whenever Miss Brown came in. She talked to them the same as she talked to everyone, bright and friendly like, and then she'd tease them about girlfriends and they'd blush, mostly Tommy because he doesn't have a girlfriend."

"Tommy's a nice looking young man. You'd think he'd have lots of girlfriends."

Joe looked over his shoulder as if making sure no one was standing behind and checking to see that the door was closed. "I shouldn't be saying anything, but maybe Strike's a little hard on Tommy. I think the boy gets embarrassed sometimes when Strike, you know, disciplines him in front of other people. Then there's the fact of Lottie being an Indian and being closer to Tommy's age than Strike's. People talk."

"Does Tommy dislike Lottie; did he ever come into the café when Lottie was there?"

Joe studied the ceiling for a moment and then shook his head. "Come to think of it, I can't say he did. Of course, not liking her...I wouldn't have any way of knowing that."

"Did you ever hear anyone say that Miss Brown was too friendly toward her students, that maybe she led them on?"

"Uh, no sir, I didn't mean to suggest anything like that. This is a small town. We know each other and we know the rules and one of the rules is that students and teachers, well…they wouldn't do anything like that."

"They have the same rules in Washington where that teacher went to jail."

"Well it wouldn't happen here." Joe's voice sounded sharp, and he seemed embarrassed by his display of emotion. "Sorry, what I meant is that everyone in town would know, and it would be nipped in the bud. Besides, Miss Brown would never let it happen. She was a real quality lady."

"We heard that Edie Coombs thought otherwise."

"Oh well yeah, I kind of forgot about that. I guess Strike told you about her—I know you can't say, but since he's the only one you've talked to, other than the boy, I mean, I just figured…well yes, Edie thought her husband, Rick, and Miss Brown were having an affair. I think all the wives thought their husbands were having a secret affair with Miss Brown because she was all the things they weren't, you know—like sexy and pretty and fun. The funny part is that if they'd just stopped to think for a moment, they'd have realized that Miss Brown wasn't interested in dead-end, pot-bellied, hick-town guys like me and the others."

Flanagan noticed him look down and pull in his stomach. "Might Rick have been an exception?"

"Yeah, no doubt that Rick was a handsome guy, some even said pretty, prettier than most women, but he was still dead-end, just like the rest of us. Miss Brown had ambition. All you had to do was meet her once, and you'd know she was a star. But Edie still got it in her head that she and Rick were having an affair."

"Did you see Edie attack Miss Brown at the dance?"

"I heard about that, but the one I know about is one time in the café—it was raining hard, a Thursday night, maybe about nine-thirty, some of the boys were in having coffee, Rick among them—Miss Brown sat in the back booth reading some school papers and eating an ice cream sundae, maple walnut—she always had maple walnut with extra walnuts and two cherries." Joe gripped the edge of the table with both hands and smiled as if tasting the memory.

"The boys left around nine-forty-five, so there was only me and Miss Brown. I didn't want to be a bother, so I sat on a stool near the front, lit a cigarette, and listened to the rain pelting against the windows, thinking, hoping Sara might call. That's when I saw headlights bouncing up the side road coming straight at the café, fast, and for a minute, I got afraid that whatever those headlights belonged to might crash right through the windows."

"I gather it stopped."

"Yes sir, it stopped all right, but not until it skidded right up against the sidewalk. Good thing it was there, the sidewalk I mean—acted kind of like a barrier, though I thought later if she hadn't slammed on the brakes, she could've of sailed clear in anyway."

"And it was Edie Coombs?"

"I heard a car door slam and then I heard cursing. Trouble was for sure about to start. I glanced back at Miss Brown's booth. As far as I know, she hadn't even looked up. In fact, I couldn't see her, tucked away in the corner as she was, and for a moment, I started to wonder if she was still there. Then the front door flew open and in stormed Edie along with a gust of wind and rain, her little white dogs all stringy and wet tucked under her arms.

Edie screamed, 'Where the hell are that bitch school teacher and my husband?' I told her that Rick and some of the boys had left for the beer parlor a few minutes before, that he'd probably still be there, and that I hadn't seen Miss Brown."

Joe leaned forward, propped his elbows on the table, and held the sides of his head.

"Well, I can tell you, she glared at me so hard I thought I'd break, but she finally spun around, went back outside, and raced off up the sidewalk toward the beer parlor, her car still against the curb, its motor running and its lights on. I ran and closed the door to the café, almost afraid to turn around, and then I heard Miss Brown laugh in that throaty way she had. She stood up and said, 'thanks Joe, I owe you one.' She didn't seem at all scared. That was one classy lady."

"So did Edie find Rick at the beer parlor?" Hutton asked.

"Yes sir, I heard that she roared in and started throwing beer glasses and cursing up a storm. Rick finally got her to quiet down and took her home. That was all about two weeks before the thing at the Friday night dance. Edie was a bit of a powder keg with a short fuse. Some figured she was mental. I figured she was just jealous of Rick. As I said, Rick was a good-looking guy, like a Spaniard or something, not that Edie wasn't a good-looking woman, but next to Rick, well everyone seemed kind of plain. It was like he was royalty or something, the way he walked and talked and moved his hands, things like that, if you know what I mean. Except next to Miss Brown. No one looked as good as she did."

"You said Rick was pretty," Hutton said. "Did anyone ever wonder if he was gay?"

"You mean like a homosexual person?"

"Yes, a homosexual person."

"He was married to Edie," he said, as if not certain Hutton understood that fact.

Flanagan figured explaining that some married people are gay would wreck Joe's simplistic view of the world. "It seemed that Miss Brown was in your café a lot."

"Yes ma'am, Miss Brown was one of my favorite customers. But that's all. I don't want you getting any ideas that she was more than that. She was a fine young lady."

"What about with your other male customers? Did they develop any special relationships with her?"

"They used to like coming in for coffee whenever Miss Brown was there, but they always left together, usually to go to the beer parlor."

"And she never went with them?"

"No ma'am. Mostly she sat in the back with her papers. But she always came out to say hello. It was funny seeing all those big men acting like school boys whenever she was around. They'd get real quiet and nervous, like they were hoping she might pick them to do some special favor. She never did though. After she said her hellos, she'd go back to her booth, and the guys would finish their coffee and go off to the beer parlor."

"Are Rick and Edie still in town?" Hutton asked.

"Rick moved away after the dance hall fight. So did Edie. California, I think. Rick's family lives over in Montana, ranchers I believe, so he shouldn't be too hard to find. They'd be the ones to tell you where Edie is. No one here keeps in touch with her as far as I know."

"Who were the others who had coffee with Rick that night?"

Joe looked nervous. "I wasn't suggesting any of them had anything to do with Miss Brown's murder, not even Rick and Edie."

"We know you weren't, Joe. All we're trying to do is get a picture of Miss Brown, who she knew, what she did, what people thought of her, that kind of thing."

Joe seemed only partially reassured. "Well, there was Johnny Burke—you met him at lunch time; he's the local grain dealer—there was Neil James, a mechanic at Bill Hedegaard's Garage—Bill's from Denmark—there was Rod Tatum—he's old man Tatum's son from Cobb's grocery store; and Al Simcoe, a truck driver. Simcoe's a bad apple, a Métis or breed of some kind—

came down from Manitoba. Drinks too much, always looking to get into a fight. Someone's always beating his can off. I don't know why he was hanging around with Rick and the others that night unless maybe Neil was working on his truck. One time he bothered Lottie, and I told him he couldn't come back whenever she was at the café, and if he did, I'd tell Strike. I also told him if he didn't behave, he couldn't come back ever."

"Does Simcoe live in town?" Hutton asked.

"Down by the skating rink in an old trailer. I don't think he's anything other than a drunk who gets in fights, though. He knows if he gets too far out of line with any of the women, someone will mess him up good."

Hutton made a few notes. Flanagan wrote down Simcoe's name. He likely had a D and D file, probably spent a night or two in the urine cell. Carson could check.

"Joe, who do you think killed Miss Brown?" Hutton asked.

"Sir?"

"Who killed Miss Brown? Surely, seeing and hearing everything that you do from the café, you must have some idea."

"Well no sir, I don't. I don't have any idea, but I sure hope you catch whoever it was. Miss Brown was a real nice lady, and so young. It's a real shame."

"Who else should we be talking to, Joe?"

"Well now ma'am you might want to talk to Dan Kiley, he's the station agent, or Johnny Burke, the grain agent, the one you met, but I sure would appreciate it if you didn't tell them I'd said anything or gave you their names."

"We won't," Hutton said.

"Joe, we meant it when we told you that everything you say is confidential."

"Yes ma'am, of course I know you wouldn't tell anyone. It's just that this is a small town and everyone sees everyone every day and one sure can't afford to make enemies."

"I'd like you to give me your daughter's phone number in Chicago. I know some people there. Maybe they can give her a hand with the modeling."

Joe studied her for a moment. "You would do that?"

"Why not?"

"Well, I mean you don't know her, and you only just met me."

"If you don't want to—"

"No, it's not that. I guess we figure people from the big cities don't care." His eyes glistened wet. He reached around to his back pocket and pulled out a squashed spiral note book that looked like it'd been there for a decade or more. Carefully, he flipped through the worn pages. "Yeah, here it is: 312 555-6789. The last address I have is for an apartment near the University of Chicago, but she told me she was moving to a new place."

Flanagan wrote down the phone number. "Why don't you give me the address that you have?"

Joe read it off.

*   *   *

Sara's in trouble.
Why?
That's a Woodlawn address. You have to find her.

Chapter 12

When Joe left, Flanagan called Carson to see if he'd been able to discover any clues to Victoria Otto's identity or fill in the blanks on Zoë Brown. He hadn't, and sounded harried. She told him so and asked why.

"Counting Miss Brown, we've got eight in here this morning."

"Christ Harry, what in hell is going on down there?"

Hutton glanced over.

"Some kid decided he no longer liked his family and started swinging an axe."

"They catch the kid?" Flanagan asked.

"What happened?" Hutton asked.

"Yeah," Carson said. "They got him. The kid's a man actually, late twenties. Apparently he's been in and out of Stadter over in Grand Forks for years, maybe all his life. When Penner and his pals stormed the place, they found the guy covered in blood standing over the bodies holding the axe."

"Penner?" Like her, Penner was a junior detective and had never handled a homicide. "How's he holding up?"

"He'll make it."

"Hold on a sec," she said to Carson. "I need to tell your friend here before he breaks something."

"Who is it?" Hutton asked.

"He wants to know who it is."

"The Grayfields," Carson said.

Flanagan repeated the name to Hutton.

"Not the Grayfields that own half the town Grayfields?" Hutton asked.

"The same—the old man, his wife, the daughter and son-in-law from California, and their three children."

Flanagan repeated what Carson said.

Hutton said, "I know the son, Llewellyn. We went to high school at the same time."

"Hutton knows the son," Flanagan said to Carson.

"Is he OK with it?"

"He wants to know if you're OK with it." She held the cell so Carson could hear Hutton's response.

"We weren't close," Hutton shouted. "I haven't seen him since high school."

"I need to know when you might get to our victim."

"Let me check with Casey." Casey Long was his 'go-to' person. "If she's not involved with the Grayfield murders, she might have something."

While she waited, she overheard Hutton talking to Penner, checking to make sure he was getting the help he needed and that he was OK in the head. She busied herself poking in her case and making a few notes on her computer because she knew Hutton wouldn't like anyone overhearing evidence that he actually cared.

"I've got a few pieces," Carson said, coming back on the line. "Just don't call Doc for a day or two. He's got the worst of it."

"I talked to him a couple of hours ago. He sounded harried, confused even, but didn't say anything."

"That's him. Won't say anything. Won't ask for help. He'll work himself to death one of these days."

Flanagan opened her notebook. "Give me what you have and ask Casey to send e-mail copies of everything she's got."

"Zoë A. Brown," Carson started. "No middle name, initial only, born in Chicago, IL, October 25th, '81, parents Sadie and Isaac Brownstein—"

"She was Jewish?" Flanagan's eyebrows shot up.

"It doesn't say for sure, but Brownstein isn't high Protestant."

*　　*　　*

It wasn't a secret. I just didn't make a habit of advertising the fact, given that there are no Jews in Largeville. And the A stands for Abbey, which in Hebrew means 'father rejoices.' He won't be rejoicing today. Nor will mother, though with her one wouldn't know.

I feel sad for them.

*　　*　　*

Carson continued, "After graduating from high school at age seventeen, she got a degree from Illinois State University in Normal, Illinois, which, before you ask, is approximately 100 miles southwest of Chicago. In 2002, she went to New York, drawn by the horrors of 9/11. She wanted to do her small part to help the city recover, so she volunteered to teach at one of the inner-city schools in Harlem. She stayed for two years, seemed to be doing an excellent job, and then abruptly resigned. The file's not clear on how or why she ended up in Largeville, although there is something about wanting to teach high school. In New York, she taught elementary."

"She goes from New York City to Largeville just so she can teach high school?"

"There's nothing more in her file," Carson said. "Maybe one of the good residents knows the answer."

"The good residents are talking a lot, but aren't saying much of anything."

"Hang on," Carson said. "Casey's on my other line."

Flanagan overheard Carson talking to Casey. "Not much," Carson said, coming back on the line. "Five-foot nine, one hundred and forty-five pounds, didn't need corrective lenses for driving, and owned a 2001 BMW."

"We've seen it. McManus gave it the once over."

"She bought it new her last year of college. No student loans either. Mommy and daddy must have a few bucks."

"What's her daddy do?"

"Dr. Isadore Brownstein, Northwestern Memorial Hospital. I guess that's the money source."

"So her daddy is a Jewish doctor."

"Yeah, it would seem so," Carson said.

*　　*　　*

My father is a neurosurgeon. His colleagues are Christian, Hindu, Moslem, and Buddhist. Why doesn't anyone ever say 'So her daddy is a Christian doctor?'

Sorry, it's just that I don't know any Jewish people. It was an ignorant reaction and I apologize.

Please take me to them. I must be there tomorrow. The will want to bury me tomorrow.

*　　*　　*

"Harry, I'm going to Chicago tomorrow. I need to talk to Zoë's parents."

"You don't have to do that," Carson said.

"Yeah, I do, and I want to take Zoë's body—they will want to bury her tomorrow. Any chance you can urge Stan along."

"I'll see. No promises."

"Harry, it's important, and have Casey get me on a flight. She can call me on my cell. She can also let the Brownsteins know I'd like to see them."

Flanagan ended the call. Hutton had finished his conversation with Penner.

"So, was she Jewish?" Hutton asked.

"Seems so."

"You're thinking her murder was racist?"

"How many times have you heard anti-Semitic slurs?"

"About as often as I hear nigger slurs, except you always know when a nigger is around. You don't always know when a kike is around."

"You know, sometimes you can be such an asshole."

"Lighten up."

"I won't lighten up, not for you, not for…anyone. I don't think it's funny. That's how it gets started. The next thing you know some ignorant red-neck decides to run around and see how many blacks and Jews and whoever else doesn't strike his fancy he can kill."

Hutton shrugged.

"Don't give me that."

"What?"

"That indifference—I've known you too long, try your act on someone who might actually believe you don't care."

Hutton studied her for a moment and then checked his notes. "Besides asking everyone if they know why she gave up New York City for Largeville, are you going to ask everyone if they knew she was a Jew?"

"A better word is Jewish."

"What ever you say, Rabbi?"

"I take back what I said—you're always an asshole."

I knew I picked you for a reason.

"I'm as guilty as he is. Maybe you'll hang around long enough to kick my ass."

Careful, you said that out loud.

"Flanagan, I'll be happy to kick your ass anytime you want."

Her face flushed. "Nothing but angry mutterings." She didn't need questions. "I wonder if Victoria Otto was Jewish."

"So you do think Zoë Brown's murder was racist?"

"It's a possibility that needs to be kept on the table, that's all. I don't think one way or the other, yet."

Casey Long called back ten minutes later. "There is a Northwest flight tomorrow morning departing at 5:02 that gets you into Chicago via Minneapolis at 8:26 a.m."

"Ugh."

"Oh, and Harry told me to tell you that Doc finished the autopsy and will ship the body. It'll be on the same flight you're taking."

"Tell Harry and Doc thanks for the fast work."

"Doc's Jewish—says her parents would want to bury her within forty-eight hours, something to do with their religion, so he put a rush on it. At least that's what Harry said."

"I didn't know Doc was Jewish, but I do know Harry isn't. How does a good Catholic boy from Boston know about the forty-eight hour thing?"

"It's a long story. Remind me to tell you sometime. By the way, Dr. and Mrs. Brownstein asked if you would do them the honor of attending the funeral. They will talk to you after."

Chapter 13

Tommy Striker sat on the long bench along the wall in Mac's Pool Hall and Barber Shop waiting for Dale Kiley to show up. He needed to talk to Dale before Dale talked to Flanagan and Hutton.

Johnny Burke, Neil James, Jock Stewart, and Rod Tatum were playing a pool game called golf on the small table in front where the locals always played golf. The large table at the back and the other small table at the far side stood silently in darkness, their sturdy legs like tree trunks planted firmly on the floor.

Racks of cues hung on the wall adjacent to each table, but none of the players at the front table used these. Their private cues hung behind a glass door in individual metal and leather containers in a locked case to which only Mickey MacKenzie, the owner of Mac's, had the key. Tommy dreamt of having his own cue there one day, maybe of carved ivory like the one rumored to be in the black and silver case that he'd never seen opened.

Next to him on the bench sat some of the local farmers, who smelled of grain dust; and Archie Somers, an old guy who had lived in Largeville longer than anyone remembered. Archie Somers smelled of stale smoke. Mac MacKenzie sat in his barber's chair in a closed off section in the front reading a newspaper. All anyone could see through the small inside window was his small head that never seemed to move.

A blue haze hung in the air from the cigarettes and cigars and pipes being smoked, and from the cigarettes and cigars and pipes that had been smoked since nineteen-sixty-five when Mac's opened for business. Brass spittoons that looked like they hadn't been emptied since nineteen-sixty-five sat at the ends of the three long wall benches.

Each of the four golf players used two snooker balls of a different color. Burke shot blue on pink. He attempted to stop the pink in front of the black to block Jock Stewart from having a clear shot. Jock was shooting red on black.

"You bastard," Jock said as Burke's ball rolled to a stop exactly where Burke had intended.

"He got you now," old Archie mumbled.

"Sure does," one of the local farmers said.

The others sitting and standing around stroked their chins or puffed their pipes or puffed on their cigars or cigarettes and mumbled agreement, their eyes glued to the table.

The chime above the front door rang. Tommy turned to look. When he saw it was Dale, he held his wrist watch in the air and tapped its face with his finger.

Dale shrugged.

Tommy pointed to the far wall and crept away. Penetrating the veil of concentration surrounding the golf table was an unforgivable sin.

"About fucking time," Tommy whispered to Dale as they took to the far bench.

Dale popped a cigarette into his mouth and offered the pack to Tommy.

"I've got my own."

Dale shoved the pack into a side pocket of his coat and produced a silver-colored lighter that he flicked open and then spun the wheel with his thumb. A smoky flame large enough to torch the town sprang to life. Tilting his head so he didn't lose his eyebrows, he touched the flame to the cigarette.

"I got your call. Why do the cops want to talk to me?"

"They want to know if any guys in town are fucking their girlfriends. I told them only one. They made me tell. I didn't want to, but they tortured me."

"Asshole."

"You're the asshole. Why do you think they want to talk to you? Miss Brown has been murdered for Christ's sake."

"Yeah, but I don't know anything."

"They got to talk to everyone. It's like they got this big blank page with a hundred blank squares, maybe a thousand blank squares, that they got to start filling in, so they ask questions."

"What kind of questions?" He took a long drag and blew smoke from his nose.

"How long your dick is; how many times you banged Miss Brown, shit like that."

"Stop being such a jerk off—I liked Miss Brown."

"That's because you were banging her."

"You're sick."

"There're two of them—one's a broad—both detectives, but they're from Minot so how smart can they be? The broad's name is Flanagan. The guy is Hutton. Hutton asks the questions; Flanagan watches your face, your eyes, your hands, everything—like a hawk. You twitch, she makes a note. You blink, she makes a note. Hutton's an asshole. I think Flanagan's hot, like she's been around, like she's seen things."

"You mean she's been around like you?"

"Hey asshole, just because I live in this shit hole of a town doesn't mean I haven't seen things."

"Looking at porn on the Internet doesn't qualify."

Tommy punched his arm.

"So what'd they ask you?"

"Dumb shit like how long I've lived here, what grade I'm in; the important thing is not to tell them anything they don't ask."

"Is that what you did?"

"Yes dickhead, that's exactly what I did. 'Yes sir, no ma'am,' nothing else."

"Yeah, well how did they get my name then?"

"They wanted to know the name of my best friend. I didn't figure there was anything wrong in telling them that."

Through the smoke circling around his eyes, Dale squinted at Tommy.

"Yeah, and since I don't have a best friend, I figured I'd give them your name."

"Figures."

"Hey, don't get all mad. I'm kidding."

"That's your problem, you're always kidding."

"Seriously, they're going to ask if you know who killed Miss Brown."

"What'd you tell them?"

"Exactly what you're going to tell them: No one from Largeville, maybe one of the guys from out of town that come to the dances to try to pick her up."

"I can't say that."

"You will if you and your old man and old lady want to continue living in Largeville."

"Why can't I say I don't know?"

"Because they'll read something into your answer, like you know, but aren't saying. They might even think you're covering for your old man or old lady, so they'll ask you a bunch of questions about them."

"You tell them about your old man?"

"What do you mean?"

"How he's always beating the crap out of you and Lottie?"

"He is not, and I didn't say a goddamn word about my old man."

"Hey, take it easy."

Tommy lit a cigarette and inhaled deeply. "Flanagan's a fox," he said through a mouthful of smoke. "I think I'll fuck her."

"Like you fuck every other woman?"

"Don't believe me then, but I'm going to fuck her."

"Your pecker will run and hide the first time it sees a real pussy."

"Fuck you."

"Maybe I'll write a song: Virgin Tommy."

"You're the virgin. Maybe I'll fuck Karen so she knows what it's like."

Dale got off the bench and started for the door. Tommy ran after him. "Hey man, I didn't mean it."

Dale continued on outside and started up the street.

"C'mon man, you know I didn't mean it."

Dale kept walking.

"Listen, I'm going to tell you something about Miss Brown that's the God's honest truth, but you've got to promise on your mother's grave that you won't breathe a word, not to Karen, not to anyone."

Dale stopped. "No bullshit?"

"I promise. No bullshit."

"What?"

"Remember that night two weeks ago when we were all in Williston at the regional Students' Union Power conference?"

"What about it?"

"Remember Miss Brown's red shoes?"

"Not really."

"Come on, the sexy red heels with the two straps around her ankles?"

"So?"

"When I found her this morning, that's how I knew it was her."

"What do you mean?"

"Just her feet were sticking out of the ditch—I couldn't see the rest of her body, but I knew it was her because she had on the same red shoes."

"That's what you wanted to tell me?"

"Do you know how I remembered the shoes?"

"You've got a pair just like them?"

"I watched her take them off."

"Whoopee!"

"I watched her take all of her clothes off."

Dale gave him a sidelong look.

"And then she took my clothes off."

"Bullshit!" Dale started to walk away.

"You don't believe me, take a look at this."

Dale stopped.

Tommy held up his cellphone and clicked through four photos.

Dale's mouth dropped open.

"We did it, man. She was fantastic, like she never wanted to stop, and then she went to sleep. That's when I took the pictures."

"Bullshit—you made them man, just like the others, and you better get rid of them before someone sees them. Someone's going to find out."

"They won't if you don't tell."

"Yeah man, but what if you lose your phone, some crap like that. What if your old man or Lottie sees them?"

"Nobody'll see them. Just make sure you keep your mouth shut."

"Hey man, I never saw a thing."

"Want another look?"

"No."

"Didn't she have a great body?"

"You're sick."

Tommy laughed. Dale started running toward the town hall.

Chapter 14

Hutton stood at the window of the town hall waiting for Dale Kiley to arrive. He saw Tommy Striker laughing and another young man running. The young man crossed the street and headed for the town hall. "You're not going to believe this," he said to Flanagan.

"What?"

"You'll see." He walked to the door.

A tall, skinny kid with slightly hunched shoulders and spiked blonde hair with streaks of red and blue and purple, shuffled in. Despite the eighty-degree day, he wore a long black coat several sizes too big that was worn through and ragged at the cuffs like a much-traveled hand-me-down. He had multiple earrings of gold and silver, eyebrow rings, a nose ring, upper and lower lip rings, a lower lip stud, and doubtless many others that weren't visible. His eyes were clear though, so he'd not been sucking up drugs or booze. He looked at Hutton and then at Flanagan.

"Are you Dale Kiley?" Hutton asked.

The kid nodded.

Flanagan stood and stepped forward. "Mr. Kiley, I'm Detective Flanagan. This is my partner, Detective Hutton." Flanagan stuck out her hand and waited while Dale Kiley removed his hand from the side pocket of his coat. She felt as though she'd gripped a dead fish and his clothes reeked of cigarette smoke.

"Please have a seat." She pointed to the chair that faced away from the window. Hutton closed the Venetian blind. Flanagan sat to Kiley's left, Hutton to his right. Kiley faced Hutton.

"For the record," Hutton said, "Please state your full name and tell us how old you are and where you live."

Dale opened his mouth to speak. Flanagan noticed his tongue stud.

"My name is Dale William Kiley. I'm eighteen. I live in Largeville."

Despite his appearance, Kiley seemed poised beyond his years. He spoke well. She could almost see his mind working, trying to anticipate the next question.

"Do you know Miss Brown?"

"Yes." He looked down.

"Do you know she's been murdered?"

He nodded his head.

"Are you sad?" Flanagan asked.

He looked up. "I guess."

"It's OK to be sad, Dale. When someone you like dies, it's OK to be sad."

He sniffled and wiped at his nose with his coat sleeve. "I'm OK with it."

Flanagan flipped open her book and scanned her notes. Hutton did the same. Kiley watched their every move. "Have you talked to anyone?" Flanagan asked.

Dale shot her a blank look.

"About Miss Brown—have you talked to anyone, say, like you parents?"

"Well my father mentioned it, that's all though."

"What did he say?"

"Like, you know, if I wanted to talk about it?"

"And did you?"

Dale shook his head.

"Tell us about your father," Flanagan said, still looking at her notes.

Dale wriggled upright. "Why do you want to know about him?"

"Don't you want to talk about your father, Dale?"

"He didn't have anything to do with Miss Brown's murder?"

"Do you know who did?"

"No, but it wasn't my father. Everyone will tell you that."

Flanagan flipped through a few more pages, stopped, and ran her finger across her notes.

Dale said, "If anyone said he did, they're liars."

"Does it always make you angry when people talk about your father?"

"No, but he didn't kill anyone."

"No one said he did, Dale, so why don't you go ahead and tell us about him."

Dale studied her for a moment, and then said, "He's the AMTRAK agent."

"Trains stop here?" Hutton asked.

Dale fiddled with his thumbs. "Maybe one freight a week—no passenger trains."

Hutton shot him a questioning look.

"I know what you're thinking."

"I doubt it, but try me."

"Since no trains stop here, you're wondering why my father still has a job."

"OK, why does he?"

"The union."

"The union?"

"In five years, when my father retires, the station can be torn down, but not until then."

"Maybe he'll take early retirement."

"They live above the station. If they tear the station down, where will they live? There are no houses other than the old tarpaper shack at the end of Railroad Avenue that isn't fit for anyone other than old Sammy who lived there until he died two years ago."

"What about in five years," Flanagan asked. "Won't they have to find a place to live then anyway?"

"My mother has family in Canada. Maybe in five years she can get my father used to the idea of living in Canada. Right now, my father says they may as well move to Alaska."

"Canada is only fifty miles north. Alaska is a long ways up there."

"The start of Canada is only fifty miles north. It goes a lot farther north than Alaska."

"Maybe they'll move near the border."

"My father says it's too depressing and too cold."

"You mean like here."

Dale shrugged. A silver-colored lighter appeared in his hands. He turned it over and over. "It's probably academic anyway because I think my father only talks that way about Canada to annoy my mother. Besides, given all the border stuff that's going on, soon Canada and Mexico are going to tell us to stay home."

"What do you plan on doing when you finish school?"

"My parents want me to go to college. Karen, my girlfriend, wants to get married. She says her father will give me a job in the garage." He smirked and looked down at his lighter.

"That amuses you."

He looked at Flanagan. "Do I look like someone who might work in a garage? Do I look like someone a garage might hire? I don't think so, not even Karen's father."

"So it's college?"

"That's what my parents want."

"What do you want?"

From his inside coat pocket, he pulled out a dozen letter-sized sheets of folded paper, dog-eared and smudged by ink stains. He straightened them out and slid them across the table. "I write music. I plan to go to New York City and write music."

Flanagan looked at the sheets. Hutton stretched his neck and tried to see. Flanagan knew nothing of music, Hutton less.

"It's a rock opera, like Rent, only it's based on Carmen rather than La Boehme."

"OK," Flanagan said. "If you say so." She gave the sheets back to Dale.

He tucked the music back inside his coat pocket. "Miss Brown knew music. She encouraged me. No one else in Largeville knows about music."

"You and Miss Brown were close?"

"Everyone thought they were close to Miss Brown. She was special, always telling us we could be whatever we wanted to be, the girls especially. Up until Miss Brown arrived, all the girls wanted to do was get married and start having kids. I mean having kids is all right, but not when you're seventeen or eighteen."

"What about the other people in town. Did they think Miss Brown special?"

"I guess."

"Did anyone not like her?"

Dale thought for a moment before answering. "Not that I can think of."

"You seem uncertain." Hutton said.

"No, I'm not uncertain—the question caught me off guard, that's all. Miss Brown was real popular—that's the only reason anyone wouldn't like her. Maybe the other teachers were jealous, but they wouldn't have killed her."

"Why did Detective Hutton's question make you angry?" Flanagan asked.

Dale's eyes squinted shut. Then he shrugged and looked down.

"Were any of the high school girls jealous? Miss Brown was pretty, and not much older."

"The girls loved her. They would have followed her anywhere."

"What about the boys?"

He looked down again. "I can't speak for the others, but I would have. Every guy in school had this huge crush on her."

"Including you?"

"Yeah, I guess so. She loved to talk about my music. I liked that."

"What about Tommy?"

"Yeah, I guess." Dale's hands made tight fists.

"You seem upset."

"I just don't want to talk about it."

"Were you angry because he was closer to Miss Brown than you were?"

"He wasn't."

"What then?"

"No one talked to her about music except me. All that other stuff didn't matter."

"What other stuff?"

"Guys saying they'd like to, you know…"

"That they'd like to what? That they'd like to have sex with her—is that what you're saying?"

He nodded.

"Did Tommy have sex with her?"

"I don't know…he…"

"He told you he did?"

"Tommy's always saying things like that. I never believe him."

"He told you he had sex with Miss Brown?"

Dale nodded.

Flanagan reached across and touched his arm. "Dale, no one will know what you tell us. Did he say he had sex with her more than once?"

"Yeah, but he's always talking about stuff like that, about having sex with every girl he sees. Like, if he sees a girl on TV, like Brittney Spears or Hillary Duff or Lindsay Lohann, he goes on about how, you know…"

"Do the other boys talk the same way?"

"I don't know. I'm with Tommy more so I hear him more—he talks about it all the time."

"Did Tommy have sex with any of the girls in school?"

"He says he did, but I never believed him."

"Who?"

"A lot, Sara Peterson, others."

"Why did you mention Sara Peterson?"

Dale shrugged. "I don't know. He talked about her a lot."

"Did he talk about having sex with her a lot?"

"Yeah."

Flanagan made a few notes. "Let's get back to Miss Brown—were any of the men in town in a relationship with her?"

Dale raised a pierced eyebrow.

Flanagan persisted. "Married men, like Mr. Peterson or Mr. Burke?"

"Nothing like that. She had two boyfriends—I guess that's what they were—who she went out with once in awhile. Everyone in town thought she'd end up marrying one or the other, but I don't think Miss Brown thought so."

"Why was that?"

"I don't know. I guess it was because she didn't seem serious. I mean, you could tell she liked them, but no different than anyone else, and I don't think she ever went out with either of them alone."

"What are their names?"

"Greg Adams and Dawson Richards. Greg has a big farm north of town; Dawson lives in town with his parents, but I heard he's leaving for Los Angeles to work for a book publisher, or something like that. He's real smart, won the Governor's Award of Excellence for top marks in grade twelve and then he won a bunch of honors at college, graduated summa cum laude."

"Did you ever see or hear of any boyfriends from other places, like Chicago or New York?"

Dale shook his head.

"Does Tommy have a girlfriend?" Hutton asked.

Dale shook his head.

"What does Tommy do—what are his interests?"

"He's either on his computer or in the pool hall. He plays a lot of pool."

ALLAN M^CLEOD

"Is there anything else you can tell us about Miss Brown?" Flanagan asked.

"Like what?"

"Did she ever say or do anything that you thought odd?"

Dale furrowed his brow. "I don't think so."

"I expect you have e-mail?"

Dale nodded.

She gave him her card. "If you think of anything, let me know."

He examined Flanagan's card and stuck it into a side pocket of his coat. "Is that it? May I go now?"

"Yes," Flanagan said and stood up. "Thank you for coming in." She walked him to the door. "Good luck with your music. Maybe you'll buy your parents that new house."

Dale gave her a sidelong look. "Maybe I will."

Flanagan rubbed at the tingling sensation in the back of her neck. She smelled the orchids.

I hope you don't believe all that he said about Tommy and me.

Did you have sex with Tommy?

Chapter 15

Flanagan returned to her chair. "Well, what did you think of that?"

"You know what I think," Hutton said. "I think the Striker kid was doing more than bragging about having sex. He was obsessed, and I think the wonderful Miss Brown took advantage of his obsession to satisfy her needs, I mean since it doesn't seem she was getting it anywhere else."

"If that's what you think, I don't want to hear it."

"What I also think is that you're refusing to accept the obvious."

"So what if they did have sex, and I don't believe for a moment that they did—that doesn't mean he killed her."

"It puts him a lot closer."

"She wasn't killed in her room. She didn't leave her room wearing only her red high heels. Where did he take her? How did he get her clothes off? How did he kill her? How did he get her to the drainage ditch?"

"He calls her. She decides to have one more go with the kid. After, the two of them lying there in the nude, she starts putting on her shoes and tells him it has to stop. He loses it and whacks her with a baseball bat."

"That he just happened to bring along?"

"Maybe the kid decided to have one last fling and then he killed her so no one else could have her."

"She hadn't had recent sex."

"Hey, I'm just tossing out possibilities. Maybe he killed her before they had sex."

Flanagan got up and crossed to the window. She opened the blind and stood with her hands on her hips, looking out at the street. The row of parked cars suggested that people must be around, but the town seemed deserted.

Some of what Hutton said made sense, but she doesn't want it to be true. She doesn't want Zoë to be the type of person who would have sex with one of her students. She turned to face him.

"Do you want Tommy to be the killer? Do you want them to be sexually involved?"

"Now whose thinking is way off base?"

"I don't think it is. You don't like Tommy so you want him to be the killer and the only way you can make it work is by having him sexually involved."

"Hey, I don't like his old man either, and I don't like Mozart Kiley—I'm surprised as hell he has a girlfriend, she must be a real winner—but I'm not running around saying they did it. You're not listening to what the Striker kid and young Kiley are saying. The Striker kid almost slobbered when he talked about the victim's red shoes and according to young Kiley, all he talked about was fucking her brains out. Well maybe he did more than fuck her brains out."

"He's a teenage boy with billions of wild hormones flying around, affecting everything he says and does and thinks. Don't you think it normal for him to fantasize about sex, to brag to his friends?"

"Just like it's normal for deranged kids to kill? Kiley reminds me of those two punks from Columbine that went on a killing rampage, except I think Kiley would shit his pants if anyone handed him a gun—not so Tommy Striker. In fact, maybe Kiley deserves another look too because I'm sure he does whatever Tommy Striker tells him to."

Flanagan returned her attention to the street. She didn't want to listen because she knew he made sense. Maybe she'd let herself get too involved. Maybe she'd made up the whole spirit thing as a way to let her decide who the killer was rather than deal with each suspect on an impersonal basis, on equal footing. Tommy Striker, though seemingly misguided, seemed like a nice young man who couldn't possible be capable of murder. The victim is this beautiful young woman who everyone loved as though she were a saint, a Mother Theresa, so she couldn't possibly be having sex with her students.

Her body tensed as she felt Hutton coming up behind, her skin a billion cilia reaching out to detect his nearness. She heard his breathing, she felt his heat.

"I know you're right. I just don't want you to be."

"I'm not right, and that's why we're a team, Flanagan, to bounce ideas around. I don't want it to be the kid either, but let's keep him in play, both of them in fact."

They looked at Dale Kiley standing across the street. A blue Mercedes convertible pulled to the curb next to Kiley and stopped. A stunning blonde with a halter top and short shorts and a body to die for got out. They kissed. Kiley slid in under the steering wheel and they drove off up the street.

"You can close your mouth now," Flanagan said.

"And he wants to be a musician?"

"Composer actually, and yes, I can believe it. In ten or fifteen years he'll be a famous composer and we'll be watching TV and telling our friends that we knew him way back when."

"I doubt it."

"I've seen your eyes tear over whenever Lawrence Welk comes on TV."

"Give me a break."

"How about Angie Dickinson? How about Peggy Lee? They're from North Dakota."

"They're a long way from Largeville's contribution to the punk rock world."

"Don't be so sure. A lot of people in Minnesota probably thought the same about Prince. You've got to learn not to be so narrow-minded, to look past the clothes and the hair and the body armor."

"Yeah Flanagan, I'll remember that." He went back to the table. From the reflection in the window, she saw him check his watch. It was getting late. Another hour and the sun would be gone and the good people of Largeville would be doing whatever it was that they did after dark on a Saturday night. Probably meet at Pete's, the men anyway, and then off to the bar. She expected Claudine Peterson was already in the bar, if what everyone said was true. She and Hutton could go to Pete's...for dinner, but the mammoth lunch still sat heavy in her stomach.

"I don't think we're going to accomplish much more here today," she said.

"Thank God. I was beginning to worry I might have to spend Saturday night in Largeville."

"I'm sure you've had worse." She walked back to the table and started gathering up her notebook and computer. "We'll start fresh Monday. We've got several more Largevillians to talk to, and we may need to revisit some of those we've already talked to."

"Keep the Striker kid and Kiley near the top of your list."

"Whatever you do don't let me forget."

"Hey, don't kill the messenger—I'm just trying to be helpful, and while I'm in the not letting you forget mode, let's not forget McManus."

Flanagan called McManus at the school. She said she needed another half-hour and told Flanagan not to wait, that she'd e-mail anything she found.

"I'll be in Chicago," Flanagan said. "Carson has my itinerary."

"Father Carson?"

"That's one I haven't heard."

"I thought everyone knew he'd studied to be a priest."

"What happened?"

"It's complicated. Better that he tell you."

Flanagan ended the call and said to Hutton, "McManus just told me that Carson wanted to be a priest."

"Yeah, he did."

"So how come I didn't know?"

"We don't tell you everything."

"Thanks."

"What can I say? I didn't know you didn't know."

"What's the scoop? And if you tell me it's complicated, that Harry will have to tell me, I'm going to kick your ass."

"No, I don't think it's all that complicated. He can fill in the blanks, but it had something to do with his wife's sister getting murdered, I mean before he was married, like when he still planned on being a priest. He doesn't talk about it. To hear him tell it, it wasn't a big deal—I mean he doesn't struggle with his decision."

Flanagan wondered why Harry had never told her. They'd been close for the last couple of years; she'd met his wife and spent time with their son, Harry Junior. Why hadn't she been told? Why hadn't she suspected something? Why hadn't she heard others talking about it? Maybe it was like Hutton said: it wasn't a big deal; still, she felt slighted, like they'd been keeping secrets.

"You coming?" Hutton waited by the door.

She grabbed her case.

"After you," he said.

She was about to step into the hallway when a gunshot like banging sounded. Her heart leapt into her throat.

"What the…" Hutton said.

They reached for their holsters.

Chapter 16

Hutton said, "Relax, it's some woman pounding on the door."

Flanagan took a deep breath. Hutton opened the door. "May I help—"

"Outta my way, mister." The woman, wild-eyed and big, barged past. "I'm here to see the lady."

Flanagan figured her at one-eighty. She wore red sweats with 'America' in large white letters emblazoned across the front of the sweater and down one pant leg. What looked like mustard was smeared across one shoulder and down the arm. Other gobs of foreign matter not as prominent proliferated. Her large breasts hung loose and bounced dangerously as she tromped forward in once white high-top sneakers. Her short black hair that looked like it had been cut with a butcher knife flipped back and forth across her forehead and her round face was the rosy pink of one with blood pressure that shot off the charts.

Hutton tried to grab her, but she moved too quickly. Flanagan braced for physical contact. "Ma'am, please calm down or we'll restrain you," she shouted.

"Are you in charge of the murder?" the woman asked, coming to a stop a foot in front of Flanagan's face.

"What murder is that, ma'am?"

"Don't play games. You know the one I'm talking about."

"We're on our way back to Minot," Hutton said. "We'll talk on Monday."

"You can wait until Monday if you want, but if you're interested in what I have to say it's tonight or never."

"This is Detective Hutton. I'm Detective Flanagan. Why don't you have a seat?"

Hutton rolled his eyes and returned to the table.

"Mommy?" A small person with curly blonde hair, barefoot, wearing blue checkered pajamas, appeared in the doorway.

The woman whipped around. "Didn't I tell you to stay in the car?"

"Johnny says I look like a girl."

The woman charged to the doorway and hollered out into the street, "Johnny, you stop teasing your brother or so help me god I'll come out there and paddle your ass so hard you won't sit for a week." She grabbed the pajama clad boy by the shoulder and said, "Now get back out there and stop being a baby. You come in here again and you'll wish you were a girl."

The little boy's eyes teared.

"Go on now," the woman said, her voice softening, and she gave him a side-of-the-sneaker love-kick in the rear. The boy grabbed his behind with both hands and ran. Flanagan thought she heard him laugh. The woman watched for a moment, and then returned to the table. "Little buggers," she said, her face fighting to stifle a grin.

"Why don't you start by giving us your name," Hutton said, opening his computer and notebook.

The woman glanced at Hutton, and then said to Flanagan, "I'm Elizabeth Burke, but I suspect you already know that."

"Ma'am?" Hutton asked.

"Don't play games with me mister. I know this town. I know what people say. I know who you've been talking to. They all talk about me."

"Ma'am, I can assure you that no one has said one word about you."

"Hah!"

"Ma'am, what is it that you want to tell us?" Flanagan asked.

Burke folded her big hands on the table. "I don't like to speak ill of the dead, mind you, but it's time someone told you the truth."

"The truth, ma'am?"

"I know everyone you've talked to said how much they loved Miss Brown, how everyone in Largeville loved Miss Brown, well, I'm here to tell you that not everyone in town loved her, not by a long shot." Burke's hands twitched.

"Are you saying you weren't a member of her fan club?" Hutton asked.

"I didn't kill her, if that's what you're thinking, but if I'd have caught her with my no good husband, I'd have killed both of them."

A child's voice screamed, "Johnnneeee!" Burke jumped from her chair and moved to the doorway faster than Flanagan would have thought her capable. "Johnny, you kids behave," she shouted, and then returned to her chair.

"Is your husband Johnny Burke?" Hutton asked.

"Ptui, ptui, I spit on his name."

"Is he why you're leaving?" Flanagan asked.

"He's a drunken bum—I don't want to say his name, I don't want to hear his name, I don't want to think about him."

Flanagan and Hutton wrote in their books.

"Was Miss Brown having an affair with your husband?"

"I know her kind, all fancy and pretty and sexy. They come into small towns looking for men who fall all over them, men who can give them what they want, and I'm sure I don't need to tell you what that is. They think it's a big game, stealing husbands, wrecking homes, and then off to the next place to start all over again, leaving nothing but a trail of wrecked lives."

A car horn honked. Burke leapt from her chair and ran to the door. "Johnny," she hollered, "you stop that this instant or so help me, I'll come out there and box your ears clean off...Yeah, well you're the oldest...Caleb, do you want me to come out there?...I will, don't you dare make me"—she took a menacing step onto the sidewalk—"Yeah, well not one more sound, you hear me?"

Breathing heavily, she came back inside and plopped on her chair, her dark eyes darting between Hutton and Flanagan.

"Are you leaving because Miss Brown had an affair with your husband?"

"It wouldn't surprise me one bit."

"Mrs. Burke, has you husband had other affairs?"

"Hah! He knows I'll kill him if he does."

"What about with Edie Coombs?" Flanagan asked.

Lizzie's eyes flashed fire. "That's crazy talk. She tried to beat up on my Johnny once. Had I not been there, there's no saying what might have happened."

"We've met Mr. Burke," Flanagan said. "He looks like he can take care of himself."

"Yeah, my Johnny's a big boy all right, but he'd never hit a woman no matter what."

"Why did Edie Coombs go after him?"

"It wasn't because they were having an affair, that's for sure. In fact, it wasn't even him she was after—he just got in the way."

"Tell us about it."

"It happened at one of our Friday night dances. Edie's husband, Rick, disappeared and she'd been storming around searching for him everywhere. Well, just about at the point where we thought we were going to have to tie her down, this Zoë woman that everyone loves prances in the side door as pretty as you please, face flushed, hair mussed, with Rick in tow. Well you can imagine: Edie attacked, screaming and wailing like a moose in heat."

"Only she got Mr. Burke instead?" Flanagan asked.

"My Johnny, big dumb ass that he is, stepped in front of Little Miss Goodie Two Shoes. Let me tell you: had I been close by, I'd have yanked him the hell out of the way and let Edie at her."

"But you were close enough to come to his aid," Hutton said.

Lizzie gave him a cold sidewise glare, and then continued to Flanagan, "Rage had consumed Edie—she flailed and scratched and punched, not caring who got in the way. My Johnny tried to get her in a bear hug, but what did he do instead: he tripped over his big feet and fell to the floor with Edie on top, still swinging and clawing? Well, I figured if Johnny wouldn't protect himself, I'd better, so I jumped in and pulled her off. Then she gets up and sails into me so I deck her and she goes down for the count."

Lizzie glanced at Hutton as if to say, 'Any more dumb questions?'

"Is Edie Coombs still in Largeville?" Flanagan asked.

"I heard she's moved to Alaska."

"Can you find out where, phone number, address?" Flanagan asked.

"I can ask around. My kid sister might know. She and Edie hung around a bit."

"What's your sister's name?"

"Mary D'Arcalengo. She's not married. Too busy beating them off, just like I used to until my Johnny said we should get married." She fingered her large diamond ring for a moment. "She's in Minneapolis—got a good job there with the city."

Flanagan slid her card across the table. "I'd appreciate it if you'd call her and then call me, tonight, one way or the other."

"If I can get hold of her."

"Either way, let me know?"

Burke shoved the card into the front pocket of her sweats. "Someone else who might know is that old busy-body Miss Reaves. She makes a point of knowing everyone's business. Used to be principal of the school here, taught every adult in town at one point or another, probably whacked their knuckles with a ruler more than once too. She sure did Johnny's and mine. She came here right after Normal School, sometime in the forties, taught until she was seventy or eighty. Even then, it was a fight to get her to retire. She was a good teacher, though. Lived to teach, to have her students excel, and don't think she doesn't periodically remind us how much better we should have done."

"Spell her name," Hutton said.

"R E A V E S. There's only one in town. She lives across the street from Howard and Hilda's place, where the schoolteachers live. You can't miss her in her long black dress and hair up in a bun—ninety if she's a day and not more than a handful of gray hair, still has her own teeth, something she'll be quick to tell you—"

"Mom, mom, dad's leaving the beer parlor." A handsome kid that looked like a miniature Johnny Burke stood in the doorway frantically waving his arms and looking back toward the hotel.

Lizzie Burke jumped up, toppled her chair, and raced out the door. Flanagan and Hutton ran to the window. The only car moving on Main Street was an old blue Cadillac that limped past Pete's Café and headed toward the railway tracks. Burke and the kid dove into the front seat of Lizzie's red Ford. With tires spinning and shooting bits of gravel against the town hall windows, they fishtailed, almost spun out of control, and raced after the Cadillac that disappeared beyond the rise of the railroad crossing. Lizzie's car took flight as she hit the same rise doing about ninety, kids bouncing around in the front and back seats like they were riding bucking broncos. Flanagan could almost hear them cheering.

"I guess that's the end of the interview," Hutton said.

"Don't worry, she'll be around on Monday," Flanagan said. "She's too much in love with 'her Johnny' to ever leave him and Largeville."

"You think 'big Johnny' and Miss Brown were having an affair?"

"Not in a million years. I'll bet money that Lizzie turns into the green-eyed monster whenever any woman looks twice at 'her Johnny'—today Miss Brown is her target, tomorrow, who knows?"

They gathered their stuff, killed the lights, and headed out to the SUV. McManus was there. She rolled down her window. "I saw you were still here so decided to wait."

"We had a last minute caller," Hutton said.

"Was that the maniac I saw flying out of here?"

"That would be her," Hutton said.

"What did you find?" Flanagan asked.

McManus handed her a file folder stuffed with newspaper clippings. "They all have to do with a woman who disappeared from Largeville thirteen years ago."

Flanagan fingered through the clippings. "Victoria Otto," she said. She felt Hutton's eyes boring into the side of her head. He didn't say anything, but she knew he'd etched a few questions into his brain.

"There are also a couple of notes about a Rhonda Striker, married to a Newton Striker from Largeville."

"He's the mayor," Hutton said. "She must be his ex."

"According to the file," McManus said, "eight years ago ex-wife Rhonda was committed to the Big Springs State Hospital in West Texas, but..." She handed Flanagan a letter.

"But, Flanagan said, scanning the letter, "according to this, the Superintendent of the Big Springs State Hospital wrote to Dr. Isaac Brownstein in Chicago saying they have no record of a Mrs. Rhonda Striker, not now, not ever." She handed the letter to Hutton.

"Dr. Isaac Brownstein as in Zoë Brownstein's father?" Hutton asked.

"The same," Flanagan said. "Zoë was looking for something, but what?"

Hutton said, "I wonder what she found."

"Or was trying to find," McManus said.

"What's the date of the letter?" Flanagan asked.

"Recent, May 1st."

Chapter 17

Tommy said, "I've been here for a fucking hour." He ducked down in the tall grass around the perimeter of the cenotaph next to Town Hall.

Dale looked at his watch. "I've only been out of there half an hour."

"Get down before someone sees you."

"It's getting dark. Who's going to see us?"

Tommy reached up, grabbed Dale's coat, and pulled him down. He took a cigarette from the pack in his shirt pocket, didn't offer one to Dale, and struck a match on his thumbnail, cupping the flame in his hands to keep it from the wind and prying eyes.

"You think he gets off on it?" Tommy asked, flicking the smoking match into the weeds.

"Who?"

"Johnny Burke. You know, seeing his old lady roaring down the street after him. I mean, what happens when she catches him—they don't have a fist fight or anything like that, may be they have a go."

"She almost ran me down."

"Could you smell it?"

"What?"

"Her cunt. It must have been pulsating when she tore past, knowing it was about to feel old Johnny's big dick."

"You're crazy."

Tommy sprang up, clenched fists, and glared down at Dale. "Never call me crazy."

"Hey man, I'm sorry, OK. I didn't mean anything by it."

Tommy clenched and unclenched his hands several times, nostrils flaring.

"Sit down man. I said I was sorry."

"Don't call me crazy," Tommy said, dropping to one knee. He smoked hard, stared out into the gathering night, and threw the smoldering butt into the street.

"You feeling rich? That one still had some smoking left in it."

"The old man left some money for Lottie. I borrowed a twenty. She'll never know and even if she does, she'll never tell him." He pulled the cigarette pack from his pocket, and rotated it in his fingers. "Think there's anything to this Surgeon General shit?"

"Maybe when you're older. I never heard of young people dying of lung cancer."

Tommy lit a fresh cigarette and inhaled a few drags. Dale played an imaginary keyboard on his pants legs.

"So what'd you tell them?"

"Like you told me, nothing."

"You were in there a long time to tell them nothing."

"They wanted to know about my old man and old lady. I told them they might move to Canada."

"You're shitting me?"

"I'm not saying they're moving, I said they might, and I'm not going anyway." His phone rang. "Yeah," he said, listened for a moment, and then said, "I don't have any money." He listened for another minute and snapped the phone shut.

Tommy knew it was Dale's old lady. "What did she want?"

"Bread and eggs."

"Took her a long time to say bread and eggs."

"The eggs have to be brown and fresh this morning; they have to come from Gamble's farm, not old man Dyck's place because she doesn't like his eggs. The bread has to be cracked wheat, not whole wheat and is has to come from Peterson's Bakery in Minot, not from Great Falls—she doesn't trust big city bakeries, thinks there's mouse shit in their bread. And then when I told her I didn't have any money, she wanted to know what happed to the ten dollars she gave me this morning, she had to tell me that money doesn't grow on trees, and she had to finish off by saying I should be more respectful of my father's hard work."

"Maybe she should move to Canada."

"It's not funny. My old lady's worried about where they're going to live."

They sat for a moment, neither saying anything, and then Tommy turned to Dale and asked, "What else'd you tell 'em? Did you tell them you were fucking Karen?"

"I said the three of us hang together."

"Did you tell them I didn't have a girlfriend?"

"You don't."

"Fuck you. What about Petra?"

"You mean the girl who is never out of sight of her parents."

"I'm going to fuck her before I leave for college."

"If her old man catches you looking at her you'll be going to college minus your dick."

"I've got ten bucks that say I do."

"Keep your money."

"What else'd you blab about?"

"They asked a lot of questions about Miss Brown."

"I hope you didn't tell them anything."

"I didn't, not about you and her, but I think they know anyway."

"Listen asshole, they don't know shit unless you told them."

"Well then they don't know shit because I didn't tell them anything."

"Why don't I believe you?"

"I told them about my music, about how Miss Brown helped me."

"Oooooh, little Dale sucking up to Miss Brown about his music. You know, they don't give a shit about your music."

"Well I do, and Miss Brown helped me."

"Hey, don't get so pissy."

"You're always saying something to hurt someone else."

"I didn't mean anything by it."

Dale said, "I got to go."

"That's all you talked about for the whole time you were in there, moving to Canada and your music?"

"I told them about Greg and Dawson."

"Those assholes—she didn't even like them."

"I said the three of them were always hanging around, that's all."

"Yeah, well they weren't always hanging around."

"Just because you had sex once doesn't mean anything, if you even did it."

"You saw the pictures, asshole. What do you think? She posed nude? Besides, we did it at least ten times."

"You're a sick prick." Dale got up and brushed his hands across the ass of his jeans. "I've got to get to the store before my old lady comes lookin' for me."

"Thought you didn't have any money."

Dale jammed his hand in the front pocket of his jeans and pulled out a ten.

"You're the sick prick. Hey, wait a minute, get down, quick. There's Flanagan and Hutton."

They bent low and ran to the edge of the cenotaph, peering out through the weeds at Flanagan and Hutton.

"Can you hear what they're saying?" Tommy whispered.

Dale shook his head.

"Let's go closer."

"They'll see us."

"Not if we stay behind that truck. Come on."

With Dale following close behind, Tommy ran hunched over along the sidewalk away from where Flanagan and Hutton were standing. After they'd gone a hundred yards, they darted into the center of the street, ran back to the one-ton truck, and ducked behind the rear wheels. Dale was panting. Tommy held a finger to his lips. Dale gave him the finger and kept panting.

Tommy inched closer. He heard Flanagan say Big Springs State Hospital, and knew who they were talking about. Flanagan and Hutton got into the SUV and pulled away. The woman they were talking to followed. After they'd disappeared over the railroad crossing, Tommy stood up.

"You hear anything?" Dale asked.

"Thanks to your gasping, nothing."

"Hey man, I'm not an athlete."

"No, you're an asshole. Did you hear anything?"

"I thought I heard something like Stings. I don't know man, it doesn't make sense. Maybe they were talking about Sting."

"All you know is music." Tommy's eyes narrowed. He looked at the two sets of taillights headed for the highway, sure they'd been talking about Big Springs?

Chapter 18

Flanagan stepped into the hard spray of the shower and let the water pelt down on her face, hoping to wash away the mucous web that encased her brain. Four hours in bed hadn't given her the recharging that her mind and body demanded. Now, catching some sleep on the plane was the best she could hope for, though if past attempts were any indication, doing anything other than gripping the armrests with every grind and bump was wishful thinking.

The spirit of Zoë Brown had gone silent and Flanagan began to think she'd imagined the whole thing. She had dreamt a lot, but of her mother who no longer had a face. At one-thirty, soaked with perspiration, she'd gotten up to check the picture on the mantle fearing her mother's face had been erased from it also. She touched her fingers to the glass as if to transfer the feel of her mother's skin, the lines of her happy smile, the sound of her laughter, the smell of her perfume, the smell of her shampoo, to capture all of it and store it in her brain.

Had her father killed her mother—not in the sense that he'd murdered her, but with his drinking and womanizing? Is that why her mother had started drinking, not much at first, maybe a glass or two of wine, but then gin and vodka? The first time her father came home and found her drunk, no supper on the table, he hit her hard across the mouth. Flanagan shuddered remembering the screams, hers, and the blood, her mothers.

After that, her mother drank more and more, and soon her father stopped showing up for dinner, but they still fought when he came home. She hid in the barn so she couldn't hear their fighting: her father's cursing, her mother's crying. She stopped having friends over; they stopped inviting her to visit. One time in the barn she'd awakened to find her father standing over her.

"Get up," he'd shouted.

He reached down and yanked her arm. "I said get up goddamn it." He pulled her to her feet. "Take off those goddamn jeans. I told you no daughter of mine is going to wear jeans."

She hesitated. He hit her with the back of his hand and sent her reeling against the horse stall.

"Take them off." He took off his belt, the one with the big silver buckle.

She closed her eyes and undid her jeans.

"Push them down," he shouted and slapped the belt across the top of the stall next to her head.

"Please don't," she said.

"It's time you and your mother learned who's the man around here." He reached over and yanked her jeans down below her buttocks, and then he started wailing at her with his belt, the buckle slashing into her with every hit. She felt tears come to her eyes, but she refused to give him the satisfaction of hearing her cry out. Later, at the hospital, it took five stitches to sew up where she'd bitten down on her lip. It took two hundred and seventeen stitches to close the cuts to her buttocks and backs of her legs. She'd pressed charges and put her father in jail, more because she was afraid he'd kill her mother. Maybe he had anyway—she was never the same after that night.

She looked down. All the scars were still there, not that she'd expected them to magically disappear overnight since they'd been there the previous day and the day before that and the day before that, ever since the bandages had been removed, only then they were red and ugly. Now they were white and not so ugly, only the memory retained its ugliness, fresh in her mind as the day it happened.

"Enough of that," she cried and reached for the shampoo. She squeezed a dollop into her hand and rubbed it into her hair, first on top and then down the long strands that hung half way down her back and over her breasts. She watched the bubbles drip from her nipples and ripple down across her tight stomach. Hutton thought Tommy a pervert for staring at her breasts. She cupped them in her hands and closed her eyes, she felt their warmth, she felt their slippery fullness, hating for the moment the special bra she wore that kept them tight against her chest, wondering what it would feel like if Hutton caressed them, rubbed them...

"Aaarrrggghhh," she screamed. "Stop kidding yourself." She toweled off, wrapped her head, and started for the bedroom.

*   *   *

"Not now." She stopped. She smelled orchids.

You didn't imagine me.

A shadow moved across the mirror on her bedroom door. "I don't believe this, whatever this is, is happening."

I felt the same about Victoria Otto.

"Who is Victoria Otto? How does she fit into all of this? No, stop! Why am I talking to you? You don't exist."

*   *   *

She rubbed her hair and stepped away from the mirror.

*   *   *

You can push me away, as I pushed Victoria Otto away, but I'll keep coming back until you find out who murdered us; that's the only way our spirits can be released.

*   *   *

Flanagan put on her bra and panties.

*   *   *

Victoria Otto didn't mean to occupy my body. She made a mistake, but she doesn't know that. The only thing she knows is that if I don't find her killer, her spirit can't join the spirits of her ancestors.

"What do you mean she made a mistake?"

Her spirit is weak, very weak. It was searching for someone else—someone who has greater spiritual connection to her ancestors than I do, but once attached to my soul, her weakened spirit had no power to find another. Probably with her last gasp of energy, she made me promise to find her killer.

*   *   *

Flanagan pulled on a pair of black slacks and a gray blouse.

*   *   *

I know you hear me. You smell me, you feel me. Please believe.

*   *   *

Flanagan snapped her watch on her left wrist, slid a jade bracelet on her right wrist, and studied herself in the mirror. She felt the spirit's shadow as though wrapped in its embrace.

*   *   *

"Why won't you answer my questions?"

I can't tell you what I don't know. Whenever you ask a question for which I have no answer, I'm drawn away somewhere, to a frightening place, a place of great unhappiness. I try not to go, but I have no control over my movements, except when I become reattached to you.

*   *   *

Flanagan put on her shoulder holster and checked to see that the clip was full. After adjusting the strap that ran across her shoulder, she reached for her suit jacket.

* * *

"Does Victoria Otto talk to you?"

No longer, though I continue to feel her presence. She is discouraged that she's been trapped for eleven years, and I greatly fear her spirit may die before she is set free.

"I didn't think spirits died."

I don't blame you for being skeptical, but I do know there's a cold place where dead spirits go, never to return. Sometimes I feel Victoria Otto's spirit beginning to grow cold, and I become fearful.

* * *

Flanagan turned out the lights, walked to the front door, and activated the alarm system.

* * *

Thank you for going to Chicago.

"Am I going to learn anything there? Am I going to find Sara?"

* * *

Flanagan stood in the dark for a moment. She no longer smelled orchids. She felt alone. She stepped outside and pulled the door shut.

Chapter 19

In the beginning light of morning, she walked to the curb and waited for Hutton to arrive, though there'd been a slight change of plans. They'd found out from Lizzie Burke's sister that Edie Coombs indeed lived in Las Vegas where she worked as a dealer at Harrah's. Armed with her address and phone number, Hutton was on his way to talk to her and there was only one way to get to Las Vegas: the 5:02 to Minneapolis, the same flight that Flanagan had to take to get to Chicago.

She'd phoned Dr. and Mrs. Brownstein and told them she planned to attend Zoë's funeral. Dr. Brownstein said they were pleased—Mrs. Brownstein hadn't said much of anything other than they would try their best to answer any questions.

Flanagan's flight was scheduled to arrive in Chicago at 8:35; Zoë's funeral wasn't until 2:00—Flanagan planned to use the morning to find Sara Peterson.

She breathed in a lungful of the fresh, fifty-eight degree air. A shiver ran through her body and she pulled her suit jacket closed. She'd thought of wearing a heavier coat but wouldn't need it once the sun came up and the temperature warmed to the mid-eighties.

A set of headlights rounded the corner. She glanced at her watch. It was 4:05. Hutton's red Jeep Cherokee stopped at the curb. She climbed in and they headed for the expressway.

"I hope this isn't a wild goose chase," Hutton said, his voice raspy and curt.

"All I know is what Lizzie Burke's sister said: Edie Coombs is dealing at Harrah's and you have her address and phone number."

"Humph."

"We need coffee. Stop at the deli up ahead."

He glanced at the dashboard clock. "We don't have time."

"We've got time. Besides, I want to talk, but I'm not going to unless you get some caffeine into your system."

"That bad huh?" Frowning, he scraped a hand across his unshaven face and licked his lips. "OK, tell me where."

"Two blocks up on your right, just past the light."

He pulled into the strip mall with the blinking red neon sign that said 'Coffee Shop - Open 24 Hours.' Flanagan ran inside and returned with two containers. "I added ice so you won't scald your innards."

"Why do they have to make it so goddamn hot?" He took a cautious sip and pulled back onto the expressway.

"So, what is it, lack of sleep or trouble at home?"

"Dorie isn't happy."

It wasn't a secret that their marriage had run into a few snags, but Flanagan hadn't meant to pry. "Sorry," she said.

"I'd promised to go to her sister's place today for a family barbecue."

"At least you can blame this one on me."

"She wants me to get a nine to five Monday through Friday job."

"Can't say I blame her."

"Her friends' husbands are lawyers and doctors."

"They don't work nine to five."

"The money seems to make that less important."

"So you're not making enough money."

Hutton took another sip and stared off into the distance.

"Don't forget you're driving."

"She wants a divorce."

"Oh shit! Bob, I'm sorry—I didn't know it had gotten that bad."

"Not gotten. She's mentioned it before."

"Peters or Campbell could have gone to Vegas."

"It doesn't matter. Tomorrow it would have been something else."

A knot formed in her stomach. Should she offer? She had lots of room, but how would it look? Forget about how it looked—how would she handle it, having him that close? She'd fought to keep their relationship professional, to keep from feeling the heat every time she brushed against him, to keep from letting their relationship be other than cop to cop, to keep from interfering with his marriage.

"What are you going to do?" she asked.

"I'll stay in the Lodge Motel for awhile. If Dore and I haven't been able to fix the broken parts, mid-August my brother has an apartment coming vacant in his building downtown."

Her face was hot—she'd narrowly avoided making a complete ass of herself. Hey, this is great, I'm crazy in love with you and I have a spare room. Oh what the hell, forget the spare room; sleep with me. No thanks. Not interested. I'm trying to save my marriage.

"I hope you and Dorie can patch things up."

"Yeah, well that seems to be the thing to try to do. Statistics aren't in our favor though."

"That's BS. A lot of cops stay married."

"Not to Dorie."

"Well, let me know if you feel like a beer and a pizza once in awhile. I would think motel living gets old real fast."

"Thanks Flanagan. I may take you up on that."

"Strictly professional."

"Yeah, I know. You don't socialize with your fellow workers or something like that."

"Something like that."

He pulled into the airport parking area and turned down the first row. There were no empty spaces. He turned into the second row.

"Stop!"

Hutton hit the brakes. "What?"

Flanagan pointed at a dust-caked SUV. "Isn't that Striker's?"

"Sure as hell looks like it."

"I think it's time we found out where Striker goes when he's not in Largeville." She called Carson's voice mail and left the plate number along with the message that if it indeed belonged to a Newton Striker, to find out where he went.

Hutton parked at the end of the second row and they headed inside the terminal. Their flight departed on time and they landed in Minneapolis at 6:25. As they started toward their respective gates, Flanagan said, "Call me when you get to Vegas."

"You want to make sure I haven't turned around and gone home?"

"For a rookie you catch on fast." She stood for a moment and watched him proceed down the walkway. Just as she'd given up on the notion that he would turn and give her a departing wave, he swung around, grinned, and touched the tips of his fingers to his temple. She pulled in a deep breath and waved back.

Chapter 20

When Flanagan's plane landed at O'Hare, she rang Sara Peterson's phone number. She didn't get an answer.

After she picked up her rental car and found her way onto the JFK Expressway, she headed for West Woodlawn. She'd driven the route several times, but it had been a few years since she'd roamed the University of Chicago campus searching for a nephew who didn't want to be found. For the first few miles nothing looked familiar except for glimpses of Lake Michigan and the Sears and Hancock towers announcing that the skyline belonged to Chicago. Near the university, she began to recognize buildings and areas that didn't seem as alien.

She continued to try Sara's number to no avail, and with each call her concern grew. She knew that Sara not answering didn't mean anything other than simply that, but she'd always had a thing about unanswered telephones ringing and ringing, each ring seeming more urgent than the one before.

At South Michigan, she turned on 63rd and crossed to South Hamilton, an area of run-down red brick apartment houses, many of them burnt out and boarded up. The few people evident were black. On the corner, several young men eyed her with what she calculated to be smoldering hatred. She felt her foot press down on the accelerator. Two blocks further ahead, she stopped in front of the apartment building with the number that Joe Peterson had written.

*　　*　　*

You shouldn't have come here alone.

I didn't. Apparently I've got you, and I've got my gun.

Keep it handy.

*　　*　　*

- 155 -

She locked the car and looked up at the building. Half the windows were boarded over. Others were broken. One or two were covered with newspapers. A few had curtains. None were clean. One of the ones with curtains had a row of plants in small pots balanced on the window sill. A cat peered down from another. Two small black faces were pressed to a window on the fourth floor. She waved. The faces vanished.

An unseen woman screamed at an unseen child. Somewhere, a baby cried. Several dogs barked. A man yelled, "Shut the fuck up—I'm trying to sleep." The dogs paid him no mind. On the railroad tracks immediately behind, a mile-long freight train crawled past, its iron wheels clunking at each join in the rails. The diesel leading the growling pack of four blasted its approach and the crossing guards lowered with flashing lights and clanging warning bells.

Little patches of grass looked tired and in need of water. The leaves of the few trees that clung to life had yellowed. No birds sang. There were no flowers or ponds—everything smelled of concrete and tar.

She made her way up the crumbling sidewalk to the crumbling steps whose railings had long since been ripped out or broken off. A yellow plastic bat handle had been jammed into one of the old railing holes. Stepping around a flattened blue Frisbee and a tricycle with no wheels, she climbed the steps to the outer door that had three rectangular holes where glass used to be.

The door hung ajar because it was missing its handle and lock. She pushed through and stepped into a small foyer. The inside metal door with a thousand dents and bashes and gashes was locked. Most of the buttons on the callbox were missing, including that for Sara's apartment, 2-C that had nothing but a black hole. 4-A looked promising. She pushed and waited. She pushed again.

"Go away," a woman's voice said. "Stop pushing my buzzer."

"I'm a friend of Sara Peterson's in 2C. Her buzzer doesn't work."

"Go away, or I be calling the po-lice."

"Please, it's important. I'm afraid she might be in trouble."

4-A went silent. After trying two other buttons that looked like they should work and getting no response, she stepped outside and phoned Sara's number. Inside a phone began to ring. She hung up and the ringing stopped. She redialed, and again the phone started to ring. It's her number, but what now. She started down the steps.

She heard a scraping sound and turned to look. The inside door had opened a crack and a large pair of eyes stared out through small glasses with round plastic frames. Flanagan stepped forward.

"Now you keep your distance or I'll be slamming this door tight."

Flanagan stopped.

"Who you say you be looking for?"

"Sara Peterson in 2-C."

"She that white girl?"

"Yes, she's—"

"She be up to no good, that one. We don't like her type 'round here, all them drugs and lord only knows what else be going on."

"I know, and that's why I'm here, to try and help her."

"Who you say you were?"

"Kathleen Flanagan, from North Dakota." She showed the woman her driver's license, thinking that flashing her police ID might not be the wisest move.

The woman studied the license long enough to commit to memory, but Flanagan didn't rush the process because she knew what the woman was really trying to do was decide whether or not to unchain the door.

"Haven't seen her for a couple of weeks," the woman said, peering up at Flanagan.

"I have her keys." Flanagan fished her own house keys from her bag. "Please let me in so I can check her apartment. Maybe she left a message."

"You have her keys how come you not be opening this door?"

Think fast Flanagan. "I only have her apartment key."

One of the little black faces she'd seen at the window poked around from behind the woman's dress. Flanagan smiled and wiggled the tips of her fingers. The face disappeared.

The woman eyed Flanagan one more time and closed the door. Flanagan's heart sank, and then the door opened half-way.

"Thank you so much," she said, and sidled inside.

"I don't usually let people in here, but you say you be helping that girl, that's what she need. Maybe you be helping her to find a new place to live."

Flanagan guessed her reluctant hostess to be in her seventies. Though worn looking, but clean, her blue print dress was dotted with hundreds of small yellow flowers and her fuzzy pink slippers had no backs. The woman was as wide as she was high, about five-six, Flanagan figured. The door slammed shut and four locks clicked into place.

Flanagan looked around. The interior was no better than the exterior. There were more holes than not in the graffiti decorated wallboard; plaster hung from the ceiling in chunks and the lone light fixture was nothing more than an empty socket dangling from a wire.

Taped to the gray elevator door, a sign on a single piece of what must have been indestructible paper evidenced by its continuing existence and that looked to be

printed by a child with a red crayon simply read: BRO-
KEN. Below, in fading ink, in a more adult looking
handwriting, were the words 'Since 1940.' A multitude
of other musings covered every other exposed area of
the paper. The one's that weren't faces or flowers instructed the reader to perform anatomically impossible
acts or had something to do with bathroom functions.
Some had been scored through, though not enough to
disguise what had been written. Had it not been for the
packing tape securing all four sides of the sign, Flanagan
figured it would long ago have slid into the oblivion of
the elevator's shaft.

The lady pressed a hand to the small of her back and
started down the hallway, swinging her hips in a slow
gait. She was severely bowlegged.

"I'm sorry. I didn't mean to have you come down
four flights of stairs."

"You be ringing, how else you expect me to open the
door? Besides, ever since I got these young uns, I be up
and down these stairs seems like a hundred times a day."

"Well, thank you. I really appreciate your help."

"This here's 1-C," the lady said, pointing to a door
with no numbers or letters. "2-C be directly above."
They proceeded to the stairs in the back. The lady
grabbed the rail and began an arduous process of swinging and hoisting herself up, one step at a time. At the
second floor landing, she pointed and said, "Your friend
lives there."

Flanagan thanked her again and stepped into the
hallway facing 2-C. She knocked loudly and said, "Sara,
it's Kate Flanagan." When she didn't get a response, she
pretended to use her keys while working the lock pick.
She felt the old woman's eyes and ears watching and
hearing every move. "Stuck," she said over her shoulder,
then the bolt clicked and the door opened a crack. "Got
it," she said. Please God, don't let there be a security
chain. There wasn't.

She heard the woman continue up the creaky stairs. From above, a tiny voice called out, "Grandma hurry, or we'll be late for Sunday school."

"I be coming as fast as I can," the old woman said.

Flanagan removed her gun and stepped inside. Her heart began beating harder and faster. The combination living/dining room/kitchen had been ransacked. Chairs and lamps were broken and tipped on their sides; cans and broken dishes lay scattered across the kitchen area, curtains and blinds had been pulled from the windows and the other floor areas were strewn with books and newspapers. She smelled gas and moved to the stove. Its burners weren't on. She suspected the pilot light. Two windows faced the back of the building. One opened easily.

She moved to the bedroom. Everything had been tossed. The closet doors were open, what few clothes there were had been scattered, and the bedding including the mattresses that had been sliced open lay on the floor.

She stepped back into the hallway. The bathroom door was ajar. She put her ear to the crack and heard dripping water. With her pistol extended at eyelevel, she nudged the door with her foot. Her body began to tingle the way it did when death was present. "Please, not Sara," she said, and kicked the door.

White legs and downward-pointing feet protruded from the water-filled tub. She clicked the light switch with her elbow and stepped closer. Emptiness filled her stomach. The young woman's long blonde hair floated to the surface. She was nude. Flanagan couldn't see her face, but knew it was Sara, and she hadn't been dead long.

She stepped out of the bathroom and called the local police. When two Chicago uniforms arrived, she showed them her ID. One of them got busy on the radio. Fifteen minutes later, two stocky detectives in matching blue-gray wrinkled suits arrived from the homicide division and took charge. The younger one introduced himself as Mike Lipinski. He pointed at the older one and said his name was Sean Murphy. "A Pollack and a Mick working together as cops in Chicago," he said. "Who could have guessed?"

Flanagan showed him her ID.

"You know the vic?" Lipinski asked, flipping open a worn notepad that he'd removed from his suit jacket.

His question was cop shorthand for 'what is a cop from North Dakota doing in a shit hole apartment in Chicago with a body?' She told him about Zoë Brown and gave him the known facts: found in a water-filled ditch, red high heels, nude, didn't drown, cause of death: head bashed in by blunt object, not raped, no witnesses, no prime suspects.

"What brought you here?" Lipinski's eyes darted about, taking in every detail of the apartment.

"I was given this address by someone I interviewed yesterday."

"A suspect?"

"He's on the list. So is everyone else."

Now Lipinski looked at her. His eyes did the talking. Come on lady, stop screwing me around. What the fuck are you doing here?

"I believe the victim is Sara Peterson. It was her father, Joe Peterson, who gave me her phone number and address. Sara had started to ask him for a lot of money to further her acting and modeling career. I wanted to talk to her, to make sure she wasn't getting ripped off, to make sure she wasn't getting in with a bad crowd."

"Looks like she found the bad crowd—mind hanging around?"

She recognized a rhetorical question when she heard one.

A few minutes later, Sara's apartment crawled with lab people taking pictures, dusting for prints, and poking at everything that might yield a clue.

"Detective," the lab person in the bathroom said to Lipinski.

Lipinski ambled to the bathroom door, listened to the lab person for a moment, and stepped inside. A moment later he reappeared. "Looks like she took it on the side of the head with a baseball bat. Too many similarities starting to crop up. Maybe we ought to talk some more about your vic."

Flanagan saw motion near the doorway and looked across at a little black face peering into Sara's apartment. "Excuse me," she said to Lipinski, "I'll be right back." She strode across to the boy. "You shouldn't be here. I'll take you upstairs."

"I've seen dead people before. I'm not afraid."

"How do you know anyone is dead?"

"That's the only reason police ever come here. They came when my mommy was shot dead."

Flanagan felt cold. She picked the boy up and held him tight. "How old are you?"

"Seven."

"And is that girl I saw you with in the window your sister?"

"Half-sister. We have the same mommy. We don't know who are daddies are."

Flanagan started up the stairs.

"JOSHUA?" The old woman's voice sounded from above. "YOU BE GETTING YOURSELF UP HERE THIS INSTANT OR YOU BE GETTING SOMETHING ALL RIGHT."

"Is that your grandmother?"

Joshua grinned at Flanagan. "That's my great grannie. Our grannie got shot dead too so all we got left is great grannie Mae. COMING."

Flanagan winced as her ear got most of Joshua's hundred-decibel response. "Maybe your mother and grandmother didn't get shot."

"Yeah they did, I saw them."

They rounded the stairs on the forth floor and entered the hallway. The old lady stood, hands on hips. The little girl came out from behind, eyed Flanagan suspiciously, and said to Joshua, "You're going to get it."

"Am not."

"Are to."

Flanagan put Joshua on the floor and he ran to the old woman.

"Don't you ever be running off that way again. How many times do I got to tell you?" She swatted his rear end. He giggled and ran inside, followed closely by the girl who said, "Told you." The old woman glared at Flanagan and slammed the door.

Flanagan stood for a moment, thinking about seven-year-old Joshua seeing his mother and grandmother shot dead, about how matter-of-factly he'd talked about it, like an everyday occurrence. Nothing in Minot compared—the people there understood nothing of how millions of Americans like Joshua and his half-sister and their great grannie Mae lived. She glanced one more time at the door to 4-A then returned to 2-C to deal with Sara Peterson's murder, to wonder what brought her to this place, to wonder how she was going to explain her murder to Joe Peterson.

"It seems," Lipinski said when she returned, "that we've got identical murders."

No questions about the young boy. No concerns about how he's handling a murder in the building where he lives. "The boy says he saw his mother and grandmother shot dead."

Lipinski gave her a sidewise look that said, What the hell you talking about, Lady?

"I was concerned having a murder in the building…"

"Look Dakota, this is the shit section of Chicago. These kids could give lectures on murder, on seeing their mothers and fathers and brothers and sisters getting killed. They've seen more and know more than any guidance counselor. Bottom line: when it's someone not in their family that gets it, they're happy."

Flanagan shook her head. "Let me know when you get your ME's report. FYI, we believe an aluminum baseball bat was the weapon used on our victim."

"So we have some loony running around with an aluminum baseball bat braining women, taking off their clothes, and dumping them in water."

"Let's hope it stops at two." For the time being, she decided against mentioning Victoria Otto.

"We found these." He handed her two eight by ten glossies. Sara's name and telephone number were printed across the bottom. "Looks like our vic is who you thought. You want to notify the father?"

"May I take one with me? I'd like to get her father to make a positive ID."

"Be my guest. We've got lots."

"I'll be back in Largeville tomorrow. I'll let you know."

"Anything else we need to know?"

Flanagan looked around at the shambles, the havoc that had been wreaked on Sara's apartment. "Our victim's place wasn't ransacked. In fact, it was hard to find so much as a hair out of place."

"This looks like a drug toss. Your vic into drugs?"

Flanagan shook her head. "Maybe it wasn't the killer."

"A possibility," Lipinski says. "Or the killer's trying to make us think drug toss. Try this on: the murder took place elsewhere; the killer brought her here, dumped her in the tub, and started wrecking the place while the tub filled with water."

"Why would the killer bring the body here?"

"Who knew you were coming? Maybe they wanted to make sure you found the body."

She stared at him, her brain starting off in a thousand different directions. "No one outside the department."

"That you know of?"

She nodded.

"Walls in Chicago have a lot of ears."

"Largeville's don't, but they're thin."

He grimaced. "Something to ponder."

Flanagan glanced across at Lipinski's partner. "He ever say anything?"

"He usually needs a couple of shots of Bushmills, and then you can't shut him up."

They watched as the gurney rolled out. The black bag was always so final, all hope extinguished. Everyone knew what it meant. It meant that Joshua and his sister and great grandmother would be happy. It wasn't anyone from their family.

"I'll call you," she said.

Chapter 21

Flanagan turned off Lakeshore onto Elm and found a parking space a block past the synagogue along the quiet, tree-lined street that ran in front of luxury apartment houses populating the area. Economically and socially, this was the other end of the spectrum from West Woodlawn. Not only weren't there burnt out shells of cars here, there weren't any old cars except one or two show-room antiques that glistened like polished gemstones.

She stepped onto the carpet-like grass that ran between the curb and the sidewalk. Black wrought-iron planters at the base of centuries old elm and oak trees encircled flower beds rich with coleus and impatiens. The temperature had climbed into the low nineties, but the stiff breeze from Lake Michigan felt cool against her face and unlike West Woodlawn, this air was fresh with the smell of money.

The stone and brick synagogue loomed prominently in the next block. A lanky man in a tailored black suit and a small woman in a black dress and broad-brimmed black hat circulated among the scores of people congregated on the large apron at the top of the steps.

*   *   *

Flanagan breathed in the aroma of orchids.
They look so sad.
"What did you expect?"
I'm not sure.
"Do you know about Sara?"
My heart aches for that poor, lonely girl.
"Do you know who murdered her?"

*   *   *

Flanagan waited until everyone had gone inside and then entered the synagogue. A strange feeling came over her, like she didn't belong, like she'd violated some ancient and sacred law. Even the air smelled biblical, ancient. She wondered if they had special seating for non-Jews. Did the women sit apart? She'd read that somewhere. No, everyone was sitting together. What about a shawl? Should she have covered her head? Were pants appropriate? She sidled into the rear pew, happily observing the absence of kneelers—high Episcopalian and Catholic services had always confused her.

A young man in a black suit came back and asked if she'd like to move closer to the front. She shook her head and took a book that she thought a hymnal from the rack and opened it. It wasn't a hymnal, more like a bible but in Hebrew and English. She put it back.

At the front of the Synagogue, Zoë's father stood stooped, his hands caressing the closed coffin. Sobs shook his body. Her mother gripped his arm with both hands.

Flanagan studied the two hundred or so people who had gathered, mostly couples, mostly the age of Zoë's parents, most of the women wearing hats, most of the men wearing yarmulkes, some fancy, some plain black. She wondered if only Jewish men were allowed to wear yarmulkes, or if all the men in attendance were Jewish why they weren't all wearing them.

The person she assumed to be the rabbi came down from the dais to the coffin and escorted Zoë's parents to the front row. He held Mrs. Brownstein's hand for a moment while they shared a whispered conversation. Dr. Brownstein sat, head hanging down, the plain black yarmulke that looked too big slightly askew.

The rabbi returned to the dais and began Zoë's eulogy. The cantor chanted the psalms and mourning prayer. All were in Hebrew interspersed with English. A man in a dark gray suit who appeared to be about the same age as Dr. Brownstein ascended the stairs to the dais. He introduced himself as Zoë's Uncle Benjamin and said he wanted to tell a story about the wildest girl he'd ever known, his favorite niece, Zoë, whom he loved as his own daughter. A titter ran through the crowd while a large number daubed their eyes.

While Uncle Benjamin fished his wire rimmed glasses and a folded paper from his suit jacket, Flanagan noticed two young men in the row immediately behind where Uncle Benjamin had sat. They seemed to be together. Across the aisle, two rows back, a woman in a black sheath sat alone. She turned and looked back. Flanagan thought she looked familiar but the veiled hat and large dark glasses obscured her face.

The audience chuckled. Flanagan missed what Uncle Benjamin had said. She tried to pay attention, but her eyes wandered back to the woman who sat with her head erect, shoulders back, and chest forward. Flanagan glanced back at Uncle Benjamin. He wiped his eyes and noisily blew his nose with a large white handkerchief that he inspected before folding it back into his vest pocket.

On the way to his seat, he stopped and kissed Mrs. Brownstein on both cheeks and embraced Dr. Brownstein. One of the two young men got up and started toward the front. He stopped and faced Zoë's parents, taking their hands in his for a moment, and then continued on to the dais.

He introduced himself as Dawson Richards and then introduced his friend, Greg Adams, whom everyone turned to look at. Adams seemed embarrassed by the attention. Richards explained that they were both from Largeville, that they were both in love with Zoë, and that one day one of them had hoped to marry her.

Flanagan sensed some in the congregation stiffening at the thought. Dawson continued by acknowledging that it was probably wishful thinking on his and Greg's part. Those who had found the idea that Zoë might marry a non-Jew distasteful relaxed somewhat. Dawson went on to explain how much Zoë had been loved by the people of Largeville, how the students of Largeville High School had so dramatically changed for the better after Zoë had arrived…

The woman in the black sheath put a gloved hand to her veil and crept to the rear of the sanctuary. Flanagan tried to get a better look, but saw only black. Even her shoulders and arms were covered with a shawl and long gloves. At the door the woman turned and looked back. Framed by the brilliant afternoon sun streaming in through the doorway, all Flanagan saw was an exquisite outline, and then the door closed.

"…as much as Largeville took Zoë to heart, she took Largeville to heart, she captured Largeville's heart." Richards returned to sit with Greg Adams, who leaned over and whispered in his ear. Richards nodded.

Flanagan dashed after the woman, pushing through the door in time to see her get into the back seat of a black Lincoln. Her chauffeur closed the door. Flanagan started down the steps. The Lincoln swerved away and sped toward Lakeshore Drive. She made a note of the plate thinking her new Chicago cop friend, Lipinski, could run a check and returned to the synagogue.

Zoë's parents came down the aisle. She stepped to one side. They walked toward her.

"You must be Detective Flanagan," Dr. Brownstein said, and offered his hand. "Thank you for coming. I'm Zoë's father, this is her mother."

"I'm so sorry about Zoë," Flanagan said, and embraced them both.

Mrs. Brownstein said, "Please ride with us to the cemetery. We can talk along the way."

"I have a car."

"After we leave the cemetery," Mrs. Brownstein said, clutching Flanagan's arm and pretending or choosing not to hear, "we'll be going to our home for a reception. We would be pleased to have you join us."

The large stones in Mrs. Brownstein's earrings flashed. Flanagan figured anything that big had to be Zircon. "I don't know...my car, I should probably be getting to the airport."

"Please, it would mean so much to us. When we first saw you come in it was as if for a brief moment Zoë had come back into our lives."

"Yes, of course I will," Flanagan said, the back of her neck and the aroma of orchids announcing Zoë's nearness.

A maroon, stretch Mercedes crawled up the street and stopped at the curb. The uniformed chauffeur got out and ran up the steps. He took Mrs. Brownstein's arm, his white gloves flashing in the brilliant sunlight. Flanagan decided that Mrs. Brownstein's earrings might not be Zircon after all.

"I could have managed on my own," Mrs. Brownstein scolded, but didn't pull away.

"Yes ma'am."

"Roland, this is our dear friend from North Dakota. She's going to ride with us to the cemetery and then come back to our home. After we get back, I'd like you to fetch her car."

"I'd be happy to, ma'am. Miss, please give me your keys and tell me which car is yours."

"No, it's not necessary. I can easily take a taxi—"

"Nonsense my dear, Roland's always looking for things to do. He'll be disappointed if he has to sit around, won't you Roland?"

"Yes ma'am."

Roland opened the limo door and assisted Mrs. Brownstein inside. Flanagan handed him her car keys and pointed to the dark blue Ford half-way into the next block. "The plate number is on the key tag."

He pocketed the keys and offered his arm to Flanagan, but she was already more than half inside, already breathing in the opulence of the large suite that made up the back seat and thinking that the practice of medicine must be grossly lucrative in Chicago. Dr. Brownstein slid in beside her.

"So my dear," Mrs. Brownstein said as they pulled away from the curb. "What can we tell you about Zoë that you don't already know? What can we tell you that will help find the son-of-a-bitch that did this?"

Flanagan glanced at Dr. Brownstein. "You'll have to excuse Sadie," he said, "but she never was one to waste time or mince words."

"I'm sorry, "Flanagan said. "It seems like such an inappropriate time for me to be—"

"Nonsense child," Mrs. Brownstein said. "If we don't get started, we don't get done. All we can do for Zoë now is find her killer." She flipped a switch on her arm rest. Roland's voice, sounding as though echoing from an orbital satellite, said, "Yes ma'am."

"Rowland, do you know how to get to the cemetery?"

"Yes ma'am."

Sadie released the switch and said to Flanagan, "I gather you haven't found Zoë's killer in North Dakota, or you wouldn't be spending you weekend poking around Chicago."

Flanagan nodded.

"OK, what is it that you want to know?

Flanagan dug her notepad from her handbag and turned on her recorder. "Do you know anyone who might want to hurt her?"

"Hah," Sadie said. "If you were talking about me, the list would be long. For Zoë, nothing, nada, bupkiss. She's like her father, such a mench—never a confrontation, never a bad word. Oy!"

"Anyone on your list who might be trying to get even?"

"Enough to murder Zoë? No, never anything like that—a bunch of meshuganas they are, but they get revenge by getting even on the next deal, or if not the next deal, the one after that, or the one after that, not by hurting my family. It's strictly business."

"What about from college or New York? Any trouble there?"

"Me. I was the big trouble. Teacher's college. What for? She doesn't need from teacher's college. She could run my business. One day it's hers."

Dr. Brownstein had been looking out the side window. He seemed used to saying nothing in Sadie's presence. "Dr. Brownstein," Flanagan asked. "What did you think of Zoë getting a degree in education?"

"Hah," Sadie said. "I'll tell you what he thinks. He thinks everyone should be a teacher. My Izzy, the only time in his life he disagrees with me."

Dr. Brownstein's eyes twinkled and wrinkled into what Flanagan took to be a wry smile.

"In one of Zoë's files, we found a letter addressed to you, Dr. Brownstein, from Big Springs Mental Hospital."

"Zoë was worried about one of her students, a boy by the name of Tommy Striker, and asked me find out what I could about the boy's mother."

"There was just the one letter."

"I only sent it a few days ago. We didn't get a chance to talk more about it."

His eyes turned heavy.

"I'm sorry. I shouldn't have brought it up."

Wrigley Field passed by on their right.

"The cemetery is two blocks ahead," Dr. Brownstein said, and put his hand on Sadie's.

"Dear, we'll talk more after," Mrs. Brownstein said to Flanagan.

They completed the journey in silence. Roland glided the big Mercedes to a stop, stepped out, and opened Mrs. Brownstein's door. She took his gloved hand and pulled herself out. Flanagan and Dr. Brownstein followed. Sadie brushed at Dr. Brownstein's suit with her hand.

"It's OK," he said.

"What, so now you're an expert?" Mrs. Brownstein asked, still brushing.

Flanagan noticed several cars pulling up and stopping behind the Mercedes, one of which was the hearse.

*　　*　　*

Mother always has to go first.
Like mother like daughter?
I didn't let her run my life, like she does Daddy's.

*　　*　　*

Mrs. Brownstein gripped Flanagan's arm. "Come dear, walk with us."

Stopping several times in what Flanagan assumed was a ritualistic march, six young pall bearers carried the coffin across the spongy grass past a majestic oak tree to a granite mausoleum the size of a small hotel with Brownstein etched above the porticoed entrance. Mrs. Brownstein pulled Dr. Brownstein to one side and let the rabbi from the synagogue follow the pallbearers. After they'd gone inside, she tugged Dr. Brownstein's arm and they entered. Flanagan noticed the others standing back and decided to wait.

"Come dear," Mrs. Brownstein said back to her. "I get the feeling Zoë wants you to see her final resting place."

After a brief service, they returned to the Mercedes for the trip to the Brownstein's home. "We aren't far from here," Mrs. Brownstein said. "And once we get back to the house, there won't be time to talk so I'm going to have Roland take the long way."

"The others will be waiting," Dr. Brownstein said.

"So let them wait," Mrs. Brownstein said. "Now dear, where were we?"

"You didn't want Zoë to get a degree in education."

"What is this didn't want, didn't want, like I had a say. They ganged up on me. What could I do?"

"You bought her a new BMW."

"Izzy bought it so she could come home on weekends. I told her she could stay there for all I cared."

"You paid for it," Dr. Brownstein said.

Mrs. Brownstein shrugged. "So what could I do? They ganged up on me."

"Did she have any boyfriends?"

"You should have known her—every boy was her boyfriend. For her bat mitzvah we tell her to invite all her friends—a hundred young men show up. They all loved her."

"How about in college? Anything serious."

"Zoë never got serious about anything except teaching. She wanted to make kids understand things, to know things, things they didn't get to see normally, like music and art and dance."

"She went to New York after she graduated?"

"Nine/eleven happened in Zoë's her first year of college. My Izzy took us to New York. He said we have to see what can happen when evil gains power. He said we have to make sure it is stopped. We stayed for a week, going down to ground zero every day to help out. We served soup to the firemen and police and other workers. So tired they were, and so sad. That first night, when we got back to our hotel, Zoë cried and said that when she graduated, she was going to teach in New York."

"She taught at a school up in Harlem," Dr. Brownstein said.

"I understand," said Flanagan, "that she stayed two years and then went to Largeville. That's quite a change."

The Mercedes slowed and took a turn.

"We're nearing the plant," Sadie said. "It's just ahead on the right."

Flanagan glanced out the side window. They were on a wide boulevard surrounded by grassy knolls and trees and flowers and small lakes hooked together by streams and miniature water falls. Periodically, a low-rise building popped up, scarcely visible from the roadway.

Mrs. Brownstein flipped the intercom. "Roland, we won't stop. Just go in and drive around the circle, and then we'll go to the house."

They passed through an unmarked guarded gate. The property was surrounded by a ten-foot high brick wall with cameras mounted every hundred feet. They continued up a small rise and then down to a circular drive that passed in front of a two-story brown brick building that looked more castle-like than a plant. Like the guarded gate, no names appeared anywhere on the building. Smartly uniformed doormen stood on either side of the front door. Flanagan sensed they were armed.

"The only Italian renaissance building west of New York," Dr. Brownstein said. "It's Sadie's one extravagance."

"Oy, such money it cost."

"Why all the security?"

"Three words: gold, platinum, diamonds."

"No parking?"

"Underground. No cars can be visible from the streets otherwise our hoity-toity neighbors complain, sheesh, such a trouble."

They drove back out through the guarded gateway and headed back to the boulevard.

"I had asked why Zoë left New York and went to Largeville."

"She said it was to teach high school, but a young man was involved."

Mrs. Brownstein seemed reluctant to elaborate, a definite anomaly.

"What happened?"

"I'd rather not talk about it." Sadie said.

*   *   *

Make her tell you.
How do you propose I do that?

*   *   *

"It might be important."

"It's over and forgotten."

"I wonder if Zoë would agree."

"She would agree with me."

"Enough to give up teaching in New York, enough to stop helping a hurt city that she so desperately wanted to help, enough to run away and hide in Largeville? Have you been to Largeville? Have you seen what a dump it is?"

Mrs. Brownstein looked out the window. Flanagan felt a touch on her arm and turned to look at Dr. Brownstein. He shook his head, a signal to back off.

"I need answers," Flanagan said. "Did you ever meet a young woman by the name of Sara Peterson?"

Mrs. Brownstein turned and looked at Flanagan, a flash of recognition in her eyes.

"She came to the house once," Dr. Brownstein said. "We gave her some money."

"Did Zoë tell her to come and see you?"

Mrs. Brownstein asked, "What's that got to do with Zoë?"

"Sara Peterson was murdered this morning."

The shock of what she'd just told them registered on their faces. Mrs. Brownstein's mouth opened. "Ach," was all that came out.

"And there's another young woman missing from Largeville, also a school teacher."

They stared hard.

"Her name is Victoria Otto."

Their expressions didn't change.

"We found several news clippings in Zoë's files that suggested she was trying to find out what happened to

Victoria Otto. If you know anything at all, it could be important."

Mrs. Brownstein said. "Always the helper was our Zoë. She calls out of the blue not to talk to her mother, who she hasn't talked to for over a week, but to say a young girl needs two-hundred and fifty dollars."

"That's when we met Sara," Dr. Brownstein said. "She didn't look well. I was concerned she might be addicted."

Mrs. Brownstein said. "I hope she's now at peace."

Dr. Brownstein said, "I told her I was a doctor and asked her if she wanted help. She said she was fine, took the money, and climbed back into the taxi. We never saw or heard from her again."

"How long ago was that?"

"Two, maybe three weeks ago."

"It was Mother's Day. I remember wondering if that poor girl had a mother."

Flanagan thought about Claudine Peterson, whom she hadn't met, her addiction to alcohol, her 'sleeping around' as one Largevillian had put it, and how she would react to her daughter's murder, but she thought more about Joe because she knew from meeting him how hard he had tried to be a good father, how proud he was of Sara, and how devastated he would be.

"You want to know about that young man in New York?" Mrs. Brownstein asked.

Flanagan nodded.

"Our Zoë falls in love for the first time in her life. She calls and says she wants to get married, that she's bringing a young man home to meet us. Izzy and I are so happy. Finally, our Zoë finds a man she wants to marry."

Dr. Brownstein clenched his hands into fists.

"So Zoë brings him home. Gott in himmel. Anderson Fleet Wellington III from Greenwich, CT. What kind of a name is that? An investment banker at the firm founded by his great, great grandfather. I don't trust him—my Izzy tries to like him. We keep our mouths shut because we can see how much our Zoë loves him."

Dr. Brownstein said, "Zoë called a couple of days later, after she and Mr. Wellington returned to New York. She told us their engagement was off, that she wouldn't be seeing him again."

"That's why our Zoë left New York. Mr. Fancypants from Connecticut broke her heart. That was just about a year ago, and when she called a few days later to say she was leaving New York, that she needed to find a place to restore her soul. North Dakota she picks?"

Mrs. Brownstein dug in her purse and pulled out a copy of an e-mail. "This arrived this morning." She handed it to Flanagan.

It was from Anderson Fleet Wellington III of Wellington Investments. 'Dear Mr. and Mrs. Brownstein: My deepest and heartfelt sympathy on your immeasurable loss. I loved Zoë deeply. Letting her go was a horrible mistake.' Flanagan handed it back.

"Now he loves her?" Mrs. Brownstein stuffed the e-mail back into her purse.

"What happened?" Flanagan asked.

"She is a Jew—that's what happened. The waspy Wellingtons from Connecticut wouldn't countenance the heir to their fortune marrying a Jew."

The Mercedes turned onto North Astor, slowed, and then stopped for a wrought-iron gate that slowly swung open. The winding paved drive led to an enormous house sitting atop the hill about five-hundred yards distant. The grounds looked hand-manicured with their array of topiary shrubs, vast flower beds with rich black earth, and perfectly shaped giant conifers, some blue, others green.

The house was a pale yellow with black roof and shutters. To one side were two tennis courts, an Olympic-sized pool, Jacuzzi, and a collection of small service buildings.

"Those are for our guests," Mrs. Brownstein said, pointing to two single-family sized homes nestling in the trees behind and to the right of the main house. "But when you come, you stay in the main house, next to Zoë's room."

The Mercedes rolled to a stop. A butler in formal attire arrived and led them up the steps through two giant oak doors that guarded the main entrance to the house.

On the drive back to O'Hare, Flanagan checked her voice mail. Hutton hadn't called. She tried his number, got his voice mail, and told him she'd see him in Minneapolis. Her flight departed on time at eight and was scheduled to arrive in Minneapolis at nine-thirty. She hoped Hutton had made his four-thirty flight so they would be on the same connecting flight to Minot. She wanted him to go with her to Largeville to tell Joe and Claudine Peterson about Sara. It couldn't wait until morning.

Predicting how Joe and Claudine would react to Sara's murder was a game she didn't want to play, but her mind played anyway. Joe would be devastated. What about Claudine? How would she react? Would she be sober enough to be sad, would she be so dazed by alcohol that she couldn't comprehend, would she simply consider it an annoying interruption to her drinking and partying? Please God, don't let it be that.

She propped her head against the window and tried to sleep, but the name of Anderson Fleet Wellington III lodged in her brain and wouldn't let go. She stared out at the darkening clouds rimmed golden by the lowering sun. Zoë's face appeared in the nearest one. She was crying.

Chapter 22

Hutton identified himself to the leggy brunette with a pretty face and sweet smile who answered the door of the well-kept bungalow on a well-kept street with lots of green lawns and manicured flower beds and trimmed shrubs. She said her name was Gwen Rydell. She and Edie lived together, as in friends, and worked together at Harrah's, although not always the same shift. Edie wasn't at home, though after assuring her that Edie wasn't in any kind of trouble, Gwen batted her long eyelashes and told him where he could find Edie.

Twenty minutes later, Hutton turned onto a street lined with small lots containing large single-family houses that, except for color and finish, looked the same. It was a new subdivision judging from the stakes and rubber and wire holding up spindly trees stuck into front lawns that were fighting for survival.

Half-way into the block, he slowed and pulled into a driveway in front of a two-car garage attached to a brown stucco split-level. The garage door was closed. If anyone was at home, they wouldn't see him because of the way the garage jutted out from the front of the house.

He rolled down his window and sat for a moment, thinking of Flanagan and wondering if she'd found Sara, wondering if she'd attended Zoë's funeral. He reached for his cellphone to call her and then changed his mind when he thought he heard a door slam.

He cocked his ear trying to hear additional sounds. The neighborhood seemed asleep. No cars, no people, no barking dogs—it seemed too quiet even for Sunday. He glanced at his watch. It was nearing one. Off in the distance a lawnmower powered up. Maybe people in Las Vegas did get out of bed on Sunday after all. He stepped from the car and walked around the garage, mounted the two front steps, and rang the bell.

Inside, a dog with a small voice barked. He remembered that someone in Largeville had mentioned Edie's white poodles. His eye caught an almost imperceptible tug at the front drapes. A man coughed. "Who is it?" the man asked.

"Is this the Derrick Smith residence?"

"Just a minute."

A chain slid, a lock clicked, and the inner door opened part way. Hutton stepped back a pace. A large man with bushy black hair and a face black with a day-old growth of beard peered out through blood-shot eyes. "Waddya want?"

"Sorry to bother you sir, but are you Derrick Smith?"

"Who wants to know?"

"I need to have a word with Edie Coombs."

"Don't know anyone by that name."

"Are you Derrick Smith?"

"As I said, who wants to know?"

Hutton showed his badge, certain that Gwen Rydell would have called Edie.

Smith opened the outer door a crack. "Put it closer."

Hutton complied.

Smith leaned forward. Hutton saw he was in his under shorts. It wasn't a pretty sight. Smith studied Hutton's badge and ID for a moment, and then said, "It says here you're from North Dakota."

Hutton nodded.

"A little of your beat, aintcha?"

"I need to ask Edie Coombs a few questions? I'm sure her friend, Gwen, called to tell her I was coming."

"You don't listen too well. I told you I don't know anyone by that name."

"And you don't understand too well. I haven't got all day. Either she talks to me here, or I go downtown, get the Nevada Gaming Authority involved, and talk to her at work."

"What is it baby?" A large woman opened the inside door a little wider and stood next to Smith. Her long black hair flowed down over a red satin robe that was cinched tight around her waist and open enough at the neck to show melon-sized cleavage. She held a white toy poodle under each arm. One barked continuously.

"Can't you make that goddamn mutt stop his constant yapping," Smith said.

"Are you Edie Coombs?" Hutton asked.

"You don't need to say nothing to him," Smith said. "He ain't from here."

"Why baby? Who is he?" She continued to eyeball Hutton in an easy way, giving him a practiced going over.

"He's with the police from North Dakota."

Edie glanced up at Smith's big, shaggy face, and then looked back at Hutton. "Why do you want to talk to me?"

"Can we talk inside?"

Smith scowled and said, "Anything you got to say you can say out there."

One of the poodles started barking again.

"Tooey, shut the fuck up," Smith said to the barking poodle. He raised his hand as if to strike the dog.

Coombs swung away putting herself between Smith and the dog. "Baby, please go get your robe, and he's only being protective so please don't holler at him."

Smith glowered and then spun around and disappeared.

"Don't mind him," Coombs said, opening the door and motioning Hutton inside. He caught a whiff of perfume that he decided he liked. She closed the door and put the two dogs down. They ran to Hutton and started sniffing his pants and would have gone for his crotch had it been lower to the ground.

"Passepartout, Tocqueville, stop this instant."

They didn't. Hutton brushed at them with his hand, which they sniffed and licked.

"They like you," she said, sweeping them to her ample bosom.

She led the way into a sunken living room and pointed him to a big stuffed chair. She sat with the dogs on the matching sofa. Had it been her place, he would have expected the pleasantly decorated room, but for a pig like Smith, it seemed an anomaly.

"Nice place," he said.

"No it isn't." She laughed pleasantly. "I had this room and the master bedroom redone. The rest of the place is a dump, but I'll get there."

"I met your friend. I hope you don't mind that she told me where to find you, though I am surprised she didn't call."

She looked up the stairs and then back at Hutton. "He and Gwen don't much like each other. She may have hung up if Derrick answered." She alternately toyed with a tassel on one of the several pillows that surrounded her and brushed at one of the poodles and then studied Hutton again. "How may I help you?"

"I want to ask you a few questions about Zoë Brown."

"That teacher from Largeville?"

"She was murdered."

"Oh my god." She got up, shooed the dogs downstairs, and closed the door. Both instantly started to bark.

"What the hell's going on?" Smith hollered from upstairs.

"Nothing baby, sorry," she hollered back, and then turned to Hutton. "When…I mean…how awful. What happened?"

"So this is the first you've heard about it?"

"Yes…but surely you don't think…"

Hutton studied her face and eyes.

"When did it happen?"

"Early yesterday morning."

"I was at the club here until four."

"That can be verified?"

"Of course. I'm a dealer. I must be on a dozen or more cameras."

"When did you last see Miss Brown?"

She stared past Hutton out the front window. "I guess you're here because you heard about our differences."

"They were described as something more than differences."

She nodded several times, still peering off into the distance. "Yes," she finally said, and faced Hutton. "I'm certain they were."

"Care to tell me about it."

"As it turns out, my problems weren't with Miss Brown as much as they were with my ex-husband."

Hutton waited.

"My ex-husband lied to me."

"And you decided to take a round out of Miss Brown?"

"He told me she had lured him into an affair. I believed him."

Coombs kicked off her slippers and Hutton noticed her perfectly shaped feet that were perfectly white and perfectly tipped with neon red nails. Her robe opened and revealed most of her full-sized leg, also perfectly white except for the large black and blue mark on her thigh. She looked down, seemed momentarily embarrassed, and clutched her robe closed.

Hutton opened his case and placed his recorder on the coffee table. "Just for the record, you are Edie Coombs formerly of Largeville, North Dakota?"

"Yes, but I no longer use Coombs as my last name. I switched back to my maiden name, Pitano, when the divorce became final."

"Fast divorce."

"Nevada marries them fast and divorces them fast. I sent the forms to Rick—two days later I had them back signed. Six weeks later, it was all over, and he was as glad to be rid of me as I was of him."

"When did you leave Largeville?"

"February 23rd."

"You seem to have a clear memory of February 23rd."

"If I'd have got my hands around Zoë Brown's neck, I might have killed her. Yeah, I'd say I have a clear memory of the day my life damn near ended, and all because of a lie."

"When did you find out that it was a lie?"

"A week later…Mary McAllister told me."

"And Mary McAllister is…"

"Lizzie Burke's sister. Do you know Lizzie Burke?"

"We've met."

"I can tell by the look on your face that you've also heard about the fight Lizzie and I had, but then why wouldn't you have? I'm sure everyone in Largeville still talks about it."

"It was mentioned."

"Odd, isn't it? Lizzie and I going at each other like that and her sister, Mary McAllister, was the only person in Largeville who understood me. To the extent I had a friend in that god forsaken place, she was it. I guess we both wanted to escape, she from her crazy family and me from a marriage that was making me nuts."

Hutton flipped through his notes and stopped to scan something he'd written. "It seems you both succeeded."

"Yeah, Mary ended up in Minneapolis and I ended up here."

"Is this where you came after you left Largeville?"

"After that morning at the school, I went home, got my two babies, Passepartout and Tocqueville, and took off, not knowing if the cops were after me or not, not knowing where I was going. I drove and drove and ten

days later I ended up in Anchorage. That's when I heard
from Mary. She told me that she was OK with everything, that she had no hard feelings because of her dumb
sister, and that she'd been to the hospital to see Rick.
That's when he told her he'd lied about Miss Brown,
hoping I'd leave. Well, guess what? It worked." She
brushed at her eyes.

"I'm sorry," Hutton said, thinking for a moment
about his own screwed up marriage.

"At first I thought it strange that he would tell her,
but that was his way; he'd never say anything to my face
and I guess he knew that by telling Mary, I'd be sure to
hear."

"Hmmm," Hutton said, not really knowing what to
say. He and Dorie had no trouble on that score. Maybe
the opposite: when they got mad, they both said to damn
much to each other.

"It's OK. I guess I loved him once in a crazy, jealous
way, but I'm recovering."

Displaying far more hairy skin than Hutton needed to
see, Smith came down the stairs in a Speedo bathing suit
with a grotesquely huge bulge in front that trumpeted his
endowment. He glanced at Hutton as if to say 'yeah,
asshole, and she loves it.'

"Hi baby," Coombs said. "Going for a swim?"

"No, I'm going to the fucking mall."

Coombs's face reddened.

Smith banged out the front door.

"He's a good man," Coombs said, though the wistful
look on her face told Hutton she didn't believe it.

She was a beautiful woman who had a pleasant per-
sonality and seemed smarter than most—why did she
have trouble picking good men? Maybe everyone wondered the same about his wife. "What does he do?"

"He's uh, involved in various business interests."

Hutton made a note to run the name of Derrick Smith
past the local police. He figured Smith for a two-bit

hood, a cheap muscle man used by some of the local money lenders to collect markers. A door banged. One of the dogs yelped. Edie jumped up and ran down the stairs.

"Look what that goddamn mutt did?" Smith hollered.

"Baby, please don't kick him," Coombs said.

"I'll break his scrawny neck."

"Baby, please go outside. I'll clean it up; I'll put them in the car, please."

SMACK! YIPE! YIPE! "Please baby, don't hurt him; he didn't mean it."

Hutton jumped up and ran downstairs. Smith pounded his large fist into Edie's face. Hutton lunged, driving his shoulder into Smiths abdomen and smashing a fist into his balls. Smith roared like a bull elephant and toppled to the floor, clutching at his groin.

"You cocksucker," he gasped, "You're a dead man."

"Not today bully boy."

Hutton helped Coombs, who had dropped to one knee and seemed dazed but otherwise OK, scoop up the two dogs prancing around in circles and barking at Smith. She managed to grab one. Hutton got the other. She looked at him through a mushy, badly swelling eye.

"Take the dogs and get in my car."

"It's OK, really. He won't hit me any more."

"Who do you think you're kidding—I saw the bruise on your leg. You stay here and he'll keep using you for a punching bag until he kills you."

"I have my car. I won't leave it."

"Think you can drive?"

She nodded. Smith grabbed her leg as she started for the stairs. She screamed. Hutton swung around and decked him on the chin. He hit the carpet, out cold. Next to him was a mound of fresh dog shit. Hutton rolled him over so that when he came to, he'd be face down in brown.

"Hurry," Hutton said. "He won't be out long."

Edie ran up the stairs and out the front door. Hutton, on her heels, gathered his case, notebook, and recorder from the coffee table and followed her outside. Edie opened the garage door jumped into a new red Buick with the two dogs. "Where are we going?"

"You've got to have that eye checked."

"I'm not going to a hospital."

"Let's argue the point later. Drive somewhere, any-where, but fast. I'll follow."

Hutton jumped into his car and backed into the street. Edie did the same, and sped away. After rounding the corner and crossing the intersection, she pulled to the curb. Hutton pulled in behind.

"I can't go to the hospital," she said when Hutton walked up. "In case you haven't noticed, I haven't got any clothes on, and I've got to take my babies home."

"Phone Gwen, tell her what happened, and have her come and get the dogs."

Edie shook her head, grabbed a tissue from the glove compartment, and blew her nose. "She's on her way to work."

"We'll figure something out. You've got to get that eye checked."

She glanced in the rearview mirror. "If he finds us he'll kill both of us."

"Is that what he does for a living?"

She took another hurried look in her rear view mirror.

"You drive to the hospital, I'll follow, and phone someone who can meet us and look after the dogs."

"I told you I don't have any clothes."

"It's a hospital for Christ's sake. The first thing they make you do is take your clothes off. Look at it this way: you're ahead of the game, now let's get the hell out of here."

As Hutton followed her to Maryland Parkway and across Vegas Valley to Sunrise Hospital Drive, he called the local police who said they'd have someone waiting at the emergency entrance. When they arrived, a patrol car sat alongside one of the ambulances. Hutton told Edie to stay put and approached the patrol car. Both uniformed officers got out. They were young and uncertain why they'd been ordered to meet a man and woman at the hospital. Hutton introduced himself and gave them a fast overview.

"The first thing we need to do," he said, "is get that young woman's eye some medical attention. If one of you can come with her and me and the other look after the dogs, we'll be off to a good start."

"You're kidding about the dogs?"

"I couldn't be more serious. The dog's names are Passepartout and Tocqueville. Come on, we haven't got all day." Hutton walked toward Coombs's car. The two dogs were jumping around in the back seat like they'd been shot full of a high-energy substance and attached to bungee cords.

Coombs stepped out and eyed the two approaching police officers. "They might know Derrick," she whispered to Hutton. "He's an ex-cop."

Hutton turned to the two cops and said, "Derrick Smith, an ex-cop did this." He pointed at the now closed eye that had become an ugly mass of black and blue and purple. "He's looking for us, but he'd better not find us. Is that clear?"

The larger of the two stepped forward. "We know Smith. He doesn't have many friends on the force, and we aren't two of them." The smaller one nodded.

"Fair enough," Hutton said. "Let's go."

The smaller one, Patrolman Cleary, accompanied them inside. Cleary grabbed a doctor who examined Coombs and rushed her off for x-rays. Before Coombs returned, Cleary sent a cruiser out to pick up Smith, but Smith had disappeared.

Hutton said, "The car in Smith's garage was a dark blue de Ville, Nevada plate DS ONE."

Cleary put out an APB and said to Hutton, "He won't get far. A lot of guys have a score to settle with that obnoxious prick."

"What about the woman? Smith won't stop."

"Until we put him away where he belongs, we'll keep someone on her."

"She works at Harrah's. Can Smith get to her there?"

"She's probably safer there than anywhere. Harrah's will make sure nothing happens on their turf, not a scratch."

Hutton nodded.

"Think she'll press charges?"

If she didn't, Hutton knew Smith couldn't be held. "I'll have her friend work on her." He looked up and saw Coombs with a tight grip on the young doctor's arm, wobbling down the hall toward them. The left side of her face was wrapped in a thick bandage. The doctor escorted her to a chair and helped her sit.

"We've given her a couple of shots," the doc said to Hutton and Cleary. "So she'll be groggy for a few hours, likely want to sleep. Here are two prescriptions, one for pain and one for swelling. She'll want the first when the shots wear off and the second when she looks in the mirror."

Hutton took the prescriptions and turned to Edie. Her head bobbed and her chin drooped to her chest. A trickle of drool escaped from the side of her mouth. He took her hand and asked, "Edie, what time does Gwen get off?"

"Mishnish."

"What is that? Midnight?"

Edie nodded.

"I'll take her home," Hutton said.

They put her in a wheel chair, took her out to her car, and strapped her in the passenger side. Cleary's partner, Hopkins, gladly ceded his dog watching chores, particularly since Tocqueville had diarrhea and the inside of the car smelled like a giant shit hole.

"You might have cleaned it up," Cleary said.

"You said watch the dogs, not clean up their shit."

Hutton got his case from the rental car and tossed the keys to Cleary. "Get rid of this for me."

Cleary nodded. "What's her address? We'll send someone out."

Hutton checked his notes and gave Cleary the address. "You'd better send a nurse to look after her until her girlfriend gets home."

Cleary said he would and signaled Hopkins, who got busy on the radio. Hutton slipped in under the steering wheel, being careful not to let the dogs out.

"And don't open the windows," Hopkins said. "The dogs might escape."

Hutton gave him the finger and drove off.

Edie lived a mile south of the hospital. When they arrived, as much as he needed fresh air, he drove the adjacent streets checking for Smith's car. After deciding it was safe, he pulled into the driveway. The dogs were going crazy and his stomach had started to revolt at the smell, but he wanted to wait until her protection arrived before going inside.

A moment later, a blue half-ton pulled up and parked across the street. A man got out and walked toward them. Hutton put his hand on his pistol. The man flashed a badge as he neared. Hutton stepped out, his hand remaining on his pistol.

"Cleary and Hopkins sent me out to keep an eye on your passenger."

Hutton examined his credentials: Sergeant Craig Lippert, Las Vegas Metropolitan Police Department.

"You alone?"

"A nurse is on the way."

Hutton relaxed. They managed to get Coombs and the dogs safely inside, Coombs on the sofa in the front room and the dogs running amok throughout the house.

Lippert returned to his truck. Edie murmured. Hutton asked if she was OK. She winced, but nodded.

A few minutes later, Hutton saw a yellow Beetle pull into the driveway. A large man with a brush cut dressed in white slacks and tunic got out. Lippert intercepted him and appeared to be asking a number of questions. The large man pulled out his wallet and showed Lippert what he apparently wanted to see because the two of them came into the house.

"This is Deane Unger from Home Care," Lippert said.

"I can stay until midnight," Unger said. "Someone will relieve me and stay until eight. If the patient needs anyone after that, all she has to do is call our central office."

"Whoever's out front will look after it," Lippert said.

Hutton gave Unger the prescriptions and called for a cab. He arrived back at the airport an hour before his scheduled departure at 4:34 p.m. After checking in, he contacted Cleary for an update: Smith hadn't been located. Next, he called Flanagan and got her voice mail. He decided to try her later and called his wife to let her know that he'd be late, but would have most of his stuff out by morning. She said she'd already called his brother to have it out before dinner. Bitch, he thought, and hung up. He called his brother and apologized for making him work on Sunday.

"I hope you're not still thinking of trying to make a go of it with that crazy woman," his brother said.

"Sometimes yes, sometimes no. Right now, no."

"Please dear sweet Jesus I hope you hold that thought."

Hutton ended the call and thought of what Flanagan had said about having a beer and pizza. Maybe she wasn't serious; maybe she'd only offered because she thought it the right thing to do. He laughed to himself. Dorie was jealous of Flanagan—if she only knew how disinterested Flanagan was. He tried her number again. She didn't answer. The ground hostess called his flight for boarding. "Hey Flanagan," he said to her voice mail, "I'm getting on the plane. Hope to see you in Minneapolis."

Chapter 23

Hutton was at the gate when Flanagan deplaned in Minneapolis.

"Good of you to let me know you were alive," she said.

"It's great to see you too."

"I must have checked for messages a hundred times."

"I called a hundred times, but didn't want to burden you with a collection of messages you'd feel obligated to answer."

"You might have left one."

"I did, just before I got on the plane."

"Well I didn't get it. Where's our gate?"

He pointed across the concourse. "They've started boarding."

She checked her watch. "Give me five minutes. I need to use the ladies' room." She handed him her case. "Look after this and don't go anywhere."

"Yes sir."

"Careful, I can still put you down."

Ten minutes later they were buckled into their seats. She told him about Sara Peterson.

"I guess that means we're going to Largeville."

"I hope Dorie doesn't mind if you move out tomorrow instead of tonight."

"Actually she would, but my brother's getting my stuff so she doesn't dump it on the street."

"She wouldn't do that."

"Yeah, she would. Did you get to the funeral?"

"Greg Adams and Dawson Richards were there. Dawson Richards spoke. It seems they truly loved Zoë; they were heartbroken. There was also a young woman there who I thought looked familiar, but she left the service early. I went after her, but she saw me coming and sped away in a limo."

The smart-looking, black flight attendant stopped at their row and asked if they'd like anything to drink. Flanagan returned her smile. The attendant reminded her of a grown up version of the little girl in Sara Peterson's building in Chicago. They ordered a beer.

"You seem upset," Hutton said.

"Just thinking about Sara Peterson and Zoë and a little girl I met in the horrible apartment where Sara lived."

"Was the little girl black?"

"How did you know?"

"I saw the way you looked at the flight attendant."

"Sometimes you amaze me."

"Sometimes I amaze myself."

They sipped their beer in silence for a few minutes. Flanagan wanted to get away from thinking about Zoë and Sara for awhile, and Hutton so far hadn't volunteered any information concerning Edie Coombs so she asked. "Did you ever find Edie Coombs?"

"Oh I found her all right." Hutton gave her chapter and verse on Las Vegas, Derrick Smith, and Edie Pitano, the woman formerly known as Edie Coombs.

"Did they find Smith?"

"Not as of Minneapolis, but they will. He drives around in a blue de Ville with personalized plates—how hard can it be?"

"You think Coombs is going to be OK?"

"Smith has her scared, but she strikes me as being tougher than the woman I saw today."

"Largeville didn't think of her as a shrinking violet. If she wasn't afraid of Johnny Burke, I cant' imagine her being afraid of Smith."

"Burke wouldn't have hurt her. Smith's a bully."

"You probably saved her life."

"I hope she knows that. She has to press charges, or Smith walks."

"I wish I'd have had a go at the sob. He wouldn't have filled out the Speedo quite as well."

Their flight landed on time at eleven thirty-seven. Ten minutes later they left the parking lot. Both looked to see if Striker's SUV was still there. It wasn't.

"Have you heard anything more from Father Carson?" Hutton asked.

"You're kidding."

He chuckled.

They both knew that if Carson had his way, a law would be passed making it illegal to commit a crime or work on a crime on Sunday.

Chapter 24

At 12:20 a.m., they pulled up in front of Joe Peterson's bungalow nestled in a large stand of trees behind the baseball diamond. A single bulb that acted as a yard and street light burned brightly from high atop a spindly wooden pole. Flanagan and Hutton silently walked up the dirt pathway leading to the only door. Flanagan checked around to the side that faced the thick trees.

"There's a light on in a back room," she said.

She searched for the doorbell. There wasn't one. Hutton rapped on the door. No one answered. He rapped again, louder. Another light came on.

"Who's there?" It was Joe Peterson's voice.

"Detective Flanagan, Joe, we need to talk."

Seconds ticked by. Flanagan pictured him standing there, perhaps afraid, wondering what was going on. "Uh, just a minute."

The door opened. Joe had on a plaid robe, white t-shirt and rubber flip-flops. He smiled when he saw them, but it was a cautious smile that seemed to know it wasn't going to be around for long.

His voice said, "Come in." His eyes said, 'What do you want?'

Flanagan and Hutton stepped into the kitchen. Coats and hats hung on wall mounted hooks to the right. Boots and shoes were lined underneath. Linoleum with worn spots covered the floor. A green fridge sat on one side of a large laundry sink and an antique looking cook stove on fancy chrome legs sat on the other side. A single light bulb hung from a wire that dropped from the middle of the ceiling that, like the walls, was a tired yellow. Centered under the light was a chrome table that had salt and pepper shakers, a sugar dispenser, and napkin holder arranged the same way Joe had his tables in the café arranged. Four matching chairs, one on each side, were pushed in under the table, all as if waiting for the next customer.

"Joe, is Claudine here?" Flanagan asked.

He looked toward the back of the house. "She's not feeling too well."

"Please go get her Joe. We need to talk to both of you."

"I think she's sleeping. I don't know if I can get her up?"

"Joe, I'm sorry to have to tell you this, but Sara has been murdered."

Joe's mouth moved as if he wanted to scream, but no sound came. His eyes screamed 'liar,' and began to fill with tears that left dark wet lines as they trickled down his red cheeks.

Flanagan put a hand on his shoulder.

"Please dear God," he whispered. "Don't let this be true." He pulled out a chair and sat, cradling his head on the table. Sobs shook his body that seemed suddenly smaller and more delicate.

Flanagan knelt beside him. "Joe," she said, keeping her voice low, "Claudine has to be told. Do you want us to do that?"

When he lifted his head, a look of hatred replaced his tears and his mouth firmed. Jumping up, he banged his fist on the table. The salt and pepper shakers bounced and tipped on their sides. "I'll get her," he said, and stomped away.

Flanagan and Hutton glanced at each other. They heard a woman's slurry voice say, "Go away...leave me alone..."

Smack. "Claudine, goddamn it, wake up." Smack.

Hutton took a step. Flanagan grabbed his arm. "He's not hurting her."

"Stop hitting me you bastard..."

Smack. "Not until you wake up, damn it." Smack. Smack.

"Aaahhhhrrrrrgggghhhhh, you asshole, fuck off and leave me alone, stop pulling my arm."

"You're coming with me even if I have to drag you every inch of the way."

"You pig. You're hurting my arm."

"I'm not hurting your arm."

Flanagan and Hutton heard a scraping sound, and then Joe appeared with Claudine hanging from his shoulder. Her feet were half-walking, half-dragging. Her fiery orange hair looked like a ball of matted yarn and her nightgown showed more of her blotchy red body than either Flanagan or Hutton wanted to see.

"You asshole. What, you want a piece of this? You think this makes you a man, slapping your wife around." She looked up, her head weaving, her eyes trying to focus on Flanagan and Hutton. "Who the fuck are you?"

Joe stopped.

Claudine found her feet and stood, head continuing to bob cobra like. She was tall and slim, skinny actually, but considering what they'd been told she'd been doing to herself for a lot of years, she wasn't nearly as bad as Flanagan had expected. Claudine gripped the edge of the table and looked back at Joe. "Who the fuck are they? They looking for a two-fer?"

"I'm Detective Flanagan. This is my partner, Detective Hutton."

Claudine snorted. "Getting drunk and screwing against some law?"

"Mrs. Peterson, we're sorry to have to tell you this, but your daughter Sara has been murdered."

Claudine's head kept weaving, but not as much. Her eyes squinted and she peered hard at Flanagan and then at Hutton, and then back at Flanagan again, as if on one level she wasn't sure she'd heard correctly, but on some other level, the message had started to register in some dark hallway of her alcohol soaked brain. She looked at Joe. Joe took her arm. She yanked away and reeled toward the table, grabbing it with both hands to keep from falling.

She hung her head between her arms for a moment, and then looked up at Flanagan and Hutton. "Get out of my house," she screamed. "Get the fuck out of my house."

"Ma'am, are you going to be OK?" Flanagan asked.

Faster than any of them would have thought possible, Claudine charged, her small fists smashing in the air and then on Flanagan's chest, tears streaming down her cheeks. Hutton and Joe started to grab her, but Flanagan told them to stay back. Soon, Claudine's energy had been sapped and she collapsed, sobbing, into Flanagan's arms. Flanagan held her for a moment, and then took her to a chair. Joe touched Claudine's shoulder.

She turned and glared, hatred dripping from her eyes. "Don't you dare touch me, you bastard. Don't you dare touch me ever again. This is all your fault. You drove her away with your touching and pawing. You and your friends couldn't leave her alone. I should have stopped you; I should have killed you, you...you...dirty, filthy bastards."

Joe glanced helplessly at Flanagan and Hutton. "She's drunk; she doesn't know what she's saying."

Claudine lunged to her feet and pushed Joe hard, sending him crashing to the floor. "You think I don't know what I'm saying, well you'd better listen and listen good you son-of-a-bitch. I want you out of this house right now. Go sleep in your goddamn little restaurant. Go sleep in the streets. Go sleep with your squaw for all I give a fuck, but you're not sleeping here and if you ever come back here again, I'll blow your fucking head off." She stood over him, her fists clenched, and then she spit in his face.

Joe got to his knees and looked up at Flanagan and Hutton. "Please, you can't believe what she's saying."

Hutton said to Joe, "You'd be wise to remain there for a moment."

Flanagan said to Claudine. "Ma'am, you're making some serious accusations."

"Ask him," she shouted. "Ask him what he used Sara for. Ask him what he made her do for his friends." She turned and spit in Joe's face again.

Joe tried to get up. Hutton held him down.

"Ma'am, I want you to listen carefully to what I have to say."

Claudine nodded. Her venom seemed depleted; she seemed depleted, but she seemed steadier.

"We'll be back in the morning. Between now and then, don't drink any more alcohol. You understand?"

Claudine nodded.

"Because we'll be looking to have a serious discussion and you have to be sober. Meanwhile, we'll be taking Joe with us until this gets sorted out."

Hutton half-lifted, half-pulled Joe to an upright position. His head hung down; he couldn't or wouldn't look them in the eye.

"Ma'am, do you have anyone who can stay with you tonight?"

Claudine had started crying again. She shook her head.

"What about Lizzie Burke? Do you know Lizzie Burke?"

Claudine's face went blank for a moment as if she had suddenly realized she had no friends. "I'll be all right," she said.

*   *   *

Call Joan Foster and Betty Hale.
Do they know her?
No, but they will stay with her.
Did you know what was going on with Sara? Is that why you sent her money? Is that why you spent so much

time at the restaurant—trying to find out if Joe was using her?

*   *   *

Flanagan signaled to Hutton that she needed a private word. They stepped away and Flanagan whispered that she was going to get Joan Foster and Betty Hale to stay the night. Foster and Hale were glad to help and Flanagan left them in charge. They took Joe back to Minot and booked him into a holding cell.

It was 1:30 a.m. when Hutton dropped her off in front of her house. "I'd like to get an early start," she said to Hutton. "I don't want Claudine hanging out there too long." She glanced at her watch. "What's your new address?"

"I'll come downtown. Save you a trip across the city."

"Make it 7:30. I'll be waiting in front."

"Yes sir," Hutton said, throwing her a salute. "Good night sir."

"Smart ass," she said, and started up the drive.

"Oh, and Flanagan?"

She turned her head, wondering what other barbs he might toss her way.

"Good work yesterday and today."

Her face felt flushed. She was glad for the night. "You too."

Chapter 25

At seven, Flanagan parked her Land Rover on Central, a block from the police station. As she started up the street, she heard the unmistakable Boston accent of Harry Carson booming from behind.

"Hey Flanagan, wait up," he said.

She turned and waited, watching his gangly frame that seemed ganglier because of the cowboy boots and thin-legged blue jeans he'd taken to wearing not long after arriving in North Dakota.

He pulled alongside, gasping for breath. "How'd you and Hutton make out yesterday?"

"Not a glitch, thanks to you."

"Too bad; I had hoped to strand Hutton in Vegas." He removed his hat, wiped his brow, and put his hat back on his head with a series of moves that bordered on ceremonial.

"He might want to talk to you about Llewellyn Grayfields."

"What's his interest?"

"He knows him from school. He says not, but I think hearing old Llewellyn whacking his family shook him up a bit."

"As soon as I get an update from Stan, I'll give him a call."

"At the same time you can ask him about Vegas."

"Any hints?"

"He had an interesting day, but I'll let him give you the details. Did you get my message about Striker's SUV?"

"I should have something this morning."

"Hutton and I are going back to Largeville. You can reach me on my cell."

They parted company once inside the building, Carson to the lab and Flanagan to the office she and Hutton shared. She checked her e-mails and printed the detailed reports on Zoë that Carson had sent. The rest were either jokes that she read and deleted, or spam mostly having to do with penis size or ability that she deleted without reading, or business that could wait.

She put Zoë's papers in her case, checked her voice mail, and headed down to the garage to get the SUV. Ten minutes later, she parked in front and waited for Hutton. She glanced at the dashboard clock. It was seven-thirty. She called Hutton on his cell and got his voice mail. "Where are you?" she asked and ended the call. She got out, walked around the SUV, and stood on the sidewalk, her rear end leaning against the front fender. Half expecting to see his grinning face peering down, she glanced up at the windows to their second floor office.

Rick Danby, looking more like a banker in his gray pinstripes than a detective, came out of the front door and ran down the steps. "Hey Flanagan, where's your dummy?"

"I gather he isn't upstairs."

"Negativo. I was the only one there."

Flanagan looked at her watch. Hutton was known for a lot of things, being late wasn't one of them. She opened the passenger door, dug her Blackberry from her case, and checked Hutton's numbers. She dialed his home number. Dorie answered on the second ring.

"Dorie, it's Kate Flanagan. I'm looking for Bob."

"Kate, you sound tensed out."

And you sound awfully chipper for someone who has just put her husband out on the street. "Monday morning." She tried to chuckle.

"I'm sure Bobby told you, but he and I have decided to go our separate ways."

"Yes, he mentioned something like that, and I'm sorry."

"Don't be sorry. It's for the best. Anyway, I haven't seen him since Friday. He was supposed to stop by yesterday to move his few things out, but he had to go out of town—like what else is new—so Joe, his brother, got stuck with the job."

"Do you have Joe's number?"

Dorie asked her to hold. When she came back on the line, she had Joe's number and the number of the motel where Bobby said he'd be staying. Flanagan recorded both in her handheld and called Joe, who said that Bobby hadn't shown up, that he figured he'd got hung up in Vegas. Flanagan got an uneasy feeling in her stomach. She called the motel. Hutton hadn't registered.

She ran inside to find Casey Long and found her coming down the stairs from the cafeteria carrying a tray with one coffee and Danish enough for four.

"Hey Flanagan, how they hanging?" She flashed her thousand-watt smile.

"I can't find Bob."

"Shit! Give me details." She increased her pace, striding down the hallway toward the operations center as fast as her stubby legs would move.

Flanagan said she'd last seen him at 1:30 a.m., he was driving his red Jeep Cherokee, ND license number ZXV 472; that Dorie hadn't seen him since Friday; that he was supposed to see his brother, but hadn't shown up; that he said he'd be staying at a motel out by the airport, but hadn't checked in.

Casey raised an eyebrow.

"If you don't have to say anything about the motel and staying at his brothers…"

Casey nodded. "Does anyone else think he's missing?"

Flanagan shook her head.

Casey got on the radio and told the police, cabbies, and ambulance drivers to be on the lookout for Hutton and his Jeep. All the police wanted to know why.

"Listen boys," Casey said, "I love you all, but you're not smart enough to be trusted with that kind of information. But here's what I can tell you: I'm making two dozen cinnamon buns tonight—whoever finds Bob gets one cool dozen."

Flanagan left Casey and ran upstairs to the lab where she told Carson about Hutton and asked if he had anyone who could go with her to Largeville. He said he didn't, not until ten. She couldn't wait.

She arrived in Largeville at eight-fifteen and drove down the eerily empty main street. As she drew parallel with Pete's Café, she saw a piece of paper pasted on the front door. She stopped and ran across to investigate. It was a hand-written sign that said: TEMPORARILY CLOSED. PLEASE COME TO THE HOUSE. It was signed: CLAUDINE.

She drove to Joe and Claudine's. Several cars were parked on the grassy area around the front of the house. Three familiar looking young boys swung through the trees and beat on their chests like young Tarzans. Flanagan took her recorder and cellphone from her case and walked up to the open front door. A dozen people milled about inside, smoking and drinking coffee. Claudine, wearing a red gingham apron over a green short-sleeved dress and waving a pancake turner in the air like she knew what to do with it, stood at the old-fashioned stove. A couple of women stood beside her. One was Lizzie Burke, still in sweats and sneakers, but with a red silk scarf tied around her neck.

"Johnny," Claudine turned and hollered in a hog-caller's voice, "How'd you say you liked your eggs, broken?" and then she laughed a raucous laugh. Several others politely but nervously joined in. Like a turtle trying to disappear inside its shell, Johnny Burke seemed to be trying to disappear inside his big overalls and green plaid shirt.

Flanagan looked around for Joan Foster and Betty Hale, but didn't see either.

Lizzie Burke walked over. "Apparently she's been going like this since around five, and I don't think she's slept a wink."

"Has she been drinking?"

"I don't think so, but she's going to drop soon."

"Did she tell you what happened?"

"She called me not long after you and your partner left. Poor Sara—I can't believe someone murdered her. Of course I came right over."

"Does everyone know?"

"Everyone here does. Maybe she's phoned others."

"Have you seen Joan or Betty?"

"I sent them home at seven. They had to get ready for school."

"Oh there she is everybody." Claudine yelled, pointing the pancake turner at Flanagan.

Everyone turned to look. Flanagan shifted from one foot to the other, not wanting to be the center of attention.

"How about some breakfast, detective? As long as you're not too fussy, we've got eggs and pancakes and coffee." Claudine let out another shrieking cackle.

"Did she say anything about Joe?"

Lizzie looked at Flanagan as though she didn't understand the question.

"It's important that I know what Claudine told everyone."

"She said that Joe had to go away. We assumed he went to Chicago to get Sara."

"Can you take over the cooking chores? I've got to talk to Claudine privately."

"Do you want me to kick everyone out?" Lizzie flexed her muscles as if ready to spring into action.

"Let's let Claudine decide after she and I have our talk."

"You may want to use the bedroom in the back. If she decides to get ornery, and believe me she can, you might need help, and the others here won't be as upset if they see me tugging on her."

Flanagan recalled how Claudine reacted when she and Hutton told her about Sara. "Be warned. She might kick up a good fuss."

"I was a trench nurse in the army and you've seem my kids. A little screaming and hollering is nothing."

"So what'll it be detective?" Claudine asked as Flanagan moved to her side.

"We need to talk, alone and now. Come with me to the back." Flanagan gripped her elbow.

"Lottie," Claudine said, "you take over the cooking chores for a few minutes?"

Flanagan glanced to her right. She hadn't noticed Lottie Striker standing next to the stove.

"Yes, of course," Lottie said. She nodded at Flanagan and then looked down. Something in Flanagan's brain tried to stir, but for the moment she had to concentrate on Claudine.

Flanagan felt Claudine stiffen and her eyes started to dart around. Lizzie grabbed her other arm and said, "It's OK honey, I'm here. Let's go with Detective Flanagan. She needs to talk to you alone."

Claudine released the pancake turner and wiped her hands down the front of her apron. She turned to Lizzie. "Will you stay with me?"

Flanagan nodded at Lizzie.

"Of course sweetheart, we won't leave you alone."

Flanagan felt Claudine relax. She and Lizzie moved to the back bedroom in unison, Claudine limp between them. They sat Claudine on the edge of the unmade double bed, its tattered blue chenille spread in a lump on the floor. Lizzie kicked the door closed and sat next to Claudine. Flanagan pulled up a stool from the mirrored dresser and faced the two of them. Claudine began to sob. Lizzie draped a big arm across Claudine's bony shoulders.

"Claudine, Lizzie doesn't know about Joe. Do you want me to tell him?"

Claudine nodded, wiping at her nose and eyes with the sleeve of her white blouse.

"Here honey, use this," Lizzie said, and handed her a tissue. "Don't get that pretty blouse all messed up."

"Lizzie, anything you hear is confidential; you can't tell anyone, not even Johnny."

"I don't care if she tells," Claudine said. "I don't care if she tells the whole world. It's his fault, all of it. He killed Sara."

Lizzie's mouth dropped open. She stared at Flanagan and then turned to Claudine. "Claudine honey, you don't know what you're saying. Joe didn't kill Sara." She turned back to Flanagan and repeated, "Joe didn't kill Sara."

Claudine's body started to shake.

Lizzie pulled her tight to her ample bosom. "You'll be all right honey. Joe will be home soon. He can look after you."

"No he won't," Claudine cried. "If he comes any-where near me I'll kill him."

Lizzie's eyes pleaded with Flanagan.

Flanagan kept quiet. She wanted Lizzie to hear every-thing from Claudine.

"You don't know what you're saying baby. You're upset."

Claudine pushed away from Lizzie's embrace and rubbed at her eyes with her apron hem, the tissue that Lizzie had given her long since reduced to a shredded wad in her bony fist. Then, with clarity of voice she said, "Yes, I'm upset. I'm upset because someone mur-dered Sara in Chicago. But I'm more upset about why Sara went to Chicago?"

"What do you mean?" The look on Lizzie's face said she wasn't sure she wanted to know.

"Joe was…" Claudine wiped at her eyes and took a deep breath. "Joe was having his way with her."

"What are you saying?" Lizzie pleaded.

"From the time she was thirteen." Claudine started to sob again. "When she told me, I slapped her and called her a liar." Sob. "So maybe I killed her too." Sob. "Maybe I drove her away as much as Joe."

"Oh no baby," Lizzie said.

"And there were others. Joe let the others have her too."

"Oh Jesus." Lizzie sprang up, fists clenched. "Don't tell me it was my Johnny? I'll kill the bastard."

Flanagan touched Lizzie's arm and shook her head.

"Joe used Sara to pay off his poker debts. Funny isn't it. They were fucking me for free and fucking my daughter for a hundred bucks."

"Oh my God." Lizzie's mouth tried to say other words, but none came.

"Who were the others, Claudine?" Flanagan asked.

"No one from here. They'd come into the beer parlor after they'd fucked Sara. They didn't know I was her mother. They'd laugh at me and tell me if I was one tenth as good as that little minx Sara, they'd pay me a dollar to suck their dicks."

"Oh Jesus," Lizzie said. "Oh Jesus, baby, I'm so sorry."

She reached for Claudine, but Claudine was too quick. She sprang from the bed, ran to her dresser, and grabbed a large figurine. Before Lizzie or Flanagan could stop her, she smashed it into the dresser mirror, spraying shards of glass in a hundred different directions. Some hit her face and blood spouted from ten different wounds. She reached for a large jagged piece of mirror and tried to jamb it into her throat, but Flanagan grabbed her arm, yanked her back, and threw her on the bed. Lizzie jumped on Claudine and pinned her flailing hands.

The bedroom door burst open and Johnny Burke barged in, followed by Lottie and two other men Flanagan didn't recognize.

"Bring some towels and hot water," Flanagan said to Lottie Striker.

"Johnny, get my bag from the trunk," Lizzie said. "Neil, you get over here and help me hold Claudine so she doesn't hurt herself more."

Flanagan yanked her phone from her pocket and called Harry Carson. After she got an ambulance on its way, she asked about Hutton.

"Don't worry," he said. "He'll turn up."

"When he does, tell him to get his ass up here. I need help."

Lottie came back with the hot water, towels, and face cloths and began digging glass from Claudine's face and daubing at her cuts.

"Hold still baby," Lizzie kept saying.

Johnny rushed in with a black bag and shouted, "Is this the one?"

"Yes sweetheart, that's the one. Now open it and come stand here beside me so I can get a few things."

Johnny Burke did as he was told.

Lizzie said, "I need you to take my place on top of Claudine so I have both hands free."

Johnny hesitated. Claudine started to heave her body.

"I'll do it," Flanagan said. Lizzie slipped off and Flanagan slipped on. Claudine seemed to relax somewhat.

Lizzie took some bottles and tape from her bag and started dressing Claudine's lacerations. After she'd finished, she and Lottie cleaned up the glass scattered around the bedroom. Claudine sobbed quietly while Flanagan and Neil James continued to hold her down.

A few moments later, the ambulance arrived. Flanagan told Claudine that she'd get a shot to calm her down and then the ambulance would take her to the hospital in Minot where her injuries could be properly treated.

Claudine nodded, her red-rimmed, bloodshot eyes round with uncertainty and fear.

Lizzie said, "Don't you worry, baby, we'll be down to see you later today and we'll look after everything here."

"What about the café?" Claudine asked.

"I can open it," Lottie said. "I mean, if you want me to?"

Flanagan turned and looked at Lottie standing off to one side, her head erect, her shoulders back, her chest forward. She still had difficulty imagining her with the likes of Newton Striker, but something besides Newton Striker stirred in her brain: a young woman sitting in a synagogue in Chicago, a young woman who ran down the steps and disappeared in a limo.

She stepped toward Lottie. The ambulance attendant grabbed Flanagan's arm. "Where to?"

She pulled him aside so Claudine and the others couldn't hear. "Check with Harry Carson. She needs to be put under suicide watch. I'll call and set it up."

The attendants put Claudine in the ambulance. One stayed in the back. Flanagan called Harry Carson and told him what was on the way. He said he'd make the arrangements and then he said, "They found Hutton's Jeep..."

Flanagan felt a cold, ugly hand tighten around her throat.

"...next to the self-storage place out on Burdick. He wasn't in it, but I've got to tell you that there was blood on the front seat—not a lot...some, is how it was described to me—and two bullet holes, both fired inside, one in the door and one in the roof."

"Oh Christ Harry, how long ago?"

"Casey just called. I'm on my way out there now."

"I don't know what to do, Harry. Tell me what to do."

"You won't contribute anything here. I'll send someone to give you a hand, to help you keep your mind on the investigation."

"Right now, Hutton is the only one who can accomplish that."

"Yeah, ditto that here, but when we find him, let's for God's sake not tell him."

"He ran into some trouble yesterday in Vegas." She told him about Edie Pitano and Derrick Smith. "It might not be a coincidence. Have someone check with the Vegas police to see if they've found Smith."

Hutton said, "I'll call them on my way."

"I'll call Edie Coombs. Do you still have her number—the one you looked up for Hutton?"

"Hold on a sec…yeah, here it is."

Flanagan recorded the number. "Call me as soon as you've had a look at Hutton's Jeep."

Chapter 26

Flanagan left Joe and Claudine's place and drove to the town hall. She dug in the console for the keys, where Hutton said he'd put them. Among the maps and citation books, her fingers felt something hard: Striker's American flag key chain with three keys attached.

As she started across the street, she saw Lottie going into the café. She taped a note on the door saying where she'd gone, went back to the SUV, and drove to the café. It was only a block, but if Hutton arrived, she wanted him to see the SUV and know where she was.

Through the window, she saw Lottie moving about. She changed Claudine's note to read: WILL OPEN AT 10 A.M. Lottie came to the door to investigate.

"You and I need to talk," Flanagan said when Lottie opened the door. "Soon the whole town will show up and leave you without a moment to yourself."

If Lottie felt nervous about being in Chicago, she hid it behind her generous smile. After Flanagan entered, Lottie bolted the door. The aroma of fresh coffee already filled the air, but not so much that she didn't smell Lottie's perfume, the same as that at the synagogue's entrance when she ran after the young woman in black. It had to be her. She was positive.

"I'm sorry, but coffee won't be ready for another fifteen minutes."

"Judging from the aroma, it'll be worth the wait."

*   *   *

The scent of orchids wafted through the air, erasing for a brief moment, all else.

Ask to sit in the back booth.

*   *   *

Flanagan clutched her elbows and tried to shake of the chill that at that moment decided to permeate her body.

Lottie looked at her and smiled. No 'Are you OK?' or 'May I get you something?', only a warm smile.

"Do you mind if we sit in the back." Flanagan didn't wait for an answer, but proceeded to the far booth. Lottie followed. They sat facing each other.

"You were at Zoë's funeral."

Lottie's face flushed. "I'm sorry I ran, but I couldn't handle talking to anyone. Zoë was a dear friend, the only one I've ever really had."

"Do you have any idea who might have killed her?"

Lottie's hands rested on the table, her long, elegant fingers stretched out, her perfectly manicured nails painted the purple of violas, the same color as her lipstick. She raised her hands from their heels, spread her fingers, and studied them for a long moment. "I don't know," she finally said, looking back at Flanagan. "Ever since Newton told me the horrible news I've been praying to the spirits of my ancestors, seeking answers, praying that she will dwell in the land of peace and plenty where there is neither disease nor death."

"I like how that sounds."

"I'm a descendant of the ancient Athapascans. My father is a chief. I am a princess. I have been raised to honor the customs of our people."

"I'm certain Zoë would appreciate your prayers."

"We talked religion often, perhaps because in Largeville, we were both minorities of one."

"So you knew she was Jewish."

Lottie nodded, her big eyes heavy.

"You knew her better than most people in Largeville."

"We spent a lot of time together, mostly right here in this booth. That's why I hesitated when you suggested we sit here. I sometimes feel her spirit close by, as I do now, and I fear I shall interfere with her journey."

"Do you believe her spirit remains here…among us?"

"I feel her torment, as though she hasn't completed a sacred life mission. We all have sacred life missions that must be completed before we can make our final journey to the land beyond."

Flanagan wondered if she should share the conversations she had with Zoë's spirit and if she did, how much she should say. She studied Lottie, who seemed in a quiet place, a holy place, her face aglow with the confidence of faith and immortality. Then she reminded herself that however strongly she felt connected, Lottie was still a suspect. Her heart beat faster as though it knew danger, danger that had been sidestepped.

Lottie touched Flanagan's hands with the tips of her fingers. "I expect you must feel Zoë's spirit also. When I saw you at Zoë's funeral, I felt that Zoë had brought you there."

Flanagan's hands grew warm. The tips of Lottie's fingers started to glow. Flanagan pulled away, blinked her eyes several times, rapidly, and reached for her notebook.

"I wouldn't know about that," she said, clearing the hoarseness that had crept into her throat. "If she hasn't been able to complete her journey as you call it, perhaps finding her killer will help."

"Yes," Lottie said. "I'm certain that must be it. Please, how may I help?"

"I'd like to ask you a few questions."

"Of course, anything." She looked confident that nothing Flanagan could ask would be beyond her ability or desire to answer.

Flanagan opened her notebook. "For the record, where were you between Friday midnight and six Saturday morning?"

"At home, alone, so I'm afraid I'll have to remain on your suspect list."

"Do you believe you're a suspect?"

Lottie interlaced the ends of her fingers and then separated them two at a time. "I believe everyone is a suspect until you find the real killer. Sometimes, the real killer isn't found and all suspects become the killer until a suspect is selected who becomes the killer." Her eyes grew heavy.

"Has that ever happened to you?"

"It happens to my people. They are falsely accused; they die for the crimes of others."

"Did you murder Zoë?"

Lottie looked into Flanagan's eyes, as if trying to peer into her soul, and shook her head.

"Do you think I believe you?"

"I know you want to believe me."

"Yes, I do want to believe you, so let's think about the other people of Largeville, men and women, who might have wanted Zoë dead."

Lottie shook her head. "There is no one."

"Did you go to the Friday night dances?"

"Not often." Like a little white cloud shunting across a big sky, a wistful look shunted across her face. "I didn't like the drinking and fighting."

"Did Tommy ever attend?"

She nodded.

"You seemed about to say something."

"We don't talk much." She pushed up the sleeves of her yellow blouse and then quickly lowered them.

"Why is that?"

"He believes if I weren't there, his mother might return."

"Where's his mother?"

"You probably know more than I."

Flanagan felt her face grow hot. "Please understand that we need to ask the same questions over and over and then compare answers."

"What I meant was that Mr. Striker has never told me."

"How long have you and Mr. Striker been married?"

Lottie shrugged. "Two years, maybe a little more."

"You seem neither certain nor thrilled."

Lottie's face grew dark and she locked her eyes on Flanagan's. "My father and I made a deal with Mr. Striker: me for oil royalty payments."

"My God, don't you know this is the twenty-first century."

"Not so much so in West Texas and not on our reservation. Our people were starving. They needed the money. My father knew Mr. Striker and Mr. Striker knew the oil companies and the governor. And I knew Mr. Striker wanted me."

"How did he know about you?"

"He checked oil and gas wells on our reservation and always stopped to give my father a box of cigars. I first met him when I was twelve, but I had already developed a young woman's body and could tell he wanted me."

"I hope he didn't get you because that's illegal, even in Texas."

"On a reservation, young women are forced to mature sexually at an early age."

"So your father decided to negotiate a trade. You were probably entitled to the royalties anyway, otherwise I doubt Striker would have been able to negotiate a single nickel. Someone was robbing you blind."

"I know that now, but at the time I had to do something to save our people, so I asked Mr. Striker if he wanted me to visit his motel."

"And he agreed."

"He laughed and told me to grow up."

"How long did he wait."

"Two years."

"Oh God."

"I knew what I was doing."

"Yes, but fourteen?"

"My spirit remained on the reservation—I wouldn't give him that."

"Is that when he brought you to Largeville?"

"I was eighteen when Mr. Striker brought me here. We got married two years later."

"How old are you?"

"I'll be twenty-one in November. We've been married for two years."

"Did you ever ask what had happened to his first wife?"

"My deal had already been made. It didn't matter to me if he had several wives."

"What about Tommy. Didn't he ever ask about his mother?"

"Not that I ever heard. He's very private. He has the whole basement to himself and it's filled with computers."

"What was Tommy's relationship with Zoë?"

"I sensed that he adored her."

"A schoolboy crush?"

"I'm not familiar with that term."

"When a student falls in love with a teacher, we call it a schoolboy crush. It happens in every school every year."

Lottie sat silently for a moment, as if pondering what Flanagan had said, perhaps trying to think of something analogous from her background, perhaps seeking some verisimilitude, and then said, "In Tommy's case, I think it was more than a schoolboy crush. Once, I heard him screaming like a wounded bear. Then I heard glass smashing. I wasn't allowed in the basement, but I was afraid he'd hurt himself so I ran down to see what had happened. I found him sitting in the middle of the floor surrounded by his demolished computers, no longer screaming, but crying like a baby."

Flanagan made several notes, and then looked up at Lottie. "I'll get back to Tommy in a moment, but did you say you weren't allowed in the basement?"

"There are rooms where I may go and rooms where I may not go."

"You're serious?"

"Yes of course. Why would you think otherwise?"

"Because it's normal, when a man and woman get married, that both have equal access to all parts of their home, that's why."

"You seem angered."

"I'm mad is what I am."

"I'm sorry if I have said something to cause this feeling in you."

"They aren't allowed to treat you like they own you."

"I have a large bedroom, I am allowed to watch TV in the family room, and I use the kitchen to cook for Mr. Striker and Tommy. That's more than enough rooms for me."

"That's not the point. It's your house too. You are entitled to go into every room, but we can talk more about that later. Let's get back to Tommy. What was his problem?"

"First, let me get coffee." Lottie started to get up.

"If I drink it, I fetch it, and while I'm up, I'll get your one."

"That's what Zoë used to do—she was the only one who ever brought me coffee. Well, maybe Joe once or twice."

Flanagan returned with two mugs. She took hers black. Lottie also. Like Hutton. Flanagan glanced at her watch. Where was he? Where was her backup? "You said you found Tommy crying?"

"He used hateful language."

"I've heard it all, if that's what concerns you."

"I hate repeating what he said."

Flanagan wanted to know but sensed pushing Lottie wasn't going to produce anything other than stony silence.

Lottie fingered her mug, slowly turning it one-hundred and eighty degrees so that the handle faced left rather than her right, so that the happy face stared at Flanagan rather than at Lottie. "He screamed, called me a fucking squaw, and told me to get out."

Flanagan remained silent.

"Then he said Zoë was a fucking bitch just like I was a fucking bitch."

"I hope you left him suffering in his misery."

"I had never seen him that upset. I told him that anger cleansed the soul, that he shouldn't feel badly about crying, that good men were capable of crying."

"How did he respond?"

"He spit in my face and told me if I didn't get out of the basement, he'd tell his father that I tried to fuck him."

Flanagan began to wonder how she'd misread Tommy by such a wide mark. Her record on reading people had been one of her undisputed strong points. "How long ago did all this take place?"

"Two weeks ago, last Saturday. Mr. Striker had gone out of town on business. We had stayed late at the dance the night before and I'd helped Joe with his Saturday lunch crowd. I felt tired and went home for a rest."

"How did he explain the smashed computers to his father?"

"Tommy told him I'd knocked them over trying to clean."

"And he believed him?"

"Mr. Striker asked me if that's what had happened. I told him if that's what Tommy had told him, then that's what had happened. I never heard any more about it."

They sipped their coffee and studied each other for a moment. Flanagan set her cup back on the table and asked, "How did you get the bruises on your arms?"

Lottie shrugged.

"You don't have to stay married to him."

"My father and I made a deal. I am honor bound to keep my end of the arrangement."

"You were lied to. He treats you like a slave. You're not honor bound to do anything except leave and press charges."

"He would find me and bring me back."

"The law will protect you. He can't do that."

"I'm an Indian. We have different laws."

"I'm not talking about Indian laws; I'm talking about the laws of the United States."

"So am I."

Lottie had responded so calmly and matter-of-factly that Flanagan didn't quite know what to say. She figured that as an Indian, Lottie had ample reason to feel bitter about the white man's laws, the laws of the people who'd stolen Indian land, but she didn't appear to be. "I'm sorry that my people have made your people feel that way, but at least I can help you win this one."

"Yes, I believe you probably can," Lottie said. "I need some time to think, and I need to communicate with my father."

Flanagan gave her a card. "Here are my numbers. Call or e-mail or stick a postcard in snail mail. I promise I wont let you down."

Someone pounded on the door. Both Flanagan and Lottie checked their watches.

"People will be anxious to get in," Lottie said. "Joe hardly ever closed, and they need a place to talk about all that has happened."

"Or it might be my partner," Flanagan said. "Let me check." She strode to the front door. There she saw a shifty-eyed man in a John Deere cap, checked shirt, and jeans trying to look inside. Flanagan opened the door and said, "We'll be open in a half-hour."

"I was a lookin' for Joe. He around?"

Flanagan studied him closely when he spoke. Like Lottie, he too was an Indian. Unlike Lottie, Flanagan felt uneasy in his presence. She smelled evil and felt her muscles begin to tense. "No, Joe and Claudine are away. Lottie's trying to get organized, and just as soon as she does, she'll open."

"Where'd Joe go? D'ya know?"

"No, and we're not sure when he'll be back."

"What about the other woman. She know where's he stayin'?"

"Sir, are you from Largeville?" Flanagan got a feeling in her gut that this might be one of the scumbags that had sex with Sara.

"No ma'am, I ain't."

She glanced up the street toward the town hall hoping to see her backup arriving. "Tell you what," she said, "if you can wait for a few minutes, I'll be able to give you that information. Is that your vehicle?" She pointed at a red Dodge Ram that hadn't been there when she came in.

"Yes ma'am."

"Give me your name."

"Art Logan."

"Art, wait for me. I'll come and get you in a few minutes." She closed and locked the door, grabbed a paper napkin, and noted Art's license plate and name.

Back at the booth she asked Lottie if she knew Art Logan. Lottie said she didn't.

"Did you ever hear rumors about Sara having sex with men from Largeville or from out of town?"

Lottie wasn't one who revealed her emotions, but her hesitation in responding told Flanagan that the question hit a nerve. "No one would talk to me about things like that."

"But did you overhear anyone or anything?"

"Here, in the restaurant, people accepted me because of Joe. But I'm still an Indian and they treated me differently. When ever I came near, conversation stopped. I felt them looking at my back, wondering if I might be part wild animal, wondering if I might let out a war cry or start dancing wildly, wondering how many white men my ancestors had scalped."

"They're probably wondering how any woman, Indian or white or otherwise, could be so beautiful."

She smiled. "You speak kindness, like Zoë."

"What can you tell me about Sara?"

Lottie looked away, the muscles on her cheeks flexing as she subconsciously clenched her teeth.

"You aren't betraying her or Joe by telling me what you can."

Lottie looked back at Flanagan. "Sara is…was tough. She knew what she wanted and what she wanted was to get out of Largeville. Joe wanted her to stay and finish school. They fought over that and most everything else, but Joe always laughed about it later, after Sara had stormed off somewhere, saying it was normal for fathers and daughters to fight like that. Once he wanted to know if I had fought with my father."

"Did you?"

She shook her head. "As a princess, disrespect of one's elders was not allowed."

Flanagan flipped to a new page in her notebook. "We've been told that Joe held poker games here in the restaurant after closing time."

She laughed. "Mostly something they call cribbage for ten cents a point."

"What about Friday and Saturday nights?"

Lottie's face darkened. "That's when men from out of town came. Sometimes they were still here when I showed up in the morning. There were always lots of empty whiskey bottles and stacks of money."

"Did they ever say anything?"

"Joe always ran them off whenever I showed up. He didn't want 'their kind' he called them around when his regular customers started arriving for their morning coffee and breakfast. One time just after I began working for him, he told me if they were there when I arrived that I was to go directly to the kitchen, to not look at them or in any way acknowledge their existence."

As Flanagan wrote a note she asked, "What did you think of that arrangement?"

"Because some of our people become easily addicted to alcohol and gambling, I've seen whiskey and cards and money before. My father tries to stop it from happening, but the young men always have to test the laws of their elders."

"I thought it was illegal to bring alcohol onto the reservation?"

"On the reservation, the laws of the white man are not the laws of my people. We deal with our own in our own way. The worse offender is not he who breaks a law but he who reports the misdeeds of an Indian to the white man. That Indian is branded a traitor of his people and is no longer welcome."

Flanagan began to wonder if what Lottie was telling her would ever be useful. Their Minot Indian problems were confined to the occasional drunken brawl at the seedy hotels where a few teeth were lost and a few beds in the overnight cells got stunk up with piss and vomit. Mostly, it was the same ones. Once in awhile a new face appeared. Once in awhile a regular face disappeared. Flanagan had never asked why, and she'd never heard her colleagues ask why. But these Indians weren't like Lottie. She didn't know if North Dakota had Indians like Lottie. "I think that there's more to this discussion that you and I need to have, but for the present, let's get back to Joe and his gambling activities."

Lottie nodded.

"Claudine has made some serious accusations against Joe."

Flanagan noticed a flicker in Lottie's eyes. "I need to tell you because you're going to hear it sooner or later, and I expect sooner because Lizzie Burke knows, not that she would tell everyone indiscriminately, but she hasn't been sworn to secrecy."

Lottie smiled. "Lizzie is a friend, not like Zoë was, but she and Johnny always treated me as a person. I can tell you this about Lizzie: if she isn't supposed to tell, not even Johnny could pry information from her, but if she isn't restricted, you are correct—everyone will know." A deep frown replaced her smile. "But I am concerned. What is it that Claudine has said?"

"She accused Joe of molesting Sara and selling her to the Friday and Saturday night poker players to settle his poker debts."

Lottie put her hands together as if in prayer, closed her eyes, and touched the tips of her fingers to her mouth. Her lips began to move. A moment later, when she opened her eyes, they were full of tears. "I don't believe Joe is capable of these wrongs; I don't believe he is burdened by this great evil."

"We're holding him in Minot until we find out what the truth is."

"I pray to the spirits of my ancestors that Sara dwells in the land of peace and plenty where there is neither fear nor want, but her father did not do this thing to her, he is not capable of this dark act."

"I'll make sure he gets a lawyer and tells his side."

Lottie checked her watch.

"You don't have to open the restaurant."

"The people will need to come and talk. I need to be here."

"Lottie, please don't stay another night with Striker."

"Do you think Mr. Striker killed Zoë and Sara?"

Lottie's question caught her off guard. She thought Striker capable, but hadn't consciously put him at the top of her list. Her main fear was him hitting Lottie again, or was it? Maybe her main fear was that Striker would kill again. Maybe her main fear was that Lottie was next on his list. "Do you think he did?"

Lottie fell silent. She looked past Flanagan to a place that seemed far off, perhaps on a distant horizon or perhaps to a time long ago or perhaps to the spirits of her ancestors.

"Lottie, do you feel a need to open the café?"

Lottie blinked her eyes several times, as though awakening, and returned her attention to Flanagan. "I want you to call me Shower Cloud," she said. "I am Princess Shower Cloud—that's my real name. Only Joe and Zoë knew. They were the only ones who called me Shower Cloud."

"Shower Cloud...I like that—tell me one thing, Shower Cloud: Do you need to open the café?"

"I owe something to Joe and Sara. I feel Sara's spirit fighting to be free, crying out for my help, and Joe needs me to be here."

"Let me have the card I gave you before."

Shower Cloud pushed the card across the table. Flanagan wrote on the reverse side and gave it back. "I want you to promise that when you leave here today, you will go to this address in Minot. This is where I live. I want you to stay with me until we find out what's going on. Tell Lizzie and Johnny Burke that you have to leave town, that you want them to look after the café, and, no matter how much you trust them or others, don't tell anyone where you are going."

Lottie's mouth tightened to a thin, firm line, and she stared hard at Flanagan. "Yes," she said after a moment, "I will do that. I do not fear him and I do not know if he killed my best friend, Zoë, and poor Sara. I do know that I have not had sex with him. I lie next to him in his bed when he asks, but I never let him touch me, and I never sleep for fear he might try to violate my womanhood. If he ever does, I'll kill him. Knowing that I am capable of killing him has kept me sane, knowing that I am capable of killing him has allowed me to honor the agreement of our people, and I have now decided to end that agreement. It is time, and I sense that my father and the spirits of our ancestors agree." She studied what Flanagan had written on the card. "Yes, I will stay with you for I believe you are my friend."

Shower Cloud, like Striker and everyone else currently on or to be added to her list, remained a suspect, but she'd sooner be criticized for offering safe harbor than face a murder that she might have prevented. She could hear Hutton saying, "Flanagan, we arrest them, not take them home." She fully intended to place Shower Cloud in protective custody, just not in jail, a white man's jail that Shower Cloud would never countenance. And thinking of Hutton, she glanced at her watch. "I have to leave, but before I go, did Zoë ever mention the name of Victoria Otto?"

Flanagan's body grew warm; her skin began to feel hot, and then she turned cold and goose bumps formed on her arms and down her back and legs. She shivered, and looked across at Shower Cloud, who seemed to be fading from sight, as if a vanishing mirage. She rubbed her eyes and looked again. "What's happening?" she asked.

"Detective?"

Flanagan felt a hand on her arm.

"Detective, are you going to be OK?"

Flanagan blinked a few times. Shower Cloud came back into focus. "Yes, I think so. Did I ask about Victoria Otto?"

Though Shower Cloud responded, "That name is not familiar to me," she had tears in her eyes.

"Zoë never mentioned her name?"

"Did she have something to do with Zoë's murder?"

"I don't know," Flanagan said, and stood up. "It's a name that showed up in Zoë's papers."

Shower Cloud got up and stood close.

Flanagan's heart began to race and she tried to step away, but Shower Cloud took her hand and held tight. A searing fire shot between their bodies and Flanagan felt as though her feet were welded to the floor. Their bodies became encased in a glowing pod.

Then Shower Cloud smiled and the glowing pod vanished. Her hand felt warm and normal and comforting.

Flanagan moved her foot. She studied her fingers. Everything seemed normal. "What just happened here?"

"The spirits of my ancestors…you will be all right."

Flanagan glanced around.

"Do not worry," Shower Cloud said. "They will not hurt you."

"No, I suspect not, but what about you? It's you I'm worried about."

Shower Cloud stood tall. "The spirits of my ancestors watch over me. I do not fear earthly harm."

Chapter 27

Whatever happened, Flanagan left the café trying to convince herself it hadn't. She stood on the sidewalk and inhaled deeply until her heart slowed to near normal. She glanced back. Statue-like, Shower Cloud stared out at the street. Flanagan nodded, not sure if Shower Cloud noticed, and walked to the SUV.

The red Dodge Ram had gone. She called Harry Carson intending to have him give the license number to Casey Long. She also wanted an update on Hutton, but Carson wasn't in his office so she called Casey Long directly. After giving her the Ram's license number, she asked where Carson had gone, figuring if anyone in the department knew his whereabouts she would.

"All he told me was to tell you he'd call as soon as he knew anything."

With her frustration nearing the exploding point, Flanagan ended the call and drove toward Town Hall. At the main intersection, she stopped and looked down the side street toward the beer parlor hoping to spot Art Logan's truck. There were two new pick-ups and an old blue Toyota parked at the curb, but no red Dodge Ram.

Past the beer parlor across the street was the AMTRAK station where Dale Kiley lived. A yellow Volvo station wagon was parked along one side. In the other direction, an old Lincoln, huge and square and brown, sat in front of a green two-story house on one side of the street and a white truck with a car-towing mechanism mounted on the back was parked in the driveway next to a gray bungalow. A man with his arm resting on the truck talked to a woman in a red dress standing on the front porch of the gray bungalow. Flanagan rolled the windows down. Their voices carried on the breeze, but not their words. The woman laughed.

Flanagan continued on to Town Hall. At the door she stopped and looked across at the red brick school. Two boys that looked to be in their mid-teens were playing catch with a football. Others, girls and boys, sat or stood in groups of two or three or four. They seemed drained of energy, even the boys playing with the football. News of Zoë's murder had obviously taken its toll, and soon they'd have to deal with Sara Peterson's murder and the whole issue of sexual abuse. Small towns like Largeville didn't have batteries of counselors that could be mobilized, but they had involved parents, parents like Lizzie Burke, and they had good and dedicated teachers like Joan Foster and Betty Hale, all of whom she guessed would be working overtime. Or maybe the kids worked it out on their own like they used to when she went to school. Rural kids were closer to death; they saw farm animals being sent away for butchering—some farms probably still did their own butchering—and still others dying from weather or old age or being killed by predators or in territorial battles. Death wasn't an unspeakable tragedy; it was part of life, but murder…she hadn't had to deal with murder when she was young. She thought for a moment of the little boy in Sara's apartment in Chicago, of how much death he'd seen.

She removed her note, unlocked the door, and stepped inside. She tried Striker's door, but it was locked and for the moment, she didn't bother picking her way in. In the interview room, she went around to the far side where she'd sat on Saturday and took out her recorder and notebook and set them on the table and put her case on the floor next to the chair.

When she flipped her notebook open she saw Edie Coombs's number that Carson had given her. She punched it into her cellphone and hit 'TALK.' A scratchy recording came on, dogs barking in the background. She identified herself, left her cell number, and hung up.

She checked her watch, wondering where her backup was and decided to phone Carson again. His voice mail answered and she started to leave a message when a black Chevrolet with oversized tires and a dozen aerials pulled up and parked alongside the SUV. "Never mind," she said to Carson's voicemail. "My backup has just arrived. Make sure you call me when you know something about Hutton."

From the doorway she watched a young man who looked no older than Tommy Striker slide from under the steering wheel and walk to the front of the car and stand for a moment, giving Largeville the once over. When he saw Flanagan, he nodded and started toward her. With his flopping blonde hair and red cheeks and small frame, he looked more like a young boy all dressed up to play cops and robbers.

"Hello Galen," she said. "Sorry to drag your ass up here. What do you think of my town?"

"I've lived in worse. When I was a kid, my old man had trouble finding work so we moved every two years or so, always to a small town."

"Thanks for coming. Anything new on Hutton?"

"The last I heard, Carson had gone to check out his SUV. I expect you'll hear before I do."

They went inside and Flanagan brought him up to speed on Zoë and Sara's murders and the interviews.

"Where's Striker now?" Galen asked.

"Short answer: I don't know. Long answer: He left here on Saturday afternoon saying he had to go to Minot and then check some wells, but when Hutton and I got to the airport yesterday morning, his SUV was in the parking lot. Carson hasn't yet found out if he took a flight."

"Yeah, well I'd say Carson's had a busy morning."

"That wasn't a complaint." Flanagan felt her face get hot. She remembered why she'd never liked Galen: sarcasm and sniping comments. Maybe it was his lack of physical size that made him act like a prick.

"Didn't say it was," Galen studied his nails. "Why don't you call Casey and have her get someone on it."

"Be my guest."

"I'm sure you know there're only three flights a day and they all go to Minneapolis."

"I'd like to know which one."

He called Casey and told her what he needed. "What's his name again," he said to Flanagan.

"Newton Thomas Striker."

He repeated the name to Casey. "Yeah, call me when you find out." He ended the call, took the chair facing the window, and kicked his feet up on the table. "Who have you got lined up?"

"Before we go any further, let's get a couple of things straight. This is my case. You are my backup. If you came here thinking otherwise, go back to Minot; or if you intend to take over, be my guest, but I won't be your backup. On top of everything else, I don't need to get involved in a pissing contest."

He looked at his nails again. "I gather this is your first case."

She smashed her hand to the table. Galen flinched.

"Yes, this is my first case and that doesn't give you license to waltz in here like God's gift to the world and smother me with your bull shit. And another thing, get your goddamn feet off the table."

He swung his feet to the floor, eyeing her carefully.

Flanagan inhaled, hoping her face didn't look as flushed as it felt.

"OK," he finally said. "I'll play by your rules. What's first on your agenda?"

Flanagan's phone rang. She glanced at the caller ID. "It's Carson," she said. Her breathing felt forced. "Yes," she hollered into the mouthpiece.

"We've found him. He's going to make it."

"Oh Jesus, thank you!" She inhaled and exhaled noisily. "Thank you dear God. What happened?"

"A good whack on the head, got a couple of bullet holes, lost a lot of blood—nothing serious."

She brushed at her eyes. "Where'd you find him?"

"Locked in one of the storage units where we found his truck—he wasn't supposed to live. Another day, maybe even a few hours, he wouldn't have."

"Harry, I've got to come in. Galen's here. He can take a couple of interviews until I get back."

"Sorry, he was the only one available."

"Yeah well, later on that. I'll be there in thirty minutes."

"I'm not sure you'll get to see him."

"Yeah, well we can talk about that later too. Where did you send him?"

"Trinity. I'll wait for you there."

Trinity was a level two trauma center, one of the best in the state. Flanagan knew a couple of Trinity's doctors, one she used to date, so she wasn't worried about bureaucratic bullshit keeping her from seeing Hutton. "What about Smith?"

"Nothing at this end. I talked to Cleary and Hopkins, the two cops he saw yesterday in Vegas. You get hold of the Coombs woman?"

"Just her answering machine. Maybe you can put Casey on her as well."

She ended the call, gave a courtesy update to Galen, and told him she had to go to Minot.

"I wouldn't have expected less."

"What the hell does that mean?"

"Hey, take it easy. I just meant that he's your partner."

Bullshit, she thought. She still wanted to hit him. "I should be back mid to late afternoon. While I'm gone, I want you to talk to Ed Gregory and Tony Perini over at the school." She looked at her watch. "Pete's café is the only game in town. I suggest you get there early, like now, and tell Lottie that you're working with me. She'll make sure you don't go hungry."

"Actually, I brought my lunch."

Of course you did, Flanagan thought, and gathered up her computer and notebook. "Here's a copy of my notes and all the information that Carson's group managed to dig up on Miss Brown." She handed him a CD.

"Brown is the teacher?"

Flanagan nodded.

"What about the girl in Chicago?"

"Sara Peterson. Everything we have is on the CD."

She started to hand him her card when a loud rapping noise sounded against the front window.

"What the hell is that?" Galen asked jumping up, gun in hand.

Part of a black umbrella with an ivory handle floated into view and gave the window another loud rap.

Flanagan strode to the window and looked out.

"Put your gun away."

Standing on the sidewalk, so severely stooped that they hadn't been able to see her, was an ancient woman with her hair in a bun and thick glasses with black wire rims and a long gray dress that exposed nothing except her head, her black-gloved hands, and her black lace-up boots. When she peered up and saw them, she shook her umbrella motioning them outside.

"Looks like you'll have company for lunch," Flanagan said, and went out to the sidewalk.

"Are you the detective I've been hearing about?" Birdlike, she cocked her head to one side and looked up. Her blue eyes were clear and danced when she spoke, her diction crisp, and her manner commanded an answer. She smelled of Listerine.

"I'm Detective Flanagan. How can I help you?"

"May, child, may, not can, and it's more like how I can help you."

"Yes, of course."

"I'm Abigail Reaves. I taught school here for fifty years, not there..." She nodded her head toward the school. "...but the old one they tore down. I hear you're investigating a murder." She looked at Flanagan as if to say, 'Well, are you?'

"Yes, you've heard correct...ly."

Reaves cocked her ear as Flanagan struggled to add the 'ly.'

Galen joined them. "This is Detective Galen," Flanagan said.

Reaves gave Galen a thorough going over and then said, "Why he's nothing more than a boy."

Galen's face tightened. Flanagan faked a cough to hide a chuckle.

"Yes, well I assure you he is a full-fledged detective and would be happy to talk to you."

"Well young lady, he might be happy to talk to me, but I'm sure he'd probably get more out of it if I talked to him."

Flanagan's face felt warm.

"And I'm sure Detective Galen is a very fine police officer, but I'd sooner talk to you."

Flanagan figured Galen wouldn't argue the point. "Yes, and I'd like that too, but I'm leaving for Minot and may not be back."

Reaves eyed Galen again and said to Flanagan, "Well I guess he'll have to do then, but I want a few things understood, a few rules that have to be followed."

Flanagan nodded.

"There is to be no bad language. I don't cotton to men..." she turned her glare on Flanagan "...or women, using bad language. Understood?" She peered at Galen, her mouth snapped shut, her lower lip covering her upper lip, her umbrella at the ready.

"Yes," he said, "I understand."

"And I expect you to speak proper English. I used to say to my students—and I've had hundreds over the years—that the rules for proper English have already been written; there is no need to make up new ones."

"Yes, well Detective Galen is especially well schooled in proper English so you'll not have a problem with him." Flanagan handed Reaves a card. "And you can reach me at any of the numbers listed there, though I'm sure you won't have any complaints whatsoever."

Reaves studied the card and shoved it into a pocket that until that moment had been hidden in a fold of her dress. "I'm glad to see you've moved into the twenty-first century."

Flanagan raised an eyebrow.

"I'm talking about e-mail, young lady. I never use the phone any more. It's far too expensive, and usually when I want to talk to someone, they're either in bed or have left work, so I dash off an e-mail. I don't know what the world is coming to with these young people. It seems to me they spend far too much time sleeping and playing and not enough time at work." She offered Galen her arm. "Help me up the steps, young man. I'll be OK after that."

"Make sure you send me an e-mail if you have anything to add to what you tell Detective Galen."

"Oh I will, young lady," Reaves said, busily negotiating the steps with Galen's help. "Have no fear of that."

Chapter 28

On her way to Minot, Flanagan tried Edie Pitano again. She got the same scratchy answering machine and started to leave a message when a live voice said, "This is Gwen." Gwen came out sounding like 'Gwane.'

Flanagan identified herself.

"Y'all's partner saved her life."

"How is Edie?"

"She's doin' just fine. Her eye's still swollen shut and she hurts all over her poor little body, but she's doin' just fine. You be sure to tell Detective Hutton."

"Detective Hutton is the reason I'm calling. He was beaten and shot. We think it might have been Derrick Smith."

"Oh, dear sweet Jesus, I'm so sorry to hear about that. It's Derrick. I just know it is. I tried to tell Edie that he was no good. Is Detective Hutton...you know..."

"He's going to be OK, but I need to talk to Edie."

"Sweetie, she's out like a light. Those wonderful nurses have been giving her all kinds of magical pills; right now I don't think she could tell you her own name."

"She...probably the two of you need to be extra careful. Smith could be on his way back there."

"Oh we will darlin'. If he shows up here, I'll blow his ugly face clean off with my trusty shotgun. He knows I damn sure know how to use it and he knows I damn sure won't hesitate."

"Isn't someone watching your house?"

"Why sweetie, they were, those nice policemen, but I sent them away. We've got neighbors to think about. Imagine what they'd say if they knew the police were sitting out there on the street watching our little ole place. The only thing a girl's got in this town is her reputation, and darlin', once that goes, you might just as well go out to work as a prostitute lady. But don't you worry none, we keep our alarms on, and we damn sure know how to take care of ourselves."

Flanagan ended the call and phoned Cleary. She got his voicemail and asked him to call. Despite Gwen sounding like she might be capable of taking on a formidable foe, Smith was a killer and Flanagan had no intention of leaving them at his mercy, particularly when Edie might be her only avenue to Smith.

Minot's city limits and the thirty-five mph speed limit sign loomed ahead. She flipped on the flashing lights and siren and continued full speed up Broadway to Burdick, and took two rights into Trinity. Harry Carson's car occupied one of the police parking spaces. A patrol car sat next to Harry's car and the chief's car and driver sat next to the patrol car. She pulled in beside the chief's car. The young constable sitting behind the wheel nodded as she got out.

"I'm Flanagan," she said.

"Yeah, I know. They said you were coming. They're in ICU."

She ran up the emergency entrance ramp, flashed her badge at the security guard, and headed for the elevators. She got off on the fourth floor and raced down the hall. Harry Carson saw her coming and stepped forward to greet her.

"How is he," she said, panting to catch her breath and clutching Carson's arm.

"Detective Flanagan," the chief said, his rich baritone echoing off the walls.

She hadn't seen him standing off to Carson's right.

"He's going to be as good as new in a couple of weeks."

She glanced at Harry and then at the chief. "Have you seen him? Has he told us anything?"

Harry shook his head.

"We've all seen him," the chief said. "Trouble is, he didn't see us. We're waiting for the doc now." He raised his arm and made a point of looking at his watch. "I'd say he should be here any moment." He turned and looked at the two uniformed officers, who nodded because that's what uniformed officers do when the chief looks in their direction.

Flanagan looked down the hallway past the waiting room and saw a nurses' station. "I need to make a call," she said, and took off on the run. At the nurses' station, she collared an aide, showed her ID, and asked her to page either Dr. Wolyshyn or Dr. Singh.

"Which Dr. Singh?"

"Jas, and have them call you. Whatever you do don't use my name."

The aide punched a button on a large monitor, and then spoke into a microphone. Flanagan heard the call go out over the speaker system and studiously avoided looking back to where the chief and Harry waited. The aide fielded a call and wrote something on a piece of paper.

"Dr. Wolyshyn will be right out," she said to Flanagan. "If you want you can meet him through there." The aide pointed to closed door on her left. Flanagan took off at a brisk pace. Wolyshyn charged out just as she arrived. She gripped his elbow and spun him around.

"This is a pleasant surprise," Wolyshyn said, allowing himself to be pushed back through the swinging door, "but I somehow suspect I'm not the object of your visit."

"My partner's in here. I've got to talk to him."

"If you mean Hutton, you're out of luck."

"Don't give me a run-around, Alex. He knows something I need to know. The chief of police is waiting just outside those doors, and if he sees Hutton first, that'll be it because he won't tell the chief squat and the chief won't let anyone else see or talk to Hutton until he re-covers—we don't have that kind of time."

Wolyshyn tugged at his chin.

She'd always hated when he'd done that, but that wasn't what ended their relationship. That would have been his other bad habit: screwing all the young nurses.

"It'll cost you dinner."

"I have a gun and could shoot you."

"But you won't."

"OK, deal, now move it." She could always put him off until Hutton had recovered enough to join them. He didn't say she couldn't bring a friend, and she had promised Hutton drinks and dinner.

"Come with me detective."

She followed his swaying tunic and grey slacks and brown Allen Edmunds soft-soled loafers—nothing but Allen Edmunds ever for the good doctor, she wondered if they were the ones she'd plopped down two-hundred and fifty for—and the premature thinning spot on the back of his head, no doubt caused by too much pillow friction. At the end of the hallway, they took a left and stepped into a room full of green gowns and caps and masks.

"We'll need to dress for this one," he said, and slipped out of his white tunic. "Here, this should be your size."

"They all look the same to me."

"They are."

"Always the smart ass." At least Carson and the chief wouldn't recognize her if they managed to make their way into Hutton's room.

"It's up here on the right," Wolyshyn said, resuming their journey.

He pushed through a door and walked across to the single bed containing a mummified looking shape to which a thousand wires and tubes had been attached that came from bottles and bags and blinking and beeping machines with screens that had blips and dots and graphs and aurora borealis-like visualizations. Then she saw that his arms weren't wrapped and the tattoo that she knew to be Hutton's. He raised a finger when Wolyshyn asked if he was awake.

"Better make it fast," Wolyshyn said to Flanagan. "You'll soon have company."

She gripped Hutton's hand, then leaned over and whispered, "It's me." She didn't want Wolyshyn to hear what she or Hutton said. Wolyshyn might not say anything to her colleagues, but he might utter sweet mutterings into the ear of some medical world ingénue who also happened to spend some of her nights with young police constables. "The chief is on his way in. I need to know if Smith did this."

Hutton groaned and moved his hand.

"What are you trying to say? Can you squeeze my hand?"

He squeezed.

"Once for yes, understand?"

He squeezed twice.

"Smith didn't do this?"

He squeezed once.

"Are you saying Smith didn't do this?"

He squeezed once.

Shit. Then who the hell did?

"Did this happen on your way home?"

He squeezed three times.

"What? Did this happen on your way home or not?"

He squeezed once.

"I don't understand. Do you know who did this?"

He squeezed once.

"Do I know who did this?"

He squeezed twice. Nothing made sense.

"Can he write," she asked Wolyshyn.

"Give it a go." He handed her a note pad and pen that he fished from the pocket of his gown.

She placed Hutton's hand on the pad and stuck the pen between his fingers. "See if you can write down the name of the person who did this to you."

The pen fell to the bed. She picked it up, held it between his fingers, and steered his hand to the paper. He ran off the edge and onto the sheets. She put his hand back. He made a few lines and loops that appeared meaningless.

"Try again," she said. "I can't read what you wrote."

She put his hand back on the paper and held the pen between his thumb and first two fingers. He made a few more squiggles and dropped the pen. Behind them, the door pushed open and three people entered. She grabbed the pen and note pad and shoved them in her pocket. Wolyshyn grabbed Hutton's wrist.

"What are you doing?" the doctor demanded.

Wolyshyn turned. "The nurse here and I were passing by and thought we heard an alarm."

The doctor glared at Flanagan.

"Pulse normal," Wolyshyn said. "Nurse, Dr. Martin will take over."

As they walked out Carson gave her the eye. She didn't return the favor and hurried back to the green gown room where she shucked the hospital garments. Wolyshyn did likewise and led her back to the nurses' station.

"Sorry I couldn't buy you more time," he said. "Can you make anything out of what he wrote?"

She looked at the two pieces of paper. "Maybe if I was three-years-old—I'll take them downtown, someone there might be able to figure something out."

Wolyshyn turned to leave. "Good to see you again, Flanagan."

"I'll call when this is over, doctor. Big Mac sound OK?"

"I'm sure I'll come up with a restaurant somewhere in North Dakota that's appropriately expensive and romantic."

"If it's not in Minot, you'll be dining alone, or at least not with me."

Wolyshyn left her with the two constables in the waiting room. To avoid having to listen to their discussion about muscle cars and NASCAR, she sat several spaces away and buried her nose in a Time magazine that she took from the scattered collection sitting on a center table. A few moments later, Harry Carson and the chief came up the hall toward them. She asked what they'd been able to find out.

"Nothing," the chief said. "His jaws are wired shut so he can't speak, but the docs assure us it's only a matter of a few days. We'll let him know you were here."

"Thanks, I'd appreciate it." She turned to Carson. "I need to see Claudine Peterson, the woman from Largeville we sent in this morning, and I'd like company."

"Something new?"

"We still have her husband in custody. I've got to know if she wants to press charges."

The five of them walked to the elevators. Flanagan and Carson got off on the third floor and identified themselves to the duty nurse. She led them to Claudine's room, which was guarded by two uniformed officers, one inside, one outside. Flanagan glanced at Carson.

Carson shrugged. "Quiet morning. Better safe than sorry."

The uniformed officer stepped out when they entered. Carson closed the door. Claudine sat propped up in her bed. Her eyes flickered in recognition when Flanagan walked up.

"Claudine, this is Deputy Chief Carson. He's working with me on Sara's case."

Claudine cast a wary eye at Carson.

"We need to find out what you want to do about Joe. If you aren't going to press charges, we've got to let him go."

Claudine's face hardened; her eyes mere slits. "Of course I want to press charges. He killed Sara, my baby Sara." Her eyes filled with tears.

"You knew what he was doing and didn't try to stop him."

"He gave her to those men, sold her like she was a whore. That's why she ran away, that's why she got killed, not because I didn't try to stop him."

Flanagan took Claudine's bandaged hand. "Do you want Sara's body shipped here?"

Claudine's eyes flashed with uncertainty—having to deal with the body moved Sara's death to the realm of cold, hard reality. Now, at least as far as Claudine was concerned; Sara's murder was no longer a mental state.

"Do you want her interred in Largeville?"

Tears tumbled down Claudine's cheeks. Her eyes begged guidance.

"I'd recommend you have her sent to one of the funeral homes here in Minot and let them handle everything. Do you have a pastor?"

She nodded, though Flanagan suspected she would be hard pressed to come up with a name.

"What about someone in Largeville who can help?"

"Lizzie?" Claudine asked, her eyes hopeful, but heavy with question marks.

"I'm sure she'd like to hear from you. Call her. She'll be glad to help."

Claudine still looked doubtful.

"You have to do this now." Flanagan reached for the phone sitting on the table next to Claudine's bed and called Casey. She explained to Casey what was needed, told her to stay with the call to make sure there were no snafus, and put Claudine on the line.

Carson shook his head when Flanagan asked him if there was anything else he needed to hear. They said goodbye to Claudine and left to see Joe. One of the uniformed officers stepped back into Claudine's room.

Fifteen minutes later, Flanagan sat in the holding cell with Joe. Carson didn't join her because he had to get back to his lab.

"How are you feeling?" she asked. He looked like he'd been on an all night binge.

Joe nodded, ran his hand through his hair, and looked down at his untied sneakers.

"I saw Claudine. She's in the hospital."

He didn't look up or otherwise react.

"Did you hear what I said?"

He flinched at the loudness and sharpness of her voice. "Yes," he said, and looked up.

"Because she is pressing charges, we're going to have to keep you here. Do you have an attorney?"

Joe nodded. His eyes looked dead.

"Joe, have you called your attorney?"

He shook his head.

"I want you to do that now. Come with me; I'll take you to the phone up front."

She led him to the desk near the entrance to the holding cell area. "Use that phone," she said. "Do you know the number?"

"No," Joe said.

"What's the name?"

"Ralph Todd or Emily Gray at Winslett Ashburn."

Flanagan picked up the phone and called Casey, who told her that Claudine had completed her call, that Elizabeth Burke had agreed to help, and that Mr. and Mrs. Burke were on their way to Minot to visit with Claudine. Flanagan asked Casey to get the Winslett Ashburn firm on the line for Mr. Joe Peterson and handed the receiver to Joe.

"They know me as Pete," Joe said into the phone. He sat in the chair next to the desk and seemed to be concentrating on not looking at Flanagan or anyone else or anything except the phone. He nodded his head as though the person on the line could see him and then said, "Yes, that's right."

"Have you made contact?" Flanagan asked.

He nodded.

"I'm going to step outside that door. I don't want to know what you say."

He nodded.

"Knock on the glass when you're finished."

He nodded, and Flanagan stepped outside. A few minutes later, Joe knocked and she took him back to the holding cell. She surmised his attorney would show up and get him a bail hearing.

"Claudine is making arrangements to have Sara interred in Largeville," she said.

Joe sat on the cot in his cell and started to cry. "I didn't do what she said."

"Your attorney will work with you on that, but you should call Lizzie or John Burke. They're helping Claudine with arrangements."

"I didn't do what she said," he sobbed again.

"Joe, listen to me, the important thing now is that you and Claudine give Sara a proper burial, for her and for yourselves. The rest will have to work through the system. Do you understand?"

He nodded and rubbed a sleeve across his nose and sniffled.

She thought he needed some positive news and told him that Lottie had opened the restaurant.

His eyes did light up for a brief moment, and then clouded over when Flanagan announced that she had to leave. She asked if his attorney was on the way over."

"Yes," he replied. "I don't know why Claudine is doing this to me."

"Just make sure you tell your attorney everything you know, no lying."

With that, she left to call Constable Cleary in Vegas. This time he answered. She let him know that Smith might not be the one who'd tried to kill Hutton. When Cleary told her that Smith was still at large, she asked him to send whatever information they had, including photographs. Maybe Smith hadn't tried to kill Hutton, but she had a bad feeling in her stomach that wouldn't go away until Smith was put away.

Chapter 29

As soon as they got seated in the interview room, Reaves said to Galen, "I assume you're going to lower those blinds. I don't want any of the town busy-bodies poking their noses into my business. Besides, it's too bright."

Galen closed the blinds and returned to his chair, opened his notebook, and turned on his recorder. "I hope you don't mind," he said.

"No, of course I don't mind. Why should I mind?"

"For the record, please state your name."

"My name is Abigail Amelia Reaves. I would like to say I was given two names that started with 'A' because AA Milne's books were among my favorites when I was a child, but of course I was already born when he wrote Winnie-the-Pooh." She paused and looked at Galen with critical eye. "I'm eighty-five, you know. Winnie-the-Pooh was published in nineteen-twenty-six."

"I didn't know that," Galen said.

"What, that I'm eighty-five or that Winnie-the-Pooh was published in nineteen-twenty-six?"

"Neither."

"You mean either…you didn't know either. Proper English, remember?"

"Yes of course. Now, what was…is it that you want to tell us…me?"

"I live across the street from Hilda and Howard Vole. They have a large home, the largest in Largeville, and when the last of their children left, they had eight you know, four boys and four girls, the girls were good students, but the boys couldn't seem to apply themselves, oh they got by and went on to become doctors and lawyers, but they weren't smart like the girls, I'd much sooner have one of the girls operating on me or defending me if my life depended on it, but of course they aren't doctors or lawyers, all married local farm boys, raising families of their own now, never come to visit either I might add, Hilda and Howard converted their second floor into four apartments that they rent to the single female teachers. They don't charge near enough, but they do it more for the company than the money, lord knows they have enough money. Before that, it was hard attracting good teachers. Oh, they'd come and look around and like the school and like the town, but when they discovered they'd have to live in a basement suite or worse, take a bedroom in a house where they lived with a family, they never stayed. Now in my time, I started teaching in nineteen-forty-two, came here in nineteen-forty-five, made nine hundred dollars a year, we were thankful to have a job, but now everything has to be handed to them on a silver platter, though I still don't think teachers are paid enough. How much money do you make, young man?"

None of your goddamn business… "Seventy-two thousand, but I have ten years experience and a degree."

Reaves's mouth dropped open. "Every teacher has a degree and they don't make nearly that much."

"Yes, we're overpaid."

"I know you're being sarcastic, young man, and it doesn't become you, but no, I don't think you're overpaid. Your kind put their lives on the line every day and one can't put a value on that. What I do think is that teachers are underpaid. They take young lives into their hands every day, young lives that they try to mold and shape, young lives that they try to prepare for a balanced and productive future, perhaps so policemen like you don't end up staring down the barrel of a gun being held by a dropout who's reached the end of his hopes, whose dreams have all been shattered."

Galen studied her face, he felt her intensity, and she no longer seemed an ancient old crow.

"Well, enough of my soapbox. As I said, Miss Brown lived across the street from my little house. I don't sleep so well when my back hurts and these last two weeks, it's been kicking up a storm; I think we're in for an early and bitterly cold winter, that's what I think. Anyway, last Saturday morning I got up to make a cup of chamomile tea. The tea kettle started whistling so I turned off the burner and filled my cup about two-thirds of the way. The other third is for brandy. Nothing works for my aching back like chamomile tea and brandy. I took my tea and brandy to my little kitchen table and sipped, enjoying the peace and quiet of the morning. It was four o'clock, and the reason I know it was four o'clock is because that's usually the time I wake up and also my old clock, that hasn't been wrong in over thirty years, chimed."

"Excuse me for a moment," Galen said and opened Flanagan's timeline recap on his computer to review the entries. Four o'clock was when Zoë may have left her room. "Sorry," he said. "Please continue."

"Well, you can imagine my surprise when I heard a car door slam. Where do you live, young man?"

"In Minot, but I was raised in a lot of small towns."

"Well then you know what a car door slamming at four in the morning means. It means someone is up to no good, being out on the streets at that time of night."

"I don't suppose you got a look at who it was?"

"Do you think I'm daft? Of course I got a look." She gripped the handle of her umbrella with ferocity and her mouth curled into a near snarl. "It was that Indian woman."

"Indian woman?"

"The one who lives with the mayor no less, corrupting that fine young boy with their common-law arrangement, or at least that's what some call it—there are other words that more accurately describe what's going on, but they shall not cross my lips."

Galen scanned Flanagan's computer file, trying to piece in what Reaves had said. "Are you talking about Newton Striker and his wife, Lottie?"

"That's exactly who I'm talking about, except she's not his wife. Everyone in town knows that, but no one will take a stand—they're all afraid of Mr. Striker and what he might do if he finds out. Well let me tell you, I'm not afraid of him and his violent temper. His words can't hurt me, and I'm certain he's not about to take a swing at an old lady."

"Does he make a habit of hitting people?"

"Oh he's a hitter, that one, and a bully, hitting his boy and the Indian all the time. They won't tell you so but anyone in town will tell you it's true."

He again referred to Flanagan's computer notes. "It says here that she's not the boy's mother."

"No, he packed the boy's mother off ten or eleven years ago, said she was sick—I'll tell you what: she was no sicker than me—and comes traipsing back to town pretty as you please with this young, greasy squaw smelling of campfire smoke, to care for the boy he said, but it doesn't take a genius to know what's going on."

"According to Detective Flanagan's notes, they're married."

"Listen young man, I didn't read about a wedding and I didn't read about a divorce, and I'm not only talking about what I read in the Minot Daily News, I'm talking about everything I read on the Internet and in all the newspapers from Texas—not one word. I told some of the people in town, but, like I said, they're afraid of Mr. Striker and most of them think of me as an old busy-body."

"No, I'm sure not."

Galen blanched under her glare.

"Finally, I wrote a letter to the governor. He didn't answer. Then I sent him an e-mail. He didn't answer that either. So I telephoned and got one of his aides, a Miss

Periwinkle, who promised she'd look into it, but of course I'm still waiting, but there's an election coming up so I'm going to go to one of his rallies and ask him in person."

"What is it that you intend to ask?"

"I intend to ask how an elected official, a mayor in the State of North Dakota, can live outside the law. If our elected officials have no respect for the law, we are but a few steps from anarchy." With a force that belied its fragility, she banged her bony hand on the table.

Galen sat for a moment, pretending to ponder the point of her outrage, and then said, "Let's get back to Saturday morning. Are you sure it was the Indian woman?" Judging from the thickness of her glasses, he wondered if she could see ten feet let alone across the street in the early light of morning.

"I can see twenty-twenty with my glasses, but I doubt you believe me so I'm going to prove it. Open the blinds."

Galen hesitated.

"Come on, young man, I haven't got all day." She thumped the umbrella shaft on the floor.

Galen did as requested.

"Is that your car there, the black one?"

Galen nodded.

"License plate QCZ 834."

"OK, you've proved your point. You have excellent vision with your glasses."

"Yes, and when I heard that car door slam, I grabbed my glasses and went to the window. It was the Indian all right, standing next to her car just as plain as the nose on my face."

"Are you one-hundred percent certain it was her?"

"Have you met the Indian woman?"

"No, I can't say I have."

"Then you haven't. If you had, you would know about all that long black hair—and I'm not talking white man black, I'm talking Indian black—done in braids that hang in circles half-way down her back. And with those beaded strips woven in, she looks like a wild woman. If you ask me, she should be dancing around a campfire somewhere."

"Did you see her face?"

"I didn't have to. No one has hair like that."

"You said it was her car?"

"Everyone knows her car, that bright red sports car that Mr. Striker bought for her, like he was her sugar daddy, and the way she drives around town with her nose in the air like she's something special, like she's better than everyone, like she's not a…well you know."

"Did you see the license plate?"

"I didn't have to. There's only one car like it in Largeville."

"OK, assuming it was her, why don't you tell me what you saw?"

"I saw Miss Brown come to her window—her room is on the front facing my place. I guess she also heard the car door."

Galen stopped writing and looked up, the silence disconcerting. Miss Reaves seemed frozen, her eyes looking like glazed marble. "Yes, go on; then what happened?" He hoped she hadn't died.

She blinked and gave her head a shake. "Indian savages murdered my grandfather—scalped and speared him to death—in eighteen-seventy-six, when my father was only six years old. He told me about it many times. He saw it happen. Not a thing for a young boy to witness. They were the same savages who murdered that brave General Custer and all of those fine soldiers over in Montana later that same year."

"You saw Miss Brown at her bedroom window?"

"She was friendly with the Indian woman, though I never figured out why. They were always sitting together in the café, laughing and talking. The Indian woman works for Pete, probably there now, tossing her hips and batting her eyes at the men, advertising her body that way…disgusting."

"Do you think the Indian woman had something to do with Miss Brown's murder?"

"There was a man with her. If you ask me, the Indian figured Miss Brown was competition, maybe made a pass at one of the men the Indian wanted. Miss Brown was an attractive young lady, maybe too attractive for her own good, wearing clothes not befitting a young woman of good breeding, those high skirts and high-heeled shoes and tight sweaters, just asking for trouble, not that Miss Brown wasn't a proper lady mind you…nothing like the Indian woman."

"Did Miss Brown join them?"

"I saw the Indian and her male companion creep toward the house and duck behind that thick caragana hedge that Howard and Hilda have running across the front of their place. Why they have to have it there and so high I'll never know—not like they have anything to hide."

"And Miss Brown came down from her room?"

Reaves looked at him askance, and continued. "After a couple of minutes, I saw the Indian woman and the man, well their shadows really, sneaking up the sidewalk and onto the porch. They opened the door—most people in Largeville don't lock their doors, but I always do, a single woman living alone, you never know what might happen—and disappeared inside."

Galen drew in a deep breath. Come on lady, he thought, come on.

"I went to turn on the television to catch the early news and when I came back, I saw the Indian and the man carrying what looked like a rolled carpet. I didn't think anything at the time other than four a.m. seemed an odd time to be moving a carpet, but when I heard that Miss Brown had been murdered, I realized what they were carrying was no carpet—they were carrying her. They killed her and carried her out and put her in the trunk of the car and then dumped her in the ditch like she was a piece of garbage."

"How do you know that? Did you follow them?"

"No, of course not, I don't drive, always have someone willing to take me where I want to go, but it didn't take me long to add two and two and get four."

"Miss Reaves, will you excuse me for a moment? I have to make a call."

"Yes, I expected once you heard what I had to say you'd have to contact Detective Flanagan."

Galen fought the urge to lash out, to tell her that he didn't report to Flanagan. "For your information I'm in charge, and I'm not calling Detective Flanagan. What I am going to do is see if the Indian woman is at the café."

"Oh she's there all right. I checked when I walked past on my way here."

"Have you mentioned any of this to anyone else?"

"Oh my no, not a single word. What kind of person do you take me for?"

Galen felt his heart beating faster. He'd show all of them: Flanagan; the chief, who thought he was incompetent; Carson, who thought he was a suck-up; the rest of them who teased him about his small size and called him junior, saying he looked like a real policeman only smaller. He gathered up his computer, recorder and notes and shoved them in his case. Miss Reaves watched hawk-like.

"Before you run off and arrest the Indian, I'll need help down the steps."

Galen gave her a long look.

"That's what you're going to do, isn't it?" She got up and hobbled to the door, reaching for his free arm. He helped her to the sidewalk.

"You sure you haven't talked to anyone?"

"Young man, when I say I haven't talked to anyone, I mean I haven't talked to anyone. Now, I'm in a hurry to get to Cobb's there across the street. They mark their produce down to half-price on Monday afternoon, getting ready for their fresh shipments during the week. With my tiny teacher's pension, I have to watch every penny you know."

"Do you need help?"

"I've been making my away around this town for sixty years, I expect I can make it through another day. Besides, haven't you got more important things to do?"

"Yes, I expect I have."

"It's high time someone put that Indian in her place. I hope you're man enough for the job."

Chapter 30

Galen jumped in his car and tore off up the street. In the rearview mirror, he saw Reaves standing in the middle of the road, watching. I'll show the old bat.

He skidded to the curb in front of the café and went inside. The Indian woman wasn't hard to spot, being the only Indian and only woman in the café.

She came out of the kitchen area in the back and walked toward him. "Are you here for lunch, detective?"

Her beauty caught him off-guard and for a brief moment, his mouth wouldn't say the words he'd so carefully rehearsed. Also, several men in groups of two and three were having lunch. They all stopped and stared. One casually nodded his head.

"Are you Mrs. Lottie Striker?" It came out more loudly than he intended.

"Yes. How may I be of service?" Her big eyes widened as she studied his face, her mouth spread into a smile that showed her perfect white teeth.

Reaves had been right—she was coming on to him just like she came on to every man. He grabbed his handcuffs from his belt and slapped one on her wrist and grabbed her other wrist hard before she had a chance to react. Her mouth dropped open, but she didn't flinch or back away. A couple of the men got up and started forward.

"Back off," he said, taking out his gun and yanking her toward the door. "Mrs. Lottie Striker, you are under arrest for the murder of Zoë Brown. You have the right…" He finished reading her Miranda rights and got her other wrist secured in his cuffs.

A bear-like man said, "Lottie, what the hell is going on?"

"I'm sure it's all a mistake," Lottie said to the big man, and then to Galen said, "Do you know Detective Flanagan?"

"Of course I know her. She works for me."

"Where are you taking me?"

"I'll ask the questions."

"Is Strike around?" The big man asked.

"No," Lottie said, "and I don't want him to know about this. I know Detective Flanagan. She'll sort this out, whatever this is? Do me a favor: ask Lizzie if she'll lock up. The keys are on the peg in the kitchen."

"You sure you're going to be OK?"

"Don't you worry for one moment, I'll be fine."

"You sure you don't want Strike to know?"

"More than anything else, I don't want him to know. Tell Lizzie I'll call her from Minot and let her know what's going on. If she hasn't heard from me by morning, I want her to come searching."

Galen pulled her out the door and shoved her into the back seat of his car. Several townspeople had already congregated on the sidewalk, either because they'd seen his car racing up the street or because Miss Reaves had rung the town alarm. In either case, Galen figured, Mr. Striker and the whole town would soon know that the Indian whore had been arrested for murder.

Chapter 31

After trying for a half-hour, Flanagan finally reached Galen on his cellphone. "Where have you been?"

"Doing my job. Where have you been?"

The hair on the back of her neck bristled. "Have you set up interviews with the principal and vice principal?"

"I don't think we'll need to do any more interviews, Flanagan. I've solved the case."

"You know Galen, you're such an ass."

"Take a look out of your window."

Flanagan got up from her desk and looked out as Galen's car pulled up and stopped.

"Keep watching Flanagan."

"What the hell have you done?"

"I expect the chief will want to know why you overlooked the obvious."

Galen opened the back door, looked up one last time, and reached in and pulled his prisoner into view. Flanagan dropped the phone and took off running, down the stairs and out the front door, intercepting Galen and Shower Cloud before they mounted the first step.

She grabbed Shower Cloud's arm. "Are you OK?"

Shower Cloud smiled, but Flanagan saw her eyes flash distrust.

"Take those handcuffs off," Flanagan said to Galen.

"She is a murder suspect. The cuffs stay on."

"Listen you sawed off little excuse for a cop, do as I say and do it now."

Galen retreated a step, but made no move to take the cuffs off. Flanagan stepped behind Shower Cloud and unlocked them with her key. "I'm sorry about this," she said.

Galen took a step forward like he might try to stop her.

"Don't even think about it or I'll land you on your ass right here for all to see."

Galen glanced up. Grinning faces looked down from every window.

"It's OK," Shower Cloud said, rubbing the red marks on her wrists. "I probably would have done the same and since I was coming to see you anyway, he saved me the drive."

"Come inside while we get this sorted out. You too, Galen, and if you want to save face, take Mrs. Striker's other arm."

Galen hesitated, but, given the audience waiting for him to make a complete and utter fool of himself, had little choice.

As they entered the police station, Shower Cloud said, "According to Detective Galen, Miss Reaves said she saw me and another person, likely a man, go into Zoë's apartment on Saturday morning around four o'clock."

"She also identified her car," Galen said.

They proceeded to Flanagan's office on the second floor.

"I'm not doing this without the chief," Galen said. "I want him to hear every word."

Flanagan pointed to the phone. "Call him. We'll wait."

The chief wasn't in. Galen slammed the phone down.

"What about Carson?" Flanagan asked. "Is he an acceptable stand-in?" Galen despised Carson.

"Do I have a choice?"

"Not really."

Galen gave her a sidelong sneer and punched four numbers. When he hung up he said, "He's on his way."

Flanagan said, "I've got two chairs besides the one I use. Either get another chair or decide who between you and Carson is going to stand."

Galen glared and brought in another chair just as Carson arrived. Flanagan introduced Shower Cloud as Mrs. Striker, and had Galen relate the eyewitness account that led to her arrest. When he'd finished, Carson asked, "Were the ID's on the car and on Mrs. Striker hard?"

Galen checked his notes. "According to the eyewitness, one doesn't have to see the suspect's face because of her long black hair that hangs half-way down her back in braided circles with beaded strips woven in." Galen left out the part where Reaves said the suspect looked like a wild woman who should be dancing around a campfire. He also left out the part about Reaves's hatred of Indians dating back to her grandfather getting scalped.

Carson looked at Shower Cloud. She stood up and turned her back, giving him a first-hand image of what Galen was talking about. Carson nodded. Shower Cloud sat down. "Tell me," Carson said to Shower Cloud. "Do other Indian women wear their hair the same way?"

"Only a princess and not all tribes observe the same customs."

Carson's brow furrowed.

"My father is chief of the Apache Nation in West Texas."

Galen jumped up from his chair. "The eyewitness said the victim waved and the victim and the suspect were good friends."

"What about the car?" Carson asked Galen.

"The eye witness said there was only one like it in Largeville."

"It's true," Shower Cloud said.

Carson gave her a 'Whose side are you on?' look.

"It's a red Mustang. Mr. Striker gave it to me as a gift."

Carson glared at Galen.

Galen started to sweat and glanced around, first at Flanagan and then at Shower Cloud. He rubbed a hand across his forehead. "This isn't my fault. If Flanagan had been doing her job, she would have brought this suspect in the first day."

"No one's blaming you for anything," Carson said. "Just relax."

"Everyone knows you and Flanagan are friends, maybe more than that for all I know."

"Take it easy, Galen. You're stepping out of line."

"Yeah, well if Flanagan had been doing her fucking job, you wouldn't have sent me to help. Maybe you planned it all to get me. Well, here's a news flash, I'm not that easy to get." He pulled out his gun, grabbed Shower Cloud around the neck, and stuck the barrel to her head.

Flanagan reached for her gun.

"Go ahead, and you'll have squaw brains all over your desk." Galen started to back out.

"Put the gun down," Carson said. His voice remained calm.

"If you think I'm taking the fall because of this fucking Indian whore…" Tears came to his eyes. "I'm not, goddamn it. I know everyone laughs at me, well not any more."

He took another step back. Flanagan sat, ready to spring. Shower Cloud remained expressionless. Carson moved to the edge of his seat, his legs tensing.

Galen's heel brushed the doorway's saddle causing him to misstep and glance down. Shower Cloud shot her elbow into his stomach, whipped around and brought her knee up to his chin, and cracked her clasped hands down on the back of his neck. Galen's gun dropped and he toppled to the floor in a heap. Shower Cloud kicked his gun out of reach and stepped aside.

Flanagan cleared her desk in a single motion. Carson, a step ahead, put a knee on Galen's back and cuffed him. Several other officers appeared with guns drawn.

"It's over," Carson said, and ordered them to stand down. "Take him to a cell," he said to one of the young uniforms.

"Where did you learn that," Flanagan asked Shower Cloud.

"My father is a chief. I tried to be the son he wanted. I had to prove myself by fighting the young men in our tribe, and I learned how to win."

Chapter 32

Flanagan escorted Shower Cloud to the second floor waiting area and told her and the desk sergeant that she was to remain until Flanagan returned. When Flanagan rejoined Carson, who had finished reviewing the case notes, they decided that Shower Cloud would stay at Flanagan's place, but under police guard. One, she needed to be protected from Striker, and two, until what had happened Saturday morning outside Zoë's apartment could be explained, Shower Cloud remained a suspect.

"And," Carson said, "she was in Chicago when victim number two was murdered."

Flanagan nodded. Her mind and heart and soul said Shower Cloud was innocent. Logic said she had to be a prime suspect.

"What are your next steps?" Carson asked.

Flanagan bristled, but knew he wasn't questioning her handling of the case. "Striker and his kid have moved to the top of the list. There's only one small problem: we don't know where they are."

"Do we know if they're together?"

"Doubtful, but we don't know for sure."

Carson looked back at his computer screen. "What about the New York boyfriend?"

"I can't connect him to Largeville or Chicago, only to victim number one."

"Recap the others for me."

"The woman in Las Vegas, Edie Pitano, knew both victims but she has an iron-clad alibi. Striker and his son knew the victims, but we don't know if either was in Chicago. The parents of victim number two were in Chicago when their daughter, victim number two, was murdered, and it seems unlikely they had anything to do with victim number one's murder. Everyone else in Largeville knew the victims, but there is no reason to suspect anyone in particular."

"What about the poker players?"

"We'll have to rely on Joe and Claudine for a list of names, but it seems doubtful any one of them had an interest in Zoë."

"Who is Victoria Otto? How does she enter the picture?"

Flanagan wasn't about to say a spirit told her. "A teacher in Largeville who disappeared twelve years ago. Her name popped up in some of Zoë's papers."

"Are we looking at three murders?"

"We don't know that Victoria Otto was murdered. Her body has never been found."

He put the tips of his fingers together and studied Flanagan for a moment. "You'd better stick to the two we've got. In fact, let Chicago handle Sara Peterson. You've got enough on your plate with Hutton out of commission."

Flanagan nodded. She couldn't tell him that she had no intention of confining her activities to Zoë's murder, that Zoë Brown's spirit wouldn't let her.

"Who else is vulnerable?"

"You mean besides Mrs. Striker and Edie Pitano? No one unless we include Claudine Peterson, victim number two's mother, and she's only vulnerable if one of the poker players murdered Sara."

"So we have three suspects who might also end up being victims, and two suspects we can't find."

"Well, four if you add Smith and the person who tried to kill Hutton to the mix."

"Remind me about Smith again."

"Edie Pitano's boyfriend, the one Hutton decked."

"And his only connection to Largeville is through Edie Pitano?"

"As far as we know." Flanagan handed Carson three sheets of paper. "Las Vegas sent these mug shots of

Smith. I'd like to put them out so our people will know what they're looking for."

"I'll get Casey on it. How do you know it wasn't Smith who went after Hutton?"

Flanagan tried to recall what she'd said. "Did I say it wasn't?"

"You said 'Smith and the person who tried to kill Hutton.'"

"Slip of the tongue."

"Not likely," Carson said.

The way he looked at her, Flanagan figured he knew she'd been in Hutton's room.

"I assume you have more interviews since Galen didn't finish the job."

"The principal and vice principal. Whether they tell us anything that leads to someone else is anyone's guess at this point."

"I'm sorry Galen ended up being a disaster. Pick two people, and I'll make sure the chief makes them available. Send one to watch Mrs. Striker. The other can go with you to Largeville to finish up."

Carson's phone rang. He glanced at the caller ID and picked up. Flanagan could tell from the way he talked that it was Casey. His brow furrowed. He hung up and turned to Flanagan. "Did you interview a young man in Largeville by the name of Dale Kiley?"

She pictured Kiley in her mind. "We did. Why?"

"He hacked into our computer system."

"Not Kiley."

"That's the name she has. As near as Casey can figure, he's downloaded our files on the murder investigation and an inventory of our vehicles together with license plate numbers."

"It doesn't fit. The Striker kid, yes, but Kiley...I can't believe it."

She got up and walked toward the door. "I'm going to Largeville. Dooley and Quigley came in awhile ago.

I'll take them with me if you don't mind. Dooley and I will find the Kiley kid and Quigley can take the interviews with the principal and vice principal."

"What about Mrs. Striker?"

"Can you scrounge up someone to take her to my place?"

"Now you're pushing it, Flanagan, but I'll see what I can do."

She met Dooley and Quigley out front. Quigley took the SUV and went to the school. She and Dooley took the ghost car. They stopped next to the Volvo wagon beside the AMTRAK station, a barn-red building that consisted of a two story house at one end and a long one story attachment containing freight sheds and waiting room from the bygone era when trains stopped in Largeville. A short, plump woman, who appeared to be in her mid-fifties, busily swept the small back porch and wooden steps.

Flanagan and Dooley approached. She stopped sweeping and peered at them through her frameless glasses.

"I'm Detective Flanagan. This is my partner, Detective Dooley. We want to talk to Dale Kiley."

"What's he done?"

"Ma'am, we need to talk to him. Is he home?"

"No, he's out with his girlfriend. What's he done?"

"Ma'am, are you his mother?"

She nodded.

"Do you know where we can find him?"

"I think they went to the show in Minot. Sometimes they go up to Canada." She leaned her broom against the railing of the wooden steps and punched her hips with her fists. "What's he done?"

"What kind of car are they driving?"

"Jesus mother," a booming voice came from behind. "What have you done now?"

Flanagan and Dooley turned to face a tall man with slicked back, thinning gray hair. He wore gray coveralls and a blue baseball-style cap, both with AMTRAK logos printed in big red letters.

"They're looking for Dale."

"What's he done?" He walked forward several paces.

"I asked, but they won't tell me."

"Sir, is Dale Kiley your son?"

The man's face tinged red. "He's our son, and I think you'd better tell us why you want to see him, or I'll have to ask you to leave."

Dooley held up a piece of paper. "Sir, this is a search warrant. We need to go inside and take a look around. We believe your son hacked into the police computers and took some files."

Mr. Kiley snatched the warrant from Dooley's hand, and from one of his overall's many pockets fished a pair of glasses that got slapped on his nose. "Hmmm," he said, grabbing his chin.

"I knew all those computers would be nothing but trouble," Mrs. Kiley said. She grabbed her broom and began sweeping more vigorously than before. Flanagan and Dooley stepped back to avoid being smothered in a tornado of dust.

"When did you say he did this?" Mr. Kiley asked, still examining the warrant.

"Between one and three this afternoon," Flanagan said.

"Well, this gives you the right to search, but we can tell you he wasn't here. He and Karen Hedegaard— that's his girlfriend—left for Estavan up in Canada about nine this morning and won't be back until late this evening."

"Has anyone else used his computer?" Flanagan asked.

"The only one he ever lets anywhere near is Tommy Striker, and we haven't seen him around here for ages."

"Good thing if you ask me," Mrs. Kiley said.

"Why do you say that?" Flanagan asked.

"She doesn't like old Strike and his kid much," Mr. Kiley volunteered.

"Why is that?"

"Not our kind," Mrs. Kiley said, and thumped the broom down.

"Could anyone have used your son's computer without you knowing?"

"We've been here all day," Mrs. Kiley said. "No one's been here."

Mr. Kiley asked, "Is this something to do with that poor woman, the one who was murdered?" He handed the warrant back to Dooley.

"For the moment, we need to take a look at your son's computer. Detective Dooley wants to get some fingerprints, and I want to examine the hard drives and storage disks. Either directly or indirectly, your son's computer was used to get into our files."

Mr. Kiley led them upstairs to a closed door with a large sign that read: PARENTS AND OTHER EARTHLINGS NOT ALLOWED.

Mr. Kiley said, "He doesn't like anyone touching his music."

Flanagan opened the door. It led to a large room lined with rock music posters. A dozen speakers hung from the walls. Two keyboards and stacks of sheet music, some purchased, some that looked home produced, likely Dale Kiley's creations, sat on a long desk in front of a wall of computers and synthesizers and other musical paraphernalia."

"That's his main computer," Mr. Kiley said from the doorway. He pointed at a Power Mac G5. Flanagan pulled on a pair of gloves and flipped through the open web pages. All pertained to music, either downloads or chat rooms or suppliers.

Dooley dusted the keyboards for fingerprints. Flanagan checked the hard drives and vast collection of CD's for any trace of police files, but turned up nothing. Dooley was reasonably certain that only one set of fingers had touched the keyboards, the same set of fingers that had touched everything else in the room.

Flanagan thought for a moment, and then turned to Mr. Kiley and asked, "Did he set this up on his own?"

"Yes ma'am, he and Tommy Striker. Tommy's a computer genius, even more than Dale."

"Does Dale carry a cellphone?"

"His mother insists on it."

"What's the number?" Kiley told her from memory. She guessed that Mrs. Kiley wasn't the only one who insisted that Dale carry a cellphone. She punched in the numbers. Dale answered. She identified herself and asked where he was. As Mr. and Mrs. Kiley had said, he and Karen were in Canada.

"Dale, I need to know if Tommy used your computer between one and three this afternoon."

"Hello Dale," his father shouted.

"Is that my father? What's going on?"

"Someone hacked into our police computer."

"From my computer?"

"I'm afraid it looks that way."

Dale remained silent for a moment. Flanagan heard him breathing into the mouthpiece. She heard a young woman's voice ask, "What's wrong? Why do you look so angry?"

"It was Tommy," Dale finally said. "He's always going through other computers. Last month he hacked into some hospital computers through my computer."

"Did he get caught?"

"The FBI or someone like that knew it was him, but they couldn't prove anything. He didn't steal anything, no files or stuff; he'd just gone in and messed around so I guess they decided to let it drop."

"Do you know where he is?"

"Hang on a sec."

She heard muffled voices and then Dale said, "Karen says she saw him at his house this morning."

Flanagan told Dale to call the moment he returned to Largeville, and she and Dooley drove to Striker's house. They sat for a moment watching the windows for signs of life.

"Looks like no one's home," Dooley said.

Flanagan told Dooley to drive to the end of the block, turn around, and stop across the road. He pulled in behind a wreck of a car parked under two giant weeping willows in front of a quaint little house that needed paint, like most everything else in Largeville. A young woman holding a baby peered from a small window, but soon lost interest.

If Tommy was inside, they needed to get him away for an hour. She also couldn't tell Dooley that she didn't have a search warrant. Hutton might let her get away with fudging, but Dooley had a reputation for obeying all the rules. So did she, except by the time they got a warrant, it would be useless. She needed to check his computers now, not tomorrow, not even in five hours, the fastest she might be able to lay her hands on a warrant assuming everyone who had to sign off agreed, which was never a sure thing.

She called Dale Kiley's cell. He agreed to help.

"You trust him?" Dooley asked.

"We don't have a choice. If Tommy Striker figures we're on to him, he'll be gone."

"What about a warrant?"

She waved the Kiley warrant in his face and stuck it back in her bag before he had a chance to eye it too closely. He nodded. She pulled on a pair of latex gloves.

A long ten minutes later, Tommy came out with Zinc, his German shepherd. As soon as they'd disappeared around the corner, Flanagan grabbed her camera.

First, she checked the two-car garage at the back of the property. It was empty. She walked along the fence, through the wire gate, and up to the back porch. She glanced back at Dooley. He gave the all clear signal. She opened the door and stepped inside a large, modern kitchen all in white except for the black and white tiled floor. A neon fixture above the double-range provided the only light that didn't come through the windows. A clock ticked. The fridge motor came on. All else was quiet.

A large archway led from the kitchen to the living room. Other than that, the kitchen had three closed doors. The one on the left looked more like it led to the basement than the other two, which looked like closet doors. She turned the knob. The door opened. A musty smell greeted her nose. She stood for a moment, letting her eyes adjust to the semi-darkness, and then tiptoed down the steps, one hand on the rail and one hand on her pistol.

Halfway down, the wall opened into a large room. Several dozen green and red and orange dots peered back at her and she heard a symphony of whirring fans. She continued to the bottom of the stairs and stopped. He had twice the equipment of Dale Kiley: a wall of blinking modems; several monitors had lists of numbers continuously scrolling; one seemed to be capturing a CNN announcer's voice and playing it back.

A high-back, black leather chair sat in front of a large flat panel screen. She decided to start there and stepped over to the large desk that would have looked at home in some business executive's office.

As she reached for a stack of manila folders and papers on the near end of the desk, her phone vibrated. "Yes," she said around the large lump in her throat.

"The kid's coming back. Do you want me to stop him?"

"Has he seen you?"

"I don't think so."

"Let him continue, but if either he or I aren't out in five minutes, make some noise." She hung up, ran to the far side of the room, and pushed through a partially open door. It appeared to be his bedroom. She backtracked to the other side and found an opening leading to a back area that housed the furnace and hot water heater. Using her pen light, she found her way around behind the furnace and crouched down amid a tangle of spider webs, trying to control the shivers running up and down her spine. After her eyes adjusted, she noticed the stack of smashed computers piled against the back wall.

A door opened and slammed shut. "Stay," Tommy said. "I'll be right back."

The basement door opened. Zinc barked.

"STAY!"

Her heart thumped so loudly she was sure Tommy would hear. Zinc would smell her out in an instant.

"Good boy."

Tommy ran down the stairs. A desk drawer opened and closed. A lock clicked and something small and metal clinked on glass. He ran up the stairs. The basement door closed.

"Good boy. Come."

She sat for a moment listening to the silence until her skin began to crawl like a horde of spiders had started to march across her body. She shivered and hurried back into the open space of the computer room, brushing wildly at her neck and arms. Her phone vibrated. It was Dooley.

"He's gone. You OK?"

"Yeah, thanks."

She returned to Tommy's desk and took out her pick. It took less than a minute to open the locks. When she started to finger through the hanging files in the drawer on the lower right, she noticed several files sitting on the bottom. She pulled them out and spread them on the desk.

As she examined the contents, her heart began to race. Everything was there: the list of police vehicles, the names and addresses of all members of the police department, even the start of Zoë's computer file containing the information that had been uploaded from their laptops.

Flanagan's address had been highlighted in yellow and next to her name, in red ink, 'A delicious piece of ass!!! I'm going to drive my big cock so far into her that she screams for mercy. Maybe S will want a piece of the action. Maybe we'll have to flip a coin to see who has the fun. Maybe we'll both fuck her, fuck her to death, or maybe I'll tell him to go fuck himself. Why should he get any?' Underneath he'd drawn a large, dripping penis. 'Why should he have a taste of the virgin cop? She's mine, all mine, to lick and fuck her brains out.'

Hutton was right. The kid was a pervert. She wanted to grab him by his shoulders and shake him until...until what...until she dispelled her anger...until he stopped being a pervert? How would getting rid of her anger help Tommy? It wouldn't, and she suspected his sexual perversion was a whole lot more than peer to peer boasting, it was a deep-grained sickness on which batteries of psychiatrists would salivate to opine. Maybe they could help, probably not. Her blood boiled as she began snapping pictures of the files' contents.

She returned the files, relocked the desk, and called Dooley who gave the all clear. She went up the steps and was about to step into the kitchen when her neck began to tingle in the way that said Zoë's spirit wanted to communicate. She waited for the smell of orchids. Nothing. Zoë remained silent. She tried to step into the kitchen but her feet wouldn't move. Hands seemed to grip her head and force it to the right.

The tingling intensified. She watched in awe as her hands reached out and grabbed two aluminum baseball bats that stood along the wall next to a pair of skis and other sports equipment.

She stepped up into the kitchen. The tingling in her neck spread to her arms and legs. She examined the bats. One had a dark stain. Bats in hand, she returned to the car and told Dooley what she'd found.

Dooley glanced at the bats.

"Zoë was killed by a blow to the head." She pointed at the stain. "And that could be blood."

"I'll look after them. You'd better stay low in case the kid returns." Dooley pulled on a pair of latex gloves and stowed the bats in evidence bags that he then put in the trunk. Flanagan called Dale Kiley and asked him if he knew were Tommy Striker had gone.

Dooley got back in.

"The kid's at the pool hall," she said.

Chapter 33

Dooley drove along the main street. The pool hall sat on their left, next to Pete's Café. Flanagan spotted Shower Cloud's red car. Striker's SUV wasn't to be seen. Dooley slowed.

"Keep going." She didn't think the whole town needed to see them take Tommy into custody.

Dooley raised an eyebrow.

"He hasn't got anywhere to run that we can't catch him."

"I wasn't questioning your decision, Flanagan. What I want to know is where I should go."

"Sorry. I keep thinking…" I keep thinking Hutton is here.

"Yeah, I know."

"Next block. That little white building that says 'Town Hall.'"

He parked at the end of the row of cars. They got out and crossed the street. Flanagan unlocked the doors and led Dooley into the interview room, and then began to question her decision. "Maybe you'd better stand outside and keep your eye on the pool hall in case he decides to make a run for it."

Dooley stepped out to the sidewalk. Flanagan stood by the window. She called Tommy and asked him to come for another interview.

"Why do you want to see me again?"

She detected a nervousness that hadn't been present Saturday. "Don't worry, it's just procedure. We need to clarify some information."

"I don't know if I can come now."

"It won't take long. We can come and get you if you like."

He was silent for a moment and then said, "Uh, no, that's OK. I'm at the pool hall. I guess I can be there in a few minutes."

"That's great Tommy. Thank you."

She told Dooley that Tommy was on the way. While they waited, she called Carson to tell him that she and Dooley were about to interview the young man who'd hacked into the police computers.

"It wasn't Dale Kiley though," she said. "It was Tommy Striker. He accessed through Kiley computers."

"Good work, Flanagan."

"Is this Harry Carson?"

He chuckled.

"I'll call you after we've talked to him. What about Hutton?"

"According to his doc, he's making good progress, but it will be tomorrow at the earliest, probably Wednesday, before he's going to be able to communicate."

"And Smith?"

"If he's here, he's laying low."

Tommy's head passed the window. "Gotta go, Harry. Tommy Striker has arrived."

She heard Dooley ask him to step inside. Tommy and Zinc came in, followed by Dooley.

"Interesting," Dooley said. "Are you a student of Hitler?" Tommy's t-shirt had Mein Kampf' printed across the front.

"Do you even know what Mein Kampf means?" Tommy asked.

"My Struggle, if memory serves," Dooley replied.

Tommy glowered.

Boy did you pick the wrong one to screw with on social history, thought Flanagan. Dooley had a PhD in history and had written his thesis on the Soviet Experiment. He became a cop because he couldn't get a teaching job in North Dakota that paid enough to support a wife and three kids. Harvard beckoned, but he refused to move his wife away from her aging parents.

"What is your struggle, Tommy?" Dooley asked.

"I think of it more as a metaphor for life. Also, it pisses a lot of people off. May Zinc stay?"

"Sure, and have a seat." He started toward the chair where he'd sat on Saturday. "No, take that one today." Flanagan pointed him to the opposite end.

He looked at her and grinned. "I know that game," he said. "Change the chairs, confuse the sheep."

"No game, Tommy. Real life."

Tommy took the designated chair. Zinc lay at his feet and snorted.

"Thanks for coming in."

He nodded.

"We talked to your friend, Dale Kiley."

"You mentioned real world—Dale doesn't live in the real world. He makes stuff up."

"You mean his music?"

"I wouldn't call what he writes music. Crap is more like it, but no, that is not what I meant when I said he makes stuff up. He lies. Ask anyone in town. Dale Kiley is a master prevaricator."

"Did Miss Brown have good taste in music?"

"She was the only one in this shit hole of a town that did."

"According to her notes, she thought Dale's music had a lot of potential."

"She was just being kind. I know for a fact that she hated it worse than I. I pretend to like it because Dale's my friend, but she truly hated his work. She told me it made her sick."

Flanagan brought up her notes on her computer screen, certain that, from the files he'd hacked into and taken copies of, Tommy had studied every word that Dale Kiley had said.

"When did she tell you that Dale's music made her sick?"

"You know…we talked about a lot of things."

"What kind of things."

"About what she thought of Largeville, about the people here, her students, how she hated all of it."

"Why would she tell you that? Don't you think that unusual?"

He shrugged.

Flanagan decided to switch tactics. "Have you heard about Sara Peterson?"

"Yeah." He eyed her carefully.

"Did you ever hear of her having sex with Joe's poker buddies."

His head jerked up. "She didn't to that."

"How about with some of the men from Largeville?"

"She didn't have sex with anybody," he said.

"How do you know?"

"I just know."

"Why does the fact that she had sex with others upset you?"

"I'm not upset."

"Yes you are. You're voice is trembling and you look like you're about to cry."

He smashed his hands on the table and jumped up. Zinc sprang up and growled. "I am not," he screamed. "I don't give a shit if she fucked the whole goddamn country."

Dooley put his hand on his pistol.

"Did you have sex with her?" Flanagan asked.

"Yes, I mean no."

"What is it, yes or no?"

"No, I didn't have sex with her." He glared at her through his tears. His hands opened and closed into fists, and then he crumpled into his chair. Zinc looked at Dooley and Flanagan and resumed his position on the floor.

"Your friend Dale said you did."

"He didn't say that."

"How do you know?"

"What I meant is if he said that he's a liar."

Flanagan studied his face. Nothing, he had lied without conscience.

"Did you love Sara Peterson?"

"No, she was just a school friend."

"Did you fantasize about having sex with her?"

"No."

"What about the other girls at school?"

"What about them?"

"How many did you have sex with?"

"None."

"So you're a virgin?"

"No, I'm not a virgin. I've had sex with…"

"Who Tommy? Miss Brown? Did you have sex with
Miss Brown?"

Tommy stared down at the table, and then looked
back at Flanagan. "No, I didn't. If Dale told you that,
he's lying."

"Did you tell him you had sex with Miss Brown?"

"No, nothing like that. That's sick. She was our
teacher."

"How did the kids at school take the news of Miss
Brown's murder?"

"It was like a funeral. Most of the kids walked around
trying to look shocked or sad."

"Why trying? Weren't they?"

"Yeah, sure, I guess, but they haven't had experience
with acting shocked or sad."

"Have you had experience being shocked and sad?"

"I wanted to look as sad as I felt. I didn't want to appear indifferent; I didn't want to seem phony."

"Have you had experience being shocked and sad?"

"Not really."

"How did the students find out about Miss Brown?"

"Mr. Gregory called everyone into the gym. Some of
the parents were there."

"Did he tell them about Sara Peterson at the same
time?"

He nodded.

"Did you know Miss Brown was Jewish?"

"What are you talking about?"

"Miss Brown's real name is Brownstein. She's a Jew."

"I don't believe you."

"I went to her funeral in her synagogue in Chicago, and I met her parents. It is definitely true."

Tommy stared.

"Why does that upset you?"

"She doesn't…didn't look like a Jew."

"What do you think Jews look like?"

"Not like her that's for sure."

"Tommy, do you know where Lottie is?"

"I heard she'd been arrested."

"Do you know why?"

"Only that it had something to do with Miss Brown's murder."

"She's a suspect. Does that concern you?"

"Not really."

Flanagan noticed a flicker of uncertainty in his eyes. "If my mother were arrested as a murder suspect, I'd be concerned."

"She's not my mother."

"Do you hate her?"

"She's an Indian."

"Do you hate Indians?"

"No, I don't, but she isn't my mother."

"Would you hate her if she were a Jew?"

"I don't hate Jews."

"Why doesn't Lottie's arrest concern you?"

"I was afraid she might be involved."

"How so?"

"I saw her leave the house on Saturday morning."

"Why didn't you tell us that before?"

"I think I must have been in shock or something, I mean, after discovering Miss Brown's body, I wasn't thinking straight. I planned to tell you, but then I heard that she'd been arrested so I didn't think it mattered."

"Where did you go on Saturday?"

"What do you mean?"

"You left town and didn't get back until last night."

"Did Lottie tell you that?"

Flanagan didn't respond.

"I was in the basement the whole time working with my computers. You can check my ISP's. They must have some sort of record of all the web pages I visited and the times."

"Where is your father?"

"He doesn't tell me where he goes and when he's coming back."

"Have you seen him since Saturday?"

"No."

"Have you talked to him since Saturday?"

"No. We don't stay in touch."

"Where is your mother?"

"What do you mean?"

"Your real mother, where is she?"

"She's dead."

"Is that true?"

"You seem shocked," Tommy said.

"If it's true, I'm truly sorry."

"She's in a hospital in Texas."

"Do you think it funny telling people your mother is dead?"

"Hey, I didn't mean anything by it. She's in an insane asylum so as far as I'm concerned, it's easier to say she's dead."

"Does it embarrass you?"

"No one wants the world to know that one of their parents is nuts."

"Have you ever visited?"

"Once, just after she was committed. My dad took me."

"Do you write or phone or e-mail?"

"I don't really remember her. My dad says she doesn't know who we are."

"So you have no contact?"

He nodded. Zinc got up and stretched. "Down," he commanded. Zinc dropped like he'd been shot.

"You've got him well trained," Dooley said.

Tommy looked down his nose at Dooley. "It's a master servant relationship. They prefer it that way."

"Tommy, do you know Victoria Otto?"

"I don't think so. Who is she?"

"She's a teacher who disappeared from Largeville twelve years ago."

"That's when we moved here, the year I started in grade one. My teacher that year was Miss Bartlett, but I didn't know a Miss Otto; I didn't know any of the other teachers except Mrs. Wilson. She lived across the street from our house."

"Did you ever hear anyone speak of Victoria Otto?"

He shook his head.

"Tommy, did you know that Miss Brown sent money to Sara?"

He looked as though he didn't know what she was talking about.

She repeated the question.

He shook his head. She could see his mind working.

"Were they lovers?"

He made a choking sound. "That's sick. There's no way."

"How do you know?"

"They weren't lesbians. They went out with men."

"Maybe they're bisexual."

"They weren't. I just know. We have a couple of lesbians at our school, always kissing and licking each other, rubbing their hands on each others breasts, daring anyone to say something. Miss Brown and Sara weren't anything like that."

"Because you had sex with them?"

"No, I already told you…"

She waited to see if he had more to say, and then said, "Tommy, I'd like to read you something if you don't mind." She attached her camera to her computer and opened the pictures she'd taken of his files.

He shrugged, though his eyes betrayed concern and wanted to see her computer screen.

"'A delicious piece of ass!!! I'm going to drive my big cock so far into her that she screams for mercy. Maybe S will want a piece of the action. Maybe we'll have to flip a coin to see who has the fun. Maybe we'll both fuck her, fuck her to death, or maybe I'll tell him to go fuck himself. Why should he get any?'"

Tommy looked like he'd been slapped. Dooley blanched.

"Do you want me to read more?"

His mouth hung open. Hate dripped from his eyes.

She raised her voice. "You wrote that, didn't you?"

"You tricked me and I'm not saying another word without my lawyer."

"You have a lawyer, Tommy?"

"My father told me not to talk to you again without a lawyer."

"I thought you said that you hadn't seen your father, that you didn't talk."

He glared.

"Who is the S that you mention in your note?"

He stayed silent.

"The S in your notes, Tommy. Who is S?"

"I told you—"

"Tell me," she screamed, and banged her fist on the table. "You think I'm playing a game here. You think you're going to walk out of here and go back to your basement full of computers. Well think again. You're going to jail, Tommy. Do you know what kind of people you'll meet in jail? You talk about fucking me. When you get to jail, Tommy, you'll find out about fucking. You'll find out because you're going to have pus dripping penises shoved up your ass ten times a day."

He jumped up and headed for the door. She grabbed his arm and crashed him against the wall. Zinc, hackles raised and teeth bared, took a snarling step forward.

Dooley jumped up from his chair, pistol in hand. "Tell him to sit, or I'll shoot him where he stands," he yelled.

"STAY!" Tommy shouted, his large eyes fixed on Dooley's pistol. "STAY!"

Zinc stopped in his tracks.

"SIT!"

Zinc sat.

"What about the baseball bats we found in your house, Tommy? Is that what you used to kill Miss Brown?"

"You're crazy if you think I killed Miss Brown."

"We got the bat, the one with blood on it. Is that what you used to bash her head in?"

"I told you I didn't kill Miss Brown."

She spun him around and slapped him in cuffs. He started to cry and pissed his pants.

She read him his rights.

He looked down at his wet crotch and pant leg. She pushed him toward the door.

"You'd better contact that lawyer your father mentioned."

"I don't know his name."

"The court will appoint one. Meanwhile, I recommend you get hold of your father."

"I don't want him to know."

"He'll find out sooner or later. Better from you."

"I'm eighteen. He can't tell me what to do."

"Discuss it with your lawyer."

"I don't want to see that son-of-a-bitch ever again." Fresh tears came to his eyes. "It's his fault my mother left."

She glanced out at the empty street. "If you walk normally, you won't attract a lot of attention."

"What about Zinc?"

"We've got a dog cage in the SUV. We'll put him in the police kennel for now."

"He won't get into the cage unless I tell him."

Flanagan nodded at Dooley. He called Quigley at the school and told him to bring the SUV to the curb in front of the town hall. When Quigley arrived, they escorted Tommy and Zinc out. On Tommy's command, Zinc went into the dog cage in the cargo area. Dooley closed the door and snapped the lock. Flanagan took Tommy to the back seat and cuffed him hand and foot to the restraint rings.

Quigley hadn't finished with Gregory and Perini, but told Flanagan not to expect any revelations. She asked him to post his notes to the computer. He took the ghost car and returned to the school. Dooley and Flanagan took the SUV and Tommy and Zinc back to Minot. Along the way she called Carson to give him an update.

"I need to see you as soon as you get back."

"Sounds serious." Her heart missed a beat. "Is Hutton OK?"

"Yeah, he's OK. It's just that we've got some trouble with Mrs. Striker."

Chapter 34

Back in Minot, Flanagan left Dooley in charge of Tommy Striker and Zinc and headed for her office. Carson was already there, eyes and slacks equally baggy, looking like someone who had something to say but wasn't sure where to start. She pointed at a chair. He opted to remain standing.

"What's wrong with Mrs. Striker?" she asked.

"McManus gave me this a half-hour ago."

He laid a phone record on her desk. She bent over to take a closer look. It was Lottie Striker's cellphone record for the past five days and showed that she'd made a call to Zoë's number at 3:55 on Saturday morning.

Flanagan straightened up to her five-foot nine and looked Carson in the eye. "Harry, I've arrested the kid for Miss Brown's murder. Lottie Striker had nothing to do with it. If you've ever trusted even one iota of my instincts, trust me on this."

"You know I want to, but the chief is on a rampage because of Galen and he's not happy that you had Pete Peterson sitting in a cell like this is some Motel 6."

"What did Lottie Striker say?"

"That's part of the problem—she won't talk to anyone except you."

"I'll talk to her, but it's nothing, or else the kid used her phone. As far as Peterson is concerned, he was homeless."

"Did the kid confess?"

"Nothing's that easy."

Carson gave her a sidelong look.

"Go to bat for me on this, Harry. I won't let you down."

"I'm not worried about me. He'll chew my ass out, but if you're wrong he'll put you back on foot patrol as quick as the flick of a cow's tail; that's if you're lucky; if you're unlucky, you'll be under the cow's tail."

"I've been there before."

"Not like this. A lot of people want you to fail."

"Because I'm a woman."

"Yeah, partly, and partly because they know you're better than them and partly because you're the most junior detective on the force—a lot of guys who've been around a lot longer have never led a case."

"They'll get over it, and between you and me, I'm not going to fail."

"You've got my vote. Let me know if I can help."

"Well, I didn't have a warrant when I took the photos of the kid's files and his baseball bats."

"Jesus Christ Flanagan, it never stops. Does Dooley know?"

"Just you and me."

"You don't make it easy."

"Harry, you look like shit. Go home and get some rest."

"We're still trying to find the kid's old man. We haven't found his SUV, and he didn't take a flight, at least not from here under his own name. We're checking other airports."

"His disappearance is more of a curiosity now that we've got the kid in custody."

"Don't ever leave any loose ends hanging out there Flanagan. They'll come back and bite you in the butt."

"Who've you got on it?"

"Casey."

"I'll keep in touch with her. If anything pops up, I'll call you, now go home."

"Why do I doubt that?"

"Go home. I promise I'll call."

After Carson left, Flanagan checked with Casey. Nothing had changed on Striker; and Smith hadn't been found. Flanagan gave her Victoria Otto's name to add to her list of people to find.

"Harry gave me her name this morning. So far, zip."

Flanagan smiled. Count on Harry to keep all the bases covered. "Call me at home if you come up with anything."

Fifteen minutes later, Flanagan pulled into her driveway. Stepping from her car, she glanced at Lenny Ebert, the undercover officer parked across the street. He saw her but didn't let on.

The television blared and she hoped the fried chicken smells wafting in the air emanated from her kitchen. The last time she'd had a decent home-cooked meal was when she'd made detective and Harry's wife cooked a celebratory dinner.

The front door was unlocked. Shower Cloud needed to be told that this was Minot, not Largeville. She stepped into the foyer, unbuckled and kicked off her two-inch heels, and walked down the hallway toward the kitchen, the hardwood pleasantly cool on her feet. "I smelled your cooking from the driveway."

She poked her head into the kitchen. "Shower Cloud?" A covered frying pan and large cooking pot sat on the stove. The burner under the frying pan had been turned off; the pot sat on a mere flicker of flame. She looked inside the pot, breathed in the aroma of golden corn on the cob slowly rotating in the water, and replaced the lid. She looked through the window on the oven door. Foil wrapping with symmetrical fork punctures encased what she assumed to be giant Idaho potatoes. She knew the frying pan contained fried chicken, but she looked anyway, unprepared for the crisp firebrick brown and rich bouquet of spices that made her mouth pucker.

She went into the hallway. "Shower Cloud?" Flanagan felt her stomach tighten and started for the bedrooms. Shower Cloud wasn't there. Flanagan ran back to the kitchen. That's when she saw the note sitting on top of the kitchen table.

"Hello Kate, I'm not running away, but there is something I have to do for Zoë. Please don't try to find me because you already have enough to worry about, and I am expert on disappearing."

She dropped the note and raced out the front door. Lenny's vehicle hadn't moved. Take it easy, Flanagan, she told herself. Don't go pushing a bunch of alarm buttons. Shower Cloud was probably right—they wouldn't find her anyway and she didn't need the chief and Carson on her case any more than they already were. She took in a deep breath and walked across the street.

"I'm going to be here for the night," she said through his open window. "I'll call if I have to leave."

Lenny didn't need to hear the offer twice. As soon as he'd disappeared, Flanagan ran back inside, turned off the stove, and grabbed the phone. She called Shower Cloud's cell, the same one that McManus said had called Zoë at 3:55 on Saturday morning.

Shower Cloud answered on the third ring. "I hope you're not angry with me," she said.

"Angry doesn't begin to cover it—not having you arrested as our principal suspect is becoming extremely difficult."

"I guess you should have locked me up."

"I'm not saying that, but we've discovered that a call was made from your cell to Zoë at 3:55 on Saturday morning. Add that to the eyewitness, declaring your innocence has gone beyond trust and instinct. My bosses, as they are kicking me off the police force, will say it defies logic."

"I saw you send the police officer away so I know you haven't reported me missing and I promise I'll be back before anyone except you knows that I've gone."

"I don't know what you think you're doing and maybe I wouldn't understand if you told me, but I do know I don't want you doing it alone."

Shower Cloud hesitated.

"Please, let me come with you, let me help you."

"Not tonight. There are one or two things I have to check."

"Tommy's been arrested. I've charged him with Zoë's murder."

Shower Cloud remained silent.

"I can't give you details, but we found enough evidence to hold him."

"Tommy is a dangerously troubled boy."

"Enough to kill?"

"Yes, but I don't believe he killed Zoë."

"What about Sara Peterson?"

"I thought she was murdered in Chicago."

"Tommy may have left Largeville on Saturday and returned on Sunday night. He denies that, saying he was in the basement on his computers the whole time."

"I don't know."

"In some explicit sex notes we found on Tommy's computer, notes that Tommy wrote, he referred to someone as 'S.' Who do you think that is?"

"Tommy has a vivid imagination. He may have made it up."

"Shower Cloud, it's vitally important that we talk. I think you know more than you're telling and I'm afraid you are putting yourself in danger."

"I'll call you tomorrow morning, and because the location of this phone can be traced, I'm dropping it into the nearest garbage can as soon as I hang up. Goodbye Kate. Please believe in me." Click.

Flanagan stared at the phone in stunned silence, but what she wanted was to scream and race around the room and hit someone. She dropped the receiver onto its base, noisily threw Shower Cloud's dinner into containers in the fridge and the pots and pans into the sink, and left for the police station. If she didn't get busy trying to find the missing pieces, or put the ones she had in an order that made sense, she'd go nuts.

Chapter 35

Flanagan told Casey she'd returned to her office and started reviewing her computer files and notes. She unlocked the double doors concealing the project board, erased the remnants of a previous case, and attached a three column grid with rows that moved up and down. Using a felt-tip pen, she listed all the names down the left-hand column that she knew or suspected, no matter how remotely, were either connected or could be connected to Zoë's murder. Then she did the same down the right-hand column for Sara. After she'd done that, she wrote the connection in the center column.

So what's missing? She went back to her computer and notes and then went back to her grid and added Victoria Otto's name at the bottom in Zoë's column and Ronnie Striker's name to the center column in a new row that she inserted under Newton Striker's name since she couldn't attach her to anyone except Newton and Tommy Striker.

"What's going down?"

She spun around. Harry Carson filled her doorway. "Jesus, don't do that. You scared the crap out of me." She glanced at her watch. "I thought I sent you home two hours ago."

"I couldn't take the pace, so I came back. Besides, McManus called. She may have something on the red Dodge."

They strode down the hall and caught the elevator to the lab on the floor above. McManus was at her desk, which was actually about ten desks shoved together in a big circle, each with two or three computers. She also had a thirty-six inch screen mounted on the wall that she used for group sessions or showing nude men, the latter her way of getting even for all the sexist comments, she said. McManus stood about five feet and weighed about ninety pounds, but she had the cockiness of a bantam rooster and the tenacity of a pit bull, and she loved dishing it out as much as she loved research.

She stood up when they entered, and then sat back down when she saw who it was.

"Were you expecting the governor?" Carson asked.

"I don't stand for the governor either, but I ordered two male strippers for dinner. I thought you might be them."

"Just two?"

"On a diet. You want the Dodge guy?"

Carson nodded, but McManus had already turned to a screen full of data. "Look at screen seven," she said, pointing to a screen whose case had '7' written on the top and sides in bold black strokes. Flanagan turned the screen around so it faced them.

The name of Lee Scranton headed the information.

"He told me his name was Art Logan."

Following the name was 1900 71st Avenue NE, Bismarck, ND, Born: October 25th, 1945; Height: 5'10"; Weight: 185; Hair: black; Eyes: black/brown; Sex: male; Race: Native American; Skin Color: brown; Scars: gall bladder, interior right leg knee to ankle from metal plate attached to shattered tibia in 1972 motor cycle accident; Tattoos: heart and two intertwined snakes on right bicep, skull and bones shield on left bicep, dagger on penis.

"Well I didn't see his penis, but that's the guy," Flanagan said. "Who puts a dagger on his penis?"

"Lots of guys and it's a good thing Ashcroft still isn't Attorney General, or I'd have to withhold that kind of information," McManus said.

Flanagan said, "McManus, you are one sick puppy. Is Joe Peterson still our guest?"

"He checked out this afternoon. Some tall blonde with legs to die for in a short green suit that even got me horny sprung him at 1:35."

"That would be Emily Gray from Winslett Ashburn," Flanagan said.

"That would be her," McManus said.

"I know Jeff Haynes over in Bismarck," Carson said to Flanagan. "I'll give him a call if you like. He might be able to find Lee Scranton or Art Logan or whatever name he's using now."

"Lieutenant Haynes?" McManus asked.

"You know him?"

"Let me see: six foot two, looks like a Greek god, nope, never heard of him."

"I hope he's not one of the Chippendale guys you're always flashing on the big screen," Flanagan said.

"The real ones I keep in a private file."

"Let's call him," Flanagan said to Carson. "Scranton and a bunch of his card playing buddies might have used Sara Peterson as their private sex toy before she was eighteen."

Flanagan and Carson were striding down the hall back to Flanagan's office when Casey Long came trotting up behind. "Before you run too far," she panted, "I just got a hit on the Striker SUV."

"Where?" Flanagan and Carson asked.

"Winnipeg International Airport. Here, the Mounties sent this."

Flanagan studied the print-out. "It says here he didn't take a scheduled flight within the past week so what's he doing parked at the airport?"

"What about rental cars?" Carson asked.

"Nothing, no rental car, he's not in the hotels, no train tickets, no bus tickets. They're checking the airport video tapes to see if they can spot him coming into the parking lot and will call me as soon as they know one way or the other."

Flanagan returned to her office to review her notes on Newton Striker. Nothing sat right with him. After a few moments she called Casey and asked her to confirm his employment with Tex-Cal and to find out who else he'd worked for.

"How far back?"

"Nothing before his date of birth."

Chapter 36

It was nearing midnight when Flanagan left her office. The streets of Minot had long since emptied of people. A few cars whizzed by, most speeding. Out of habit, she glanced at the license plates. All were locally registered. She had never figured out a Minot resident's need to rush from one point of nothing to another point of nothing, but they all did.

The streetlights' orange glow produced a host of ghostly shadows, some growing shorter and others growing longer, as she walked along the sidewalk leading to the parking lot. She passed a long-vacant lot the size of a city block left by the hotel developer who purchased the property and razed the old tenements before running out of money. The head-high weeds that grew around the perimeter gave off a powerful odor that made her think of the sloughs around the farm where she'd grown up, the ones where she'd ride her horse and while he grazed, she would lie in the long grass upwind from the stagnant water and watch the clouds drift across the giant sky.

The signs spaced every twenty-five feet along the chain-link fence read 'KEEP OUT.' None of the locals were crazy enough to climb the fence, but drifters often did and she didn't want to make an easy grab target. She felt for her pistol and moved to the road.

At the next corner she crossed to the well-lighted lot where, during the day, over two-hundred cars parked. Now there were fewer than ten. She had parked well apart from the others, something she tried to do whenever she worked late, so no one could lurk around her car without being seen.

Thirty feet from the car she dug her keys from her handbag and clicked the remote. The horn sounded, and the interior lights and headlights came on. That was normal. What wasn't normal was the large manila envelope stuck under the windshield wiper. She thought only of Shower Cloud, and her footsteps and heart speeded to a rapid pace.

Pulling on a pair of latex gloves, she opened the envelope by slicing the blade of her pocket knife under the flap. Inside was a single sheet of paper on which a map had been drawn. She held it to her nose and smelled Shower Cloud's perfume. Though not really expecting to see her, still she glanced around at the other cars.

She fished a penlight from her console and studied the map from every angle, looking for a clue that would trigger a thought process, something that would place the sketched area into a familiar location. Nothing clicked. She phoned Casey, hoping she hadn't gone home.

When Casey answered, Flanagan said, "I'm sitting in my car looking at a hand drawn map that I can't figure out. Are you going to be there for a few more minutes?"

"Penner hasn't gotten the ax murder out of his system yet so I told him I'd buy him a couple of beers. In his present state, I'm probably not going to get him into the sack so why don't you join us?"

"Where?"

"TJ's, where else?"

"I'll see you there in five minutes." TJ's was one of the cop hangouts, had been for fifty years.

When Flanagan arrived, Casey and Dirk Penner were seated at a table along the far wall. They weren't hard to spot since they were the only ones there. Casey, who had changed into a white t-shirt and blue jeans, waved when Flanagan came in. Penner turned his head and smiled when he saw it was her.

"You sure I'm not interrupting anything," she said, walking up to the table.

"I'm glad you're here," Penner said, his black eyes shining. He had on a multi-colored checkered shirt open at the neck and jeans. Flanagan didn't check, but she knew he'd be wearing cowboy boots.

"Ditto," Casey said. "Get you a beer?"

Flanagan nodded and Casey hollered at Dewey, the bartender, to bring another round.

"One's my limit," Penner said.

"Bullshit," Casey said. "Tonight you don't have a limit."

"I heard about your case," Flanagan said to Penner. "Sorry your first one had to be all blood and brains, but none of them are pretty."

"The violence is what got to me," Penner said.

"Some car wrecks are violent. Try to think of it as a car wreck."

Penner nodded and the look in his eyes intensified.

"Let's see your map," Casey said, sliding a fresh beer across the table toward Flanagan.

"Where's mine? Penner asked.

"I don't want to force it on you."

"Just give me the damn beer."

"Are you going to look at my map?" Flanagan took a sip from the frosted mug, letting the aroma of the ice-cold beer work its way up her nose and the bubbles tickle her face.

"It looks like a trail map," Casey said, carefully placing the sheet of paper on the table a safe distance from the beer.

"What's the writing?" Penner asked, peering at the, to him, upside-down map.

"Some kind of shorthand," Casey said.

"That section in the middle could be water, maybe a lake," Penner said, and pointed at the Rorschach-like drawing, "and that could be a river."

"That's my guess," Casey said.

"The question is: What lake? What river?" Flanagan asked.

"Penner," Casey said, "you're the fisherman. What do you think?"

"If it's in North Dakota, it could be any one of a dozen lakes and half-a-dozen rivers, but there's only one river that I know of that runs through a piece of water that size."

"The Missouri?" Casey asked, her eyebrows raised.

"Yes, and if it's the Missouri, the water has to be Lake Sakakawea."

Casey turned the map to give him a better look. After studying it for a moment, he became more animated and said, "The 'X' might be the dam. And this line coming down from the top might be Route 83. It is, I'm certain of it, and this is Route 200." He pointed to a line running horizontal to his Route 83 line.

"What are the hieroglyphics?" Casey asked.

Penner shook his head and tugged at his chin.

"They might be Athapascan," Flanagan said.

Penner and Casey looked at her.

"The person who left this is Athapascan."

Casey grabbed the map from Penner and squinted at the tiny lettering on the right-hand side. "Either of you have a penlight?"

Penner dug a Swiss Army knife from his pocket and handed it to Casey. She clicked a button and a spot of light hit the map. "Any chance of a magnifying glass," she said as she focused on the writing.

Both Flanagan and Penner shook their heads.

Casey looked across at the bar. "Dewey's part Indian and speaks a little Cree. Mind if he takes a look?"

Flanagan wasn't sure she wanted an outsider seeing something that might contain information that should be known only to the police, but also feared that time might be a factor and she didn't want to wait until morning.

"He's practically one of us," Casey said.

Flanagan raised an eyebrow.

"I use him as a translator when we get a bunch of drunks or prostitutes who can't or won't speak English. He knows to keep his mouth shut."

"Go for it," Flanagan said.

"Hey Dewey," Casey shouted. "Put a 'Closed' sign on the door and get you butt over here. We need to pick your brain."

Dewey broke into a toothy grin. He flicked a few switches and turned the sign on the door around so that 'CLOSED' faced out.

"This is Detective Flanagan and this is Detective Penner," Casey said when Dewey got to the table. "Sit here next to me."

Flanagan and Penner nodded. They didn't shake hands. Dewey sat as instructed, his eyes on Flanagan and Penner.

"Relax," Casey said. "They aren't going to run you in for selling booze to minors and letting the ladies of the night sit at your bar after the cops go home."

Dewey's face snapped in Casey's direction, his mouth open.

"What, you thought I didn't know? Listen, this isn't about any of that, we want you to take a look at this map and tell us what it says."

Dewey's shoulders relaxed.

"And like everything else we do," Casey said, "this is between you and us. You understand?"

"Yes, of course," he said, and then nodded at Flanagan and Penner as if for good measure.

Dewey had the shiny black hair, dark brown eyes, and broad face of an Indian. Flanagan guessed he weighed two-hundred pounds and not much of it fat. His blue jeans looked as though they'd been bought for a smaller body and his cowboy boots with their intricate tooling looked custom made. The red cowboy shirt he wore opened at the neck revealed several gold chains. A gold Rolex was strapped to his powerful looking left wrist and a gold chain encircled his equally powerful looking right wrist. He wore a large ruby ring on the ring finger of his right hand. Flanagan wondered where he got his money. It wasn't from bartending and it wasn't from cop tips.

"We're trying to figure out what that is," Casey said, moving the map closer to Dewey, but with her fingers maintaining their firm grip. She shone Penner's light on the writing.

Dewey leaned forward until his nose practically touched the map. After a moment, he said, "It appears to be directions."

"Can you tell us what it says?" Flanagan asked, taking out her notepad and pen.

"I think so," Dewey said, continuing to study the letters and numbers. Flanagan appreciated that he hadn't tried to look at the rest of the map. "It's not written in Cree, but it looks familiar."

"It may be Athapascan," Flanagan said. "If that makes a difference."

Dewey nodded. "This line is the road behind the Garrison Dam." He pointed to a line on the map next to ten small circles. "And these circles are surge tanks."

"So it is Sakakawea," Penner said.

Yes, and these are the banks of the Missouri river." Dewey pointed at a wandering set of parallel lines. "Here, west of the turbine house, is a twenty-foot embankment with a lot of trees on top. It says to go to the point on the embankment where the southwest corner of the turbine house lines up with the west side of the second surge tank. There you will find a stone marker. From the stone marker, walk thirty paces due west and ten paces due south."

*　　*　　*

Flanagan felt a cool breeze on her face, a cool breeze that smelled of orchids.

She's showing you where Victoria Otto is buried. She's at the dam at Sakakawea. I'm certain of it. That's why I had such a powerful vision of her when I took my class to Sakakawea the day before I was murdered.

She told me she'd never heard of Victoria Otto.

*   *   *

"Why do I get the feeling you're going there tonight," Penner said.

"Is there anything more?" Casey asked Dewey.

Dewey shook his head. Flanagan thanked him. Casey pulled the map away and handed it to Flanagan. Flanagan checked her notes and looked at Penner. "You want to come?"

"Wouldn't miss it," Penner said.

"I'll let everyone know you'll be late tomorrow," Casey said, "but you ought to call Harry first to let him know what's going down."

"Let's let him sleep for a couple of hours until we see if there's anything to call him about. He looked bone weary tonight."

"He doesn't worry well. I think your partner getting clobbered put him over the edge."

"Hutton's due to wake up tomorrow"—she checked her watch—"better make that later today. If I'm not back, call me as soon as he's talking."

"I expect he'll call you before he talks to anyone," Casey said.

Flanagan thought she heard something in Casey's voice and gave her an extra look. Casey ignored the unspoken question.

"We can drop you," Flanagan said as they got up and started for the door.

"I go north, you're going south. I'll take a cab. Hey Dewey, thanks for your help and remember, your lips are sealed."

Spot Flash

Dewey was busy cleaning their beer mugs and wiping their table. He looked up and said not to worry, that he was glad he'd been able to help.

Flanagan and Penner stopped at the precinct and, after checking to make sure it had lights with working batteries, a compass, shovels, and a host of other digging tools, took the SUV that she and Hutton usually used. They got to the embankment at three a.m.

The stone marker was easy to find. Shower Cloud had made certain of that. Using the compass, they located due west and Flanagan counted off thirty paces. "Now ten paces due south," she said, her voice a whisper. Her spine hadn't stopped tingling since they'd found the stone marker and she didn't expect it would stop for some time. She felt Zoë everywhere; close enough to touch, to smell, to feel her breath.

"...eight, nine ten," she finished counting and stopped. The light of the twelve-volt spot cut through the underbrush as though it weren't there and ricocheted off tree trunks, casting a million darting shadows. "There, what's that?"

Penner focused the light where Flanagan pointed. All she saw was a growth of wild prairie rose bushes lush with bright pink flowers. Penner moved the light. "There," she said. A cross made from two tree limbs stuck from the ground.

Flanagan recognized the beaded strips that held the cross together, the same beaded strips that Shower Cloud wore in her hair. An envelope was tied to one of the strips. She removed it and read the note inside: 'Kate, I knew you'd find her. I love you, Shower Cloud.' She handed the note to Penner.

"Strange that she wrote this in English but not the directions."

"I think she was being careful. She didn't want anyone else to figure out what she'd done—I think she knew I'd figure it out."

"She never heard of phones?"

"For the moment, she has good reason to not trust them."

"I'll get the shovels," Penner said, and started toward the SUV.

Flanagan called Harry Carson to let him know what they'd found and asked if he wanted to be in on the dig.

"Is it fresh?"

"No. My guess: I think this is where she was buried twelve years ago."

"How did you find her?"

Flanagan hesitated. "Lottie Striker."

"Is she with you?"

"Yes," she said. She hated to lie to him, but she didn't have time to walk him through every step since Shower Cloud had disappeared.

"She's too close to this," he said. "Don't let her out of your sight or we'll both be looking for new jobs."

Her face grew hot. "I won't," she said.

"I want you to call me as soon as you get back, and if you find anything other than a body, call me immediately. If I need to start creating a story for the chief, I want all the lead time I can get."

She ended the call and Penner arrived with the digging instruments, bagging paraphernalia, and camera.

After she'd taken several pictures, she poked at the soft ground with her shovel. "I'd be surprised if the animals haven't dug her up."

"Too close to the dam, too many people around," Penner said with authority. "The big animals disappeared a couple of decades ago. The only animals left are squirrels, skunks, and badger. Besides, she may be down a ways."

They started digging.

Penner shuddered.

"You sure you're up to this?"

"It's just another car crash, right?"

"Right."

They found her four feet down, wrapped in a heavy-duty plastic tree bag that had partially decomposed. Before cutting the remainder of the bag away, Flanagan took several more pictures from different angles.

"No dress," she said as they began to peel away the plastic, "which means it has either decomposed or she wasn't wearing one. Must be nylon panties—they would have lasted another twenty years, same for the bra."

"Want me to do that?" Penner said, reaching for the camera.

Flanagan nodded. She figured he'd be better taking pictures than getting too close to what was left of Victoria Otto.

Penner pointed to the watch and rings. "It doesn't appear that robbery was the motive."

Flanagan shook her head, wondering how Victoria Otto and Zoë Brown and Sara Peterson were connected, other than all having lived in Largeville. Maybe that was the only connection.

After they'd packed everything in bags that they stowed in the SUV, they sifted through the grave to make sure they hadn't missed even the tiniest shred, Flanagan took several pictures of the empty grave, and they filled in the hole. Penner started back to the SUV with the shovels.

"I'm going to look around," she said. "I won't be but a few minutes."

"I'll get a GPS reading if you want." Using their new GPS receivers combined with the stationary receivers the state had installed, he could pinpoint the location of Victoria Otto's grave to within an inch.

"Good idea," she said.

After fifteen minutes, Flanagan returned to the SUV empty handed. She hadn't really expected to find anything, but didn't want someone from the department start poking around and finding an important piece of evidence that she and Penner had missed, like a baseball bat with hair, blood, and bone fragments.

They got back to Minot at 7:15 and rang the bell on the ambulance entrance to the ME's morgue. One of Stan Jackson's new young associates answered and relieved them of Victoria Otto's remains. "Tell Stan that I'd like a full report by nine," Flanagan said.

Shock registered on the associates face. "I don't think..."

"Relax, I'm kidding. Tell him that either Harry Carson or I will call later this morning with particulars." She turned to Penner. "I'm going to hang out until Stan and Harry get in, maybe grab a few zzz's during the day. What about you?"

Before he answered, her cellphone rang. It was Casey.

"The Mounties found Striker," Casey said.

Flanagan waited for her to say more. The line remained silent, a Casey trademark. Let the drama build. "Where?"

"In Canada, but not Winnipeg?"

"Casey, I love you and you're the greatest, but I'm too tired—please just tell me what you know."

"In Regina."

"And?"

"He's dead."

"Any idea when?"

"Ten o'clock Saturday night."

Chapter 37

When Carson arrived, Flanagan told him what she and Penner had uncovered and that Striker had been found. Before Carson had a chance to start firing questions, Stan Jackson called. Flanagan handed the phone to Carson who asked Jackson to determine the cause of Victoria Otto's death as soon as humanly possible. Even from across the desk, Flanagan heard Jackson say "Goldangit Harry, this isn't a goldang auto body shop," and then he hung up.

"Tell me what we know about Striker," Carson said to Flanagan as he handed her the phone.

"He was murdered, head bashed in, at ten on Saturday night. They found him in a storage warehouse near the Regina airport."

Carson's left eyebrow cocked skyward. "I thought they found his SUV in Winnipeg."

Flanagan's phone rang. It was Casey again.

"Did you get my e-mail?" Casey asked.

"I did, thank you," Flanagan replied. Casey had sent all the information on Striker. "Harry's with me now. I've given him the news."

"Before anyone asks, I sent him a copy."

"I'll tell him." She nodded at Carson and pointed to her computer. He got the drift.

"That's not why I called."

"I'm putting you on the speaker." She punched a button. "OK, go."

"I got on the Mounties case up in Winnipeg about their airport cameras."

"I thought they were sending a report."

"That's what I mean: I hadn't received anything so I got on their case."

"And do they have anything?"

"Camera's came up zero."

"And that's why you called?"

"It seems someone got confused between kilometers-per-hour and miles-per-hour. The driver of Striker's SUV got a speeding ticket at five o'clock Sunday morning."

"How far is it from Regina to Winnipeg?"

"Three-hundred and fifty miles plus or minus."

"So Striker gets whacked around ten on Saturday night, someone hops into his SUV and hightails it to Winnipeg to throw us off the trail"

"The someone was a woman."

"A name Casey, a name."

"Sylvia Smith."

"Who the hell is Sylvia Smith?" Carson asked.

"Forty-two-year-old white female, North Dakota driver's license, address and phone number in Bismarck."

"Did they ask why she had Striker's SUV?"

"The vehicle is registered to Tex-Cal Oil in Houston. She had ID that said she worked for Tex-Cal."

"And she just happened to be in Winnipeg at five o'clock on Sunday morning?"

"She told them she had to meet Tex-Cal people flying into Winnipeg from Minneapolis and then they were all flying to Calgary. She sounded real, she looked real, and they believed her story."

Or, Flanagan thought, if Shower Cloud had masqueraded as Sylvia Smith, she ended up in Regina with Striker, killed him, and then, to cover her trail, drove to Winnipeg where she flew to Chicago in time to murder Sara Peterson and then attend Zoë's funeral before flying back to Minot.

"Did she fly to Calgary?" Carson asked.

"They're checking that now."

"Let us know when you find out," Carson said.

Flanagan terminated the connection. "They won't find any record of Sylvia Smith flying out of Winnipeg," she said to Carson.

"I think you're right and as much as I know you think Lottie Striker is innocent, I think she owes not only you, but everyone, detailed answers for her whereabouts since Friday night."

"You thinking what I'm thinking?"

"What, that she had motive and opportunity?"

Flanagan's stomach knotted.

Carson continued, "The chief will arrive soon. I don't need to tell you he'll want one of his famous briefings as soon as he finds out we're now talking four potentially related murders plus a near murder if you add Hutton."

Flanagan nodded.

Carson stood to go.

"Harry, I think you'd better sit down for another moment."

Carson's eyes asked 'Why?' and he remained standing.

"Shower Cloud...Lottie...has disappeared."

Carson sat.

"She's the one who gave me the map to Victoria Otto's gravesite."

"And then took off?"

"Well she didn't physically give it to me." She told him about Shower Cloud's disappearance earlier in the evening, finding the map in an envelope under her windshield wiper, and Dewey at TJ's helping decipher what it said.

Carson sat forward. "Do you think she killed the women? Do you think she tried to kill Hutton?"

"I'm having trouble knowing what to think. Part of me wants to believe her; part of me feels angry and betrayed; part of me worries about what she might try next."

Carson gripped his chin and studied the top of her desk.

"I can understand why she might kill Striker," Flanagan said, "but I can't make myself believe she did. And the three women and Hutton make no sense at all."

Carson looked up. She could see his mind churning, no doubt trying to patch together a story for the chief.

"Do you think Hutton will be able to tell us anything, like today?" she asked.

"If we're lucky, and that's a big if."

"I need to talk to him, Harry."

"You mean again?"

Her cheeks grew warm. "So you did know?"

"Kate, you'd better tell me what you can. I'm not going to spill to the chief, but I've got to be firmly on your side when he starts asking why we can't produce Lottie Striker."

"First, I need to talk to Hutton." She picked up the phone, called the hospital, and made contact with Alex Wolyshyn. They talked for a few minutes and Flanagan hung up. "Harry, why didn't you tell me he'd slipped into a coma?"

"A coma? Honest to God Kate, I didn't know. How bad?"

She eyed him carefully. He'd never lied to her and she got the feeling that record continued. "It wasn't a deep coma and he's responding well, but still, I should have been told."

"Kate, believe me, had I known, I'd have told you immediately."

"The chief knew, someone damn well knew—I'm his partner for Christ's sake."

"I promise you this: I'll find out, but not now. We've got too much at risk already and taking on the chief on matters of protocol, no matter how important, isn't going to advance our cause."

Flanagan hoped that being left out of the loop was only an oversight.

"He may come out of it as early as today."

"I expect you'll be the first to know. Call me when you hear anything."

"You're the second person to intimate that. I don't know why I would be, but I hope to be among the first."

"I asked because I thought you might have set it up that way with your doctor friend. Others might think that because they think you and Hutton are close."

"We're partners for Christ's sake. Of course we're close."

"That's not what I meant, and you know it."

Flanagan's face flushed. "Harry, if it goes beyond partner closeness, I'll let you know."

"Fair enough, but I'd like to know if he contacts you."

"Fair enough."

Flanagan's phone rang. It was the unctuous Ripley Blakewell, attorney at law, whom everyone in North Dakota knew wanted to be the state's next Republican senator and therefore involved himself only in cases that attracted a lot of press.

"To what do I owe the pleasure?" she asked, mouthing his name to Carson.

"I'm representing Mrs. Claudine Peterson in the case against her husband."

Of course you are, thought Flanagan. Sara Peterson's case would likely get CNN coverage twenty-four/seven for at least a day or two.

"Mrs. Peterson asked if you would consider attending Sara's funeral this afternoon, two o'clock, in Largeville."

"Please tell her I will if I can get away."

"My client would like you to be there, and if I were you I'd make sure of it. Just so you know, I'll be having dinner with Chief Unger later this week."

The hair on the back of her neck bristled. She could picture him sitting at his fancy, oversized desk in his gray pinstriped suit and white shirt with monogrammed

French cuffs and gold cufflinks, flashing his gold Rolex watch, and rubbing his hand on his slick-backed black hair, his constantly pinched face with its squinty smile unfortunately not hiding his black pea-like eyes that stared like a snake's, a face that at the moment she'd like nothing better than to smack.

"I gather Mrs. Peterson has decided to file charges."

"Out of consideration for poor Sara, charges aren't to be filed until tomorrow morning so her father will be able to attend the funeral."

"That is considerate of you," Flanagan said, and hung up. "How did she end up with that asshole?"

"Everyone knows Blakewell," Carson said. "Ask anyone on the street for the name of a good lawyer and ninety-percent will say Blakewell."

"What do the other ten-percent say?"

"They plead the Fifth."

Flanagan barely had time to chuckle when the chief's voice boomed down the hallway. Carson stood up. "Let me handle this," he said. "You might want to keep a low profile for the next few hours."

"If you need me, I'll be at Sara's funeral."

Chapter 38

Flanagan went home and slept for three hours. At noon she got up, showered, and called Alex Wolyshyn for an update on Hutton. Nothing had changed, though everyone still optimistically thought he would wake up sometime that day. Next, she called Carson to see what had happened in his meeting with the chief. Carson wasn't in. She decided against leaving a voice mail in case the chief was within earshot when he played his messages. She called Casey and asked if Tommy Striker continued to be a resident of the jail.

"He made bail at ten-thirty this morning."

"Who's his council?"

"Ripley Blakewell."

"I should have guessed. Who put up bail?"

"Well we know it wasn't his old man," she said. "Yeah, here it is—cash, twenty-five thousand, anonymous guarantor."

Flanagan ended the call, angry at herself for thinking that Shower Cloud might have provided bail.

She put on a simple dark pant suit with two-inch matching heels, strapped on her shoulder holster, and made sure the ammo clip was full. After checking in the full-length mirror and hating how big-boned she always looked, she left her bedroom and walked down the hallway to the front door.

Absently, she reached for the cellphone that always sat on the hall table. It wasn't there. She checked her bag and then went back to her bedroom thinking she might have accidentally left it on her dresser or the night table. After a few minutes of searching, she decided she'd left it at her office.

She set the alarm, locked the door, and proceeded down the steps toward her car. The back of her neck began to tingle, not the Zoë tingle, but the early-warning system tingle. She checked the street for signs of vehicles or people that seemed out of place, but all seemed normal.

The air was still and hot. A baby cried. A woman hollered at a child. The child hollered back. Distant sounds were in the air: traffic, airplanes, a jackhammer, but they were not obtrusive—more like background music. The sun glinted from her windshield. She adjusted her sunglasses and then stopped, frozen where she stood. Someone was in her car.

Instinctively, she felt for her pistol and took a step laterally toward the trees lining the driveway. They were small trees, but better than nothing and the angle would give her a clearer view because the sun wouldn't be directly in her eyes.

The passenger door opened. Flanagan reached for her gun. "Step out and put your hands on top of the car," she said.

The person hesitated.

"NOW!" Flanagan hoped she didn't attract the attention of everyone in the neighborhood, but wasn't willing to take a chance that whomever had decided to occupy her car might be armed.

The person got out and stood up. Flanagan moved two steps farther to her right. The person came into clearer view as the sun's glare no longer impeded her line of sight. The person turned to face her, placing her hands on the roof of the car.

"So you decided to make an appearance." She started forward, lowering her gun, but not putting it back in its holster.

"I'm sorry I ran out on you," Shower Cloud said. "I know I created big problems, but there were some things I needed to do on my own."

"Like draw a map to Victoria Otto's gravesite?"

Shower Cloud nodded.

"Thank you for that, but you told me yesterday that you didn't know Victoria Otto."

"I didn't mean to mislead, and I hope you can forgive me."

Flanagan holstered her pistol. "Take your hands down," she said, "and get back into the car."

Shower Cloud did as she was told. Flanagan slid in under the steering wheel and slammed her door. She called Carson to let him know that Shower Cloud could be removed from the 'missing person's' column. While she waited for him to pick up, she turned to Shower Cloud and asked, "Other than the map, what kinds of things did you need to do?"

"Where is she?" Carson asked, his voice coming on the line.

Shower Cloud urgently signaled Flanagan to hang up.

"She's with me Harry, but something's come up—I'll have to call you back."

"Flanagan, don't you dare hang up—"

"This had better be good. Harry Carson's a good friend who has not only saved my skin, he's saved yours. Without him, there would have been cops everywhere looking for you and I'd likely be fired or working nights, locking up hookers and drunks."

"When Zoë first asked me if I'd ever heard of Victoria Otto, the name sounded familiar, but I didn't know why. Then, when Zoë got murdered, I felt I had betrayed her by not doing more to help her find this person she had been seeking."

"And now you've done that." Flanagan glanced at her watch. Sara Peterson's funeral started in forty-five minutes.

"I believe I owe you the whole story, to tell you why it became important for me to dishonor the bond of trust between us by lying and running away as I did."

"Did you murder Zoë or Sara Peterson or..." Flanagan realized that Shower Cloud may not know about Striker.

"No," Shower Cloud said. "I could never do that. Zoë is my friend; Sara's father is my friend, though I guess my behavior has given you good reason to ask."

"Have you murdered anyone, ever?"

"No. Please believe me."

"Striker is dead."

"I know."

"Who told you? We didn't tell anyone." Tommy and his lawyer, Ripley Blakewell, had been told, but she was certain neither of them told Shower Cloud.

"It is easy to lose one's trust and so very, very difficult to find it again."

"Does that mean you won't tell me who told you?"

"It means you won't believe me and I dare not tell you more things you won't believe."

"Someone tried to kill my partner."

Shower Cloud shook her head and looked away.

"You know, don't you? You know who killed them and who tried to kill my partner."

Shower Cloud turned to face Flanagan. "I think it would be best if I told you the rest of the story."

"Yes, I think it would."

"After I talked to you, I called my father and asked him to end my marriage. I was married on the reservation under Indian law and only my father, as chief of our tribe, has the authority to end such marriages. He told me the spirits of our ancestors had never sanctioned the marriage but that they had sent me instead to find the killer of another Indian girl, a schoolteacher in Largeville, who disappeared, never to be heard from again."

Flanagan's eyebrows shot up.

"I knew then why Victoria Otto's name had sounded familiar when Zoë first mentioned it."

"Victoria Otto was an Indian girl from your father's tribe?"

"White Owl was her Indian name. She was from the Hidasta tribe. The Hidastas are part of the MHA Nation,

three affiliated tribes that consist of the Mandan, Hi-
dasta, and Arikara peoples located on the Fort Berthold
Indian Reservation that surrounds Lake Sakakawea.
When White Owl left her tribe to attend Minot State
University to obtain her teaching degree, she changed
her name to Victoria Otto."

"You seem to have learned a lot about her in such a
short time?"

"I was put in touch with White Owl's father, the
tribal chief of the Hidasta, who told me her story. I told
him I thought I could find White Owl and have her body
returned for a proper burial. He told me that only I could
do that, that the spirits of our people would guide me."

"You aren't even from their tribe. Why were you selected, and how did you know where to look?"

"I can tell by your voice that you don't believe me so
telling you won't serve any useful purpose."

"I'm sorry, but you have to admit that what's going
on here doesn't happen on a daily basis."

*   *   *

*Please, you've got to believe her. It is the only way
you can release Victoria Otto's spirit.*

*   *   *

Shower Cloud smiled. "She's with you, isn't she?"

"If I promise to believe, will you tell me?"

"Close your eyes and take my hand. I want you to
feel the spirits of my ancestors. I want you to hear what
their voices have to say."

Flanagan hesitated, and then took Shower Cloud's
hand.

Shower Cloud began to hum, low, like the sound of
Indian drums beating, and began to sway to and fro, her
eyes closed. She gripped Flanagan's hand hard. "Close
your eyes," she said.

A vision began to take shape in Flanagan's mind, a
vision of Zoe standing atop a two-hundred-foot em-

bankment rising above a huge body of water. Zoë eyes were closed. Girls and boys surrounded her. Close your eyes, Zoë said, and try to think of Sakakawea, try to picture her in your minds, try to let you minds travel back to 1804 and 1805, the time when Lewis and Clark wintered here, the time when they took Sakakawea with them to serve as their guide...

"She's upset; she's not seeing Sakakawea."

Shower Cloud whispered, "Your voice will frighten the spirits; you must listen to what they say."

Flanagan took a deep breath. Sweat began to drip from her forehead as Zoë fought the image that tried to occupy her mind, not the image of Sakakawea, but the image of Victoria Otto.

Flanagan found herself atop the high embankment next to Zoë. Help me, Zoë cried, I'm going to fall. Flanagan reached for Zoë's hand, and then her mind began spinning like it had been caught in a giant whirlpool. She stepped back to regain her balance. Zoë fell, down and down and down. No, Flanagan screamed.

And then she and Zoë were standing west of the Garrison Dam's turbine house on a twenty-foot embankment with a lot of trees on top. Zoë took her hand and led her to a growth of underbrush and rose-brambles. This is where I'm buried, Zoë said, except it wasn't Zoë's voice. It wasn't Zoë.

"Who are you?" Flanagan asked, pulling away, except she wasn't Flanagan, she was Shower Cloud.

"Mark it well, my daughter, so your detective friend can find me," the voice said.

"Why her?" Shower Cloud asked. "Why not me?"

"My spirit dwells with the spirit of your friend, Zoë. Her spirit dwells with your detective friend. Only your detective friend can set us free. Mark it well, and then walk ten paced due north and thirty paces due east from this very spot. There you will find a stone marker."

Flanagan opened her eyes.

Shower Cloud had stopped humming and she was crying.

"As soon as her remains can be released, I'll make sure they're sent to the proper place."

"You are going to Largeville to attend Sara Peterson's funeral."

Flanagan glanced at her watch. "I must leave now."

"I present a problem?"

"Your being there presents a problem—everyone in Largeville believes you murdered Zoë and may have murdered Sara."

"I have a favor to ask."

"If it's coming with me, I can't do that."

"I don't want to go with you, but I must be there."

"I've already told you why I don't think that's a good idea, and besides, I need to take you downtown. I've broken every rule in the book and then some and if it weren't for Harry Carson, we wouldn't even be having this conversation. If I betray his trust again...well, I don't want that to happen."

"You need to go to Sara's funeral."

"I feel an obligation to go, but I don't need to. Mainly, I'm staying away from the police station at Harry Carson's request. He figured if the chief saw me, he'd want to know where you are, but of course that is no longer a problem."

Shower Cloud opened the door and stepped out.

Flanagan reached for her pistol.

"Shoot me if you must, but I'm going to Sara's funeral. No one will know I'm there, and afterward, I promise I'll come with you...no more favors. You can take me to see your chief."

"Shower Cloud, please don't make me do this." Flanagan aimed her pistol and started to get out.

"If you don't shoot me, and I know you won't, I'll be gone before you get out of the car."

Flanagan hesitated. She knew Shower Cloud was right about the shooting part and suspected she'd come in a distant second in a footrace. "Why is it so important that you attend? I can understand you wanting to go out of respect for Joe, but he's about to be charged with raping and allowing others to have sex with Sara."

"I believe he's innocent. I know him better than most, and he is too much of a father to do or allow anything like that—he loved Sara. She was his life. And he has always been kind to me, but he's not the main reason I want to go."

"What is?"

"The killer of White Owl will be there. The killer of Zoë will be there. The killer of Sara will be there. The killer of Mr. Striker will be there."

Flanagan blinked. Shower Cloud had disappeared. Flanagan jumped out of the car and ran around to the passenger side certain Shower Cloud had simply ducked down, but she had gone. Flanagan ran to the street.

The air was still and quiet. She heard distant sounds like waves splashing on a far shore, like far away drums beating a call to war, like the chants of a thousand Indian braves dancing beyond the heavens, but Shower Cloud had disappeared with only the diminishing scent that proved her presence lingering for a few brief seconds.

Chapter 39

When she arrived in Largeville, Flanagan drove the length of Main Street to take another look at the town that hosted so much grief: three murders in two days; first Zoë, one of its beloved; second Sara, one of its own; and third Striker, one of its own who no one yet knew about, and add to that, Joe and Claudine and Tommy and Shower Cloud, tragedy among the living.

Pete's Café sat dark, Town Hall sat dark, Largeville High School sat dark. There were no cars on the streets, not even in front of the bar. Largeville had become a ghost town. She saw neither Shower Cloud nor any sign of her, nor had she really expected to. She made a U-turn and drove back to the main intersection. There, she turned left and headed down the dusty road toward Central Church.

That's where all the cars had gone. They filled the streets and grassy shoulders all the way up to the residents' fences, they filled driveways, and they filled the large parking area around the adjacent curling and skating rink. Flanagan parked behind John Burke's old blue Cadillac that sat at one end of a long row of cars.

Two hundred or more people stood on the sidewalk and the wooden steps leading up to the double front doors of what had once been a pretty white church that was now in desperate need of paint, hammers and nails and boards, and several window panes. It had a grand-looking cupola that had been pushed slightly atilt by a branch of one of the many overhanging Cottonwoods that surrounded the property.

Big Johnny Burke, face scrubbed pink, body bulging from a blue suit, tie askew, was one of the people on the steps. He stood off to the side puffing a cigarette that he tried to hide in his cupped hand. Periodically, he turned and blew smoke out of the side of his mouth, away from the others standing nearby. When he saw Flanagan he waved. Flanagan nodded. He motioned her up the steps. She hesitated, and then figured the top of the steps offered as good a vantage point as any to survey the gathered and try to spot Shower Cloud.

Many a nervous eye was cast in her direction as she made her way forward. Some whispered to their neighbors and heads turned. She looked for anyone that might be Shower Cloud: a beautiful, dark-skinned woman in any kind of disguise shouldn't be that hard to discern from the white-faced Europeans that composed the people of Largeville.

"The church is full," Burke whispered as he shook her hand. "All the school kids."

"Where's Lizzie?"

"She's inside with our oldest. He wanted to go. The others are with a sitter."

"Anyone you don't know here?"

"Several. Maybe they're Joe or Claudine's people from up near the Canadian border."

Burke took a puff that he inhaled deeply and then looked at her carefully. "Are you looking for anyone in particular," he asked, wisps of smoke seeping out of his nose and mouth with each word. He coughed and waved his big hand in front of his face. "Sorry," he said. "I don't like blowing smoke on anyone."

"The only thing I don't like is that it smells too good, and no, I'm not looking for anyone in particular." Telling him about Shower Cloud, Lottie to him and the others in Largeville, would be too complicated, particularly with Striker's murder.

"Joe and Claudine will be glad you're here."

She sensed he had more to say. "Is there something on your mind, Mr. Burke?"

"Please, call me Johnny."

"OK. Is there something on your mind Johnny?"

"I've heard a rumor about old Strike."

"What did you hear?"

He leaned over and whispered in her ear, "That they found him murdered up in Regina."

"I wouldn't know about that," she said. As far as she knew, only Tommy Striker and Tommy's lawyer, Ripley Blakewell, had been told. Shower Cloud knew also, but Flanagan hadn't found out who told her.

"Everything seemed so normal last week…Jesus, now look at it: three wonderful people dead, Tommy's been arrested, Lottie's been arrested, and old Strike's been murdered."

"Tommy's been released on bail and Lottie shouldn't have been arrested."

"You know, I was in the café when that young whippersnapper of a cop came in. Everyone thought he was making a mistake. I tried to stop him, but Lottie, well she'd have none of that. She went along peaceful, though she did say something strange now that I think about it: she told me not to tell Strike."

Flanagan sidestepped his unspoken question with one of her own. "Are either Lottie or Tommy here?"

Through the open doors of the church the organ music stopped. Flanagan glanced inside. Johnny tossed his cigarette. The pastor in his white surplice and purple and black stole slowly made his way to the pulpit. Flanagan suspected he'd never seen the Peterson's inside his church before, though Largeville being a small town, he surely knew who they were.

At the conclusion of the fifteen minute service, the pastor asked if anyone had anything at all they'd like to say.

After an awkward moment of stifled coughs and sheepish looks from those in attendance, Claudine, dressed in black lace and dark glasses, got up from her front row pew and, legs shaking, mounted the steps leading to the chancel and crossed to the pulpit. She removed her glasses. Her eyes were puffy and red rimmed and she looked old and tired, like any mother attending her daughter's funeral. She gripped the pulpit's top with her thin hands and lifted her head until it seemed that her eyes were focused on every person in the church.

She began to speak in a whisper and people strained to hear. Then her voice gained strength and volume as she told of Sara's life in Largeville, of her friends, many of whom were in the church and she thanked them for coming to pay their respects, and then she talked about Sara's special friendship with Zoë Brown, how, during the past few months of their lives, Zoë had been the only mother Sara had. Claudine began sobbing. Lizzie Burke started to get up to go to her aid, but Claudine waved her off. She daubed at her eyes with a tissue she removed from the sleeve of her dress. After a moment she continued.

"I have just one more thought I'd like to express: Sara and Zoë were wonderful young women—they deserved to live. If I could exchange my useless life for theirs I would do so gladly."

Flanagan rubbed under her eyes. Others were crying openly, particularly the hundred or so students in the church. The organ began playing. Flanagan wasn't totally surprised to see Tommy Striker and Dale Kiley among the six young men who got up and went to the front of the church to stand behind the open coffin while the viewing procession, consisting of most of those gathered inside and outside the church, began its long, head-bowed trek. Tommy saw her and curled his lip. Tommy's lawyer, the great Ripley Blakewell, who was sitting in the row behind where Tommy had been sitting, turned to peer with his beady eyes.

When the others in Blakewell's row joined the viewing line, he made his way to the back of the church to talk to a woman standing next to the side doorway.

Johnny Burke excused himself and joined the line of mourners. Flanagan stood to one side studying everyone going in or coming out. So far, she hadn't seen anyone even closely resembling Shower Cloud. She glanced back inside the church. Ripley Blakewell continued to talk to the woman, who had moved through the doorway and now stood immediately outside the sanctuary.

Shower Cloud's whispered breath felt cool one her ear. "She's your killer."

A hand with a vice-like grip prevented Flanagan from turning.

"It's best that she doesn't see you talking to me."

"What…"

"She has a car waiting in the lane along side the church."

Flanagan looked back to where the woman and Blakewell had been standing. They'd disappeared. She raced down the steps to the lane in time to see a dark blue Lincoln speed off, spewing dust and gravel that prevented her from seeing the license plate.

She ran for her car. A familiar-looking red Ram pickup pulled up and blocked her path. She didn't recognize the driver but knew it was Shower Cloud.

Flanagan motioned Shower Cloud to move over, clambered in under the steering wheel, and slammed the gear shift into D just as the six young pallbearers started down the church steps with Sara's coffin. The people standing on the sidewalk began spilling into the street and blocked their way.

"You drive," Flanagan said. "I'll see if I can move them out of the way."

Johnny Burke saw their dilemma and came to their aid. After a couple of minutes, they got clear. Shower Cloud said she saw the car heading south on Main Street. They took off after them.

"Who's the woman?" Flanagan asked, and reached for her ringing cellphone. She checked the caller ID.

"I've got to answer," she said, and hit 'TALK.'
"Harry, this is a real bad time—"

"Hey partner."

"Oh my God." Tears came to her eyes. "Hutton, is that really you?"

"Yeah partner, it's really me, back from la la land."

"Thank god; I've been worried sick."

"I knew you cared."

"Before you let your head get too big, it's not that I care—I just hate doing all your damn work."

Shower Cloud pointed at the car ahead. Through the dust, the tail lights of the Lincoln flashed bright red.

"Hold on a minute," she said to Hutton. "Who's the woman?" she asked Shower Cloud.

"Tommy Striker's mother."

"Holy shit!"

The Lincoln stopped at the highway. Flanagan pulled around in front and got out, pistol in hand. Using the truck box as cover, she aimed at the driver and shouted, "Everyone out of the car, now!"

The back door opened. Flanagan tightened her grip on her pistol and told Shower Cloud to stay down.

"Put that away, detective, before someone gets hurt."

It was Ripley Blakewell. Flanagan thought she would puke.

"Where's the woman?"

"Why detective, whatever are you talking about?"

"You know goddamn well what I'm talking about."

"There's no one but my driver in the car." He stepped a pace to his left. "Be my guest, detective. I'll even grant you look without a warrant."

"Tell your driver to get out and the two of you step away from the car."

"Now is that really necessary, detective?"

"Yes sir, it is. Do it now!"

"As you wish, detective, but your chief is going to enjoy this story when he and I have dinner tonight."

Go fuck yourself, Blakewell. "I'm sure he will."

Blakewell's driver extracted himself from the front seat and the two of them moved five feet from the car where Blakewell stood grinning and the driver stood glaring.

After Flanagan checked the inside of the car, feeling sicker by the moment, she said, "Pop the trunk."

"Detective, I can assure you that I don't transport my clients in the trunk of my limousine."

"You want to wait while I get someone up here with a warrant?"

Blakewell signaled his driver to open the trunk.

"Thank you," Flanagan said, trying to sound a lot more confident that she felt.

"Any time, detective, and I truly hope you catch whoever it is you are after."

Yeah, I'll bet you do. Flanagan got back in the truck and watched Blakewell and his driver turn onto the highway and disappear from view.

Shower Cloud pointed at the phone.

She grabbed it from the seat and shouted, "Jesus Hutton, sorry."

"What the hell's going on Flanagan?" It was Harry Carson.

"What happened to Hutton?"

"His nurse came in. She's about to chase me out of here. What's going on?"

"You mean other than making a total ass out of my self with the great Ripley Blakewell?"

"Flanagan, what ever are you talking about?"

"No Harry, I'm not nuts." She told him what happened and about Tommy Striker's mother.

"I thought she was supposed to be in a mental institution in Texas."

"The last thing we saw was a letter from Big Springs Mental Hospital to Dr. Brownstein, Zoë's father, saying it had no record of a Rhonda Striker having ever been a patient."

"Does it fit? Is she the murderer?"

"It does and she is, Harry, and I'm going back to Largeville. I've got to find her."

"Not without backup, you're not, and that's an order, Flanagan."

"By then she'll be gone, Harry. If Dooley's around, tell him I'm at Striker's place."

"I'll get him, but you wait for us, damn it."

"Gotta go, Harry. If you can't find Dooley, call me on my cell when you turn off the highway. I'll give you directions."

Chapter 40

Flanagan and Shower Cloud headed back to Largeville. Shower Cloud pushed herself back and punched her fists into the seat. When she spoke her voice had turned into a gasping monotone. "She's…not…in…Largeville."

"I don't mind telling you that you're starting to spook me out, but if she's ahead of Blakewell we'll never catch her so Largeville's our only chance. Any other ideas you care to throw on the table will be greatly appreciated."

"You--told--him--you'd—be—at--the--house."

"Yes, he's meeting us there."

"Look--in--the--garage."

"Striker's garage?"

Shower Cloud nodded.

Flanagan turned at Striker's house and pulled up to the garage at the back of the property.

Shower Cloud continued to sit board-like, her eyes blank and clouded over. "Look--in--the--garage," she said again.

Flanagan removed her pistol from its holster and crept to the side of the garage away from the house. She peered in the small window, gasped, and dropped to the ground. A blue Lincoln sat inside. She crawled around to the doors and checked the dirt—fresh tire tracks. She sniffed the crack between the garage doors and smelled the still warm exhaust fumes.

"She's--not--there."

"Jesus God, don't do that," Flanagan hissed at Shower Cloud who'd come up behind.

Shower Cloud opened the double doors with a key she took from her pocket and stood aside. Flanagan was convinced it was the right car and called Carson.

"We're almost there," Carson said.

"We're in a red Dodge Ram alongside," she said.

"Stay put, Flanagan. Do you hear me?"

"I hear."

"And another thing, make sure you keep Lottie Striker in sight. We're not out of the woods on her yet, not by a long shot."

Flanagan and Shower Cloud went back to the truck and waited for Carson.

"I sense you thinking about me," Shower Cloud said.

"You were in a strange place."

"The spirits of my ancestors guide me when I am lost. Sometimes it is their voices that speak."

"They spoke to me. I'm not Indian."

"Yesterday, when you took me to your home, they told me something terrible was about to happen to you."

"That's comforting."

"When I look at those I love who love me as I am, I see a golden aura wrapped around their bodies. If they love me in the same way, they see a golden aura wrapped around my body. The spirits of my ancestors say that this gift of mutual love is confined to their descendants, but Zoë had a golden aura. I first saw it the night she was murdered, while she ate dinner at the restaurant with her two friends, and then when they left I became frightened—I did not know what it meant. I prayed to the spirits of my ancestors for guidance, but they couldn't help me."

"You were frightened because Zoë had an aura and wasn't Indian?"

"I loved Zoë deeply. Seeing her aura meant she loved me deeply, and I was glad. I didn't care that she wasn't Indian—I cared that she loved me. To answer you question, seeing her aura didn't frighten me; what frightened me was NOT seeing her aura—when she left the restaurant her aura had disappeared."

"And what did the loss of her aura mean?"

"It could mean several things: that she no longer loved me because I had stolen the love of one who loved her; that I no longer loved her because she had stolen the love of one who loved me; that she was going to die an unnatural death."

Flanagan felt her heart beating faster.

"Then yesterday, when you intercepted Detective Galen and me in front of the police station and tried to figure out why I'd been arrested, your aura temporarily disappeared. I was afraid Detective Galen was the cause, the danger, but as we went into the police station, I noticed a man and a woman sitting across the street in a blue Lincoln Town Car watching. When I placed myself between so you were out of their line of sight, your aura came back."

Flanagan gave her a questioning look.

"I would have said or done something to move you out of their line of fire had your aura not returned, even though you and your two fellow officers would have thought me mad."

"You really believe I was a target?"

"Later, when I was driven to your home, I noticed the Lincoln parked on your street a block away. I asked the young police officer to pull into the driveway close to the house because I didn't feel well, but the real reason was that I didn't want the two occupants of the Lincoln to see that it wasn't you."

"That's why you left—you led them away by making them think they were after me."

"I had to. They would have killed you, like they killed the others."

"How did you know all of this? How can you feel so certain?"

"I know Zoë's spirit talks to you as it talks to me."

"I thought it could only talk to one person."

"Her spirit can talk to many hearts and minds, any that will listen, but it can only attach to one."

"Zoë's spirit doesn't know who killed her."

"The spirit of Victoria Otto knows. It knows Tommy's mother killed all three of them, but her spirit is week and can help us no longer. It is up to you, you must do the rest."

Flanagan eyed the house. "Is there any other way out except the two doors?"

"If one were desperate, there are windows all along the far side, but she isn't there."

"You seem certain," Flanagan said.

Shower Cloud nodded in a disconnected way.

"Something's wrong," Flanagan said.

Shower Cloud gazed at her with unseeing eyes. She put a hand to her throat and gasped for air and emitted a horrible gurgling sound. Flanagan tried to grab and hold her arm, but Shower Cloud pulled away and cowered in the corner. Then she stuck her fingers into her ears and began to scream ear piercing screams, and her body began convulsing and she started to choke.

Flanagan dove for her hand, frightened when she felt how cold and rigid it had become. With her other hand, she forced Shower Cloud's mouth open and jammed her fingers inside to make sure she hadn't swallowed her tongue.

Shower Cloud began to chant, "um-wah-wah, um-wah-wah," and her eyeballs bulged out. "I--see--death," she said. Her voice had an echo and had changed back to the monotone that Flanagan had heard before.

"Shower Cloud," Flanagan shouted, and shook her back and forth, being careful not to bash her head against the side of the cab. "Talk to me. Where do you see death?"

Shower Cloud blinked and her eyes cleared. Her hand warmed and became supple and she took a deep breath.

"You were in a trance. You saw death."

Shower Cloud sagged and laid the back of her hand against her damp forehead.

Harry Carson and Trevor Dooley roared up in one car and Dirk Penner and Oswald Quigley in the other. Flanagan got out and talked to Carson.

"The car's in the garage. No one's inside."

Shower Cloud joined them. Her eyes were sunken and strands of sweat-dampened hair lay across her forehead.

"Are you all right, Mrs. Striker?" Carson asked.

"My spirit is in turmoil," she said.

Carson looked at Flanagan.

Shower Cloud said to Flanagan, "I need to tell you something before you go inside."

She took Shower Cloud by the elbow and walked her to the front of Carson's car where they were out of earshot of the others.

Shower Cloud turned to face her. She had tears in her eyes. "Tommy is there. He's dead."

"No, don't say that. That can't be true. He was at Sara's funeral."

Shower Cloud shook her head. "His throat's been cut."

"Did his mother kill him?"

"I don't know. I can't see anything more."

Flanagan rejoined Carson and told him what Shower Cloud had said.

Carson glanced at Shower Cloud.

"She had a vision. It's not the first. She also told me that Tommy's mother isn't here."

"Christ Flanagan."

"Harry, I believe her."

"Yeah, but visions?" Carson looked askance. "Whatever happens Flanagan, this stays between you and me."

Flanagan nodded.

"What can she tell us about the house?"

"Ask her."

Carson motioned Shower Cloud over. She drew a detailed diagram, including closets and the attic entrance and all of the nooks and crannies in the basement, explaining clearly what each was.

Carson asked Flanagan. "How do you want to do this?"

She telegraphed her thanks—he could have taken over, pushed her aside. God knows, he had more than enough reasons. "You and I should take the back, Oz and Trev the front. After the main floor is clear, they take the upstairs, we'll take the basement. Dirk, you stay with Shower--Mrs. Striker."

"I need to come with you," Shower Cloud said.

"I know you do," Flanagan said, "but I can't permit that to happen. I want you to stay here with Detective Penner until we get back."

"The doors shouldn't be locked," Shower Cloud said, "but in case they are, here are the keys, this one for the front and this one for the back."

"We'll go in at the same time," Flanagan said. "Dirk, give us a signal."

Penner moved to the road where he could see both doors and when they were in position, gave the 'go' signal. Once inside, the four of them made quick work of the main floor. Quigley and Dooley went upstairs. Flanagan opened the basement door and heard music she didn't recognize.

"Do you want me to lead?" Carson whispered.

She shook her head and started down. The music became louder. Computer screens lit up. She saw Tommy's body lying face down in a black pool that she knew was blood. She started toward him, Carson at her back, pistol drawn. Then they heard Tommy's voice and froze.

"It's coming from the speakers," she whispered. "And there, look at the screens."

"TELL--DALE--I--LIKED--HIS--MUSIC. THIS--IS--HIS--OPERA--OF--THE--SPIRITS--OF--DEATH. I--THOUGHT--IT--APPROPRIATE." As Tommy said each word, it crawled across his seven computer screens in red block letters animated to appear as though they were dripping blood. "AND -- I'M -- SORRY -- I -- USED -- HIS -- COMPUTER – TO -- HACK -- INTO -- ALL -- THE -- OTHERS. DETECTIVE -- FLANAGAN -- I -- HOPE -- YOU – GET – THIS – MESSAGE – BECAUSE – I – LIED – TO – MY – MOTHER – ABOUT – HAVING – SEX – WITH – YOU -- AND – MISS – BROWN – AND – SARA – AND – THE -- OTHERS. I'M -- SORRY. THAT'S – WHY – SHE – HAD -- TO KILL -- THEM. I'M – SO -- SORRY. PLEASE – FORGIVE -- ME."

And then the message started again. Flanagan knelt and felt for a pulse that she knew wouldn't be there and shook her head. She saw the knife lying next to Tommy's outstretched hand.

They checked the rest of the basement and found nothing. Quigley and Dooley appeared at the top of the steps and came down. Carson told Dooley to bag the knife and he and Flanagan went up.

"I want to tell Shower Cloud," Flanagan said.

Carson nodded, and called Doc Jackson to come and pick up the body.

Penner and Shower Cloud were on the back porch. Flanagan embraced Shower Cloud.

Flanagan said, "It looks like suicide."

"Was his throat cut?" Shower Cloud asked.

Flanagan nodded.

"It wasn't suicide."

"I'm sorry, but it—"

"I must go to him."

Flanagan looked at Carson. Carson nodded. She led Shower Cloud to the basement where she sat cross-legged next to Tommy's body, closed her eyes, and began to chant. Flanagan stood by the steps and waited. Five minutes later, Shower Cloud got up and took Flanagan's hand.

"Thank you," she said. "I prayed to the spirits of my ancestors to guide his soul."

Chapter 41

Carson said, "Until Rhonda Striker is taken into custody, I'm keeping someone on you 24/7. You're the only one on the kid's list who isn't dead." Penner volunteered for the first watch.

Their best chance at finding Rhonda Striker lay with Ripley Blakewell. They agreed to meet at seven a.m. and Carson, Dooley and Quigley departed for Minot.

It was early evening by the time Doc Jackson and one of his young medical assistants arrived. After they departed with Tommy's body, Penner, Shower Cloud, and Flanagan drove back to the church to get Flanagan's Range Rover. "I meant to ask before," Flanagan said. "Whose truck is this?"

"Pick me up on Main Street in front of the pool hall," Shower Cloud said, and drove off.

Flanagan and Penner hopped into the Range Rover and followed.

"She doesn't seem to want to tell you about the truck," Penner said.

"You'll find that she does that."

As soon as Shower Cloud got in, Flanagan said, "You didn't tell me who owns the truck."

"You met him once. He told you his name was Art Logan."

That's why the alarm had sounded in her mind. He was the guy at Pete's Café, the guy who played poker with Pete, the guy whose real name was Lee Scranton from Bismarck, the guy with a dagger tattooed on his penis. How in God's name had Shower Cloud hooked up such a disgusting character?

"He's not who you think he is."

"Why don't you enlighten me?"

"When he came to the café he wasn't looking for Pete, he was looking for me."

"I checked him out. The Bismarck police are search-ing for him."

"They know who he is and they aren't looking for him; he works for them undercover."

"You're kidding?"

"Lee Scranton's real name is Bear Owl. When he left the reservation of my father's people, he joined the navy and became the first Indian Navy Seal. Then, he spent a few years, maybe ten, with a secret international counter-insurgency unit whose very existence was bur-ied deep within the Pentagon. When he turned fifty, he retired and moved to North Dakota. He has a small ranch outside Bismarck, but he misses the action so once in awhile he does undercover work."

According to the file, Scranton wasn't a person you'd take to church or have for dinner; he was the type of person you kept your daughters from and double-locked doors if he set foot in the neighborhood.

"His file said he had a number of tattoos in odd places, also major injury scars that didn't come from any form of military service."

"I doubt he has tattoos. Athapascans believe that one's body is not theirs to desecrate. Battle scars are an-other matter—they're considered badges of honor put there by the gods."

Flanagan figured his file could have easily been falsi-fied, doctored to throw anyone who got too curious off his trail. Carson might be able to find out. She made a mental note to check later.

When they returned to the police station in Minot, Flanagan warned Shower Cloud that she would be called upon to make decisions concerning Striker and Tommy.

"I will contact Mr. Striker's family in Texas. I sus-pect they will want both bodies sent there after you have finished with your work. If they want, I will accompany the bodies; I feel I owe them that."

"You don't owe them anything the way they mistreated you, the way they treated you as their slave."

"I was using Mr. Striker as much as he was using me. You freed me from my guilt when you told me my father and I'd been tricked, but it doesn't change why I did what I did. For that reason, if the family requires my involvement, my further services until Mr. Striker and Tommy are placed where their spirits might find peace, I will make myself available."

"That will take a couple of days. Until then, I'd like you to stay with me, to help me find Tommy's mother, to let me know what you sense, what you feel, what you think."

Shower Cloud stood and walked to the window. Her pale gray dress highlighted her shapely body as though she were standing there nude. She looked down at the street and shivered. When she turned, her eyes were filled with tears.

"By asking me to help, by believing, you honor me, you honor my people. Do not be alarmed by my tears for they are happy, like a spring rain, but my fears are like a raging storm that comes quickly from a distant horizon, driven by angry winds. I will stay with you; I will protect you. Like the storm she draws near."

Chapter 42

Edie Pitano returned to the casino on Tuesday night. She wasn't allowed to deal until her the bruises on her face could be completely covered by the casino's magic makeup girls, but her boss said she could work the security monitors. Gwen changed her schedule so they had the same hours. She dropped Edie at the front door drove down the ram to the underground lot. Edie waited at the top of the escalator next to a row of slots busy with a mix of people ranging from barely old enough to plenty old enough, ranging from black to white, ranging from skinny to fat, ranging from well-dressed to the jeans and t-shirt crowd.

She watched two ladies that looked to be in their nineties with a large tin can full of quarters strapped to the fronts of their wheelchairs. One of them had to maneuver around the hoses from her oxygen tank. A skinny black girl with a thin t-shirt and no bra reached over and gave her a hand. They shared a brief smile, and then attacked their machines with renewed vigor.

Edie glanced at her watch. Parking the car was a two minute chore—it had been ten minutes since Gwen dropped her off. She walked to the escalator and looked down. Ginger, one of the bell hops, raced up the moving steps two at a time. Edie grabbed her arm and asked if she'd seen Gwen.

"Not a soul," she said.

A knot formed in Edie's stomach. She ran down the escalator. Gwen's car was in the second row at the far end, where she usually parked. The knot in her stomach grew larger. "Gwen?" she called. The only response was an echo that bounced among the pillars.

She took several steps forward. Something cold hit her arm. She jumped back like she'd been shot. It was only a drip from the overhead pipe. She brushed her arm dry. The escalator scraped and a door banged shut. A shiver ran through her body.

The inside light of Gwen's car was on. She heard the pinging of the door alarm and started to run. 'PLEASE,' a voice in her head shouted. 'PLEASE LET HER BE OK.'

She got to the end of the first row. The pinging grew louder and more urgent. She clutched at her chest. Her lungs burned and her head felt like it might explode. She kept going.

The car door was open. Edie stopped, afraid to take another step, afraid of what she might find. She forced her foot ahead--one step, and then one more. Then she saw blood, lots of blood. She screamed and ran back to the escalator and vomited.

A security guard ran down from the main floor. "Someone reported seeing a car door open and blood on the floor," he yelled.

"Gwen's car," Edie cried, and pointed.

Ginger ran down. She pulled Edie aside as four more security guards raced past.

"What happened?" Ginger asked.

"That fucking asshole Derrick," Edie sobbed. "Gwen's missing. He's killed Passépartout, cut his head clean off." Edie vomited again. "I'm going to kill that mother-fucker."

It was after four a.m. by the time the casino's security unit and the police had all their questions answered, at least until someone thought of more. Edie decided to take the casino up on its offer for a room in its secure section, but wanted the police to take her home first. She was certain Smith would have taken Tocqueville, but she had to make sure.

The police cruiser pulled into the driveway and Edie jumped out and raced inside, the policeman right behind. A thirty-second search told her that Tocqueville was gone. She slumped to the chair next to the phone and brushed the tears from her eyes.

"You have messages," the young policeman, Corey Payne, said.

She glanced at the blinking light, its purpose not immediately evident to her tired brain, and when her brain finally figured out what the light meant, she picked up the receiver and accessed her voicemail. A woman's voice burned into her ear.

"You weren't very nice to Derrick. We can't allow that to happen again so we sent you a message. Sorry it had to be so violent, but it's really all your fault you know—were you not such a whore, none of this would have happened."

"What is it?" Payne asked.

Edie hoped her rage didn't show. "My mother, going on about how I never call."

Payne nodded. "They do that."

"Now I want you to listen carefully," the woman's voice continued, "or we'll have to send another message and sweetie, I guarantee it will be more violent than the first. If you force us to slice the other one, we'll send you a recording. You should have heard the first little bugger cry like a castrated calf."

The woman laughed a loud, insane laugh.

"I think the second one will cry even louder, don't you. He strikes me as a good crier. Your friend too—she's got a big mouth, but it's not working right now."

"You bitch," Edie screamed, tears again flooding her eyes.

"Are you all right?" Payne asked.

"I'll be fine. I just need to get through this. Would you mind waiting in the car?"

He hesitated, and then nodded and left her alone.

"But of course what happens to them is entirely up to you, isn't it? So bitch, here's what you must do to save their lives: you must meet me at the Largeville ball diamond at nine o'clock tomorrow night. You remember the ball diamond don't you, the place where you enticed innocent young boys to have sex, the place where you let them kiss your large breasts, the place where you let them put their hard virgin cocks into your big wet cunt, all because you weren't getting any from that queer husband of yours."

Edie fought back an urge to scream and smash the phone.

"And make sure you bring that bitch, Detective Kate Flanagan, with you. I can't wait to show you what we do to women who make it a practice of stealing the virginity from young men, ruining their lives by preventing them from ever having pure sex with their virgin wives. Tell her to leave her gun and cop friends in Minot. If you do that, your friend and dog will be set free. We don't have any quarrel with them, but don't be so stupid to think we won't torture and kill them if you don't do exactly as we say."

The door opened. She erased the message as Payne walked into the kitchen.

"Anything?" he asked.

"Other than the message from my mother, there are three calls that I haven't listened to."

"Don't erase anything," he said.

"I erased my mother's call. You surely wouldn't have wanted to hear her go on and on about her ungrateful, uncaring daughter."

He managed a wan grin.

"Do you want to listen to the others?" She turned on the speaker without waiting for his reply and pushed the 'play' button. From the caller ID, she already knew the woman hadn't called with an addendum, so she really didn't care that Payne heard the calls from friends and telemarketers.

After Payne listened, he said, "I guess you can erase those."

She packed a small bag with clothes and toiletries. Then she went to her closet and from a shoebox on the top shelf at the rear, removed a Smith and Wesson 4040 that Gwen had given her as a birthday gift.

"Are you nuts?" I've never even shot a gun."

"Hon, every single woman in America needs one of these. I'll show you how to clean it and use it. After that, what you do with it is your business, but they make damn good company."

They'd gone to the range twice. Edie managed to hit the target once out of sixteen shots.

"I told you," she'd said to Gwen.

"Hon, if it's livin' or dyin', your aim will get better real fast."

Edie shoved the six inch pistol into the bottom of her makeup kit, hoping it made it past security.

When she got to the casino, a security guard, Steeg, whom she'd gotten to know, accompanied her to her room. The bell captain carried her bag and told her if she needed anything to call him--that everything was on the house. She signaled Steeg that she wanted him to stay.

The moment the bell captain left, she said, "I need to get to the airport without anyone knowing. I have—"

Steeg pointed at the chandelier and air vent.

Edie nodded.

"What time," he whispered.

"Six a.m."

Steeg glanced at his watch. "I'll be back in one hour. Oh, and give me the gun. You won't get anywhere near a plane carrying that."

Chapter 43

Shower Cloud refused to let Flanagan out of her sight and went with her to the precinct for her seven o'clock meeting with Carson.

They put out a warrant for Rhonda Striker and wanted to issue a warrant for Blakewell also, but the chief shot that idea down because of Blakewell's growing political clout. Carson tried to argue, but the chief told them he didn't plan on being unemployed even if they did. That ended the discussion.

Hutton called to say that if they didn't get him out of the hospital, he was going to go crazy and start throwing things. Carson called Hutton's doctor to find out what was going on, told him Kate Flanagan was with him in his office, and put him on the speaker phone.

"Because he's such an ornery bastard," Hutton's doctor said, "we can't wait to get rid of him, but his wife threw him out and he needs a place to stay, someone to care for him, someone else to holler at."

"He can stay at my place," Flanagan said. "Shower Cloud is a trained nurse." She wasn't, but Carson didn't need to know that.

Carson eyed her suspiciously, but finally agreed with Hutton's doctor that provided Hutton stayed off his feet for extended periods, didn't go into the precinct, and checked in at the hospital every morning for the next ten days without his attitude so the nurses could take his pulse and check his blood pressure, he could be released to Shower Cloud's care.

It was noon by the time Shower Cloud and Flanagan got Hutton settled on the sofa in the living room, TV remote in hand. Flanagan put his small suitcase in the guest bedroom and moved Shower Cloud in with her. For lunch, Shower Cloud served egg salad and cucumber sandwiches with the crusts removed, and tea. They ate in the living room to keep Hutton company. He took an egg sandwich that disappeared in one bite.

"I'm sorry we don't have anything more masculine, like a side of beef," Flanagan said.

"Compared to the crap I've had to eat the last few days, this is heaven." He grabbed two more. "Though when you're out, you might pick up a few six-packs of anything that says 'beer.'"

Harry Carson telephoned at four to say the chief yelled at him for letting Hutton out of the hospital and to report that Blakewell had conveniently disappeared and no one in his office knew how to reach him. To raise a few eyebrows, Carson had dispatched a blue and white to Blakewell's mansion next to the golf course, but he wasn't there either and his household and garden staff didn't know where he'd gone.

"Did you tell the chief Hutton was here?"

"I told him Hutton seemed to be making remarkable progress and then his pager went off and he bounded down the hall."

"Thank god for pagers."

"Tell Hutton to behave, or he'll end up at my place sleeping with my kids."

"I'll be sure to let him know."

"Another reason I called is to tell you that Joe and Claudine Peterson are here with their lawyers and want to talk."

"I thought Blakewell was Claudine's Lawyer."

"No more. A young fellow from one of the other firms seems to be her counsel. Joe has Emily Gray."

"Harry, I'll need a ride. I don't want to leave Shower Cloud and Hutton without wheels."

Flanagan saw Shower Cloud raise an eyebrow and spent the whole time between ending the call and the police cruiser arriving trying to convince her that she would be safe, that she would go nowhere alone. Shower Cloud walked with her out to the driveway. "You must promise," she said. "I feel the darkness—the storm is coming."

It was five-thirty when Flanagan arrived at the interview room where Joe and Claudine Peterson had been waiting with their respective attorneys. Despite carrying the burden of Sara's murder and funeral, Claudine appeared ten years younger. She wore a smart pale blue dress with matching heels. The dress showed off her slender, shapely body and her face had been made up in a pleasant way, not thick like the first time Flanagan saw her. When she shook her hand, Flanagan smelled a sweet perfume, not the overpowering cloud of 'hooker cologne' that had nearly knocked her over two days before.

Joe wore blue jeans and a clean white shirt. He looked the way she imagined he always had, certainly the way he had since she'd met him the previous Saturday, eyes red-rimmed and bloodshot with puffy blue bags sagging beneath, though no doubt accentuated by Sara's death and Claudine's accusations. He seemed confused and tentatively stuck out his hand.

"Please sit," Flanagan said. Joe sat, but Claudine and the two lawyers remained standing. So did Flanagan. Joe got back up.

"I wonder if we, Joe and I, might talk to you alone," Claudine said.

"That's up to you," Flanagan said to Emily Gray and the young lawyer. "It's fine with me."

Emily Gray didn't look emotionally distraught by the idea so Flanagan guessed her departure had been previously discussed. Gray spun on her three-inch heels and left without a word. The young man trotted along behind.

Claudine dropped into a chair. Joe sat her left, hands folded on the table. Flanagan looked at Joe. His hands twitched and he looked away. She looked at Claudine.

Claudine moved her handbag to one side, and then put in on the floor.

"Who wants to start?" Flanagan asked.

Claudine looked at Joe. He motioned with his head that Claudine should go first.

"Well, we were at our house yesterday," Claudine said. "You know, after the funeral. A lot of people were there, family mostly, from Bowbells, the little town where Joe and I used to live, and all our friends from Largeville, more than I knew we had."

Joe nodded, his eyes fixed on Claudine like she was some stranger who had recently captured his imagination.

"The women from all the churches brought food, more food than Joe cooks in that little restaurant of his in a month." She shook her head. "We still have most of it. I put some in Joe's refrigerators and some in our freezer at the house, but I'm afraid the rest will go bad." She studied her nails. Flanagan waited.

"Anyway, around nine, after most everyone had gone—including Joe who said he wanted to do some work at the restaurant, the same damn place he always goes when he needs to get away from me."

The look she gave Joe was more matter-of-fact rather than mean.

"Except for Lizzie and John Burke and a few others, they were still there. Finally, I guess everything hit me so I went to the bedroom and sat on the edge of our bed and had myself a damn good cry.

"After a few moments, maybe ten or fifteen, when I felt enough in control to return, I looked in the mirror and saw a horrible mess, mascara and makeup all smeared and running together. I reached into my dresser for my emergency touchup supplies, and I've got a lot." She tried to chuckle.

"Anyway, that's when I saw the letter that Sara had sent a few days before she was killed, a letter I'd never opened. It was tucked alongside with her report cards and vaccination records from school."

Claudine reached down and took a tissue from her bag and wiped her eyes and blew her nose. She looked at Joe, as if asking his permission to proceed. Joe nodded.

"When I saw it was a Mother's Day card, I started to bawl all over again. She hadn't given me a Mother's Day card in years. When I stopped bawling my head off, I opened the card. She'd written a letter."

Claudine wiped at her eyes with her crumpled tissue.

"And then I marched out to the kitchen, borrowed Lizzie's car, and drove to the restaurant, Sara's letter in my hand, and pounded on the door. When Joe didn't answer, I tried the handle. The door was open and I stepped inside. I called his name. Then I heard him crying and found him crumpled down in the back booth, looking like a little boy, sobbing, with no one to comfort him."

Joe sniffled. Claudine reached for her bag. She handed Joe a tissue and took a fresh one for herself.

"I slid in beside him and as the two of us sat there in that little booth, I told him I was sorry, I asked if he thought it was too late for us to start over. And then we held each other and cried together for a long time. And then we talked about Sara, about how good she'd been as our daughter, about how we'd failed her as parents, about how she still loved us to the end."

Claudine reached across, gave Joe's hand a squeeze, and then reached back into her handbag and took out a letter-sized piece of pink paper, folded once. She handed it to Flanagan.

"Here's her letter. We'd like you to read it."

Flanagan opened it and began to read.

Hello Momma, don't keel over in shock or anything like that. It's really me. I'm sorry I left the way I did, but some ugly things were happening. Two men from

Daddy's Saturday night poker games were forcing me to have sex and told me if I didn't, they would kill Daddy because he owed them money and then they'd tell everyone that you were a slut, that you had sex with them whenever they wanted.

I wanted everyone to think I'd left because I'd turned eighteen, that I despised you and Daddy, and maybe I did for awhile, but mostly I figured that by disappearing I couldn't be used to get to the two of you. Crazy huh?

Anyway, I called Daddy a couple of times to make sure he was OK. He wanted me to call you, but I told him I wasn't ready. It's hard, Momma, when a girl finds out her momma's been sleeping around.

My life's a mess, momma, and as soon as I get straightened out, I'll come back to Largeville to see you. I've talked to Zoë Brown some, she was my teacher, and she's trying to help. She sent me some money once and wanted me to live with her parents, but I wasn't ready for anything like that. You should see their place. It's like a castle.

Sorry momma, I didn't mean to run on and on. I'll be home before you know it and we can have a long talk.

Love, Sara.

Flanagan blinked back the tears. Claudine held Joe's hand like she'd never let go. "I've told my lawyer to drop the charges against Joe," she sobbed. "Joe says he doesn't blame me, but I don't know why not—I've done nothing but treat him real awful."

Flanagan handed Sara's letter to Claudine. "What are you going to do now?" she asked. "Where do you go from here?"

"Joe, you tell her darling." Claudine laughed self consciously, as if the word 'darling' was a stranger to her lips. Flanagan guessed it probably was.

Joe hesitated.

"Come on Joe, you know better'n me, better'n anyone."

"Well," Joe said. "Lizzie Burke introduced Claudine and me to some man, Art Logan I think his name is, who wants us to keep the restaurant open."

"He's interested in the Friday and Saturday night poker games is what he is," Claudine said.

Joe nodded. "It seems he's after these two fellas from Bismarck, has been for some time, and found out by askin' at bars and strip joints all over the state that because so many police are looking for them, they only come out anymore to play big-money poker in Largeville and other small towns that got no police."

"They're the ones that was having their way with Sara. If Joe and I find them, we're apt as not to kill them."

Flanagan studied the two of them, certain they would kill anyone who'd hurt Sara. It would ease their guilt for having failed as parents. It would ease their pain for having driven her away.

"The only thing," Claudine said, "is this Logan guy scares me." She laughed. "That's funny, me being afraid of some guy. Can you imagine? I think I can trust him, I want to trust him."

"Is he Indian?" Flanagan asked.

"Yes, but that's not why, though, it's because of these awful tattoos and scars. They give me the willies."

Flanagan couldn't tell them about Art Logan aka Lee Scranton aka Bear Owl, but if Shower Cloud's information was correct, Logan was OK.

Joe said, "If Lottie'd still been around, we'd of had her talk to him. She knows about Indians."

"I know of him." Despite what Shower Cloud told her, Flanagan wanted to check with Carson to see if the police in Bismarck had uncovered anything on Logan. "When are you thinking of starting?"

"Tomorrow morning," Claudine said. "I told Joe we had to keep busy."

"She's going to be my new waitress." They smiled nervously at each other.

"I'm way out of practice, though. It's been ten years since I've done anything like that."

"You'll do real well," Flanagan said, "but I have to tell you something that you may not want to hear."

Their expressions turned to question marks. Claudine pulled at the tissue that was now a wad; Joe's cheek twitched.

*   *   *

Please don't tell them. What purpose will it serve for Joe and Claudine to know that she was an addict? It won't help Sara; it won't help Joe and Claudine. Joe and Claudine need to do something for Sara; that's what they need and that's what Sara wants.

I'm sorry, but they need to know the truth.

*   *   *

"These men that Art Logan is after are dangerous. Maybe you'd be better off getting the police involved."

Joe and Claudine's faces relaxed. Joe said, "Logan told Lizzie and Johnny that these guys know all the police because they've been in and out of every jail in the state. He says they can smell police for miles."

A knock sounded and the very blond and very beautiful Emily Gray from Winslett Ashburn stuck her head in the door. "Joe, all the charges have been dropped. You're free to go when you're finished here."

Joe stood and said thank you. Emily told him to thank Claudine, said that she had to run, and would talk to him later. She nodded at Flanagan, a call me nod, and closed the door. Flanagan remembered that Ripley Blakewell had started out representing Claudine, but she was almost certain the young man who'd been with her wasn't with Blakewell's firm.

"Excuse me for a moment," she said to Joe and Claudine, and ran after Emily Gray. The young man was beside her, trying his best to keep up with her leggy strides.

"Emily?" Flanagan called out.

Gray and the young man stopped. Gray introduced the young man as William Ellison from the Bates, Hitchcock firm, and then sent him on his way, telling him she'd touch base later. Ellison's face and ears turned crimson and disappeared down the hallway.

"I see another of Minot's young lawyers has been smitten by the beautiful Emily Gray."

"Until he gets on the other side in a court room and then he'll hate my guts. What's up?"

"Ripley Blakewell. I thought he started out representing Claudine Peterson."

"He dropped her like a bad penny just as soon as he smelled bigger green."

"As in Rhonda Striker, Tommy Striker's mother."

"You mean Tommy *and* his mother. I hear they are both clients."

"In Tommy's case, *was* his client."

Emily's face asked the question.

"We found him yesterday afternoon. It wasn't pretty."

"God, I don't know how you do it, Kate. What happened?"

"Looks like a suicide. Doc Jackson's working on him now."

"Sorry, I sidetracked. Your interest is in Blakewell."

"We're trying to find him."

"Let me know when you do. We've had to delay two court appearances this morning because that sneaky SOB is quote unquote out of town."

"I'll call you," Flanagan said, "as soon as we find the...him."

Gray said over her shoulder, "Hey, I'm your friend. You can call him an asshole in my presence anytime you want."

Flanagan returned to the interview room. She told Joe and Claudine that she would call about Art Logan and then escorted them to the front of the building. Joe said they'd each brought a car, but couldn't remember where they left them. Flanagan pointed them to the parking lot and watched as they walked across the street and down the sidewalk, trying to find a rhythm, relearning how to move as a couple.

She returned to her office and called Shower Cloud and Hutton. After hearing they weren't about to kill each other, she went to see Carson about Art Logan.

"Sorry," Carson said. "Jeff Haynes, my friend in Bismarck drew a blank. Is he still of interest?"

She told him about Joe and Claudine Peterson and what Shower Cloud had told her about Logan.

"I have another source." He turned and called someone's direct number from the phone on his credenza. Her innate curiosity made her watch; his innate need for secrecy prevented her from doing so, but she could tell from the movement of his hand that he hadn't punched in Bismarck's area code.

She tried to hear what he said, but he spoke so softly that she heard only a few words. He hung up and spun around in his chair. "What you've heard is accurate. My contact wanted to know if Logan's cover has been blown."

"Who's Logan?"

"Figured as much," Carson said.

"Who'd you call?"

"A priest in Washington."

"I'm sure, and by the way, you've never told me that story."

"What story?"

"The one about you being a priest that everyone knows except me."

"That's a dinner conversation."

"When we put a wrap on this, I'll remind you. Oh, and FYI, Emily Gray told me Blakewell missed two court appearances this morning."

"That guy has a way of vanishing, but we'll find him."

Flanagan went back to her office and called Joe to tell him that Art Logan checked out OK. Then she went to the morgue to see if Doc Jackson had anything to report on Tommy. She found him in the slice and dice room with Tommy on the table. Usually, seeing a victim stretched out didn't bother her. Tommy did.

"Wasn't suicide," Doc Jackson said, barely looking up. "Look at the cut. He was taken from behind. Besides, he was left handed. He also had a belly full of Benzedrine and gin. By the time he was killed, this boy was in major conflict."

"They tried hard to make it look like suicide."

"I gather there was a note—usually is."

Flanagan nodded. "Not hand written, but I knew this kid—only he could know the things the note said."

"That's the funny things about suicide notes, even real ones—many believe they contain some kind of hidden message, some reason this person decided to take his own life. Maybe they do, maybe they don't, the point being you'll never know, so don't knock yourself out over it. The sustainable facts in this case are booze, drugs, and murder, not suicide."

Flanagan went back to her office and called Carson to tell him what Doc Jackson said.

"You think his mother killed him?"

"I don't know what to think anymore. Harry, can you hold on for a sec, I've got another call coming in?" She put him on hold without waiting for an answer and hit the flashing button. "Flanagan," she said.

"Is this Detective Kate Flanagan?"

"Yes, who is this?"

"My name is Edie Pitano. I need to see you."

Flanagan's mind raced. Edit Pitano? Edit Pitano? Edie Coombs! The woman from Vegas. "Where are you?"

"I'm at the airport here in Minot." She began to cry. "Please, you and I have to go to Largeville tonight or my friend will be killed."

"Whoa, hold on a minute. What are you talking about?"

"They have my dog. They're going to kill my dog."

"Who's going to kill your dog?" Carson's call went dark. She'd explain later.

"I can't talk here. There are too many people. I need to see you."

"Take a cab to the police station. Tell the desk guard to call me as soon as you arrive."

"I can't come to the police station—they'll think I'm getting the police involved. She said they'd be watching; she said if we got the police involved, my friend will be killed."

Think Flanagan, think. "Go to TJ's bar." TJ's was where she'd met Casey and Penner the night she'd found Shower Cloud's map. "Every cabbie knows TJ's. I'll meet you there."

When she hung up, Carson stood in her doorway. "What's going on, Flanagan?"

"Sorry Harry, I didn't mean to leave you hanging."

"That's not what I mean?"

"Oh, the phone call? Shower Cloud. She's not used to dealing with Hutton's constant demands."

"TJ's bar?"

"She's got my neighbor who used to be a nurse to baby-sit, not that Hutton needs a nurse. I told her I'd meet her at TJ's for a drink, give us both a chance to unwind."

Carson looked askance. "I don't want to get a call and have to run to the chief with another Flanagan cock and bull story."

"Trust me Harry, nothing's going on."

He started away, then turned and said, "Watch yourself Kate. I'm getting rather used to battling your causes, but I'd never get used to you not being here." And then he was gone.

Flanagan took a deep breath and phoned Shower Cloud to tell her she'd be late, to tell her not to worry.

Hutton answered. "She's been in the bedroom humming up a storm," he said, "wailing, one minute sounding like a tribe on the warpath, the next like a nest of songbirds. I've never heard anything like it."

"Listen Hutton, I'd love to chat, but I have to meet someone. Don't wait up and tell Shower Cloud not to worry, that I'm not alone."

"Why do I get the feeling you're about to do something stupid."

"I'm...not. I'll save that for when you're back, and meanwhile, make sure you eat your strained peas."

Her face felt hot. She took a deep breath and hung up before he got to her any more than he already had.

Chapter 44

"This is close enough," Flanagan said. She got out of the cab a block from TJ's and stood on the curb, her stomach feeling like it held a huge rock. All the danger signs were there, but she hadn't seen anything that rang alarms. She called TJ's and asked for Dewey. When he answered, she reminded him who she was and told him not to say her name out loud.

"Yes, uh, yes, I remember."

"I'm to meet a woman there, big, curvy, and blonde, if she's not wearing a wig."

"She's here at the table where you sat."

"Is there anyone else in the bar that you don't know, or who doesn't seem to belong?"

"No, just the usual."

"Any cops?"

"Not for another hour."

"I'll be there in a few seconds. When I come in, don't look surprised or happy to see me and remember, don't say my name."

The goose bumps and bristling hair remained as she opened the door and stepped inside. Edie looked exactly as Hutton had described, filling every square inch of a large pair of jeans and white shirt. She fidgeted with her hands as though about to leap out of her skin and started to get up when she saw Flanagan enter. Flanagan signaled her to remain seated.

Two men at the bar gave Flanagan the once over. She ignored them and they went back to their beers. The alcoholic eyes of others seated at tables followed her across the floor. She winked at one and several of his stubbled pals that looked like dirt laughed.

"Beer, miss?" Dewey asked, coming up behind.

Flanagan motioned to Edie. Edie nodded. "Two Rolling Rocks," Flanagan said, and sat facing Edie.

Edie told her about the casino, about finding Passé-partout in Gwen's car, and the phone call.

Dewey returned with two beers and two glasses. Flanagan gave him a ten and told him to keep the change. Edie shoved the glass aside and chug-a-lugged half the bottle.

"That crazy old bitch intends to kill us all, doesn't she? She's totally whacked out."

A couple of heads turned in their direction.

"Sorry," Edie said.

Flanagan leaned forward and spoke in a voice that only Edie could hear. "Tell me what she said, every word. Did you keep a copy of her message?"

Edie shook her head. "I was so furious and upset that I erased it. It was sick, disgusting."

"I'm sorry you had to go through that, but I need you to tell me as closely as you can what she said."

Edie shivered.

"It could help us."

Edie struggled through recreating the message, pausing frequently to blow her nose and wipe her eyes.

"I don't know what she's talking about, having sex with young virgin men. First of all, I don't think I've ever had sex with a virgin man—not even Rick was a virgin—and I sure haven't been in a ball diamond for sex or any other purpose. The whole idea is revolting."

"There're a couple of things you need to know. I believe the woman you saw in the casino and who called and left the message is Rhonda Striker."

"That young Indian woman that Striker married?"

"No, his first wife."

"I remember hearing about her. Everyone said she was strange."

Flanagan nodded. "Her son, Tommy, is the virgin young man to whom she refers. It seems Tommy had wild sex fantasies about every woman that struck his fancy, you, me, Zoë Brown, Sara Peterson and several other girls at his high school, movie stars, you name it. I think the reason he had these fantasies is because his mother constantly harped at him about the evils of having sex with dirty women, I think she described in detail the act of having sex, I think she showed him how to have sex, using herself as the model, and pounded into his head that every woman other than her was dirty, would ruin his chance at pure virgin sex."

"Jesus, no frigging wonder old Newt had her put away."

"I also think that she became obsessed with Tommy, that she beat him if she thought he'd had sex with another woman, beat him until he finally admitted that he had. But of course he hadn't, so he made up all these stories and the more she beat him, the wilder his escapades became."

Edie shook her head.

"Unfortunately, Tommy's been murdered. I think his mother could no longer handle the notion that he might actually be having sex with someone else."

"Oh Jesus Christ, I'm sorry." She crossed herself. "That poor kid. His old lady killed him?"

"I think so, just as she murdered Zoë Brown and Sara Peterson."

"Dear Lord Jesus, I didn't know about Sara." She crossed herself again. "What are we going to do? She's got Gwen and Tocqueville."

Flanagan handed her a paper napkin to wipe the tears from her eyes. "My poor Passepartout. He didn't do a thing to her. Why did she have to kill him?"

"You know she's plans to kill us."

Edie nodded. "I've got to go. You don't have to come, but I've got to go."

"Your friend and dog will be killed if I don't."

"Right, *my* friend and *my* dog—you don't have anything personal invested."

"She tried to kill my partner, that's personal. She plans to kill me, if not tonight, then later. That's personal. Besides, two stand a better chance."

Chapter 45

Harry Carson had watched Flanagan get into a cab and wondered why she hadn't taken a police vehicle or asked to be driven home. When he asked Casey if she knew where Flanagan had gone, she didn't, but told him that she found out that Rhonda Striker's maiden name was Smith and she had a brother named Derrick.

Carson checked his watch. Flanagan should be home by now. He called her number.

"Kate?" Hutton answered.

"Where is she?"

"You don't sound like Kate and you sure as hell don't look like Kate."

"I'm worried. I saw her get in a cab."

"What the hell is she doing in a cab?"

"Is Lottie Striker there?"

"No, and you're the second person in the last minute who's called looking for her."

"Who was the first?"

"I don't know. Hey, I'm sick here. I barely have enough energy to get to the damn phone. What'd you expect?"

"Yeah, and I'm Dr. Spock, not some nurse you can sweet-talk into an extra minute of massage. Was it man or woman?"

"Woman; said she was a friend of Kate's, but now that I think about it, it seems odd."

"What?"

"She called from Kate's cellphone. Did Kate lose her phone?"

"Not that I know of. Did Lottie Striker say anything before she left?"

"She asked if I had my gun and told me to keep the doors and windows closed and locked. What's going on Harry?"

"I think Flanagan discovered where Zoë's killer has gone after her. Lottie Striker's gone to help. I've got to find them."

"I'm coming with you."

"No, you're not. First, I have no bloody idea where they might be so it makes no sense to have two of us roaring around in the dark, and second, I need you there to answer the phone in case either of them calls in."

"Bullshit!"

"Call it what you will, but that's the way it's going to play. I'm still pissed that you wrecked my Jag— consider this partial payback."

"Full payback old pal, and call me every ten minutes, or I don't give a shit what you say, I'm out of here."

"First, I'm not your pal, and second, have you got your gun?"

"Yeah…"

"Do as Lottie says, and turn off the lights. I'm not so sure you're out of the woods on this either."

"Whaddya mean?"

"I've just found out that Tommy Striker's mother's maiden name is Smith. She has a brother named Derrick."

"The Vegas asshole?"

"Yeah, the guy you kicked in the balls. My guess is they tried to take you out the first time and they're not finished."

"I'll be waiting."

"Just do as Lottie and I say and play it smart for a change. Flanagan doesn't want your blood all over her furniture."

"She's got white shag carpet everywhere."

"Maybe you should go sit in the bathroom."

"You better call me."

"As soon as I get downstairs, I'll call your cell and leave the connection open. Will that make you happy?"

"It'll do for now."

Carson called Casey. He wanted to swap cars and dropped off his keys. If the Smiths had been watching Flanagan and Hutton, they would also likely know the schedules and vehicles of everyone connected to them, particularly a maroon Jag with vanity plates that read 'ND COP – 1,' another thing that pissed the chief off. Casey's five-year-old blue Volvo wagon blended into any landscape and because she wasn't a cop, her comings and goings likely weren't on the Smiths radar.

He got Casey's car and headed for Largeville, back to Striker's house. Something in his gut told him that's where Flanagan and Shower Cloud would be. He called Hutton from his backup cellphone, told him to keep his big mouth shut for a change, and left the connection open.

Chapter 46

After they left TJ's, Flanagan rented a car, and because it would be important when they got to the ball diamond, they checked what the lights did when they turned the ignition off. Edie drove. They arrived in Largeville at ten-fifteen p.m.

"Do you know where the dance hall is?" Edie asked.

"Flanagan nodded.

"The ball diamond's immediately west," Edie said. "What should I do?"

"Is there another road?"

"There's a back lane. We can get close without being seen."

"Take it," Flanagan said. "If we go straight in, she might figure we're too confident, that we have backup."

"God I'm scared." Edie said.

"We'll be all right." Flanagan hoped she sounded more confident than she felt. "Just take it easy."

Edie turned right, drove past the church where Sara's funeral had been, and then turned left onto a lane that ran between several houses. They crossed a street and the lane continued on through a thick stand of trees and shrubs.

After they'd gone several hundred yards, the lights of a small house came into view. "That's Joe and Claudine's place," Edie said.

Flanagan recognized it when they got closer. People moved about inside. Four cars were parked at varying angles in front. One belonged to Lizzie Burke. She didn't recognize the others. A hundred yard past, they stopped next to a fence.

"Kill the lights," Flanagan said.

Edie hit the switch. The ball diamond sat to their immediate right, but it was too dark to see anything.

"I can't do this," Edie whispered.

"Yes you can," Flanagan said. "I don't know what's going to happen, but when it does, it'll likely happen fast. Listen carefully to everything I say and when I tell you to do something, do it like there's no tomorrow."

Flanagan's eyes began to adjust. She watched Edie swallow hard and clench her fists.

"When I say 'go,'" Flanagan said, "get out quickly and shut the door. Try to not make noise and remember, the inside lights don't immediately turn off so stay down."

Edie nodded.

"Stay as low as you can and wait for me by your door."

Edie nodded again.

"Go," Flanagan said in a loud whisper.

They slid out simultaneously, their doors clicking shut. Flanagan pushed the limbs of the scratchy shrub overgrowth to one side and crept through the waist-high grass. She paused behind the car, making sure to stay low so she didn't provide an easy target. She poked her head around the corner. Edie stood by her door like a statue.

"Get down," Flanagan whispered, and started toward her.

Edie didn't move.

Flanagan's body began to tingle. The hair on the back of her neck bristled.

A woman's voice said, "Stand up and put your hands against the car, or I'll blow her head off."

Flanagan felt as though she'd been kicked in the stomach. Like an amateur, she'd allowed them to walk right into a trap. They should have parked in an open space.

"That's right, bitch. Take your time. I've got all night."

When Flanagan had her hands on the car, the woman said to Edie, "Now we're going to walk slowly toward her and you're going to get her gun, understand?" The woman jabbed Edie in the back with a baseball bat. Edie grimaced and lurched forward a step.

"Where's your gun?" the woman asked Flanagan.

"You said no guns."

"If you're lying, I'll shoot your friend's ears clean off her head."

"I'm not lying."

The woman shoved Edie another step, and then another until they were next to Flanagan.

"OK bitch," the woman said to Flanagan. "Now real careful like, I want you to remove your jacket and drop it at your feet."

"I'm sorry," Edie whispered to Flanagan. "I didn't see her until it was too late."

"My fault," Flanagan said.

"That's right girls, get your visiting in now. You don't have much time."

Flanagan heard a sickening crack and Edie slumped to the ground. Flanagan spun around. The woman had smashed Edie in the head.

"She's not dead yet," the woman said, "but she will be if you brought a gun."

"You're Tommy's mother, aren't you?"

The woman jammed the bat into Flanagan's midsection. Flanagan doubled over, clutched at her stomach, and gasped for air. When she could breathe, she stood upright and looked straight at the woman.

"Tommy lied you know. You didn't have to cut his throat. He made up all those stories about having sex to keep you happy."

"You shut your mouth, bitch."

Flanagan figured if she got her mad enough, she might make a mistake, or Edie might recover and get her from her blind side. "You had sex with him, didn't you, and when he told you about all the others, you couldn't stand it, you went into a jealous rage and killed him."

The woman screamed, "Whore!" and swung the bat. It caught Flanagan with a glancing blow to the shoulder and back of her head. She rolled to the ground from the force of the impact and lost consciousness. When she came to a few minutes later, her jeans and blouse had been undone. Rhonda Striker stood over her, baseball bat in one hand, pistol in the other.

"I felt you real good, sweetie. You were right, you didn't have a gun. Now get on your feet and drag your friend to the ball diamond, to that dugout there." She pointed with her bat at the third base side. Flanagan glanced over at Edie who remained unconscious. Her clothes had also been undone.

Flanagan struggled to her feet, did up her jeans and blouse, and rubbed at the lump on her head.

"Don't worry, that was just a little something to get your attention," the woman said. "I use both hands when I want to cause serious harm, like I did to your partner."

"You messed up on that one. My partner's fine."

"Not any more he isn't." She cackled.

Flanagan felt sick. "What do you mean?"

"You see bitch, you're not as smart as you think otherwise you would have found out that my maiden name is Smith, Rhonda Smith, though everyone in my family calls me Didi. Do you know why? Because my baby brother Derrick couldn't say Rhonda, that's why. He called me Didi."

"Derrick Smith from Vegas."

"He's taking good care of your partner and that dirty squaw. Don't you worry, though. No bats this time—bullets for your partner. My guess for the squaw: first he'll have his fun and then slice her up with his hunting knife. Now grab that bitch's arms or legs, I don't care which, and start dragging."

"Do you beat Derrick and make him tell, like you did Tommy? Like Tommy, does he make up stories to keep you happy? Is he going to make up a special story about having sex with the Indian girl? Like Tommy, has he ever had sex with anyone except you."

Rhonda swung the bat and hit Flanagan in the knee. Flanagan screamed and fell to the ground, gripping her knee and rolling back and forth on her back in the grass. Tears filled her eyes and she gritted her teeth to keep from crying out again.

"What about your husband," she gasped. "Why did you kill him? Because he stuck you away and married a young woman."

Rhonda kicked her in the ribs. "Go ahead and have your fun, bitch. You don't have much time."

"And what about Victoria Otto? You killed her too."

"Oh yes, she was my first. Don't you see, when we moved here she was Tommy's grade one teacher and she got it into her head that Tommy was being sexually abused, started asking him all kinds of embarrassing questions. I had to make her disappear."

"Tommy said he didn't know Miss Otto."

"I erased her from his mind. I couldn't let him remember."

"But Newton found you with Tommy one day and put you away. No wonder Tommy was so screwed up."

"You whore! You and the others, you're all the same. You couldn't leave him alone. You all wanted him: you, that Jew teacher, that big lump of shit"—she pointed the bat at Edie—"that whore daughter of Joe and Claudine's, all of you, you dirtied him, you ruined him. He told me everything. He sent me e-mails with every sordid detail, and I cried myself to sleep every night knowing how my baby, my gift from heaven, was being abused. Don't you see? I had to stop it. I prayed every night, asking God what to do, and finally He told me: 'You have to kill all of them,' He said. 'That is the only way.'"

"Did he tell you to kill Tommy?"

Rhonda poked her hard with the bat. "Get up. Start dragging your friend."

Flanagan struggled to her feet. The pain in her knee shot up and down her side, but it remained functional. Edie groaned and her shoulder twitched. "Can you hear me?" Flanagan asked.

Edie didn't respond.

As Flanagan grabbed Edie under the arms and started to turn her around, Flanagan's knee gave way and she crumpled to the ground.

"What's the matter cunt, can't move the fat cow?"

"She shouldn't be moved." Flanagan struggled to her feet.

A car at Joe and Claudine's started, and the head-lights came on. It came in their direction.

"Don't do anything stupid," Rhonda said, and stepped behind Flanagan. She jammed the gun into her back. Flanagan winced as the barrel dug into her tender ribs.

The car slowed and stopped. The driver's window lowered. "Everything OK miss?" Johnny Burke asked.

"Just getting some air." Rhonda said. "Our friend drank a little too much."

Flanagan prayed Burke would recognize her and fig-ure something was out of whack.

"I know how that feels," Burke chuckled, and drove on.

Flanagan's heart sank as the taillights of Burke's car turned left at the main street and disappeared.

"OK, move it," Rhonda said, and shoved Flanagan forward.

Flanagan knew she couldn't drag Edie one foot let alone all the way across to the ball diamond. She had to buy time, hoping against hope that someone would see them, would come to their aid. "I have a confession, Mrs. Striker. I did have sex with Tommy. So did Edie. We laughed about it just this afternoon in TJ's bar.

Tommy told Edie that having sex with her was the best, even better than with his mother."

"You shut your filthy mouth."

"And that's exactly what he told me. He said that having sex with his mother was the worst."

"You lying whore!" Rhonda screamed and ran forward, swinging the bat.

Flanagan put up her arm to deflect the first blow and reeled to her right on impact, grabbing her forearm certain it had been broken. If it had been they were about out of time, because she didn't stand a chance with only one good arm. "Maybe you didn't have sex with Mr. Striker. Maybe Derrick is Tommy's father. Maybe that's why Tommy was strange, from in breeding. Is that what happened, Didi?"

Rhonda swung again, but Flanagan rolled out of the way.

"How are you going to tell God that Tommy's father is your brother?"

Rhonda slugged Flanagan across the back. Any lower, and it would have knocked her wind out, but most of it caught her across the shoulder blades.

"Who was the better lover, your baby brother or your son? Or maybe Newton."

"OK slut, now you see your friend die." Rhonda turned and shot Edie in the leg. "The next one goes in her eye."

"That's not your style. I thought you had to smash us with the bat. Why the bat, Rhonda? Did your father abuse you with a bat? Did he have his way with you? Did he steal your virginity?"

Rhonda screamed something unintelligible, dropped her gun to the ground, and gripped the bat with both hands. Flanagan curled up in a ball to fend off the blows and tried to roll toward Rhonda's gun. The first blow crashed across her knees.

*   *   *

She saw orchids.

You'll be OK now. Close your eyes.

But I failed you. I didn't catch your killer. I'm sorry.

*   *   *

Rhonda struck another blow, this time at Flanagan's head. A yellow light shot across the sky. So this is what dying is like, Flanagan thought, and her world went dark.

Chapter 47

Hutton checked the doors to make sure they were locked, managed to drag a chair from the kitchen to the front window, and turned off the inside lights, leaving the rear and front porch lights on. He sat looking out, gun in hand.

Lottie…he'd forgotten about Lottie. His energy about spent, he staggered back to the kitchen and called her cellphone. The message said she wasn't answering calls. He remained in the kitchen for a few minutes to regain a little strength and then, still gripping his gun, made his way back to the front window hoping to not shoot himself in the foot.

He picked up the cellphone with the open connection to Carson. "Harry, answer if you can hear me." He waited. No response. He said it again. Still no response. He again made his way back to the kitchen where he phoned Casey, hoping she was still on duty. She was. He told her that when Carson checked in to have him call on Flanagan's land line, that Lottie hadn't returned.

"I can hardly understand you," she said. "You sound terrible."

"I don't feel so hot either. Better get some backup to Flanagan's place a.s.a.p. I'm expecting company and I may need help."

He hung up and crawled back to his vantage point near the front window. The front yard was awash in light and anyone coming up the walk could easily be seen. Including Lottie you idiot. She always comes in that way and you've made her into an easy target. Using the last of his strength, he crawled across to the front door and turned the porch light off by reaching up with the barrel of his pistol.

The phone in the kitchen rang. "Shit!" His head throbbed. His stomach felt like it was tearing apart inside, but he had to answer. He lay on his right side and managed to claw across the room. By the time he got there, voicemail had picked up. He lay on the floor panting for breath, soaked in his own sweat. The phone rang again. He set his gun down and pulled himself up by grasping onto a chair.

"Yes, hello," he gasped. Click.

He dropped the receiver to the floor. The room started to spin and he sunk to his knees. His eyes went out of focus and he thought he was going to vomit. He passed out. Several minutes later he opened his eyes. The dizziness remained, but his eyes had cleared. Shadows sharpened. He smelled stale smoke and gin and wondered if he'd crossed a few wires in his brain. Digging his fingers into the carpet and inching his hand along, he felt for his gun. He sensed movement. His hand touched a shoe, no, it was a boot...the pointed toe of a man's boot.

"What's the matter tough guy? Not feeling so tough? Where's the squaw?"

Hutton recognized Derrick Smith's voice and tried to think where anything was that he might use as a weapon. A stool or chair wouldn't work because he wasn't strong enough to lift let alone swing them. The fireplace was ten feet to his right. Maybe in the dark, he could roll past Smith and get his hands on the andirons.

He rolled over, gritting his teeth to keep from gasping. Once more, he told himself. God it hurts. He stretched, hoping to feel the brickwork of the hearth. His fingers brushed against something rough and hard. Just a little further, if I don't rip my guts apart.

"That's far enough, asshole." The toe of Smith's boot crashed into Hutton's rib cage, knocking the wind out of him and breaking a couple of ribs in the process. He cried out from the impact and contracted into a fetal position, grabbing at the side of his chest.

"How does it feel, tough guy?"

Smith kicked him again, this time harder and in the kidneys. Hutton blacked out. When he came to, he was on the kitchen floor, the lights under the cabinets had been turned on, and Smith's dark outline sat on a counter stool.

"I hope you don't mind a little light. I like to see pain."

Hutton glanced at the door.

"Are you looking for the squaw?"

Hutton glared at Smith.

"I know she's around somewhere. Don't worry; she'll be back before I leave. You might not see her though. Too bad, I've got a special treat for her." He cupped his had on his crotch and laughed.

Using every ounce of energy he had left, Hutton dove at Smith's legs. It wasn't enough. Gasping, he lay in a crumpled ball at Smith's feet.

"I thought this was going to be more fun," Smith said, picking up an aluminum baseball bat that leaned against the wall. "I thought you'd at least try to run away." He tapped the bat on the palm of his hand. "Get up. Stand on your feet, you son-of-a-bitch. I'll show you what happens to anyone who punches me in the balls."

"You didn't do too well last time," Hutton said.

"Get up," Smith shouted, and bashed the bat against a stool, sending the stool crashing to the counter.

Hutton tried to move. He couldn't stand without help. He reached for the counter top. Smith swung the bat. Hutton saw it coming and let go just before it smashed his hand. It careened off the granite counter top with a loud metallic clank and flew from Smith's hands.

"You cocksucker," Smith yelled, dancing around shaking his hands. "You're going to pay for that." Smith pulled out his pistol. Keeping it pointed at Hutton, he picked up the bat. "Spread your hands on the tile."

"I thought you were going to shoot me. Lose your nerve?"

"Spread your goddamn hand."

"You want to beat the shit out of me, go ahead, but I'm not spreading my hand."

Smith raised the bat. "Say goodbye to your knees you dumb bastard."

Hutton gritted his teeth and braced for the hit. The bat landed on his leg, but it didn't hurt. He heard a crash and opened his eyes. Smith lay on his back, a bullet hole between his eyes.

"You all right?"

Hutton turned his head. "Fair shot."

"I was aiming for his shoulder. Guess the gun jumped."

"They'll do that in inexperienced hands. Thought you were going to Largeville?"

"It was only a hunch. I didn't know where Flanagan had gone, but I did know you needed help, thanks to leaving our cellphones connected."

"Did you find Flanagan?"

Carson shook his head.

"You should've gone to Largeville. I was doing OK here."

"Yeah, it looked like it. Sorry I interrupted."

Hutton tried to sit.

"Where's Lottie?" Carson glanced around.

"She didn't come back. I hope she's—"

"I ducked my way around the entire house and didn't see any sign of her. Besides, I expect if he'd run into Lottie, Lottie would have won."

Hutton managed to prop himself up on an elbow.

"If I were you, I'd stay right where you are until the ambulance arrives."

"Harry, I'd sooner be dead than go back to that hospital. We've got to find Flanagan. Help me up. You've got to get me to Largeville."

"Quigley should be getting there about now. When I heard you having trouble, I sent him and Penner. They were already north of the city and could get there a lot faster than I could."

Hutton put his hand up.

"Can you breathe OK? You're not coughing up blood?"

Hutton grimaced. "Breathing hurts like hell and I might be coughing up a rib or two, but no blood."

Carson's cellphone rang. "Hold on a sec," he said to Hutton.

"Go ahead. I'm not going anywhere."

Carson looked at the incoming number. "It's Penner." He snapped the phone open. "You find her?"

Chapter 48

The two coffins sat side by side.

"Where these going Doc?" the driver of the hearse asked.

Doc Jackson snapped off a rubber glove. "To hell, as far as I'm concerned."

"We've already made that delivery today."

"Take them to the airport. They're being shipped back to Texas."

"Are these the two they won't have to hang?"

"Yeah, now get the hell out of here. You miss that goldang plane and you'll drive them to Texas."

"Yes sir, Doc. We're on our way."

To the sounds of dripping water and the squish squish of his thick crepe soles, Jackson walked across the wet cement floor and stared down at the two bodies lying on the stainless steel tables that were no more than three feet apart. "And two more tomorrow," he said to the empty room. He pulled sheets over Newton and Tommy Striker's faces. "Two more tomorrow." He looked at the row of body drawers. "And two more the next day."

The phone on the wall near the door rang. He stared at it for a moment, wondering whether to answer, and then trudged forward, removing his once white smock and tossing it across the back of a chair.

"Jackson," he said. "Yes, goldang it, I'm coming."

Chapter 49

Harry Carson stood on one side, Hutton on the other, looking down at Flanagan. "Is the Doc coming?" Hutton asked.

Carson nodded.

Shower Cloud entered as if on the air and took her place next to Hutton. She closed her eyes and put the tips of her fingers under her chin, standing motionless, it seemed not even breathing.

Doc Jackson shuffled in, weariness hanging from his sagging face. He stood next to Hutton.

Shower Cloud began to chant, low at first, a deep sound in the back of her throat, and then she began to sway ever so slightly and her voice grew louder and higher in tone and more urgent until it seemed an entire chorus of voices and the dum-dad-da, dum-da-da of beating drums had joined in. And then she stopped. Carson, Hutton, and Doc Jackson stared hard, tears in their eyes.

When Shower Cloud opened her eyes, they were milky orbs that secreted a cloud-like substance into the room. "I must go now," she said, and vanished into the mist.

"Wait..." A fragile voice cried out.

Carson, Hutton, and Doc Jackson's heads snapped round.

"Wait," Flanagan said again, her voice sounding stronger.

Hutton grabbed her outstretched hand and clasped it to his chest.

"Please...please...don't let her go."

"I'm sure she'll be back soon," Carson said, stepping forward and looking down at Flanagan.

"Yeah, I'm sure of it," Doc Jackson said, looking at the doorway as if expecting her to come back at that very moment.

She smelled orchids. "Do you smell the flowers?"
Hutton nodded.

*   *   *

Don't search too hard for her.
I need to find her. I need to know what happened.
One day soon you will find the answers to your questions. And now, I too must go. Thank you for setting us free.
You and Victoria Otto?
Yes, and Sara—Sara's with us...

Chapter 50

Flanagan opened her eyes and peered up at the ceiling. It wasn't hers. It wasn't a ceiling she recognized. Her brain told her not to move—still she tried to turn her head. Her brain had been right. She clamped her eyes shut and gritted her teeth as the searing pain shot from her temple back through her skull and down her spine. She would have writhed and screamed but those parts didn't seem to be working.

When she opened her eyes, the room appeared bleary through her tears of pain. She blinked several times. Someone moved. She saw a shadow. It came nearer.

"It's about time," the shadow said. "I was beginning to think you'd sleep all day."

After a brief moment, her brain connected the dots. "Hello Hutton," she said, surprised that her voice seemed to be working fine. "What happened? What is this place?"

"This place is a hospital. You've had a bit of a bump on the head."

Flanagan felt her brain begin to whirr, like it had broken loose inside her head, like it had decided to go its own way. Edie Coombs! She and Edie had gone to Largeville. The ball diamond! Tommy's mother! That horrible baseball bat!

"Where's Edie. Is she…is she OK?"

"Other than a good knock on the head and a bullet hole in her leg, she's fine. You can visit later if you're up to it."

Flanagan lowered her eyes until they hurt. Her left leg was wrapped in a cast that stuck into the air. Cautiously, fearing another jolt of pain in her head, she tried to wiggle the toes of her right foot. She couldn't tell if they'd moved or not.

"You're not paralyzed," Hutton said. He grabbed her right foot and started to give her a massage. "You feel this?" he asked.

She couldn't nod her head, but she managed a smile—never before had anyone touching her foot felt as fantastic. She closed her eyes to savor the moment.

Pain shot through her head. Her brain wasn't yet ready to let her feel good. It made her see Edie on the ground. Tommy's mother had smashed her in the head with the bat. And then she hit me, first in the leg and then on the arm, and she shot Edie in the leg. She hit me again and I fell down. She kept hitting me...

Flanagan opened her eyes. Hutton stopped massaging her foot and moved to the head of the bed where she could see him more easily. He put his hand on her forehead. "Can I get you anything?"

"I thought Tommy's mother had killed us. What happened? How did we get here?"

"Your doctor told me not to talk about it, not for a few days."

"Horseshit!" Her brain no longer hurt, it no longer felt disconnected. She reached her left arm up, the one not in a cast, and touched his face. He hadn't shaved. She touched his lips. He kissed her fingers. "Horseshit," she whispered.

He took her hand in his, clutching as though he might never let go. "Quigley and Penner arrived and found you and Edie with the woman and a lot of blood on the ground. At first, they feared all of you'd been killed, but only the woman was dead."

"How did Tommy's mother..."

"You got her with your knife. That must have been a hell of a thrust—her head was damn near rolling around on its own."

"But I didn't...I don't..."

"Jesus Flanagan, no one knew you carried a knife strapped to your ankle. By next week, the chief will have all of us wearing them."

She gripped his hand as hard as she could. "But I don't carry a knife. Don't you get it? It was Shower Cloud. She killed Tommy's mother."

Hutton's face blanked. He lowered her hand to the bedcovers and gently gripped her shoulders. "You need to rest. Your doc was right. I shouldn't have told you as much as I did."

"No, listen to me. I don't carry a knife. Shower Cloud saved my life."

"OK, and who is Shower Cloud?"

"Shower Cloud, you know, Striker's wife, she worked at Pete's Café, she looked after you when we took you to my place, she…"

Hutton bent over and kissed her on the nose. She squeezed her eyes shut to try and stop the tears of anger and frustration wanting to explode. "You're right," she said. "I do feel tired. I think I'll try to sleep."

Chapter 51

A week later, Flanagan had recovered to the point where she could sit up in bed, feed herself, and take little rides on the wheelchair, mostly to the bathroom. Hutton had practically lived at her bedside, which worked out well since, according to the chief, he was supposed to still be in the hospital anyway. Edie and her friend Gwen had visited several times. Gwen even brought Tocqueville once, but didn't succeed in getting him inside the hospital. Quigley and Penner had found Gwen and Tocqueville, bruised and dirty and in Gwen's case, ready for a 'goddamn' good fight. They were locked in the trunk of the Lincoln in Striker's garage.

Harry Carson had been to see Flanagan every day, as had Doc Jackson. Casey bopped in and out with all the local gossip. Flanagan finally got up the courage to ask Casey if she'd ever heard of an Indian woman known as Shower Cloud. Casey hadn't.

Jay Singh breezed in one morning to take her temperature and feel her body. "Strictly professional," he said.

"Then stop smiling," she said.

After he'd poked her few more times, he said, "You have a gentlemen caller. Actually, he's been here every day since you decided to grace us with your presence and every day I've told him that you couldn't have visitors. He never argues, just leaves and then reappears at the start of the next visiting hours."

"Who, for God's sake?"

"Speaking in that tone to your doctor won't win you any awards."

"I have friends, a lot of friends, with guns."

Singh smiled. "He says his name is Running Bear."

Victoria Otto's father. Flanagan's stomach flinched.

"Shall I bring him in?"

"I'd like to meet him. Is Hutton around?"

"He wanted me to tell you he had to go to the police station this morning, but he'll be back before noon. Would you sooner wait until he was here?"

"I'm not sure. Did this Running Bear person say what he wanted, why he wanted to see me?"

ShowerCloud.

"So far, the only words I've heard him speak are: 'Miss Flanagan, please.' He's a refined looking gentleman, if that helps, you know, shirt and tie, all the trimmings."

"So he's not a crazed killer seeking revenge is what you're saying?"

"I keep forgetting you're a cop. It sounds to me like you'd sooner wait for your pal."

"In one sense I do. In another I don't."

"So what's it going to be, officer?"

"I'll see him, but not in here, in the visitors' room in full view of others."

"If you need privacy, I can get you a corner of the doctors' lounge."

"Let's start with the visitors' room. Will you help me with the wheelchair?"

Fifteen minutes later, Jay Singh wheeled Flanagan into the visitors' room. There were three people waiting, one elderly looking man seated next to one elderly looking woman, and one ancient man in a light brown suit, shoulder length gray hair, skin as dark and wrinkled as a prune, and a big white smile. He stood as soon as he saw Flanagan. She saw that he held a Stetson with several colorful feathers tucked into the band. A tooled leather briefcase sat next to his feet.

"Running Bear, this is Detective Kate Flanagan. She's agreed to meet with you, but I can only allow a few moments."

"Thank you," Flanagan said to Singh. "I'll be fine. Please sit," she said to Running Bear.

Running Bear did so, embracing her with clear, black eyes. As soon as Singh was out of earshot, he said, "The reason I have come is to thank you for freeing my daughter to the spirits of our ancestors."

"Ever since she disappeared fourteen years ago, we have carried the burden of her torment each day, each moment, each second, as she struggled to be free of our earthbound ways, to join our ancestors in the place where our spirits live in eternal peace and happiness."

"Your daughter is Victoria Otto." Flanagan began to feel warm. The hairs on her arms stood on end.

"We called her White Owl."

"Yes, I remember." *S h o w e r C l o u d.* "You're chief of the tribe."

"Yes, the Hidasta tribe. We're on the Fort Berthold reservation that surrounds Lake Sakakawea. My wife, Swift Deer, apologizes for not coming today, but she wanted me to convey her thanks as well and asked that I give you this note." He reached into his inside pocket, extracted a folded, note-sized piece of paper, and handed it to Flanagan.

Flanagan reached for it, and then jerked her hand back. The paper had started to glow a brilliant golden color. *S h o w e r C l o u d.* She reached again, but her hand wouldn't stop shaking. She could no longer see Running Bear, only the bright glow that now seemed to fill the room, and then she steadied her hand and snatched the paper, gripping it between her thumb and fingers. The glow subsided. Running Bear smiled. Flanagan drew in a deep breath and carefully opened the note.

I hate to impose, an ancient hand had written, but it would mean so much to Running Bear and me if you would attend our tribal ceremonies to celebrate White Owl's release to that great place beyond the far horizon.

On her behalf, we wish to honor you for making her voyage possible. The note was signed Swift Deer.

"I don't know what to say," Flanagan said.

"Please say yes. It would mean so much to all of us."

"I don't know how long…"

"We will wait for as long as it takes you to heal."

The note began to feel warm in her hands, and she looked down at the golden aura surrounding the paper. She looked back into Running Bear's eyes, into a face that wanted her to say yes more than anything else in the world. "I am honored," she said. "How do I contact you?"

Running Bear handed her a card that contained his telephone and fax numbers and e-mail address.

"You have your own website?"

Running Bear chuckled.

"I'm sorry." Her face felt hot.

"Please don't apologize. Even I forget how far we've come, maybe because I'm not sure all of this so-called advancement is for the better."

Flanagan gripped the arm of her wheelchair in a futile attempt to adjust her position.

Running Bear leapt to his feet with the agility of a twenty-year-old. "I've kept you too long. Please, may I take you to your room?"

"Ordinarily I'd say yes, but I need two nurses to get me into the bed. Fortunately, they've given me this pager so all I have to do is push this button and help will magically appear."

She showed him the red button as she pushed it, following which a woman's voice said, "We'll be right there, Miss Flanagan."

"And some advancement serves a purpose," he smiled. A moment later, when the two nurses arrived, Running Bear bade her goodbye.

That afternoon, Emily Gray with her dark suit that made her look like an assistant DA from Law and Order, came to talk about Ripley Blakewell. Emily was determined to take Blakewell down and wanted Flanagan's help.

"If we don't get this bastard he'll be our Senator," she said, pacing the floor like she was possessed, her high heels clicking on the tiles. "It's bad enough that the people in North Dakota have to put up with this clown, but we don't need to let the rest of the country think he is what North Dakota's all about."

"I'll help in any way that I can," Flanagan said, "but rather than in the courtroom, I'd prefer you oppose him as a candidate."

Gray gaped at Flanagan. "You're serious," she said when she got her mouth working, which in Emily Gray's case was a split second.

"There's no rule barring a thirty something female hotshot running for the office of US Senator just because she's a knockout blonde with great legs."

Gray threw out her chest. "Don't forget the tits."

A week later, Flanagan got her release. Her leg had healed to the point where she could manage a walking cast. They put a short arm cast on her arm and made her wear a specially constructed helmet to protect her head. Edie got released the same day and Gwen drove her and Passepartout back to Vegas. Flanagan had talked to Edie several times about Shower Cloud, hoping Edie would remember seeing her, but the only thing Edie remembered was getting knocked on the head and she had no recollection of an Indian woman having ever lived with Striker.

Dr. and Sadie Brownstein visited on the third and second last days before Flanagan's release. They established a scholarship fund in Zoë's memory and asked Flanagan to help them select a student from Largeville whose college tuition and all expenses would be paid by the fund. Flanagan told them that Zoë would have wanted the first pick to be Dale Kiley; that she would have wanted Joe and Claudine Peterson to be the ones that helped select future students; and that she would have wanted the fund to also be in memory of Sara Peterson. They agreed and the fund was set up as the Zoë Brown and Sara Peterson Pursuit of Excellence Fund.

Flanagan let Joe and Claudine Peterson tell Dale Kiley that he'd been selected for the first award. Kiley was scheduled to attend Julliard that September.

Before Dr. and Sadie Brownstein returned to Chicago, Flanagan told them of the black lady with two great grand children living in Sara's apartment. Sadie said she would contact her as soon as they got back because she needed an experienced person to supervise her kitchen and household staff.

Saying he needed to talk to her about a few things, Harry Carson drove her home from the hospital. She could tell he had a lot on his mind and several times she had to keep from blurting out, 'Yes Harry, for Christ's sake what is it?' With each passing block, the silence hung heavier in the air until it became hard to breathe. They pulled into the driveway.

"Would you like to come in?"

"It would be better if we talked here," he said, his face more drawn than she'd ever seen.

Tentacles of unease encircled her stomach.

"Kate, you know I've wanted you to become a full detective for some time, that I've supported you at every turn, that I've gone to war with the chief on your behalf."

"I know that, and don't think for a moment that I don't appreciate what you've done."

Carson continued, as if she hadn't spoken. "I'm afraid this last thing with Shower Cloud is more than I could fight."

"I'm not getting the promotion, is that what you're trying to tell me?"

"The chief wants you to take six months."

"SIX MONTHS? Jesus Harry, that will kill any chance I had—"

"It's not negotiable, Kate. I've tried every trick I know, some I made up as I went along, but he won't budge."

She didn't care that tears flooded from her eyes and tumbled down across her cheeks. "You saw Shower Cloud, Harry. You know she exists. I didn't make her up."

He shook his head and looked away.

"Don't do this to me Harry. You, Hutton, even Galen know she's real."

"Hutton told me about the voices."

"I can't explain the voices. Actually, one voice, Zoë Brown's voice, but it was as real as yours or mine, and now it's gone, just as she told me it would be, once her killer was found and brought to justice. I don't know why she picked me, but if it helps solve murders, is it such a bad thing? Jesus, we use psychics and fortune tellers and every other weapon at our disposal, but as soon as a cop hears a voice, she's labeled unstable?"

"It's not only the chief. I'm worried about you too Kate. You damn near got yourself killed. If it wasn't for that knife—"

"That wasn't my knife. I didn't kill Rhonda Smith and you know it. If Shower Cloud hadn't been there, you wouldn't have to worry about me—I'd be dead."

"Here's what I can promise: you take the six months and you'll come back exactly where you left off."

"You mean as some guy's bag carrier."

"I'll make sure you are given every chance to become a senior detective."

"Where's Hutton, or didn't he have the guts to get in on the blood letting?"

"That's not fair. For a lot of reasons, I wanted to be the one who told you. For as many reasons, and you as well as anyone know what they are, I didn't want Hutton involved."

"No, I don't know Harry. What are Hutton's reasons? Why didn't you want him involved?"

Carson gave her a long sidelong glance. "You really want me to spell it out?"

Yes, damn it, I do."

"Kate, wake up, the guy's nuts about you."

Her mouth dropped open. He may as well have punched her in the stomach.

"Yeah, and it doesn't make my job any easier. When you come back, one of you is going to have to move to a different department, maybe in another state."

A horn sounded from behind. They turned their heads to look. "Speak of the devil," Carson said.

Hutton pulled to the curb in his Jeep. Carson started to get out, but stopped when Flanagan touched his arm. "Thanks Harry," she said. "I'm sorry if I gave you a hard time, and I'm likely not finished with that part of this conversation, but for now I need some alone time with Hutton. You and I'll continue later if you don't mind."

He took her hand and squeezed. She got out. Carson backed down the driveway and headed up the street, waving at Hutton as he passed.

Hutton looked at Flanagan, hesitated, and then started slowly the street, his hands jammed in the front pockets of his jeans.

Flanagan met him at the end of her short driveway. "Are you working undercover as a cowboy?"

He tried a grin. It didn't work. "I'm off for two weeks, chief's orders." He looked down and kicked the toe of his cowboy boot at a blade of grass that had managed to grow in a crack between the road and curb. "Harry told me about your leave. Sorry."

"I can handle that. What we need to talk about is us. Harry seems to think you're nuts about me, to use his words."

Hutton's face turned red.

"Did he happen to tell you that I'm also nuts about you?"

He looked at her as if uncertain about what she'd said.

"Yeah, I'm afraid you heard correctly." She stepped closer, her heart about to leap from her chest, and took his hand. "And so now what do we do, detective?"

He made a funny sound in his throat. "You're the senior on this case," he said, "but if you want my opinion—"

She smelled his body, she felt the heat from his hand, and she wanted to taste his saliva, to feel his hands caress her breasts, to feel him deep inside the hot wetness between her wide-spread legs, over and over until she felt him explode. She gave his arm a tug. "Come with me," she said, her voice husky. "I'm way past opinions. I hope you can navigate around all this hardware."

Chapter 52

Two days later, when she and Hutton decided it might be wise to add food to their relationship and get Flanagan to the hospital for her daily checkup, one of which she'd already missed and had to up Wolyshyn's bribe to two dinners to keep him from calling Carson or the chief, Flanagan asked Hutton if he'd drive her to Lake Sakakawea. When he said he would, Flanagan phoned Running Bear, who said Hutton was welcome and asked if they could come that day. She and Hutton left from the hospital after Singh reluctantly gave her an overnight pass in exchange for a bottle of outrageously expensive champagne that Hutton gladly placed in his outstretched hands.

When they arrived at Fort Berthold, Flanagan read the instructions that Running Bear had given her over the phone. Running Bear wasn't hard to find: his instructions were perfect, and Fort Berthold wasn't any larger than Largeville. After they had been introduced to Swift Deer, whose health had recovered, she and Running Bear escorted them to the Tribal Center where a 'Banquet of the Dead' for White Owl had been arranged. Flanagan was transported by six young Indian men who carried her on an ornately hand-carved chair covered with a beaded robe that wouldn't have been out of place in the State Art Gallery.

In all, over a thousand Indians had gathered in a large tiered circle. They fell silent when the procession led by Running Bear and Swift Deer approached, and then parted, creating a six-foot wide path from the perimeter to the circle's center where White Owl's remains had been wrapped in deerskin and placed on a pyre amid a gigantic mound of fresh fruits and vegetables.

After Flanagan's throne-like chair had been lowered and placed between similar chairs where Running Bear and Swift Deer sat, Hutton was led to a place next to

where fifty young Indian men with feathered head and
arm bands sat, all dressed in beaded white leather vests
and pants. Their bodies and faces had been painted in a
way that Flanagan had only seen in movies.

Running Bear extended his arm and then moved it in
an arc to his right. A group of fifty women from various
locations within the circle began to chant and descended
toward the center, like people at a revival meeting coming down to be born again. Their chanting grew louder
and they began to clap their hands and when they had all
arrived they began to sway from foot to foot and drew
around White Owl's remains. Chanting gave way to
wailing and moaning. This went on for approximately
ten minutes and then stopped. The women knelt on one
knee, placed their hands palm down on the ground, and
lowered their heads. Nothing moved, and other than the
snapping of the fire and a distant coyote's howl, not a
sound could be heard.

Flanagan flinched when the fifty young men sprang
to their feet with a loud roar and leapt over the kneeling
Indian women. They landed silently on their moccasined
feet, bent arms extended perpendicular to their sides,
fingertips almost touching, hands palm down in front of
their chests. Their heads jerked to the right, and then to
the left. Several unseen drums began to beat out:
DUM...dum dum dum Dum...dum dum dum. The
young men's feet began to keep time by stamping on the
ground, faster and faster. They turned to their left and
began to move clockwise, their stamping feet and the
pulsating drums as one. Their swung their arms with
such vigor that they seemed destined to take flight and
bent forward at the waist as if preparing for takeoff, but
their forward progress was glacial. Their feet were a
blur, and they began to chant in time with the stamping
of their feet and the DUM...dum dum dum DUM...dum
dum dum rhythm of the drums. After a few moments
they were a frenzy of motion and their chants, like those

of the women before them, reached a maniacal pitch. And then they stopped, frozen in their positions. The drums slowed and gradually became silent.

Running Bear stood and gazed at White Owl's remains surrounded by the outer circle of kneeling Indian women and the inner circle of young braves, all frozen like ice statues. The feathers in Running Bear's headdress fluttered in the breeze that stiffened and ebbed as ocean waves. He turned and took Swift Deer's hand. She rose with the elegance of a ballerina and stepped forward to stand at his side. Together they viewed what lay before them: those gathered in celebration of the dead; the long tables of grains and berries and meat, the exact same grains and berries and meat that their ancestors had found when the Hidatsa first came there seven hundred years earlier. They viewed the coming darkness of the night dotted with campfires and they viewed the golden footsteps of the setting sun as it marched below the distant horizon where a sky of deep purple met rolling hills of blue and black.

"Come," Running Bear said to Flanagan and held out his hand. "Stand with us."

With the help of two young braves she easily stood and stepped forward. Running Bear and Swift Deer parted, leaving room for her to stand between. She looked over at Hutton, whose eyes were locked on hers, and she felt the electricity that flowed between them.

"We go now to commit White Owl's remains to the spirits of our ancestors," Running Bear said. "Please walk to the sacred circle with us. I shall lead the way. Swift Deer shall follow me, and you shall follow her in the place where Princess White Owl would have been."

Flanagan felt the strong, gentle hands of the two braves lift her from the ground as she stepped in behind Swift Deer. The tribal elders, who had been seated behind them, joined the procession. The drums began a low rumble. Still the dancing braves hadn't moved. To Flanagan, it seemed as though they'd turned to stone.

They arrived at the stand on which White Owl's remains had been placed, bound in white deer skin that had been intricately beaded over half its surface. Running Bear raised his arms toward the heavens and began chanting. Swift Deer took Flanagan's hand. An elder stepped forward and sprinkled what looked like water but smelled like rose petals along White Owl's shroud. Another stepped forward and touched a torch to the dried twigs and branches that had been placed beneath White Owl's remains.

Running Bear's chants grew louder. The Indian women who had been kneeling sprang up and added their voices. The braves that had been frozen in their dance locked their arms together and stepped forward, also chanting. Flanagan felt Swift Deer's grip tighten. The fire leapt up and consumed White Owl and the chanting grew louder and more urgent. And then the burning twigs and branches and stand holding White Owl collapsed into the burial excavation underneath and the chanting ceased. Smoke billowed from the hole that had become White Owl's grave. All heads bowed. And then there was a loud scream, a cry to the heavens by everyone assembled. Flanagan jerked her head up, not certain what had happened. Chills raced up and down her spine. And then everyone cheered.

Through the clouds of smoke, a beautiful Indian girl, Flanagan guessed eighteen, dressed in the whitest of skins that were beaded the way White Owl's shroud had been, the way Swift Deer's dress was, stepped forward. Her hair braided with feathers looped down to her waist. She bowed before Running Bear, who put his hand on her head and said something that Flanagan didn't understand. The girl then bowed before Swift Deer who put her hands on the girl's shoulders and repeated what

Running Bear had said. The girl then came and stood before Flanagan.

Flanagan felt the hair on the back of her neck stand on end. Goose bumps covered her body and raced to and for. A golden aura appeared and wrapped itself around the girl.

Tears came to Flanagan's eyes. The girl reached up and wiped them away with her finger.

"Thank you for finding my mother's killer," she said. "I have lived her torment waiting for her spirit to be freed. And now it has."

"I didn't—"

The girl put a finger to Flanagan's lips. "Shhhh," she said. "My mother, White Owl, is a direct descendant of Bird Woman, or Sakakawea as she is more commonly known. They and I know what you did, how you risked your life, and for that they and I are forever in your debt."

Flanagan searched for words that wouldn't come.

"And they and I know that because of us your abilities have been called into question."

"I can live with it," Flanagan managed to say.

"They will change their mind once you are healed."

"I'm not so sure—"

The girl's aura grew brighter. "Believe me, they will. And I ask you to stay here so we can make your healing complete. You will be my guest. You will be the guest of Running Bear, my grandfather and Swift Deer, my grandmother. You will be the guest of my father, Bear Owl, whom you may know as Art Logan or Lee Scranton. You will be the guest of all of our people."

Flanagan glanced back toward Hutton. "I don't know...my, uh friend..."

"Detective Hutton is welcome to stay." She signaled two young braves to get Hutton. "I noticed that you shivered just then. Let us walk to the table of bounty where the fires of celebration are warm. It's not far, and two of my brothers will assist you." She turned and smiled and Flanagan saw her full face for the first time.

"You are you her, aren't you? I saw the golden aura, but how—"

She took Flanagan's hand and pressed it to her chest. "Yes, I am Shower Cloud. White Owl was my mother."

THE END

To keep track of the progress of his new novels, please visit McLeod's website: http://wammac.web.aplus.net/index.html

This is the address of 'Extra Wry...with a twist!,' McLeod's weekly political and business commentary blog: http://extrawry.blogspot.com/

This is the address of 'Smartblurbs!,' McLeod's short story blog,! http://smartblurbs.blogspot.com/

Watch Lulu's bookstore for other McLeod novels: http://books.lulu.com/category/1491
Two Paige Harrington mysteries, Dance a Silent Death and The Praetorian File are due out later this year.
In Her Own Blood and The Gin Ride are due out early next year.